JEM SPEARS

STARLIGHT AND CINNAMON

Starlight and Cinnamon

An International Love and Misadventure novel

www.jemspears.com

This is a work of fiction. All of the characters, organizations, and events portrayed in this novel are either products of the author's imagination or are used fictitiously.

Printed in the United States of America.

Spear Stone Press | Cincinnati, Ohio

First Edition

Editor: May Peterson

Cover by Ana Grigorio-Voicu

ISBN 978-0-9963034-8-4

Library of Congress Control Number: 2025913738

For everyone who's suffered at the hands of internet trolls. May your harassers encounter their own Aetos Kaukasios.

Content Guidance

I'm the type of person who will go to great lengths to read all the spoilers for a story if I suspect, in any way, that it might contain something I need to prepare myself for. In this book, I would want to know that it contains the following, even if it's just a line or two:

graphic sex
stalking
online harassment, including rape and death threats
toxic work environment
mention of sexual abuse (no details)
mention of animal testing (no details)
misogyny
boundary issues
vomit

Contents

San Francisco, June 2015

Chapter One

Daphne hurried down the wide and sterile hallway, its overhead lights flickering on like the eye of a sleeping giant as she approached and closing back to darkness as she passed. She thought it wise to assume that the sudden alarm echoing through the otherwise empty basement had been tripped by her actions and wasn't just a coincidence and wise, again, to adapt to this new information.

Unfortunately, wisdom usually appeared too late in a Daphne Plan to be of any practical use. Like *after* she accidentally set off a security system.

Despite the piercing siren, she heard her sneakers squeaking against the linoleum, taunting her for her lack of planning. She thought the footwear would be more true to its name, but hadn't taken into account the type of flooring. She should have done more research. On everything. Or asked Mattie for help.

So that was two mistakes at least, but Daphne wasn't one to keep score. That was for people who had to reflect on how things went wrong and, historically, if she acted as though everything would go her way, it usually did.

Her shoulder was beginning to ache, and she adjusted her grip on her small companion's hand.

"How you doing, Coco?" she whispered.

The diapered chimp grinned up at her like she recognized her name. She probably did. Daphne wasn't sure what kinds of experiments they were doing on Coco and her friends. While she pictured the rage-monkey opening scene of *28 Days Later*, she hadn't prepared for it, and was relieved to find the test subjects if not friendly, at least not aggressive. Maybe they were testing how animals reacted to kindness.

Unlikely. They were still kept in cages.

Coco doddered along, cooing at Daphne like an old woman excited to take a field trip out of the nursing home.

A skittering sounded from down the hall, followed by a crash. As much as Daphne had wanted to pull a Pee-Wee Herman and gather armfuls of animals and handfuls of snakes, that wasn't the purpose of her break-in. Illumination, not liberation. Eventual liberation was someone else's cause to take up. Her strength was in calling attention to wrongdoing, then giving the information to the people who knew what to do next.

But that didn't mean she couldn't immediately help some poor animals in the process. And if opening their cages caused a little mischief? All the better.

"You want up?" She asked Coco, propping the stairwell door open with a plastic stopper she had brought. The monkey turned to her and held out her arms like a child, and Daphne's heart gave a little twinge as she picked up the toddler-sized creature. She wasn't an animal activist and she didn't have the temperament for children, but seeing Coco so trusting and vulnerable made her want to fight for her.

There was always a chance that the whole endeavor could serve a greater purpose beyond getting attention. Beyond satisfying her penchant for participating in monkey business. Maybe this time, her antics would make a positive impact in the world. The poor animals would be freed, the labs fined, her father embarrassed, and the love of her life would realize how utterly magnificent Daphne was and become completely, epically devoted to her.

Or maybe the monkey would bite her face.

"Please don't bite my face, please don't bite my face," she whispered, taking the stairs as fast as she dared. Coco's soft fur and friendly attitude had lulled Daphne into forgetting that she was still a wild animal, and one that had been confined and possibly abused. There was no telling what the monkey might do.

At some point in a normal Daphne plan, she would finally think her way through the wishful parts and find her way to the "wait oh wait this might have been a terrible idea" part. The monkey's breath against her cheek reminded her that there were monkey teeth just behind it and she wondered for the first time if there was a better way to achieve her goals. One that didn't involve teeth.

Already gotten this far, she thought. *Let's just see it through.*

At the top of the stairs, she toed another stopper into place to keep the door open a crack as she glanced into the hallway. Red warning lights flashed, but the auditory portion of the alarm seemed confined to the basement labs. No one in sight. Daphne slinked across the hall to another stairway, trudged up to the second floor that overlooked the atrium, and made her way to the enclosed skywalk that would take her to the adjoining library.

"Eee?" Coco asked, her arms still wrapped around Daphne's neck.

"I'm not sure if they'll have coffee there or not," she replied. "I would think amateur sleuths would require some kind of stimulant for their late-night sleuthing. So. It's likely."

Coco stared into the distance as if considering what she said.

As they reached the skywalk, voices rose from the lobby, and Daphne hurried across. Her arms and back ached from carrying her kidnappee. For some reason, she thought a monkey would weigh less.

"Almost there," she whispered, her breathing just starting to feel like work. Running footsteps sounded from behind her, the pursuers too far away to have seen her and still too close for her liking. Especially when she was just a few steps away from the end.

She pushed open the door and let out a sigh when her sneakers hit the thin carpet of the library. The air felt lighter and smelled of turned pages, oil, a touch of plastic, air conditioning. The room she was looking for was down one more hallway, but it might have been a world away from the gleaming and uncomfortably scentless building she'd just left.

Hurrying down the quiet hall, she didn't pause to gather herself or her breath before walking through the open door and into the middle of the Hayes True Crime Club's weekly meeting. Two dozen strangers stared up at her. A few people gasped, several more stood. Someone dropped their water bottle.

Daphne finally spotted Rosaline sitting in a plush chair, watching the unexpected interruption of her club's meeting with a look of soft confusion that only made her more beautiful. A pen rested thoughtfully against her full lips, and relief filled the pockets of doubt that Daphne had been ignoring in her own mind. Rosaline would notice her now. Remember her. And when Daphne asked her on a date, she would say yes.

"Hey," Daphne said breathlessly. "Any of you lose a monkey?"

***

The security office at Makamerah was disappointingly mediocre. For a building that housed animal testing they didn't want anyone to know about, the two-room office with half a dozen monitors, one desk, and no separate area to hold suspected criminals screamed afterthought. Daphne had been detained at malls nicer than this.

She'd been in this situation before, though rarely. It had been nearly a decade since the last time, and she couldn't pretend she didn't know the cause: When she schemed on her own, she got caught. When she schemed with her two usual partners in crime (this was not a statement of guilt), she got away with it. Her ego had insisted she try this project solo, no sister Mattie, no BFF Rin, and it landed her exactly where she should have expected.

The head of security—a tall Latina woman who confiscated Daphne's bag, phone, and wallet—told Daphne she would be held until the building owner decided whether to press charges.

"What charges would those be, do you think?" Daphne had asked.

"For one, breaking and entering—"

"I had a key," Daphne interrupted. "No breaking involved. And I'm not sure 'entering' is a crime?"

"—theft of property," the woman continued, gritting her teeth.

Daphne snorted. "I disagree."

"And your actions have made that clear. Now Mr Redgrave is going to express his counterargument."

"Okay." Daphne shrugged. "I guess I'll just cool my heels here while Mr Redgrave decides how to deal with me."

The officer squinted at her. "You should start taking this seriously."

"Doesn't seem to be much I can do about it at this point."

The woman stared at her another moment, gathered Daphne's belongings, and walked to the door.

"Stay put," she said, and left.

That had been two hours ago.

For most people, two hours without their phone would be torture. Daphne used the time to evaluate the security setup. Cameras and their angles, the work schedule and duty roster on the wall, the handbooks and manuals just sitting on a shelf right in the open. This must have been the first time they actually had to hold a person of interest. Either no one had tried to break in before or they called the police when it happened. Judging by their Standard Operating Procedure, Daphne guessed the former.

When the door to the room opened again, Daphne was flipping through a binder labeled "Training Manual," feet propped on the desk.

"This is fascinating," she said without looking up. "*No* taser training is required before receiving the weapon. Absolutely wild."

"So glad you're enjoying yourself."

She lowered the binder and smiled at the woman in the doorway. A little shorter than average, a little heavier than average, marble blue eyes, golden-brown hair pinned into a messy bun, and skin, brow, and jawline that mirrored Daphne's own. Her navy-blue sweater complemented her blue and green plaid dress, and Daphne would bet money that she was wearing matching bike shorts underneath.

"Mats," she said in a playful growl. "What a pleasant surprise."

"Daph." Mattie leaned against the door frame. "If you're done snooping and stealing, I've been told I can collect you. Please tell me you're done. It's after midnight."

Technically, Mattie had seen thirty birthdays, but in practice, she had always channeled the personality of an old woman. Even when they were kids, playing dress-up in their mother's closet, Mattie would go for conservative colors and layers while Daphne turned bright, tasseled scarves into wrap dresses and slid her feet into too-big, crystal-covered Jimmy Choos. Mattie kept tissues in her pockets. Daphne carried pebbles and a slingshot.

Their brains were similarly wired, though, in a way unlike most people's. So unlike most people's that they had learned early on it was best to hide it—much easier for Daphne than for her sister. Mattie's strengths were in navigating narratives and emotions, while Daphne worked best with numbers and spatial awareness. Their talents supplemented each other's, making Mattie the perfect "crime" partner.

Although Daphne sometimes found it difficult to read people's emotions, she knew her sister well enough to tell that she was exhausted and upset. Upset from the late call to pick her up, and exhausted because of it? Upset because Daphne had gone scheming without her? Something unrelated? She would take her to Shake & Quake and they'd talk about it.

Daphne snapped the binder shut and tossed it onto the desk. "Don't suppose you've seen my bag?"

Mattie held aloft the once-white messenger bag.

"Excellent." Daphne stood up and took it. She pushed aside the slingshot and water bottle to find her wallet and make sure nothing was missing. "Milkshakes. My treat."

"Now?" Mattie glanced at her bare wrist.

"Come on." She opened the outer door. "You're already dressed. Awake. Upright. Feet moving. So let's point those piggies toward a little late night treat and I can say thank you in the form of drinkable sugar and carbs."

Mats snorted but followed her sister out. The security officer walked past them into the office, frowning at them. Daphne gave her a nod of acknowledgment but magnanimously fought the urge to smirk. The woman's job was going to get a lot harder in the next few weeks. It felt mean to act snitty on top of that.

As they left the temperature-controlled building behind, the night embraced them like an old friend. It was a mild midnight, only slightly damp, and the competing smells of restaurants had mostly dissipated over the hours between dinner and insomnia. There was a hint of garlic, steamed noodles, something umami, but the amorphous scent of city dominated the hour.

Mattie's silence was expected, but even so, Daphne wondered if something had happened to make her quieter than usual. She hadn't asked any questions. Didn't scold her—playfully or seriously—and didn't complain about staying out even later. Mats would tell her at some point. She always needed some time to think things through. Hopefully four blocks was long enough.

As Daphne predicted, their silence lasted the walk, entering Shake & Quake, sliding into their usual booth under the soft overhead lights, and opening the slightly sticky menus they'd had memorized for years. The place was about half full. Despite being open twenty-four hours, it somehow managed to operate off the radar of rowdy drunks. Approaching the wee hours of Friday morning, the customers were mostly college kids and the sleepless.

"Snickerdoodle almond milkshake," Mattie told their server. "With a shot of—Daph, how long is this story going to be?" Daphne pressed her lips into a line and squinted into the distance. Turning back to the server, Mattie said, "Okay, with a shot of espresso, please."

"Mexican Mocha shake, as is," Daphne ordered, "if you would, and a giant cinnamon roll to share."

Mattie's reticence lasted until their shakes arrived and they'd taken a sip. She sighed and let her shoulders relax, finally looked up at Daphne, and drawled, "So?"

Daphne gazed out the window to the nearly empty street. "It could have gone worse."

Mats laughed at that, and a weight lifted from Daphne's shoulders. She hadn't messed everything up with her sister, then.

"Oh, I know," Mattie said. "The fact that I wasn't asked to pick you up from a hospital or a police station was sort of a good indication of that."

"Who asked you to pick me up?"

Mattie leveled a look at her. "Our father."

"Shit, Mats, I'm sorry." Daphne sat back, jiggling the foot that was crossed over her leg. "Son of a dick. I didn't know he'd do that."

Mattie shrugged. "I figured. He knows me well, though, because the message he left didn't start with 'This is your father, pick up your phone.' Must have known I'd only listen to the first sentence because it was 'Daphne is in trouble, please go pick up your sister at this address.'"

"Smart." Daphne swirled her chocolate shake with the metal straw. She shifted against the plastic cushion, disliking the feel of it against her leggings. "That's super shitty, though. He could have just directly told his security officer to release me. Oh. Bothering you is his way of punishing me."

"Figured that too."

Silence crept back in for a moment. Mattie used the side of her fork to cut a piece of the warmed cinnamon roll.

"What went wrong?" She asked, eating the bite of pastry.

Not "I'm disappointed in you" or "You would have gotten away with it if you'd asked me for help." Daphne did love her sister.

"Well, I got caught," Daphne said.

"Details, Betty."

Daphne narrowed her eyes at her spy name. She, Mattie, and Rin came up with their spy names when they formed the Honest Mischief Alliance, a group dedicated to righting injustices and making the bad guys look ridiculous. The Alliance never grew past its three founding members, and despite having twenty-plus years to evolve since its inception in grammar school, the schemes were still usually based on wearing disguises, sneaking in somewhere, and exposing the nefarious goings-on to the world. Mattie calling Daphne "Betty" was a subtle way for her to say, "You would have gotten away with it if you'd asked me and Rin for help."

"Well, my darling *Vanessa*," Daphne emphasized Mattie's spy name. "What went wrong is that I mistakenly thought that a True Crime club wouldn't reveal the name of their informant—that's me—to the police. So when they told Makamerah security that I brought the monkey to them, it wasn't much of a leap to figure out I must have been the one who released her."

Mattie paused her fork midair. "Monkey."

"Did Dad not tell you that part?"

Mats shook her head. "So you were caught because you trusted the wrong people. We can learn from that. But why did you do whatever it is that you did? And why didn't you ask me for help?"

Daphne's fingers slid along the side of the tall milkshake glass, feeling the cool condensation and smooth texture, and took a moment to figure out what she should say.

"I wanted to be able to impress you with the story of my solo scheming this weekend, after it all worked out and Rin was here."

"If you waited a day, Rin could have helped, too. Then you would have had all three members of the HMA available for capering. Her plane is in the air by now."

"The True Crime Club meets on Thursdays, though," Daphne explained. "If things didn't work out, you'd be none the wiser, and I wouldn't be as embarrassed about the other reason I did it."

"Which is?"

Daphne swallowed and rested her hand on her still-jiggling foot to still it. "Well. There's this girl."

Mattie lifted an eyebrow. "Oh."

"Yeah. She's great. She's incredible. She's into amateur detective stuff and animal rights, so..."

"Monkey. Detective club. Got it."

"And then, when it worked, I'd have an incredible girlfriend *and* one successful solo mission. And now I've got—" Daphne flicked a pastry crumb off the table. "Neither."

"She didn't appreciate the monkey?" Mattie said around a mouthful of cinnamon roll. "What a snob."

Daphne snorted. "I was sort of escorted away before I could talk to her."

"Text her now?"

"I don't have her number."

"IG? Facebook?"

"Neither."

Mattie stared at her. "Daph, how do you know this girl?"

Daphne shifted in her seat and looked out the window again. "I met her at the bookstore."

"Mmmhmm. You went up and said, 'Hi I'm Daphne, you seem really interesting, here's my number, what's your name.'"

"I was *going* to..."

"Daph."

"I was going to!" She bit her lip and brought her gaze back to her sister. Mattie wouldn't judge her for causing mischief. But she *would* judge her for this part. "I heard her talking to her friend on the other side of the bookcase, and when I turned the corner and saw her...you have no idea, Mattie. She's so beautiful. My brain stopped fucking working. I had to duck back into the other aisle just to breathe again. She talked about the True Crime Club and a vegan dish she was going to try for dinner."

"Oh my god, you've never met this girl."

"This was my chance! What a good meet cute! Can you imagine?"

The problem was that Daphne couldn't stop imagining. And when something got into her mind like that, she had to see it through to its conclusion, whatever that might be. She had to know, one way or another, the one reality of a situation, so she could stop thinking about the infinite possibilities of it.

Mattie's eyeroll was stuck toward the ceiling, as though there were answers there.

"Mats." Daphne reached across the table to take her hand. "I can track her down. She's out there right now, wondering who's that beautiful woman who rescued a lab animal. Hell, she's a detective, it's more likely she'll track *me* down."

"She's not a detective. She listens to a specific genre of podcast." Mattie took a breath. "I love you, Daphne Redgrave, and I will do anything for you, so please, please, the next time you have a plan, tell me first." She held up a hand as Daphne started to interrupt. "At least so I know how much trouble you could have gotten into when I get a midnight call from our father telling me you need to be picked up and escorted out of somewhere that may or may not require bail.

"Also," she continued, "to give me the opportunity to dissuade you from wearing the most anti-stealth robbery outfit ever."

Daphne huffed and held up her arms, presenting her lightweight white silk bomber jacket with matching white tank top, leggings, and sneakers. "Do you think they saw me?"

Mattie guffawed. "Pretty sure the International Space Station saw you and mistook you for a new star."

"Love to hear it," Daphne said, grinning. "Makes it more likely Rosaline will come looking for me."

Chapter Two

Occasionally, Daphne would walk into work as early as eleven in the morning. Between the physical toil of the previous night's scheming and the emotional toil of failing at said scheming, she ended up walking through the company's glass-and-brass doors closer to one in the afternoon. She wouldn't have gone in at all if Mattie hadn't texted at noon telling her Rin's plane had landed at SFO. They'd meet up for dinner, and Daphne felt like she should put in a few hours beforehand.

The office manager, Violet, greeted her at the front desk, holding out several celebrity gossip magazines as Daphne passed by.

"Anything interesting?" Daphne took the magazines, glossy pages sticking to her fingers.

"A surprising number of positive LGBT articles." Violet pushed her sliding glasses up her nose and turned back to her computer.

"The Supreme Court decision on gay marriage is due soon," Daphne said, flipping through the pages. "Maybe it's sympathetic magic, designed to draw out a positive outcome."

"From your lips to Saint Marsha's ears."

Daphne glanced around the quiet office. She hadn't received any texts from her boss over the past few days, but something could have come in for her that morning. "Is there work for me?"

Violet shook her head. "Not that I've heard. They're wrapping up the Eastman case now, that was the big one. I know we have a few more in the pipeline but I don't know if they need you on any of them."

Such was the nature of her work. She thanked Violet and made her way through the bright office to her desk. Nobody would mind if she worked on some personal things, but those personal things only needed a fraction of her attention, and she had come in looking for a challenge.

With her differently-working brain, it would have been difficult for Daphne to maintain a 9-to-5 work schedule at a traditional office. Fortunately, the thing that made her mind different was exactly what made her perfectly suited to her role at Diophantus Consulting, the public-facing name of the one-stop corporate espionage firm.

"Consultant" always sounded like a made-up job to Daphne, along the lines of "researcher" or "theorist"—those titles that men gave themselves for sitting around *thinking* of things. "Corporate intelligencer forensic accountant consultant" even more so, but as Mattie liked to say, everything was made up. And if men were going to do it and make money, Daphne was damn well going to do it and make money. Of course, it required not a small amount of secrecy, so as far as her family and friends knew, she was, simply, an accountant.

She got such a thrill from being underestimated.

The midday light diffused through her office, and she fought the urge to set the large, tinted window to a darker setting. The sunshine would keep her awake and focused, even if it meant suffering its bright discomfort. She settled into her bouncy desk chair and turned on the computer. Two things to finish today before dinner if she could, unless Diophantus ringleader Clarissa did have a job for her.

The security system assessment at Makamerah was the easier of the two—Daphne basically just had to fill in a form. It wasn't her area of expertise, but she paid attention when their sec expert, Brad (who of course called himself a "sexpert"), shared his knowledge and findings, and she was confident that—in this case at least—she could mimic it.

An hour later, she was drafting the email to her father.

> Hi Daddy, Attached is my final assessment of your security system and protocols at Makamerah LTD. In short, it sucks. I guess this is what you get when you decide to value cost over quality? I've made a few suggestions, but a more comprehensive analysis and overhaul would require a formal acceptance of my services, and I'm not sure you can afford me. For this initial assessment, I've given you the "friends and family" discount, so the total is

Daphne paused. He could definitely afford her, but she was definitely not interested in working for him. She didn't really expect him to pay her anything, either, since it was obviously a ruse to cover what she was really doing in that building. He'd see through it. She'd ask for a few thousand, then. An average amount for that kind of security assessment.

Except he had called her sister in the middle of the night to worry her about Daphne. He just as easily could have called the building and told them to let her go. She was glad Mattie unblocked their father's phone number for whatever reason, but Mattie had always been the scapegoat in the family, and their parents' treatment of her was problematic at best. So Daphne would add the "bullshit tax," and if he paid her anything, she'd give it all to her sister.

> US$8,000.00 (Eight thousand US dollars). I accept direct wire transfer and checks. Forgive me, but I couldn't find the email address of your AP department. Would you be a dear and forward this to them?

> XOXO, your favorite daughter, Daphne

Considering it was early morning in Auckland, she didn't expect a response for a few more hours, if ever.

In the meantime, her officemates had returned from lunch, nodding to her when she happened to make eye contact. Her phone pinged, and she opened a text from Rin: "Who's Rosaline?"

"An excellent question, Rin-Rin," Daphne murmured aloud.

Daphne:
My soon-to-be-girlfriend. Details at dinner.

Rin:
Details now instead.

Daphne:
Rin-Rin, I am WORKING. With NUMBERS. Mats can't entertain you on her own?

Rin:
This sounds more fun.

Daphne:

I'll tell you everything tonight.

Rin:

You stole a monkey for this girl?

Daphne:

it wasn't... ok look...I BORROWED a monkey

Rin:

...

Daphne:

The numbers need me. See you at dinner. Take a nap.
Also: YAY THAT YOU'RE HERE! I love you!

Rin:

I will nap, but I won't forget. Prepare your answers now.
Can't wait to see you! Love you too, muppet.

Her Kiwi friend was also on Auckland time, and Daphne was going to use the unavoidable jet lag to her advantage. She and Mats would get their best friend onto San Francisco time soon enough. But a little afternoon nap never hurt anyone.

Rin wanted to know who Rosaline was, and so did Daphne. She'd done the cursory internet stalking, but after she discovered that her mysterious crush's club met at the library adjacent to the Makamerah—which Daphne had recently uncovered some very interesting secret-animal-laboratory information about earlier that same day—it seemed like destiny was forcing her hand. Brad had helped her get a key card, she thanked the stars her father had never removed her security clearance across the board, and she was on her way to some light larceny in the name of love.

Her work computer had access to a bunch of software and websites that allowed them to do broad investigations and background checks. From offshore accounts to marriages in the most far-flung locations to unacknowledged children to WebKinz activity and archived social media and blogging sites, there wasn't much Daphne couldn't dig up. This also wasn't her area of expertise, but the software made it easy. She was reading from Rosaline's old LiveJournal when Clarissa approached her desk.

"Did you ever have a LiveJournal?" Daphne asked. Clarissa was fifteen years her senior and reminded Daphne of her aunts, if her aunts had been anarchist hackers in the 90s. The tech wiz had built Diophantus from scratch, using their vast network of computer geeks to create a full-service business that offered everything from tech support and security assessment to accounting and straight-up corporate espionage, which Daphne thought was disappointingly unlike what movies made it out to be.

"If you think I ever dabbled in LiveJournal, I invite you to find it." Clarissa grinned enigmatically as they slid into the chair across from her. They'd never outgrown their "Matrix" phase, with their short, angled hair dyed black with one blue streak that matched their eyes, and sharp-lined, tactical Acronym clothing. When they first met, Clarissa said their pronouns were they/them and identified as "androgynous" because "anything more specific would give the government, oligarchs, and megacorporations too much information," and they wanted to keep Big Brother guessing.

Daphne had loved them immediately.

"Ah, so you scrubbed it," she guessed. Clarissa didn't so much as blink in acknowledgment. "How's Eastman wrapping up? You need anything else from me? You got something new for me?"

"What are you doing on LiveJournal if you're between jobs?" Clarissa asked.

"Busted," she sang, sitting back in her chair. "I met a girl. My future wife. Now she just needs to know who I am."

"Does this have anything to do with your antics at the Makam-erah building last night?"

Well, shit. She shouldn't have been surprised that it'd gotten back to Clarissa, but this was fast.

"It may have," she confessed.

"To get her attention?"

"To give her a mystery to solve that would help animals. She's vegan."

"I heard there was a monkey involved."

"People keep saying that," Daphne muttered, shaking her head. "Coco had very little involvement, really."

"Coco, is it?"

Daphne looked up to see Clarissa on the verge of laughter, but she couldn't join them—her defeat was still too fresh for her to laugh about it.

"Sucks you got caught, though," Clarissa said, successfully suppressing their giggles. "You should work on that."

"You sound like my sister."

"Your sister is a smart woman." Clarissa rose from the chair and cracked their back. "Eastman is all but done, nothing more needed from you on that. I'm meeting with a potential client tonight. Will you be around the next few days?"

"Plan to be."

Her boss nodded. "There are rumblings out there. Haven't made their way to me officially yet, but I can sense a shape on the horizon. Keep your phone on."

"Sure thing, captain." Daphne made a salute. They rolled their eyes and turned to leave.

"At this rate, you'll never see my LiveJournal."

"Wait, I retract my sarcasm, come back," Daphne called after them, but they pretended not to hear.

***

By the time her phone made a strange chirping noise a little after five o'clock, Daphne was deeply lost in the internet. Once she had re-discovered LiveJournal, she slid into a hunt for more nostalgia, reading her own old posts, and Mattie's, and Rin's, then moving to Tumblr to see what she could find there. When she remembered the purpose of her initial search—Rosaline—she hopped back to the Diophantus database for anything else that might tell her more about her crush.

The problem was that, despite the wealth of information Daphne was able to find, the glimpse into Rosaline's past didn't say much about who she was now. Her few recent posts indicated she might like...clubbing? Hmm. Daphne might be able to get into that.

Her phone lit up and gave a different trill, and she pulled herself from the depths to check her notifications. The first alert had been from her bank: she'd received a deposit of $8,000. The second was a reply from her father, and she brought it up on her desktop.

Kia ora Daphne,

It's so good to hear from you. Seems like San Francisco is keeping you busy. I may not know your true motives for breaking into that building, but I would have remembered asking my favorite daughter to run a security assessment on it. Regardless, your assessment is appreciated, and in line with previous independent findings. As one of our smaller buildings, it unfortunately gets overlooked when it comes to upgrades. I have directed people to focus on its improvement and won't be needing further services from you.

I have wired US$8,000.00 into your account. Can you tell me how you discovered that it was one of our buildings, or will that information cost me another eight grand?

Love, Dad

Huh. Yay for the money, but beefing up security would make it harder for activists to expose the animal testing. Daphne hadn't really thought that part through.

Then again, the True Crime Club had just *handed* her over to security like she hadn't given them an entry point to a potentially juicy investigation, so maybe she'd done all she could for them.

Hi Daddy, Makam merah = "red grave" (or close enough). I see what you did there. I'm going to find all your buildings.

Thank you for your prompt payment. Use Mattie against me again and I'll block your number and email for five years.

Love, your favorite daughter, Daphne

Her father wouldn't test her. He knew she was stubborn—as stubborn as him, as stubborn as Mattie, as stubborn as their other siblings and his siblings and basically the entire Redgrave family. And she really was his favorite. Daphne was the youngest, the stereotypical baby, and he wouldn't risk losing her. As much as her parents seemed to believe it was their responsibility to make Mattie tougher, they believed it was their responsibility to keep Daphne safe. It made no sense to either sister.

She didn't wait for a reply. She'd spent too long on the computer, too far in the past, and needed late afternoon sunlight and Rin's laugh and scallion pancakes and pork and chive dumplings and a cleverly named cocktail. Her stomach growled. Better text them that she wanted dumplings.

It took a minute to shut down the computer and gather her things. On the way out, she passed Brad, just coming in. Daphne was never sure if he meant to look more like a himbo or a frat boy. Tall, muscular, and tanned, he most often wore shorts and a fitted polo shirt. He loved a little mischief, but his bright smile and sometimes vacuous eyes gave the impression that he wasn't too smart. He reminded her of Thor.

Daphne was pretty sure that he—like her—preferred to be underestimated. And like Clarissa, preferred to keep people guessing.

"You got *People?*" He yawned, pausing on his way in.

"On my desk. There's some juicy gossip. More queer stuff than usual, too, so that's nice."

Brad's face lit up. "That's great! I mean, it always should have been mainstream, but now people have more opportunities to educate themselves, and they can join in the fight for gay and trans rights..." He trailed off, frowning. "But the judges have already made their decision on gay marriage, even if they haven't told us yet, so it's too late for the articles to sway them. And it's 2015 for fuck's sake, it shouldn't have taken this long to affirm queer people's right to marry, if that's what these nine overlords decide, and—"

"Brad, hey," Daphne said, raising her hands in surrender. "We all know you're an ally. You don't need to prove it."

He puffed out a breath. "Sorry, Daph. You're right. I'll save it for the gym. Oh hey, I heard you got caught last night at the Makamerah. It wasn't the badge I made you, was it?"

"Of course not. Your work is always flawless," Daphne said. Brad ducked his head at the compliment. "It was human error. By that I mean I trusted humans I didn't know, and they made the error of turning me in."

"Bummer. Didn't get arrested, though. Your name keep you out of jail?"

"Yes, my daddy intervened," Daphne said with a sigh. "More intrusively than I expected. In fact, if we get an official request to upgrade that building's security, we should pass. Even though they might offer a ridiculous amount of money."

"How much we talking?" Brad smiled mischievously.

"Enough that you'd say yes, if it were up to you. Good thing it's not."

Brad pouted.

"I doubt they'll come to us anyway," Daphne continued, adjusting the strap of her bag and backing up toward the elevators. "Unless my spy skills are hereditary, my father shouldn't know I'm connected to this place."

"Stranger things..." Brad trailed off, heading into the office. "No monkey thieving tonight."

Daphne shook her head and pushed the button for the elevator. She had broken into a building and a secret laboratory, released a bunch of animals, stolen one of them, exposed the illegal go-ings-on to a group of so-called investigators, and got caught for the first time in a decade, but the only thing anybody wanted to talk about was the monkey.

She was never going to hear the end of this.

Chapter Three

It was a longstanding tradition that the Redgrave sisters would take Rin to their favorite restaurant the first night of her visit. They'd eat there many more times over the course of her stay, but there was something punch-drunk magical about celebrating the three of them, reunited, eating dumplings and overlooking the Bay and its inescapable fog, while Rin's jet lag softened her more than alcohol ever could.

The evening was cooler than usual, hills and skyscrapers blocking the sunset that people on the west side of the peninsula would bask in for a while yet. But it wasn't too chilly to eat on the patio. That was their place, and they would be out there no matter how cold it got.

Daphne arrived late deliberately, knowing her sister and best friend were already sitting, already drinking, already snacking. She loved walking onto the patio and seeing her two favorite people in the corner, laughing and enjoying themselves, unaware she watched them. A little voyeuristic, but she was also certain that when she died, that would be the scene greeting her in heaven.

"Daph!" Rin called, standing up, her fatigue-lowered inhibition giving her a goofy, lopsided grin. Daphne grinned back and hurried over before the Kiwi could lurch from the table.

"Rin-Rin!" Daphne shouted as she threw her arms around her. "Five months is too long!"

"Aw, Daph," Rin said, squeezing her tighter and planting a kiss on her forehead. "You could always move back to Auckland with me."

Daphne pulled away and made a face. "No thanks. It's not you. It's everything else."

Rin laughed, deep and low. She was taller than both sisters, which wasn't saying much in Mattie's case, but she also tended to wear boots or sneakers with high soles, and with her muscular build, it wouldn't be inaccurate to say she towered over most people. Shoulder-length auburn hair framed her face in soft waves, a little frizzy, like she hadn't brushed a comb through it since getting off the plane seven hours ago. She gazed at Daphne through tortoiseshell glasses, the patio lights catching her hazel eyes. They mismatched, just a little, and Daphne had taken to saying she had "Cumberbatch eyes." To which Rin would unerringly roll them.

With one arm still around Daphne, she pushed a stray strand of blonde hair out of her face.

"Love the platinum bob," Rin said.

"Bob-*ish*. I'm bringing it back."

"If anyone could, it would be you."

Daphne beamed up at her. Her love for Rin was incomprehensible to most people. Neither of them had any interest in becoming lovers. Their bond was something beyond friendship that didn't include making out.

Mattie cleared her throat. "Can you two moon-eye each other sitting down?"

"Ugh!" Daphne scoffed, and they released each other and sat down. "Mattie, it's Rin-Rin."

"I know. I'm the one who met her at the airport."

"Ohhh, it all comes out," Daphne said playfully, narrowing her eyes.

"What? That I do freelance work from home and had the time to meet our missing piece at the airport with an oversized milk chocolate bar after her sixteen-hour flight? Is that what's coming out? That I'm a good friend?"

Daphne sucked in a breath to reply, but Rin cut in. "You're both the best friends. There's no competition. I can't love you the same, because you're different people, but I love you the same *amount*." The girls quieted, letting Rin express her emotions. It may be normal when she was tired or drunk, but it was uncharacteristic of her otherwise, and the sisters knew to honor it when it happened.

"Mattie brought me chocolate," Rin continued, "and Daphne brought me the story of how she got caught stealing a monkey from a secret laboratory in a building that belongs to her own damn family."

"Speaking of family..." Daphne couldn't avoid telling them about her misadventure forever, but she could stall with the right opening, and she took it. "How are your parents, Rin?"

The Kiwi rolled her Cumberbatch eyes and took a sip of her cocktail. "You're trying to delay the inevitable, Daph. They're doing well. Business is doing well."

"Nipple is well? That's so good to hear," Mattie said, trying not to smile. "So sad when nipple does poorly."

"Hate a bad nipple." Daphne bit her lip.

"Two decades of the same joke, and it's just as unfunny as the first time."

"You can't own a company whose acronym is NIPL and not expect teasing!" Daphne cried.

"Yeah, you should expect nipple to be teased," Mattie added, and Daphne laughed.

Maintaining her façade of being above it all, Rin said, "North Island Pinnacle Leisure is doing quite well, you absolute muppets.

Just because you'd rather chew your own arms off than work at your family's business doesn't mean I'd do the same, you utter shoeboxes. So if you're quite finished? Daphne. Break-in. Monkey. Go."

Rin had a seemingly infinite well of patience, but neither woman wanted to test its depths. They cared for her too much. Daphne took a breath, stared at the ocean past her friends, and gave them an exaggerated grimace. The server arrived and set down a drink for her, two plates of dumplings, and a stack of scallion pancakes for the table.

She took a sip of her favorite cocktail—the staff knew them so well—and reached for a pancake while catching Rin up on her and Mattie's eventful evening.

"What I'm hearing," Rin said between dumplings, once Daphne had finished her story, "is that you rushed into a situation that ended up requiring a shit ton more recon, snuggled with an animal that could have bitten your face off, trusted wanna-be *investigators* not to snitch, alerted your father to your deeds, and roused Mattie with worrying, all for a girl you've never met."

Daphne sighed and poked at a dumpling. "That's a fair assessment."

"Daph."

"I know."

"It's fine." Mattie shook her head. "I got Shake & Quake out of it. And a fleeting feeling of superiority. One day, I'll fuck up just as bad, and you two can lord it over me."

"Oh! I also got you money!" Daphne said.

"You don't need to pay me, Daph, I'm your sister. I'll always pick you up from the security office or jail or hospital or—I guess now I should add 'emergency veterinarian' to the list."

Daphne snorted, but her sister wasn't wrong. "Not money from me. Our father paid me for my fake services. I wasn't expecting it and I don't need it, but he bothered you, so you've earned it."

Mattie straightened in her chair. "It's his money?" she said thoughtfully. "I suppose he owes me. Does he know it's going to me?"

Daphne shrugged. "I didn't tell him. Doesn't mean he doesn't know."

"Okay," Mattie said, after a minute in thought. "Yeah. Sure. How much is it?"

Daphne gave her a wicked smile. "Eight grand."

"Shit," Rin said. Mattie's eyes went wide.

"It's less than nothing to him," Daphne said, looking away from her big sister in case Mattie wanted to cry. She usually did. It wasn't a big deal, but she knew Mattie always felt self-conscious about being soft and emotional all the time. "But that's, like, a little bit of security for Mats."

"Thank you," Mattie said, her voice just above a whisper.

"Love you, sis." Daphne winked.

"I love you, too." Mattie dabbed at her eyes with a napkin.

"I love you both," Rin said. The sisters expressed their love for her too, but before the table could spiral into a competition of who loved each other more, Rin ordered them more dumplings and shifted the topic back to Daphne's escapade.

"So this girl."

"Rosaline," Daphne said, feeling dreamy.

"Dear god," Rin muttered.

"Beautiful. Animal activist. Book lover. Athletic. Not completely self-absorbed, if her LiveJournal is any indication. BA from Northwestern—"

"Wait, *LiveJournal*?" Mattie nearly choked on her Mexican mule. "She still actively posts on LiveJournal?"

"It's still around," Daphne said defensively, not quite answering the question. "As a writer, you should appreciate when different written forms survive."

"Yeah, but as an adult human in 2015, I judge," Mattie said, wiping droplets of her cocktail off her chin with the heel of her hand.

"Okay, so you've internet stalked her but not actually met her in person." Rin smiled, but her eyes got soft, and Daphne knew the look of pity when she saw it.

"I saw her in person, but I was so overwhelmed by her beauty that I wasn't able to speak." Daphne crossed her arms. "Besides, she knows who I am now."

"The girl with the monkey," Mattie said under her breath.

Rin made room on the table for the new dumplings and put a few on each of the girls' plates while the youngest of them reconsidered the advisability of her actions.

"Whatever happened to that other girl?" Rin asked, lightly.

Daphne narrowed her eyes. "What other girl? There was no one before Rosaline."

"Mmm," Rin mused. "Deirdre, wasn't it? She played the harp? Or, no—"

"The Irish dancer!" Mattie yelled, pointing at Rin. "Right, right. Since then there's been—oh, what's her name? The dog groomer?"

"Ulyana," Rin drawled, remembering. "God, you almost adopted like, three dogs for her." Daphne pouted. "But then, wasn't there someone, ah, I want to say Jennifer or something. Jennis?"

"'Jennis'?" Mats nearly snorted her drink up her nose. "Like 'Dennis' but with a J? No, it was something like...Jeffrey?"

"Janice?" Rin asked.

"Jenjamin." Mattie said with confidence.

"Her name was Jean, and the two of you are assholes," Daphne cut in.

"Oh right!" Rin said, giggling. "And her job was..." Rin wheezed. "She was like, a chakra chanter or something?" She was out of control, and Daphne had to steer them back to a place where they weren't making fun of her slutty heart.

"She was a holistic energy interpreter, and she made more money than either of you. And none of these people matter because none of them are Rosaline."

Mats and Rin went on like they hadn't heard her, listing more women that Daphne would have wrecked her life for in the past. It wasn't her fault she continually fell for people who couldn't match her intensity. Or who were afraid of it, not entirely irrationally. When she was drawn to someone, she wanted to go all in. And if they wanted to go all in too? Daphne would never stray.

It was hard being a Leo.

She had set her phone to silent so it wouldn't interrupt her dinner with her two favorite people, but if they were going to criticize her love life as if she weren't sitting right next to them, she damn well would check her socials while they did.

Nothing from her boss, nothing more from her father. Her social media was awash with gay pride posts, between the Supreme Court ruling on gay marriage that was supposed to be released soon and San Francisco Pride in just over a week. All the queer people she knew were a bundle of nerves, and she didn't know what she would do if her eventual marriage wouldn't be recognized in the States.

Rin was right: there was always New Zealand. Daphne, like most of her siblings, was a dual citizen, and could move back if things got too prickly in California. She hoped all the time that it wouldn't come to that.

She opened what she called her Shady AF Finsta, which followed thousands of accounts but muted all of them except whichever woman she was recently obsessed with. There was no doubt in her mind that this was completely inappropriate, and no doubt that it was still on the shallow end of the creepiness that happened across the internet.

Rosaline hadn't posted in over a month, and Daphne had no expectation that that would change, but lo and behold, as she opened the app, a new photo of her crush appeared: her cheap red wig shimmered under the fluorescent lights of a well-stocked costume shop, the sequins of her cropped, red top making a constellation of refracted light. Her arm was draped over the shoulders of a guy with a similarly dark complexion and identical pursed lips, and his green and gold steampunk glasses reflected the phone.

> Last-minute costume shopping with my baby bro! Guess what I'm going as? Summer Solstice, here we come! #mermaidlife #TheIntermittentSF #IntermitentSolsticeParty #SummerSolstice2015

Damn. She even made the duck face look good. And she'd be at the Intermittent's costume party? Daphne couldn't have planned it better herself. All that wishing, and finally, a lucky break.

"What are you smiling about, Daph?" Rin's head was cocked in curiosity. She and Mattie had finally overcome their giggling and unfair judgment of Daphne's pattern of attraction. For now. "Find someone else to fall in love with?"

"So soon?" Mocked Mattie. "And I wouldn't call that a smile, that is an unabashed, uncontrollable grin if I ever saw one."

Daphne held up one hand in surrender as she slipped the phone into her jacket pocket with the other. "I'm gonna focus on you two, I promise. In fact, I promise that I won't actively pursue Rosaline while you're visiting, my Rin-Rin."

Rin's smile turned into a look of suspicion. "Aw, you'd do that for me, Daph?"

"Of course." She hesitated. "But..."

"I knew it."

"Here it comes," Mattie chimed in.

"*But*," Daphne stressed. "I think that, if she somehow tracks me down, or we find ourselves in contact with each other another way, we'll have to allow for some pursuit on my part. If the fates align us."

"If the fates align." Mattie toasted.

"I've tried arguing with fate," Rin admitted. "It never works. I agree to your terms, you crafty cabbage, but do you? No manipulating the strings, no 'accidentally' running into each other? You can handle that?"

"Absolutely." Daphne leaned forward. "Now, let's review our plans for the solstice party tomorrow."

Chapter Four

Nestled at the edge of the Castro District, The Intermittent slouched its three stories of once-white panels and faded green trim against a florist on one side and a pharmacy on the other. In daylight, it was an unassuming building, becoming the unremarkable background of everyday life like so many city façades.

At night, it was a beacon of joy.

It was a rave, glowing bodies sidewinding throughout the dark halls to the EDM tattooing its rhythm against every wall and floor. It was a funeral reception for community members so beloved that the people celebrating their life wouldn't fit in a single house. It was the unsupervised, alcohol-fueled, mansion-wide high school party from every movie that never happened to anyone in reality. Sometimes, it was invitation-only, sparking rumors of everything from being rented out by a famous musician, to the dark rituals of a secret order, to a sex party.

For the summer solstice, it was an annual masquerade sponsored by Cheung Technologies, and only the people with the most creative or over-the-top costumes could get in. Not a weekend went by that there wasn't some costume party happening in San Francisco, but the Intermittent's solstice party was Daphne's favorite. She could never be mistaken for someone who was good at planning things, but she made sure to connect with her favorite designer every February, so she could have the perfect outfit for June. Halloween who?

Their Lyft wound through the throngs of cars and people and dropped them off nearly in front of the building. Daphne's excitement muted her worry of getting her dress and shoes dirty before she even got in the door. The trio were dressed as Mucha prints: Daphne as *The Moon*, in a dark blue strapless dress that was more bulky, loose fabric than structured garment, and its matching crown of oversized flowers. Mattie chose *Amethyst*, her hair swept up in a topknot, a poof of gem-colored satin cinched at her waist with a messy bow, delicate chain straps holding up a swathe of white muslin meant to be a shirt. Rin dressed with practicality in mind, a monochrome of chocolate brown boots, tights, tunic, and dramatic, voluminous cape, nailing Mucha's print of Sarah Bernhardt as Lorenzaccio. Daphne and Mattie should have been barefoot—not a good idea in the city—so they compromised with thin ballet flats that nobody would see anyway, beneath bunches of fabric and almost-trains.

"It's Mal!" Daphne shouted as she reached the curb, pointing toward the entrance.

"I thought he always worked the solstice," Rin said.

"He does. I'm just glad I don't have to work too hard to charm our way inside."

"You would love it." Mattie reached up to make sure the flowers in her hair weren't slipping. She and Rin had opted for contact lenses so they wouldn't compromise their looks, and without glasses to adjust, Mattie had to fiddle with something else.

People gathered down the sidewalk, everyone dressed up and joyful and beautiful, and as much as Daphne wanted to get inside the building, she slowed down to appreciate everyone she passed, falling in love dozens of times among the tassels, the glitter, the feathers and silk. She brushed against the tweed jacket of Sherlock Holmes, its rough material contrasting the satiny feel of her dress in her clutched hand.

It could have easily been overwhelming. The fact that she always fell for every woman didn't mean she didn't have a hard time dealing with people in regular social settings. That everyone was beautiful and seemed happy and kind helped, as did focusing on the costumes. She loved fashion, and touching the different textures grounded her.

Mattie, too, would have been panicking at this point, but she had taken edibles when they left her apartment, and she had a clever pocket inside her dress that she'd filled with more.

"Daphne," Mal purred as they stepped up to the door. She beamed and threw her arms around him as he stood up to greet them. He rocked her back and forth and kissed her temple. "Been wondering when you'd show up."

"Who, me?" She said innocently, making her eyes wide. "Have I been on your mind, Mal?"

"All three of you," he said. "You're my favorite part of the evening. Three beautiful, intelligent women. One who could math me under the table. Another who could kill me with a love letter. And another I'd let top me anytime, day or night. Looking good, Rin." He ran his eyes over her and rubbed his chin. Rin blushed about five different colors and muttered something unintelligible.

"You gonna let us in or what?" Daphne asked impatiently.

He laughed. "Protocol, love. You're all stunning, but you know I need more than that."

"Rin, I get," Mattie said. "She could just be someone from the Renaissance. Me, you could guess. But Daph should be very recognizable. And once you get her, you'll get the theme, and the rest of us."

Mal looked them over, thoughtful. The three spread out as much as they could and struck different poses.

"Familiar, I'll give you that. You'll have to tell me."

"Mucha!" Daphne said with a sigh. "I'm *The Moon*, Mats is *Amethyst*, and Rin is Sarah Bernhardt in Lorenzaccio." She opened her phone and showed him the pictures she'd taken of the art ahead of time.

"Damn," Mal said. "Shit, yeah. You could do one of those living art things, recreate it in real life. May I?" He gestured with his phone. "One at a time, in your poses, then all together."

They posed under his direction and gave him permission to post the photos online.

"Excellent," he said, putting his phone away and grinning at them. He reached over and opened the door and gestured them inside. "Thank you for indulging me. Have a memorable night, ladies." Daphne gave him a quick peck on the cheek as she passed him and turned around to squee at her friends as she stepped inside. Her joy was contagious, and the two of them grinned at her as they followed her in.

What they loved most about the Intermittent was that it wasn't clearly an event venue. They didn't rent out one room or one floor at a time; when someone wanted it, they had to take the entire building. The largest room was on the ground floor and had a raised stage in one corner, the best place for a band or DJ. Other rooms had couches and footstools, tables and folding chairs, comfy chairs, desks. There wasn't a kitchen, but there was an area where caterers could set up, and every floor had its own bar.

Unlike at the raves or suspected sex parties, the ceiling lights were on. Not too bright, but enough to be able to see and appreciate everyone's costume, the entire point of the evening. Similarly, the live music in the ballroom was being piped through the rest of the building at a level that made conversations manageable. If it weren't for the absolute chaos of the guests, one might even describe the event as classy.

Every room was a swirl of color and sound and movement, radiating delight and possibility. Even in places with more couches than floor space, guests spoke animatedly, flitting about, showing off their costumes, embracing friends. Laughter flowed through the rooms like the music, like the dresses and ribbons and their thoughts. Daphne relaxed, letting the vibes take her where they wanted, and the atmosphere made her as comfortable as the THC-laced chocolates had made Mattie.

The three of them stuck together, Mattie a little doe-eyed now, swaying to the music in the main hall.

"You interested in Mal?" Daphne asked Rin, voice only a little louder than normal, to be heard. "You don't say you hate his flirting, but you don't say you like it, either. I figured you'd tell him if it was inappropriate, but if you were putting up with it just to get in tonight, you didn't have to do that."

Rin smiled and glanced around the room. "Yes, I'm interested. I was going to slide into his DMs in a bit. Too many people around."

"On the DL in the DMs," Mattie drawled.

"Just the way I like it," said Rin, bringing her gaze back to her friends. "Nobody's business but me and my partner." Daphne returned her smile and went back to covertly looking for Rosaline.

"Either of you see a red-haired mermaid here?"

"Are mermaids vegetarian?" Mattie swayed, staring in fascination at the glittering gold beads adorning a stranger's locs.

"Mermaid?" Daphne repeated. "Anyone?"

"They can't eat fish, because that's themselves," Mattie said, getting weepy. "They can't eat their own tail."

"I've seen about a dozen mermaids, mate," Rin answered. "Are you waiting for someone?" She narrowed her eyes. "Daphne. Is Rosaline here as a mermaid?"

"What? No. I don't know." Always perceptive, Rin. "I saw someone who looked cute and thought they might be coming in, so now I'm keeping an eye out for them." Technically not a lie. "Red wig, red sequined top. Also mermaidy."

"By Odin's beard, what a bounty of beauties we have here!" The too-close deep voice with a terrible English/Asgardian accent made both Rin and Daphne jump, though after five years, they should have been expecting it.

"Brad," Daphne said, as he swung an arm around her in a side-hug. "We talked about startling us, remember?"

"It's Thor tonight, uh." He looked over her costume. "Flower...fairy? Queen? Of the night?"

"Hey bro," Rin said, inclining her head. He nodded to her and Mattie, who was fixated on his shiny hammer. Brad was so talented at playing dumb that while they knew that he and Daphne worked together, they never probed any further when he told them he "did stuff with computers."

Brad's girlfriend stepped from behind him, significantly shorter and thinner than he, mouth pressed into a line and eyes wide, communicating the best she could with her expression that she had tried to talk him out of wearing his Thor costume for the fifth year in a row. Her long black hair was parted in the middle with a braid on each side, and she wore a simple black shift.

"Wednesday Addams," Mattie cooed, reaching for her. "Kiera, Kiera, Kiera," she sang.

"Happy Solstice, Mattie. Hello, loves." Her English accent blended melodiously into the party's sounds. Kiera glanced at their costumes but landed on Daphne. "Ah! Mucha! *The Moon.*

So you two must be other subjects of his, though I'm sorry to say I don't recognize which. You did a great job, though."

"All kudos go to my designer," Daphne said, putting her hands up. "I couldn't sew to save my life. I just come up with the ideas. Like Brad—uh, Thor, here—comes up with the idea for his costume every year."

"Mmm," Kiera hummed, giving Daphne a thin smile and blinking too fast. "Five years now. Four years without couples costumes. I love couples costumes."

"You can be Jane again anytime!" Brad said.

"Or Sif, or Fandral," Rin chimed in.

"Loki," Mattie said, with an air of finality. "Definitely Loki."

Kiera's eyes lit up at that. "Oh, that one's good. I can do that. I'll have to channel more femininity than usual, but." She shrugged and gestured to her dress.

"Have either of you seen a red-wigged mermaid around?" Mattie would be inseparable from Kiera and Kiera loved spending time with her, Rin needed privacy to try to hook up with Mal on her own terms, and Brad was—well, he was Brad, he would figure it out—so Daphne didn't feel like she was technically abandoning any of them if she went to look for Rosaline more thoroughly.

Brad and Kiera squinted at each other, thinking. "No redheaded mermaids," Brad said. "But I definitely counted two of your exes here, Daph."

"What? Who? Where?"

Rin laughed. "It would be more surprising if she didn't have any exes here. I saw Penny and Kate Three on the way in."

"We also saw Kate Three." Brad nodded. "And Micky."

Micky? Great.

Daphne was of the opinion that things worked out as they needed to. So she was pretty good at acting graciously when her romances ended. After all, her list of crushes was long. When a relationship didn't blossom into something lasting, she could just move to the next person who caught her fancy. No hard feelings. She knew she would love again.

Micky was not of the same opinion. Despite the two of them knowing from the start that they weren't compatible, Micky wanted them to put way too much effort into staying together, even if it meant being miserable, and Daphne was not interested. They broke up, Daphne moved on, and Micky started bad-mouthing her across the city. San Francisco might have a higher density of lesbians than most other places, but it was still a close community, and Micky's behavior was downright shitty.

If it weren't for the fact that she would be acting like every terrible man in a position of power, Daphne would have had her coworkers go in and delete Micky's IG and Facebook accounts. In the end, it seemed like too extreme a reaction, and she was proud of herself for demonstrating restraint.

She hadn't thought of that ex in three years. If she believed in signs, she'd call her appearance at the solstice party a bad one. Ominous. If she believed in signs, she might have decided to leave instead of looking for Rosaline. But if she had to base all her actions on avoiding former lovers, she would have to move out of the country.

"If you all are good, I'm going to mingle," she told the group.

Three floors and forty minutes later, Daphne had to admit that Rin was right. There were a lot of fucking mermaids at the party. But none of them seemed to be Rosaline. Rin was also right that there were an awful lot of exes at the party. Usually, that wouldn't have been a problem. But between Micky showing up, not being able to find the woman she'd set her sights on, and wandering through an entire building where every room showed Daphne glimpses of people who no longer loved her (if they ever did to begin with), the cumulative setbacks were stoking the embers of what she knew would become a full-blown panic attack.

She needed to get out of the building. She needed air. She needed to not think about having a panic attack and how awful it would be, because thinking about it always catalyzed it.

The room was the biggest on the third floor, at the front of the building, with a slightly less frenetic vibe than the ground floor, despite the large bar area and twirling disco lights. She knew from previous parties that there were balconies to the front, and though she couldn't see them through the forest of bright and glittering bodies, she had to trust that they were still there.

As she reached the glass balcony door, the person on the other side turned so Daphne could see her face. Shit. *The chakra chanter*, she thought. As if Rin mentioning her the night before had summoned her back into Daphne's life. At this point, the friendliest of exes was an unwelcome sight. Daphne turned back and made her way across the packed room, while the little phantom-gray worms began their writhing in her periphery, making their own way toward the center of her vision.

The hallway was nearly as crowded, and she kept her head down, field of vision shrinking, sounds becoming muffled, her heart beating too fast and breath coming too slow. She wasn't watching where she was going, the faces, the fabrics in her way, her goal of outside and fresh air now one of the back balconies. Someone grabbed her arm, and as she tried to slip free, they grabbed her other arm, and she looked up into Micky's face.

Because of course.

"Híjole, Daphne, you look like shit."

"Fuck off, please." She managed to slip out of her grip and throw herself back into the crowd. Passing out in front of her ex was not an option, and her destination was only one hallway and just a few rooms away.

"Daph, are you okay?" The crowd thinned toward the back of the building, and Micky didn't follow her. There was one door in particular she was looking for, at the end of a quiet hall, usually used for storage and usually locked. Luckily, Daphne was usually curious and usually insistent, and several events ago, she learned how to jiggle and lift the knob at just the right angle to open it without a key.

Only a few guests in the hall, at the juncture with the main one, and Daphne could see there wasn't anyone down by the door she needed to get to. It was darker, or maybe that was just her narrowing vision. She stopped trying to hide her heavy breaths as she got there, jiggle-twisted the knob a few times, and staggered into the dark room, flinging the door shut behind her. The curtains were open, and no one was on the balcony, so she let a sob slip past her lips as she opened the glass door and dropped to her knees in the fresh air, clinging to the cool, wrought iron bars and willing the creeping darkness back where it came from.

It was so stupid. She was so stupid. Nobody reacted this way to seeing any ex-lover that wasn't one's biggest heartache. There was no reason for her brain to panic like that, and certainly no reason for her body to listen to it and follow suit. What a traitor. And during her favorite party, too. When she could be making out with a cute girl or getting mesmerized by the dancing lights with Mattie or, hell, having a dorky dance-off with Brad.

She tried focusing on all the nice things she could be doing, but beneath it all ran an undercurrent of her irrational panic like a news ticker that just said DANGER! CAN'T BREATHE! DANGER! DANGER! AIR! NEED AIR! over and over again.

Her vision had cleared, but she shook, still, her breath coming in large, wheezing gasps. Air was getting in. It would pass eventually, even without trying, without getting water or lying down or going home. She turned off the stream of good thoughts and let the danger ticker run its course, letting her mind and body do whatever the fuck they wanted to do. Breathe louder? Fine. Shake uncontrollably? Sure, why not. She couldn't embarrass herself anymore.

"Okay," said a voice from the shadows. "It's time for me to step in."

Chapter Five

Daphne gasped, but since it wasn't any different from what she was already doing, the effect was lost in the noise. Her fight-or-flight spiked again, because what she really fucking needed was being snuck up on in the dark when she thought she was alone and having a meltdown.

The shadows at the far end of the balcony moved, and—she presumed—the speaker with them. Daphne didn't hear their footsteps as they came closer, but it was possible her loud breathing drowned them out. The moon was just more than a sliver, and she couldn't see any more than the outline of the person approaching her. Their costume was blocky, but didn't make a sound when they walked. When they got to Daphne, they reached past the door into the room and flicked a switch that turned on the zig-zagging lines of fairy lights strung over the balcony.

Daphne winced away from the sudden light, dim as it was, and she was about to glance up at the stranger's face when they squatted on one knee next to her. Eye-to-eye now, but Daphne started at their boots, dark and shiny, loose crimson pants tucked into them. Layered squares of dark red and leather with slate-colored tiles at the belt, chest, and shoulders, a flowing red tunic buttoned tightly at the wrists. Familiar. So familiar, but she couldn't quite catch it, so she finally looked at their face and regretted it immediately.

The woman's dark eyes enthralled her, and Daphne's world shrank down again until all that was left was that face: heart-shaped with high cheekbones, small mouth but full lips parted like she was about to speak, perfect eyebrows shaped to complement the angle of her eyes and lifted in concern. Between the silver moon and golden lights, she couldn't guess at the color of her skin, but her hair was black and pinned up with a decorative teal comb with a mother-of-pearl magnolia design.

Mulan, Daphne thought, distantly.

"One time," Mulan started, "my party and I were exploring this abandoned house on the outskirts of Barovia." She nudged Daphne with a bottle of water, then set it by her knee. "Old and decrepit. Animals living in the walls and chimneys, but also disembodied voices, angry spirits, mutilated bodies, traps, the undead: this horror house had it all. Haunted. Super, super haunted."

Her voice is like music, Daphne thought.

"Anyway, we're only level-one characters and we have a feeling the DM is angling for a TPK—he was kind of a dick. As soon as we walk in, we know it's a death trap."

Mulan shook her head and laughed, her face animated, never taking her eyes off Daphne. "We get *slaughtered*. A spirit spooks the bard, and he falls into a closet where a broom literally beats him to death. Our cleric reaches for a doorknob on what turns out to be not a door, but a mimic, and it swallows her whole. A mirror shimmers and as some horrific thing is about to crawl through it, the already bleeding ranger shoots it with an arrow but rolls a one—a critical fail—and the arrow bounces off the mirror and strikes him in the throat. His damage roll is so high, he dies immediately—"

It's a game, Daphne thought. *What does this have to do with anything? Does she think I'm someone else?*

"—leaving the barbarian and me. Her dump stat is intelligence, so the DM lures her to another mimic that had taken the shape of a plus-two ax, and that was that. So my party is dead and it's down to me, a baby sorcerer with three total spells, and I realize he's going to kill me either way, why not try something ridiculous? I say we need a total do-over. He laughs and tells me to roll persuasion. I roll a natural twenty. He frowns and says to make a wisdom saving throw. Another twenty on the die. My friends are getting excited. The DM obviously doesn't want a do-over, so he tells me to roll a d100."

She paused and smiled at Daphne, who thought there was nothing she wouldn't give to be on the receiving end of that smile for the rest of her life.

"I roll a goddamn 100. Everyone's cheering, except the DM of course, and he asks how I'm going to ret-con everything. I tell him I suddenly wake up in a panic and find myself in bed back at the inn. It's morning, we haven't traveled to the house yet, and we're all still alive. It was all a dream."

She had no idea what any of that meant, but Daphne beamed up at Mulan, caught up in her enthusiasm.

"The DM was pissed, so we left and found a new one. Anyway, I think about that a lot. How that was the luckiest I'll ever be in my life. And I wasted it on three dice rolls when I could have just walked away." She shook her head but had a fond look on her face. "It was a great life lesson."

Daphne waited for her to say something else, but silence fell between them, and she realized she wasn't wheezing anymore. Her breath came easily. She lifted her hands from the bars and reached for the bottled water, and she wasn't trembling.

"A vivid story," Daphne said. The words sounded like stones in a tumbler, and she cleared her throat and swallowed some water.

"And I'd hate for you to think you've wasted your time, because I liked hearing it, but I don't know you. And I don't know what most of those words even mean."

Mulan gave a light snort. "Are you feeling better?"

Daphne nodded. "Almost normal." Her heart was still beating fast, but for reasons unrelated to the panic attack.

"First I thought you were just crying," she said. "I didn't want to interrupt if that was the case. Everybody deserves a good cry. But then it was more like a panic attack, and whatever you were doing to try to manage it clearly wasn't working. When focusing on it doesn't work, confusion sometimes will. So I startled you and told you a story that would keep your interest or your confusion or both, and I picked one long enough to give you time to recover."

"Are you a witch?" Daphne took another swig of the bottle. The panic attack had knocked her off her game. She was usually so good at flirting.

The woman's eyebrows twitched. "Are you?"

She thought about it for a moment, then shook her head. She put the cap back on the bottle and gestured with it. "Mulan," she guessed.

"*The Moon*," she replied. Beautiful, quick-thinking, nerdy, and she knew Mucha. Daphne was in so much trouble.

"You're really living up to your costume. Out here, rescuing people." She set down the bottle, grasped the railing and pulled herself up with a grunt, then tried to lean against it at a flirty angle. "Making them not feel stupid for needing rescuing. So warrior. Such brave."

Mulan pulled herself up beside Daphne. "More like 'so learning, such practice.' I'm a counselor. I specialize in—well, the San Francisco Special: tech company burnout. Lots of high-pressure jobs, and this place chews them up and spits them out. If they're lucky, they'll land right onto my couch." She licked her lips and glanced up to The Moon, who hadn't yet taken her eyes off her. "I don't mean to sound rude, but your panic attack was the easiest stress response I've had to deal with today."

"Oho." Daphne laughed. "I'll try to give you more of a challenge next time."

"Please don't," she groaned. "I'd really prefer it if you were easy."

"Oh, you have no idea how easy I am." She grimaced and bit her lip. Usually, straightforward was the way to go, but this felt different. The woman smiled wider, and gave Daphne a once-over that she could practically feel.

"I'm familiar with the moon," she said, nodding as her eyes found Daphne's again. "That 'monthly changes in her circled orb.'" She took a step closer, and Daphne had to tilt her head back just a little to keep eye contact. She could feel heat radiating from her, and drew on reserves of restraint she had no idea she had to not close the distance with her lips.

"Are you living up to your costume, too?" Mulan whispered, reaching up to outline a petal in Daphne's flower crown, then cupping the side of her face. "Are you as inconstant? Are you as variable?"

"I am like the moon." Daphne swallowed, distracted by the feeling of the warm palm against her cheek. "I'm brightest at night. I'm always making calculations to stay on my path. And I would argue that she's always been constant. She always remains herself. It's how others perceive her at different angles that changes. That's not her fault."

The woman tilted her head, considering.

"Also," Daphne added, whispering. "I'm like, really beautiful. Moon-style beautiful. Fae beautiful."

"And unattainable?" she asked, leaning in even closer.

"Not that."

Their lips met, and Daphne's world shrunk again. All that was left were the atoms where they touched, still sending information to her brain somewhere: soft lips moving against hers, caress against her cheek, the feeling of her partner's arm snaking around Daphne's lower back and tugging her closer. One of Daphne's hands clutched at the warrior's fabric like at her dress earlier, noting the difference in textures, and her other hand rested against the woman's smooth neck, thumb making circles against her jaw.

Not to be outdone, Daphne's other senses kicked in, trying to overwhelm her. Beyond the linen and paint smell of the costume and the professional-smelling hair products, she found a spicy, resinous scent she wanted to swallow. Voices drifted to her from far away, and her mind, unable to focus on anything but the woman and the kissing and the feeling, let them drift away again so as not to disturb whatever life-changing thing was happening to Daphne at that moment.

And at that moment, she realized she had never been kissed before. Because *this*. This was a real kiss. All those other times she thought she kissed someone paled now like faded photographs compared to the bright dawn of real life. All those times she thought she was making love, as meaningless now as a naïve fantasy eclipsed by reality.

She could have floated there forever, in her arms, against her lips, poetry and philosophy blooming fractals in her otherwise shut-down mind, but logic slipped in somehow—the first time it was ever unwelcome—and Daphne started thinking of things again. Namely, that it was unlikely that one kiss could actually change someone's entire life. And secondly, as romantic as it sounded, not knowing her name would make it hard to get a second date. Or, for that matter, a first one.

They were both reluctant to stop, and as their lips slowed, Daphne held her tighter. She returned the gesture with equal pressure, and trailed kisses down Daphne's jawline, to her ear.

"I think you look more like starlight," the woman whispered. "All sharp, bright shards piercing the depths of night."

The smallest sigh escaped Daphne's lips. It could have been a line. She could have been saying what she thought Daphne wanted to hear. But Daphne was going to throw caution to the wind and assume she meant it. In which case, it was the most romantic thing anyone had ever said to her, which made her equal parts thrilled to hear it and not a little melancholy that she was twenty-eight years old, had had a number of lovers, and had never been spoken to with the care and tenderness of this person she hadn't even known ten minutes ago.

"I can be starlight," Daphne said. "As long as I can still wear *The Moon*'s outfit." The woman laughed and pulled back from Daphne with a final kiss against her neck. They stood beneath the dim lights, looking at each other.

"So," Daphne said.

"So?"

"So," she said, more definitively. "I think the most important question now is—"

"There she is!" A voice thundered from behind Daphne and the two of them stepped apart to look. On the closest balcony to theirs, still in the dark, five or six people gathered, crowded at the railing, jostling and waving to them and speaking a language Daphne didn't know.

"Cinnamon!" the closest one called, someone in a dark steampunk or Gothic Lolita costume. "We've been looking for you everywhere!"

"Are you in that locked room? No wonder we couldn't find you."

Someone in the back of the group said something in what Daphne thought might be Mandarin, and the rest of them laughed.

"We're coming over," shouted the Klingon, and the group pushed their way back inside. The last person on the balcony stayed where she was, a tall Asian woman in a white astronaut suit, sans helmet. She looked between Daphne and Mulan with an unreadable expression before following the group in.

"Um," Daphne said, turning back to the woman whose arm was still around her waist.

"Ah," she said at the same time, and let go of Daphne, looking sheepish. "My friends. I should probably—"

Someone pounded against the room's locked door, louder and longer than necessary, Daphne thought.

"Your friends—"

"It's all falling apart without you!" they shouted through the door.

"They're not helpless. Usually." Mulan gave Daphne an embarrassed half-smile.

"I get it. I also have, um, friends." Daphne floundered. This wasn't how it was supposed to end, and there were a thousand things she wanted to know, and her brain wouldn't provide the question for even one of them. She rummaged around in the math part of her brain, thinking there was an answer there, but it failed her, too.

"Echo left for the Twinnings party already, and we can't find Emma!"

"Shit," the woman said, stepping into the still-dark room but turning back to Daphne. "That is a problem. I have to go. I'll see you around, Starlight."

She gave Daphne a brilliant smile, but there was something in her eyes, regret, or an apology, then she walked through the room, opened the locked door, and left in a crowd of flounce and shouts. The astronaut hung back long enough to shoot Daphne a dirty look, then followed the others.

Daphne stood for a moment, gazing at the rectangle of orange light filling the door frame on the other side of the room. She touched her lips and glanced up at the fairy lights, letting her eyes unfocus so they were filled with smudgy golden blotches of light and remembering being described as "sharp, bright shards." One thing clicked in her mind, finally, and she sagged in relief. She could do a lot with a profession. She could do even more with that and a name. And she'd gotten one.

Cinnamon.

Chapter Six

Cinnamon Cheung felt something precious slip away from her as she left behind the scene as still and tender as a quiet pool at midnight, and dove into the loud, harsh party she had found enjoyable just an hour before.

She had just...kissed her. She had stood there and flirted and then leaned in and kissed that beautiful woman who was as full and incandescent as the moon herself, cocky and fragile and shameless and pale. When Starlight collapsed onto the balcony—how could she ever call her anything but Starlight, now?—Cinnamon had taken one look at that art nouveau wraith, crumpled and full of pain, and wanted to gather her in her arms and kiss away her pain.

It was a frankly ridiculous reaction.

Cinnamon didn't want to go around saving damsels. Although that was sort of her job, in a figurative way, helping people navigate the stress of working in the tech industry. But she wasn't a hero, and she didn't seek out romantic relationships hoping it would be based on the other person needing her help.

She also didn't get crushes or want to kiss strangers or fall for anyone, not since getting dumped by the only serious girlfriend of her life seven years ago. The memories of that heartbreak warred with the excitement of feeling attracted to someone after so long and the uncertainty of what it meant. Had these years just been a dry spell? Was she able to want a partner again? Did kissing her first mean that Cinnamon wasn't, in fact, as broken as she thought?

"I said, where are you?"

Cinnamon jumped at the loud voice by her ear, and turned to see Ying-Li leaning in as close as she could, given the stiff and unwieldy collar of her astronaut suit. She was staring at her with a frown of half concern and half disappointment.

"Sorry," Cinnamon said, raising her voice to be heard in the crowd. "There's a good chance Emma is holding court in one of the smaller rooms. And if Echo's already gone on to the Twinnings party, we'll meet her there once we find Emma. Not a catastrophe. Yet."

Ying-Li glanced away but seemed unsatisfied with the answer. They moved with the rest of the group from room to room, floor by floor, looking for their lost friend, who they found in the caterer area, talking with the servers about the benefits of unionizing.

"Who was that girl?" Ying-Li leaned against the wall in a pose that might have made the question seem casual if Cinnamon hadn't picked up on her irritated tone.

It had become clear to Cinnamon over the past few weeks that Ying-Li Wu wanted to be something more than friends. Cinnamon's parents had introduced them, presumably hoping to make a love connection for their daughter and a business connection for themselves. Ying-Li's family was well connected, and even though Cinnamon didn't work for Cheung Technologies, she suspected that her happiness was not at the top of the list of things her parents wanted out of the match they had set up. When she told her parents that the best they could hope for was that they'd become friends, they said they were fine with it, but winked and added that love could bloom from the most unexpected friendships.

Ying-Li had been disappointed that romance wasn't an option, but reaffirmed that she wanted them to remain friends. With their growing closeness, Cinnamon suspected that she still hoped for something more than friendship, and knew that she had to sit down with Ying-Li again and draw some clear boundaries. But for now, she would make the bad choice to ignore it.

"Where?" Cinnamon asked, playing dumb.

"The one on the balcony." The rest of their friends had joined Emma in her impromptu outreach, leaving the two of them by the door in relative quiet. "With the blue dress and flower crown."

"Oh, she was dressed as Mucha's *The Moon*."

"Yeah. Is that who she is? The moon?"

No, thought Cinnamon. *She's obviously Starlight.*

"I didn't ask," she said.

"But you were kissing her." It wasn't a question.

"It seems like the perfect night for kissing strangers." She let some wistfulness into her tone, not wanting to telegraph all her emotions, but not wanting to minimize what had happened. *What* had *happened?*

"So you didn't get her number?"

Cinnamon shook her head. "No number, no Insta, no sun sign, no blood type, no name."

With a smirk, Ying-Li relaxed against the door frame. Yeah, they were going to have to review their boundaries again soon.

When their friend had been collected, they made their way outside to wait for their cars. Ying-Li had a personal driver and would take half the crew, but the other half opted for a rideshare. The night was young, but Cinnamon didn't have any mixed feelings about leaving her family's party early. Her sister, Echo, had already left, and it wasn't like everyone knew Cinnamon was a Cheung. She wasn't there as a representative of her family's business, but because she loved the solstice costume party as much as the rest of the community did, making a point to attend every year, like so many other people.

An idea popped into her head. Starlight's costume was specific and meticulous.

"I'll be right back," she told her friends. "I have to go check something real quick."

She jogged back to the front door, weaving through the costumed guests and their clouds of smoke. Mal was letting in a minotaur and a Medusa when she approached him.

"Hey, Mal," she said.

"Hey, Cinnamon. Mulan. Did you forget something?"

"No." She smiled. "This might be a weird question, but there was a girl in there, I don't know if you remember letting her in. Strapless dark blue dress with lots of fabric, like she has to pick it up and carry it, with a big flower crown, white and pink. Average height, very blonde hair. Blue eyes. The costume is a Mucha print, The Moon."

"Ah!" Mal snapped his fingers. "Right, Mucha. That's Daphne. She and Mattie and Rin came as a Mucha set. They're here every year."

Daphne. That sounded right. Soft syllables following the hard D, like she demanded attention and, once having it, whispered what she wanted. It suited her. But not more than "Starlight." Plus, Cinnamon liked the idea of calling her something nobody else did. Something she didn't have to share.

"I don't have her number." Mal smiled slyly, guessing at her intentions. "But I did tag her in the photo I posted of them on Instagram."

He turned his phone so she could see, and she took hers out and tracked down Starlight's page from there. She hovered over the "Follow" button, then closed the app. It might be too rash to friend her so soon, after a few minutes of talking and one kiss. Cinnamon had never been so impulsive before.

She glanced up at the building, thanked Mal, and rejoined her friends. If she was still thinking about Starlight in the morning, she would reach out. In the meantime, she had another party to go to.

***

"Mats, I gotta go. How you doing? Want me to take you home first?" Half an hour later, Daphne found Mattie on the second floor, sitting on a slate gray couch between Kiera and the Cleopatra whose gold-beaded locs she'd been hypnotized by when they first got here.

"I'm good!" Mattie shouted. "The edibles are wearing off just in time for me to make a very good decision."

"Oh?" Daphne raised an eyebrow. "That would be a first."

"Daph, this is Iggy, a friend of mine from work." Kiera gestured toward Cleopatra.

They exchanged pleasantries, and Mattie said, "I think I'm going to hang out with Iggy tonight, so don't let me stop you from whatever it is you're doing."

Daphne glanced at Kiera, who nodded that it was okay, silently vouching for the stranger Mattie was going home with. They trusted Kiera, and if Mats wasn't high anymore, that was as safe as they were going to get. Daphne kissed her sister, promised to call her in the morning, and said goodbye.

She found Rin in the next room, relaxed in an easy conversation with Brad. When she got close enough to hear them, she panicked for a moment that he had told Rin the truth about their job. He was rattling off numbers and acronyms, and Rin was nodding along like she knew what he was talking about.

"It'll be slightly different for you, obviously," he said as she approached. "Height, weight, metabolism, sleep quality, stress, sex, what you eat, every body has its unique biosphere. The base plan is the same, but it's *necessary* to tweak it to fit your needs."

"Should have known Thor would be talking workout routines," said Daphne. Brad gave her a wink.

"You're all flushed," Rin said. "Did you find Rosaline?"

"What? Who?" Daphne frowned. "Oh. No, no. She's not in the running anymore."

"Dear god Daphne, you only stole a monkey for her, like, yesterday." Rin gave her an exasperated head tilt.

"Never gonna live that down," she muttered. "No, I've..."

She let herself trail off, remembering how one of the points of the Makamerah Solo Plan was to win herself a girlfriend before Rin and Mats even knew she had a crush. She hadn't wanted to tell them anything about Rosaline before it was definite.

They teased her about her love life and on one level, it didn't bother her. Her sense of self wasn't rattled by their eyerolls or sighs. They loved her, and she loved herself, and they meant well. But it must be getting under her skin if she thought she had to keep her feelings to herself. She'd talk to them about it the next time they were all together. Even if she hadn't consciously known she wanted them to stop, some part of her brain had.

In the meantime, she'd keep quiet about Cinnamon. She smiled to herself. Cinnamon would be her secret, hers alone, to keep just for her. For a while. She wouldn't even share her name.

"I know that look." Rin shook a finger at her, bringing Daphne out of her reverie. "If you didn't find Rosaline, you at least found someone. And something wonderful happened. I love the look of Daph in love."

Daphne smiled wider at that. Rin did love her, and just wanted her to be happy. "I am having a wonderful time, and it has nothing to do with Rosaline. In fact, I'm going to go chase the feeling alone, unless you feel abandoned."

"You're leaving?"

"I think my princess is in another castle."

Brad and Rin both nodded knowingly.

"Sounds like Mats will be going home with Kiera's friend," Daphne explained. "And I don't want to outright abandon you without your permission."

"Then hereby you have my permission to abandon me forthwith." Rin flourished her hand and made a little bow.

"You have keys to Mats' apartment?"

"I do. But I don't plan to use them tonight."

Daphne and Brad ooo'd at her. "Look at you go!" Daphne playfully punched her arm.

"Who's the lucky, uh." Brad glanced at Daphne with a little bit of panic in his eyes, forgetting for a moment how to make a gender-specific phrase more gender-neutral.

"You can say, 'who's the lucky pal?'" She suggested.

"This feels like a trap," he said.

Rin laughed. "Close. How about, 'Who's the lucky Mal?'"

"Yes," Brad said, drawing out the word as he nodded. "Rin for the win."

She shrugged. "We'll see what happens. Where are you off to, Daph?"

"I have to find a magical and possibly fictional place called The Twinnings Party."

"I'm pretty good at finding things," Brad offered. "Maybe I can help?"

With his secret professional services, he meant. Not just googling it. As long as it didn't blow his cover, Daphne would welcome the help. It would get her back to Cinnamon quicker.

It only took him five minutes to find it. With a high five for Brad and a kiss for Rin, Daphne left the Intermittent on a quest to find the actual love of her life. And if the love of her life liked Dungeons & Dragons, well, she could certainly do worse. At least she didn't have to kidnap any primates.

"Yo Daph," Mal called to her as she left. She retraced her steps to him, gathering the smooth dress fabric in her arm so it wouldn't drag on the sidewalk.

"You'd better treat Rin well," she said, pointing a finger at him. "Communication, consent, honesty, respect. And also fun and pleasure."

He held up his hands in surrender. "You just described my only sexual mode. But before you go, would you be interested in pursuing your own pleasure tonight?"

She stared at him blankly. "Are...are you asking me to join you and Rin? Or are you asking me to join you instead of Rin? Because if it's the first one, then, um, no thank you. You're great and I like you but I'm very lesbian. And Rin is my best friend but I'm not interested in her sexually. But if it's the second one, you're terrible and I hate you and Rin is my best friend and I can't believe you'd try to get with me after making a date with her."

"Okay, slow your roll, hot stuff. First of all, you're not my type, and I don't just mean lesbian. Second, I've had a crush on Rin for two years, and I don't want to share her. And third, I was just going to let you know that a gorgeous and successful woman who's way out of your league was asking about you earlier. Described your costume, asked your name. I sent her to your Insta. But again, out of your league."

Daphne's eyes went wide. "You did that for me?" Her voice got high and small.

Mal side-eyed her. "For all the good it did me."

"I knew you were the best," she said, grinning. "Wait. Why is she out of my league? Wait more, was she dressed as Mulan? Or was it someone else?"

"Oh, it was Mulan. Otherwise known as Cinnamon Cheung. Of Cheung Technologies."

Daphne again stared at him blankly.

"Cheung Technologies like the host of this solstice party you love so much."

She sucked in a breath. "Whoa."

"Yeah, whoa. But I don't mind giving a sister a hand. She followed me on Instagram earlier. In case you wanted to track her down yourself."

"I have the best friends," she said, giving him a peck on the cheek. "You have my blessings regarding Rin."

"Didn't require them," he called after her as she walked away. "But I appreciate them anyway." He shook his head and muttered to himself about the force of nature that was Daphne Redgrave.

Chapter Seven

"I'm too old for this shit."

Echo Cheung stretched against the doorframe like a cat, and Cinnamon didn't think it had anything to do with leaning into her Catwoman costume. The party at the Twinnings estate was aimed at more of a college crowd, and neither of the Cheung sisters were having a good time.

Cinnamon snorted. "What could someone possibly be too old for at thirty-two?"

"All-nighters. Molly. Fuckboys."

"I'm with you on the first two, but I can't even imagine you giving up the third."

Letting her gaze roam around the room, Echo shrugged. "Maybe it's just a matter of cutting back on the fuckboys, like they're cigarettes. Have one every few months. And if I remember correctly, you were always too old for ragers and drugs."

"You make me sound like a prude."

"If the frock fits."

Cinnamon shot her a look and went back to watching her friends, who were dancing wildly in the middle of the room, while her mind wandered back to the kiss on the balcony.

"How's it going with Ying-Li?" Echo took a sip of something from a blue Solo cup, and Cinnamon wondered if their young hosts were upset they couldn't get red ones like they had in every teen movie.

"What do you mean?"

"I mean that when mom and dad introduced you, you weren't interested. Then you got to know each other. Became friends. And now tonight, whenever you look at her, you get this dreamy look in your eyes." She gave Cinnamon a calculating glance and a small shrug. "Her connections *would* help the business. If you ended up getting together."

"No." There was an edge to the word that she hadn't meant to use, and she shifted uncomfortably. "I wish I did have feelings for Ying-Li, because it would make things easier for all of you. And it would be a way to contribute to the company without, you know, giving up my own life, my own career."

"As the future CEO, I'd like to make it clear that I didn't set you up and I won't ever ask you to sacrifice your happiness for a fucking company."

Fierceness glinted in Echo's eyes, and Cinnamon softened.

"I know. I know you value family more than work, and love over politics. If I get a dreamy look, it's not Ying-Li, I'm just thinking of some—something else."

"Some*one*!" Echo shouted, pointing her finger at Cinnamon. "You were going to say some*one*!"

"No!" Cinnamon could feel her ears warming in a blush. God-damn sisterly intuition. People nearby turned to see what the shouting was about.

"Yes! You get goofy when you think of a person! Who is it?"

"It's nobody! I don't! I'm—I just—"

Echo grabbed her arm and led a reluctant Cinnamon through the house and outside into the relative quiet of the garden. "Two thousand eight," Echo started. "End of your senior year at Berkeley. That was the last time I saw that look, and you were head over heels for that girl in your program. You don't talk about it, but you

don't fall in love very often—no, let me say this." She held up a
hand as Cinnamon took a breath to interrupt. "Your way isn't my
way, and I don't understand it, but I don't have to. I just want you to
be happy, and if you look happy when you think about someone,
you might as well tell me about it so I can tell you I support you."

"I'm not in love," Cinnamon said, rolling her eyes. "I only...I only
just met someone."

"Spill."

"There's nothing to spill! I met someone at the Intermittent
earlier, and she seemed cool, and that's it."

Echo narrowed her eyes. "No. There's more. Who is she?"

"She didn't tell me her name."

"Look Ms Psychology, you can't pull one over on me. That just
means *she* didn't tell you her name. You found it somewhere else."

She weighed her desire to keep Starlight to herself with wanting
to tell the world about her, starting with her older sister. But
Echo was clever, and would figure it all out with few details,
so Cinnamon wouldn't have to tell her much. She brought out
her phone and opened Instagram to Starlight's page, turning the
screen so Echo could see.

"Oh wow, pretty," she said, taking the phone and swiping with
a thoughtful look on her face. Cinnamon had scrolled through
dozens of Starlight's posts on the ride to the Twinnings party
and could guess what Echo was reacting to, from the first place
archery trophy to holding up the Leaning Tower of Pisa to last
year's Pride event, where Starlight's denim jacket was plastered
with the words "Trans Ally." Cinnamon folded her arms and impatiently waited for her sister to finish, when Echo suddenly lowered
her arms and pinned her with a look.

"For fuck's sake, Cinnamon."

"What?" She tried to glance at what was on the phone.

"What's her name?"

"Mal said it was Daphne," Cinnamon answered. Why?"

"Daphne what."

"Daphne what what?"

"What's her last name?"

"Well I don't know! I just met her!" A knot of worry crept into her gut, and she reached out for the phone. Echo pulled it back, then held it in front of Cinnamon's face.

"'Annual family picnic, sans Mats.'" Cinnamon read it aloud. It was posted in February, a selfie Starlight had taken with a group of people who were obviously related. They stood on a field of green grass, with an office building in the background. Starlight was the only one who looked like she was genuinely having a good time, and Cinnamon smiled without thinking about it. She couldn't see anything wrong with it, or anything Echo might object to. "So?"

"So look at the name on the building. Look at the hashtags. Tap it and see who's tagged."

Cinnamon did. "Redgrave. I don't get it."

Echo sighed and handed back the phone. "This is Daphne Redgrave."

"Yes, okay, Daphne Redgrave." She stared at Echo. Echo stared back.

"As in the Redgrave Group."

"Whatever you're trying to tell me, I'm clearly not getting it," Cinnamon said, a bite in her words. Kissing Starlight had been a too-short moment of peace and contentment in her otherwise stressful life, and every moment that took her further away from it made her more reactive and brittle.

"The Redgrave Group is one of our biggest competitors. Our parents set you up with Ying-Li because—well, because they only know, like, five lesbians and two of them are married—but also because her family's business can help our family's business. If you're not attracted to her, that's totally fine. But if you introduce a Redgrave as your new girlfriend, it looks like you went out of your way to deliberately find whoever our parents would disapprove of the most."

"They couldn't be so..." Cinnamon trailed off. She was going to say they couldn't be so single-minded, but it wasn't until Echo had really committed to being a part of the business that they became more flexible about what and who they found appropriate for Cinnamon to study, pursue, and date. There was a possibility that they would view her dating a Redgrave as a personal betrayal and not a coincidence.

"I didn't go looking for one of our mortal enemies to make out with," Cinnamon said, her mind whirring.

"Look, usually I'd say, fuck it. But the timing feels awfully convenient for it to be a coincidence."

"What the hell does that mean?"

Echo sighed and glanced around the yard. Nobody was really within hearing distance, but as her responsibilities at the company increased, so did her paranoia.

"I can't give you details, obviously, but we're looking into buying out a couple of our lesser competitors, as well as some tangential start-ups to integrate into our system. We're sort of in a delicate position for a little while, and if someone were to infiltrate us, they could potentially destroy—"

Cinnamon burst out laughing. "*Infiltrate?* You sound like a political thriller."

"Corporate espionage is a real thing, and it can take down entire corporations." Echo always enunciated things more precisely when she was trying to mask her anger, and she was hitting each syllable with the careful intonation of a teacher speaking to her unruly student. "If someone is good enough at it, they can apply pressure to just the right spot, and CT will fold.

"I don't want to see you hurt," Echo continued. "I don't want the business to hurt, either. I'm just asking you to take a minute to look at it from my point of view before you go eloping with our competition's daughter. Can you know for sure she's not a corporate spy? That she hasn't targeted you as the weakest link to gain entry to our secrets?"

That seemed unlikely. If someone *were* trying to get to Cheung Technologies through her, their research would never have predicted her assertive behavior that night, anyway. Cinnamon herself hadn't predicted it. The first time in almost a decade she wanted to kiss someone, and she went for it. Her spirit had been high earlier, light and free and seen and accepted, and it wasn't fair of Echo to try to take that from her.

"You know, here I thought we were bonding like regular sisters over a crush. But apparently, there's no other reason why Daphne Redgrave would even notice me at all, if it weren't for my family name on a company that I have absolutely nothing to do with."

"That's not what I meant," Echo whined, pinching the bridge of her nose.

"Doesn't matter. I'm not having a good time here. I think I'll go home."

"Cinnamon—"

"No, it's fine. We can..." She sighed. "Think about what you want to say to me, and I'll do the same, so when we speak again, in daylight, after a good night's sleep, we can communicate clearly and not hurt anyone's feelings."

"Sure," Echo said lightly. "Of course."

"If you see the others, tell them I said bye."

While they'd been celebrating the solstice, night had moved closer to dawn, and as she crossed the lawn to find her way back to the street, Cinnamon wondered why she couldn't have told her friends to go on without her while she stayed at the Intermittent with Starlight. She shook her head and muttered to herself about being an adult and resisting peer pressure and living in the moment. After calling for a rideshare, she flipped back to Instagram and, angry with herself for hesitating before, hit the "Follow" button on Starlight's page with a combination of frustration, anticipation, and hope.

***

By the time Cinnamon got home, the night had settled into the damp stillness of a too-early Sunday morning. Her agitation had faded, and the only thing that felt off was an unrelated paranoia. Listening for anything out of the ordinary, she turned a slow circle in front of her house and watched the shadows for movement. When she was sure everything seemed normal, she entered the house, shut off the alarm, and did a quick search through every room, closet, and cabinet. She needed to know the windows were locked and that she was alone.

This routine was fairly new, and she hated it. While she had always maintained a healthy dose of suspicion, her recent hobby was drawing some unwanted attention, and the extra precautions were necessary.

These wee hours of the morning were already way past her bedtime, but she was too wound up to fall asleep. She stood in the kitchen, looking around for something to do that didn't require particular attention and might eventually lead to rest. Secret Hobby didn't meet either criterion, as it required focused attention to detail, and she would make a mess of it if she tried. She loved baking and used it as a tool to let her mind work through mental challenges while her hands and memory were busy making something delicious, but she was too distracted to use an oven. But mindlessly creating a complex RPG character was her equivalent of adult coloring books. She didn't have to ever use the characters, but it was a great exercise in creativity and relaxation.

After changing into red sleep shorts and bra and combing her waist-length hair, she grabbed her D&D books and notebook, threw on a red sweatshirt, and plopped into a lounge chair by the pool.

She had been making characters for roleplaying games so long that she didn't need the instructions, which was good, because she couldn't concentrate on written words. Starlight poked into her focus like the actual stars in the sky, demanding an amount of attention that, despite Cinnamon's eagerness earlier in the night, seemed too much, too soon. In the moment, she was present and all in. Hours after, her interest hadn't waned, but she'd tried to temper it with reason.

Twenty minutes later, as she was halfheartedly deciding what kind of weaponry to give her half-orc ranger, a rustling in the bushes on the far side of the pool made her go still. The flood lights in the pool were on, and there was enough dim light to read by from the kitchen behind her. But she was mostly in darkness, and if she stayed very still, anyone coming toward her from that side of the property wouldn't realize there was a person sitting in the lounge chair. She slowly stretched out to feel her phone on the side table in case she needed to call for help.

Her hard-beating heart crept toward her throat as she listened for another sound that wasn't supposed to be there.

And there it was, another rustle, followed by a twig breaking. Then a thud, and someone whispering "Ow." Another thud. "Fuck."

Cinnamon's fear was beginning to transform into a suspicious curiosity when the hedges parted and Daphne Redgrave tripped into the yard face first with another "Fuck." Cinnamon took a breath to say something, but thought better of it. As much as she'd wanted to see Starlight again, her fear of being tracked down by a stranger was equal to the thrill that this woman must have read as much into their kiss as she did herself, to the point where she employed drastic measures to see her again.

It was terribly dramatic.

And apparently Cinnamon was a sucker for a grand gesture.

Starlight lifted her head and spat out some grass with a "pfthfthfth" before pushing onto her knees and rolling her shoulders. She sat back with a sigh and brushed the dirt off her dress—still *The Moon*—adjusted it so it wouldn't fall off, then stood up and dusted off the rest. Cinnamon watched in silence, curious to know what the Redgrave girl would do when she didn't think she was being watched, when she was committing a crime and determined in her pursuit. If that was, in fact, why she was there.

The Moon shook her head, reaching up to pick leaves and stems out of her hair. Even at this distance, Cinnamon wondered at its stark white color, reflecting even the smallest bit of light like a compulsion to announce itself. Her shoulders and arms were nearly as pale, though they were now smudged by her impromptu squeeze through the bushes. The trespasser licked her hand and rubbed at her chin, evidently feeling the dirt smeared there when she fell.

Satisfied with her cursory ablutions, Starlight picked up the train of her dress, huffed, turned, and slowly made her way toward the house. Her eyes darted from the illuminated kitchen to the second-floor windows, across the yard and pool, and finally on the chair with the shadowed, person-shaped lump. She stopped short, shoulders tensing, and squinted, hand lifted against the light to try to see better.

"Uh. Cinnamon, right?"

The moment stretched as Cinnamon decided how to answer. Maybe she was being naïve—Echo would tell her so, if she found out—but she wanted Starlight's intentions to align with her own. She wanted something uncomplicated and sweet, but also a little reckless. If that was a terrible decision, that would be a later problem.

"Starlight," she said confidently, like she'd been expecting her. "Have you followed me home?"

The not-unwelcome intruder visibly relaxed and smiled rakishly into the shadows.

"Well, I thought, maybe you'd like to kiss some more."

Cinnamon's heart did a little flip before sliding down through her gut, leaving a trail of warmth that settled low enough to make her blush.

"Because I want to kiss you some more," Starlight continued, walking toward her. "And you seemed to enjoy it too, and then you asked Mal about me, and then you followed me on Instagram, and..." She stopped short when Cinnamon didn't respond, worry crossing her face as she glanced up at the house again.

"Oh fuck," she said lightly. "I crossed a line, didn't I? Christ. I'm sorry. I wasn't thinking about anything except seeing you again, and when I'm focused like that I can forget things like the concept of time or why border hedges exist."

"It is sort of a lot." It would have felt less invasive six months ago, but that wasn't Starlight's fault. "You clearly went through a lot of trouble to get here, and we're both awake, so, make it up to me by sitting with me and telling me how the hell you got my home address."

The trespasser gave her a sheepish smile. "To keep me distracted until the cops get here?"

"I don't call the cops on lesbians." Cinnamon snorted. "Assuming, of course."

"Oh no, you're right, big time lesbian here. Was hoping that was clear when I kissed you back."

"Sort of suspected, yes."

They stared at each other another moment until Starlight gestured toward the pool. "If there won't be kissing right away, do you mind if I...?" Cinnamon inclined her head, and Starlight hiked up her skirt, kicked off her flats, and plopped down, lowering her legs into the water with a sigh. She took her phone out of a pocket and set it on the stones of the patio behind her.

"One of your friends at the Intermittent mentioned leaving for the Twinnings party. I've been there before, and took a chance that that was where you would be." She swung her legs in the water, watching the ripples. "When I got there, you'd already left, so I asked someone where you went. They didn't know, so they asked someone else, and after a while, someone said you'd gone home." She shrugged. "I asked for the address, and they gave it to me."

She looked up at Cinnamon's heavy sigh. "They just...gave you my home address."

"I didn't think it was weird because I'm used to things going right for me," Starlight said. "But I can see how that would be a problem from, like, a security standpoint."

"Do you remember who it was?"

"Someone in a costume? Who was also drunk?" She bit her lip like she was trying to think.

"It's fine," Cinnamon said, waving a hand. "I should remind everyone not to give out my personal information anyway."

"For what it's worth, I was very convincing." She tilted her head and smiled.

"I have no doubt." Cinnamon let her eyes wander over Starlight, imagining trying to resist her easy seduction. Echo's warning slipped into her thoughts and she wished she could ignore the uninvited suspicion. "Do you know who I am?"

"Mal told me," Starlight said, nodding.

"Did you know before then?"

"No?" she drawled, a little confused. "Do you know who I am?"

"Thanks to Mal and social media, Daphne Redgrave. You should know I don't have anything to do with my family's business."

"Why is that something I should know?"

"In case you're a corporate spy looking to infiltrate and destroy it through the weakest link by seducing me."

She burst into laughter. "Oh, no!"

Cinnamon folded her arms. "Okay, well, I'm glad, but also, that response was kind of rude."

"No, no, it's just, that sounds like an awful lot of work. I mean, I could do it, but you seem really nice, so if I was sent by my family to pretend to like you just to make them richer, well. I would be fucking terrible at it. Also, I don't work for my family's business either, in any capacity. Well, I did just charge my father, like, ten grand but that was mostly a joke and anyway, I'm giving that money to my sister that's been cut off."

"If you don't work for them, what do you do?"

Starlight wrinkled her nose. "I'm an accountant."

"No shit."

"Yeah. I'm good with numbers and I like it, it's satisfying. Creating order from chaos and all that. Then I don't feel bad about creating chaos everywhere else."

Cinnamon laughed at that. It made sense, from the little she'd seen of her life, the party, her Instagram. Showing up at her house a few hours after midnight, uninvited.

"If you don't work for your family, why are you worried about..." Starlight wiggled her fingers toward her. "Corruption through seduction?"

"I hadn't been. But my sister found out that we kissed, and she's going to take over the business soon. She got in my head."

"Ugh. I hate that for you. But I like that you're already telling people we made out." She smiled slyly. "So instead of working at Cheung Technologies, you became a therapist."

Cinnamon blushed thinking about their kiss, before the rest of what Starlight said caught up to her brain. "Yeah. Business meetings, making deals, profit margins, R&D. I've never been interested in any of it. I always wanted to do something that helped people, instead."

"Mmm," Starlight said, thoughtfully. "Are you going to tell me I should be in therapy?"

"Everyone should be in therapy."

"Trick question. I already am. This—" she gestured toward herself. "—is me, therapized."

"Dear god."

"Not quite. But I'm working on it." She winked.

There was no reason for Cinnamon to believe that Starlight was telling the truth. She never used to be so cynical, but things changed, and she had to change with it. She knew it was unlikely—or just stupid—for someone to target her based on her family ties. If anything, she'd be targeted for her own work or her Secret Hobby, and Starlight didn't seem like the type of person who would be involved in that.

Cinnamon closed her book and set it on the side table, stood up, and stripped off her sweatshirt and shorts.

"What. Is happening." Starlight grinned as Cinnamon tossed the clothes back on the chair and walked to the pool in her red bra and light blue underwear.

The water was warm, heated against the always-chill of San Francisco after dark and before dawn—the only time Cinnamon was regularly free to swim. It was warmer than the night air, but not by much. She descended the steps and ducked beneath the surface, popping up closer to Starlight, still in the shallow end, keeping her shoulders submerged.

"You travel back and forth across the city to find me," Cinnamon said, slicking the wet hair out of her eyes. "You get to my house, sneak onto my property using the most inconvenient route possible, and make choices that in legal terms include stalking and trespassing."

Starlight winced to hear it put that way.

"So," Cinnamon continued, gently waving her arms back and forth in the water. "Why aren't you in the pool with me right now?"

Chapter Eight

Daphne looked surprised by the question, but it was only a moment before she smiled wickedly and dropped into the water, submerging dress, crown, and all.

Cinnamon watched her take the two strokes beneath the surface to reach her, her arms so pale in the bluish underwater light that they looked like they'd never known sunlight; dark dress blooming behind her like ink dropped in a water glass. Starlight was an undersea creature, somewhere between a sea witch and a naiad, something beautiful and fragile that sailors would dash themselves on rocks for before they noticed her mouth full of needle-like teeth.

She reemerged a few inches from Cinnamon's face, a burst of midnight beauty and silver stars falling like a sheet of fireworks, her breath a wisp of raspberries and mint—what nebulae must taste like, spinning unseen in the depths of the universe.

Water ran into Daphne's eyes no matter how much she wiped it away, thanks to the silk and plastic folds of petals and leaves in her flower crown sloshing trapped water whenever she moved her head. Cinnamon laughed and Starlight grinned and reached to hold her face in her hands, fingertips trailing sparks against Cinnamon's jaw, her cheeks, over her ears and into her hair. She pulled them closer, a question becoming a promise. Ink-blue eyes took up all of Cinnamon's vision, and she didn't have time to mourn them fluttering closed before a brush of lips against hers, light, and wet, and tasting like chlorine, and her eyes closed too, and she let herself lean into the starlight.

Despite kissing her first—was it only hours ago?—and despite basically asking to be kissed this time, Cinnamon felt like she was at Starlight's mercy. She never liked giving up control, but she was starting to think she never liked having it either, and that surrendering to these unexpected feelings and this tornado of a woman would be, among other things, a sort of relief.

Starlight's tongue flicked against Cinnamon's lips, sparking a desire that burned a fuse from her mouth, past the agitated butter-flies of her stomach, right into her groin. Cinnamon grabbed her around the waist, the costume's silky fabric feeling strange in the water, and returned the kiss with a desperation that felt sloppy. But she couldn't help herself.

Time suspended for both of them, as fluid as the water pressing against their bodies. The women were lost in each other, all roam-ing hands, and mouths slick more from kisses than pool water. If Starlight had any reservations about kissing a stranger, tracking her down, breaking into her home, and making out in her pool, Cinnamon couldn't tell.

Eventually, her mind returned from oh-my-god-I'm-kiss-ing-this-beautiful-woman and started asking all sorts of irrelevant questions. Like "are we sure she's not a spy for our parents?" and "are we sure she's not a spy from BDMT?" and "it's been seven years since we've been attracted to someone, we thought we couldn't be, what the fuck is wrong with us?"

Cinnamon pulled away slowly. Starlight darted forward to steal one last peck on her lips.

"I—" Cinnamon said, frowning. "I don't usually do this."

"Make out with beautiful strangers in your pool at 3 o'clock in the morning? Whyever not?"

She just...hadn't. She'd never done this before. But she was doing it with Starlight, so either the way she operated had changed for the first time in twenty-eight years, or this was a very specific reaction to very specifically Starlight.

"I don't usually kiss on the first date." That was close enough to the truth.

"Well," the midnight naiad said with a twinkle in her eye, "we haven't had a date yet, so, technically, you still haven't."

Closing her eyes, Cinnamon bit back a sigh. Starlight's breath tickled her face, warmer than the night air, warmer than the water and their skin.

"Are you a fan of finding loopholes, Starlight?"

"When they suit me."

"Are you always so reckless?"

"You have no idea."

"And do you always bend the world to your will?"

"Regularly."

She had said as much, before. Cinnamon had no doubt. Rich, cisgender white girl. Brought up to believe the world was hers for the taking. But she also had her own career, outside her family's business, just like Cinnamon. Maybe the will she worked was one of love, and justice, righting wrongs as much as mischief for mischief's sake. She did sigh, then, and opened her eyes to see Starlight again.

"Has that always worked out for you?"

Starlight looked past her, and up, into the trees, then into the sky, still a deep blue with sunrise yet a few hours away.

"Always." Her eyes met Cinnamon's again. "In the long run. Though in some cases, it's immediately clear." She glanced down and back again, somehow checking her out even though most of their bodies were under water.

"I can't tell if you're being cocky or truthful."

Starlight shrugged. "Bit of both."

Cinnamon laughed. The spell wasn't broken, exactly, but her brain and body and emotions were all demanding different things, and she knew trying to make decisions in that state would result in disaster. Especially when another person was involved.

"Come on," she said, grasping Starlight's hand and leading them both toward the pool steps. "Let's dry off. You can stay here tonight. I can't kick you out in your condition, I'd worry whether you got home okay."

"I'm staying the night?" Starlight wiggled her eyebrows. "Why Cinnamon, you horny devil."

Once out of the pool, Cinnamon got a pair of fluffy towels out of a plastic trunk and handed one to Starlight. The relatively warmer pool water had made the chilly night air uncomfortable, and the women dried off quickly. The dripping Moon shook the trapped water out of her flower crown and kicked her soaked dress into a pile as she wrapped the towel around her.

Even though she knew sex wouldn't be a good idea, Cinnamon couldn't help letting her eyes wander over the other woman's body. Warmth spread through her chest, her limbs, up into her cheeks. What if it wasn't a good idea to let her stay at all?

"If I asked you to leave, would you just break in again?"

"Oof. Okay." Starlight adjusted the towel under her armpits and picked up her dress to wring the water out of it. "First, if you asked me to leave, I'd go, no questions asked. I would leave you my number and a note saying you should call and we should go out, but I'd leave it up to you. Second, I'm not sure I technically 'broke in' the first time? So I can't really do it 'again'?"

"Your understanding of law is fascinating." Cinnamon picked up her dry clothes and D&D book. "Do you always define crimes so loosely?"

Starlight winced. "I'm a work in progress," she mumbled, stopping in her dress-wringing to look at Cinnamon. "I like you. And I'd like the chance to see if you and I have something together before I go messing it up. So if you want me to leave, I'm gone. You want me to stay, put me on a couch, lock me in a separate room, whatever. You want to share a bed, maybe kiss, maybe not, maybe more, I'm down. It's up to you, Cinnamon."

Her name danced in Starlight's mouth, a warm melody that belonged to Starlight's voice as much as it did to Cinnamon herself. She wanted her to stay. She also had to believe that she was doing what she needed to protect herself: for her heart, but for her career and physical safety too.

"I have clothes you can wear. We'll hang your dress up in the laundry room. You can share my bed, if you like. Kissing would be nice. We can see where it goes from there."

Starlight smiled and bowed her head. "I'm all yours."

***

The last day of spring and the first day of summer had too much in common to be able to distinguish one from the other, unless someone took the calendar very seriously, or unless—like Daphne—they had woken up in Spring single and empty, and in Summer the next morning in the bed of the perfect woman and with the knowledge that their life had changed forever.

The brightness of late morning tried to peek around the bedroom's wide mahogany blinds, but only succeeded in a muted, diffused light. Just enough to glow through Daphne's eyelids and rouse her from her eighth hour of sleep. Unwilling to open her eyes just yet, she noted the unfamiliar texture of the bed sheets and stretched her legs straight out, pointing her toes and feeling the silkiness against her. Much softer than her own. A blanket heavier than hers. The pillow had a faint resinous scent, like a witch shop, and beyond that was the bready, buttery smell of someone baking.

Cinnamon. Daphne grinned and stretched across the bed to pull Cinnamon closer. When her arm dropped onto the otherwise empty bed and not the woman she was expecting, she finally blinked her eyes opened and looked around.

She was alone in the bed, and if the cool temperature of the sheets was any indication, had been for a while. She sat up, her shifting clothes sending up a puff of chlorine and whatever Cinnamon used to wash her laundry—orange and pine. The dark, old furniture and honey-colored walls gave the room a sense of warmth and comfort that Daphne had found lacking in the more modern—but still spectacular—kitchen and bathroom she'd seen. The door to the hallway stood ajar, several jewel-tone shawls hanging from hooks behind it.

If Cinnamon had wanted her out, she wouldn't have just left her there to sleep. Daphne yawned and nestled back under the covers, giving herself a few more minutes before getting out of bed.

She replayed the night before in her mind, unable to stop grinning. It had just been so goddamn *romantic*. Beautiful, nameless stranger coming to her rescue. The flirting, the *kissing*. Being kissed first was a rare event, because she was always so eager and never thought about what might happen afterward. But she had been overwhelmed by the party that was somehow heavily populated by her exes (not really a mystery: she had a lot) and confronted by her many failures. It was no wonder her mind had had enough. She was recovering by the time Cinnamon had leaned in to kiss her, but she hadn't quite gotten around to her usual level of kiss-first-think-later.

And apparently, Daphne's senses had still been scrambled when she'd decided to follow her to her house and crawl through her non-euphemism bushes on the chance that Cinnamon might like to spend more time with the woman she left behind at the first party.

Daphne groaned, embarrassed all over again. It had worked out. But it was still too much. *Well, tone it down from now on*, she told herself. Sure. That would happen.

It was a good sign that Cinnamon had asked her to stay the night, even if they hadn't done more than kiss. Sleeping beside each other was intimate in its own way and required more trust. Cinnamon had fallen asleep first. It sounded like she had an Actual Adult Job with Actual Adult Hours and wasn't used to staying up until almost dawn making out with strangers. Cinnamon had kissed her one last time, said she was going to fall asleep, turned onto her back, and that was it.

Daphne had watched her as her breathing evened out, dark lashes against light, golden-sand cheeks, lips parted, dark eyebrows with the barest hint of a frown. The whorl of her ear reminded Daphne of a koru—a spiral Māori symbol of an unfurling fern—and she wanted to reach out and trace it with her fingertip. How on earth she'd been able to land the most gorgeous woman in San Francisco, she had no damn clue. But she felt very, very lucky.

The morning-slash-afternoon was slipping away, so she threw off the covers and got out of bed, trying and failing to not smile like an idiot. The smell of bakery had become stronger, and it was joined by coffee and some kind of breakfast meat, Daphne was sure. Cinnamon had loaned her a pair of teal jersey shorts and a white, cropped tee that said "Maybe Baby" in hot pink script. Daphne loathed it and never wanted to give it back.

On the way downstairs, she grabbed her phone and threw on a sapphire-and-gold shawl, partly to cover the shirt and partly to combat the chill. She stopped in the bathroom just outside the bedroom, then decided to indulge her curiosity a little and look into the other rooms on that floor. One door hid a linen closet, and another, a guest bedroom that looked like a spa. Daphne grinned. She would have been comfortable there, but Cinnamon had wanted them to share her bed. Very good sign.

The third closed door was locked. Her lockpicking set was at home, but she could get it open using a variety of metal beauty tools she'd seen in the bathroom. Daphne was cursed with thinking of the most problematic solutions to a problem first. She took a deep breath and was overwhelmed by the aroma of bread, butter, meat, and chocolate. Her eyes widened. It smelled like Cinnamon must have taken something out of the oven.

She hurried downstairs, following the smell of breakfast like a cartoon character drifting on the trail of fresh-baked pie. With the sun at its highest point, light didn't stream into the modern open floor plan, but the wide windows and pale earth tones reflected the brightness of the day into the entire house.

Cinnamon stood in the kitchen, her back to Daphne. She had already gotten dressed for the day in black leggings and a teal tank top, her hair secured in a top knot. The most casual of outfits, but desire still stirred Daphne, watching the slight curve of Cinnamon's hips, her bare arms, her elbows, for heaven's sake—the perfect silhouette. The drip coffee maker sputtered and coughed, and Daphne squinted at it as she hopped onto one of the bar stools at the large island.

"You have a La Cornue stove but a Mr Coffee drip," Daphne said as she adjusted herself in the chair. "I have to know the story behind that."

Cinnamon looked up from her baking sheet and gave Daphne a smile. A smudge of chocolate streaked across her forehead and into her hairline, adorable enough for Daphne to leave it, though another part of her wanted to lick her clean. "Good morning to you too. I was wondering when you'd be up."

"My only rule is that I have to wake up while brunch is still being served somewhere in the city. And it's only—damn, it's before noon? I could have gotten in another two hours. But whatever smells you're brewing drew me here like a siren's song. Are you sure you're not a witch?"

"There's an espresso machine over here, if you'd rather have a latte or something. You'll have to make it yourself, though. I haven't learned how."

Daphne slid off the chair and walked around to the other side of Cinnamon, whistling low when she saw the machine. "So shiny. Why don't you use it?"

Not looking up from placing sprigs of thyme on what smelled like ham and cheese croissants, Cinnamon playfully slapped Daphne's reaching hand away from the pastries. "It was a house-warming gift from my sister. I lived in the dorms at Berkeley and got used to terrible coffee. When Echo first visited me here, she saw my cheap coffee maker and had the DeLonghi delivered a few hours later. Before she even left. She's the only one who uses it."

"Echo?" Daphne dumped coffee beans into the hopper while the water heated up.

"My sister."

"Hippie parents?"

"Hardly." Cinnamon washed the thyme off her fingers and start-ed placing squares of chocolate on, most likely, chocolate crois-sants. "They wanted to fit into the rich-people club, and knew rich white people name their children ridiculous things. But instead of naming us after cities or cars, they chose English words they liked the sound of."

Daphne pulled a carton of soy milk out of the fridge. "I get it. My siblings are Hayden, Kyle, Ola, Matalina, and Topher. I won't even get into their kids' names. But you could have had it so much worse. And I like your name. I like saying it, and I like that it's yours."

Cinnamon blushed and finished stacking the croissants onto a platter. "Patio okay? It's in the shade now."

"I'll be right out. I'm going to make you a latte, too. You must think I'm just a beautiful, bumbling idiot. Since I can't dazzle you with how good I am at mazes and numbers, and I left my slingshot at home, I'll have to rely on my barista skills to convince you I'm worth keeping."

"Why would I think you're not worth keeping?" Cinnamon asked over her shoulder as she took the platter and her coffee mug outside.

Grinding coffee beans answered her, and the hiss of the steam wand. Daphne watched out the floor-to-ceiling back windows as Cinnamon set out napkins and plates and piled hers with one of each croissant. Daphne came out a few minutes later, carrying two white porcelain cups. The one she set in front of Cinnamon had a little foam art ghost in it.

"Did you give me a ghost?"

"Yeah," she answered, sitting down. Her own latte just looked like a blob. "I practiced on this one first and it came out terrible, but I'm happy with yours. Because the story you told me."

Cinnamon blinked.

"The story. At the Intermittent." Daphne slipped two croissants onto her plate. "I don't remember the details, but it was a haunted house, right? And everybody died, but you did something lucky and saved them and somebody was pissed off about it. See? I was listening. As much as my anxiety brain would allow. Fuck, what is this, ham and cheese? My god. Here I was thinking I was going to impress you with a latte."

Daphne watched Cinnamon take a careful sip of the latte, in case she hated it and Daphne had to remake it or accept that her new crush preferred disgusting drip brew. But Cinnamon raised her eyebrows and kept drinking. Daphne counted it as a point in her favor.

Daphne might have had a habit of falling in love anytime, anywhere, for any reason, but she felt there was something special about her attraction to Cinnamon besides Daphne getting kissed first, and Cinnamon's radiant, warm beauty, and the opportunity to make out almost immediately. Beyond, even, homemade croissants. She was eager to see if the ease she felt could be prolonged by another hour, another day, stretching, maybe, across the rest of her life. Daphne closed her eyes and indulged in the fantasy of a stable, long-term relationship and its accompanying buttery breakfasts.

***

"Why would I think you weren't worth keeping?" Cinnamon asked again. She didn't want to interrupt what looked like a reverent worship of her baking skills, but Starlight's comment about being worth keeping had bothered her. Starlight opened her eyes and licked the meaty cheese oil off her fingers.

"What do you know about me?" She wiped her fingers on the napkin. "I mean, what have you heard about me?"

Cinnamon shook her head. "Nothing. Nothing before last night, when I went looking for you on Instagram. Why?"

Even with the sun near its zenith, it wasn't very hot out. Bright, yes, blinding. Starlight pulled the shawl a little tighter and squinted across the backyard. While she was busy thinking, Cinnamon drank her in, from the small, pale foot skimming across the concrete, delicate tendons tracing the top of it, to the shape of her in her shorts and tee. The gold in the shawl should have drawn out whatever warm undertones were in her skin, but it was obvious that she belonged to the cool night, silver and white aura coming alive with midnight. Even in the sun, Daphne was still Starlight.

"I've thought, more than once," Starlight said slowly, "That I must have met all the lesbians in San Francisco at this point. Or, if not, that they all knew of me, and had Opinions."

Cinnamon pulled a turtle face and brought the latte mug to her lips again. "I can't imagine why."

Starlight gave her a thoughtful look, the blue of her eyes more prominent in the noon sun, the sapphire of the shawl highlighting their color.

"We should go on a date."

"Is this not a date?" Cinnamon gestured to the table. "I made you croissants. You made me coffee. It's a breakfast date."

"I crashed your alone time on a balcony." Starlight shook her head. "I crashed your party. I crashed your house. I crashed your bed. And now I crashed your breakfast. I want the chance to show you I can be thoughtful. I can plan stuff. I can build something as beautifully as I can wreck it."

And how beautifully she did wreck it. Seven years. For seven years, Cinnamon was content with her life. She had her friends, her family, her career, her hobbies, and if she didn't have someone to share her bed with, it was because she didn't want someone to share her bed with. If she ever felt lonely, if she ever cried, it wasn't because she needed anyone. It wasn't because she thought she was broken and would never love again.

Then this impossible woman stumbled into her life. Literally. Several times. Cinnamon knew her for a total of twelve hours, and eight of those hours were sleeping. She cracked her defenses and let the starlight in, and Cinnamon didn't know what to do or why, now, this practically-a-stranger felt like the woman she was supposed to let in. Before she could respond, Starlight's phone chirped in her pocket.

"Sorry," she said, taking it out. "It might be work. Yikes, two percent battery."

Cinnamon cleared her throat, trying to get her emotions to back down. "I have a charger, if you need one."

She sighed and sat back in the chair. "Sorry," she said again, fingers flying over the screen. "It is work. They took on a new client and want me to start with them tomorrow, and that means reviewing the case today. They want me in the office in an hour."

"I was going to ask if you wanted to go hiking this afternoon."

Her fingers paused above the phone, and she wrinkled her nose.

"You know. As a date," Cinnamon continued. "Or dinner tonight, if you're working this afternoon."

Daphne added furrowed brows to her face of dislike, and Cinnamon laughed. "Or dinner tonight because you hate hiking?"

"Swimming, cool," Daphne said, resuming typing. "Food, great. Sex, perfect. But I'm assuming hiking takes place outside. I'm not interested in outside for the sake of outside." She stopped typing and smiled at Cinnamon before returning her attention to the phone. "Well, unless there's archery. But I'm very interested in you, so if that's what you want to do, give me a few hours to research it and buy appropriate clothing and gear, and—god-dammit."

She slid her phone onto the table. "Battery died."

"Here." Cinnamon grabbed the phone and took it into the kitchen. Daphne picked up one of the chocolate croissants and followed her, taking a bite and pausing to lean against the doorway in pleasure.

"Oh Jesus," she said, closing her eyes. "Would you be cooking dinner, too? How the fuck are you single?"

If only there was an answer to that. From a junk drawer, Cinna-mon brought out a cord and plugged in the phone. "I'm assuming you can't exactly show up at work wearing...that."

"You'd be surprised," Starlight sighed, climbing up onto the island stool again. "If you could call me a Lyft, I'll wrap my still-damp Moon dress around me, plop on my flower crown, and head home to change before going in."

Cinnamon slid her own phone across the island as she made her way out of the kitchen. "The app is on the first page. I'll check your dress. You can wear those pajamas home anyway." She turned back and let her gaze wander over Daphne. "That way, you'll have to see me again to give them back."

The grin on Daphne's face could only be described as lupine. "Oh, Cinnamon. As if I needed an excuse to see you again."

Chapter Nine

An hour later, as Cinnamon was putting away the leftover crois-sants and cleaning the kitchen, her phone chirped a cascade of text message alerts.

Daphne:

made it just in time!

Still smell like chlorine, it's distracting.

:)

This is Daphne bye

*btw

dammit autocorrect

Also I just realized your name is Cinnamon and you bake pastries. Fate?

Sure enough, Starlight had created herself as a contact in the phone, either while Cinnamon was sleeping or when she ordered her rideshare. And all of her contact info was there: name, cell number, address, email, usernames across a bunch of different social media. Going into the edit function, Cinnamon changed the name to Starlight, who had already set it up with a picture of herself biting into the chocolate croissant, eyes closed. Cinnamon laughed, but she was going to have to change the photo as soon as possible to one that didn't hide Starlight's best feature.

Her imagination flashed her a quick image of the woman, naked and pale against Cinnamon's red sheets, waiting for her, and the jolt of desire was so sudden and so like electricity, she nearly dropped her phone.

Not that kind of picture, she admonished herself, trying to breathe around the tangles of want that had appeared throughout her body. *Her eyes. I meant her eyes.*

The new image in her mind was a close-up of her face, midnight eyes glossy, lips red and swollen from kissing, and of course, just below the frame, wearing absolutely nothing...

"Get a grip," she snapped, shaking her head to dispel the fantasy, which didn't disappear so much as lumber back into the dark corners of her mind with a growl of discontent. She planted her feet on the floor and found her balance, closed her eyes, and took a few deep breaths. It seemed to be Starlight's style to rush into things, but Cinnamon preferred to feel certain, even if it meant going slow.

Cinnamon:

> Glad you got home okay and got to the meeting on time.
> My name and my baking are not fate, just coincidence.
> Still want to try for dinner? I should have asked if you
> have any allergies.

She slid the clean baking sheet into its cabinet and glanced around the kitchen, making sure she didn't miss anything. Hiking had sounded great an hour ago, but now that she was alone at home, she wanted to stay alone and at home. Swim in the pool for a bit, relax, then pour a glass of wine and head upstairs to work on her Secret Hobby until, possibly, dinner with a date. Her phone made another series of chirps.

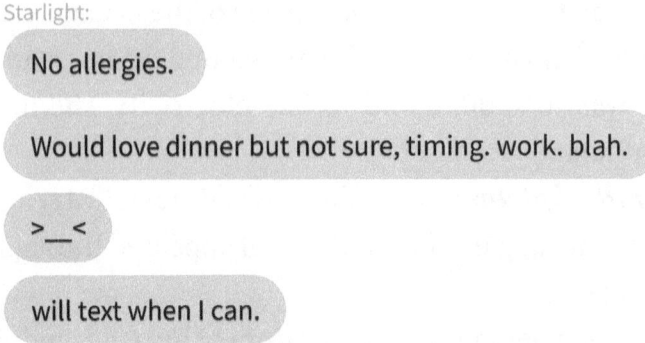

Starlight:

No allergies.

Would love dinner but not sure, timing. work. blah.

>__<

will text when I can.

As she closed the text app and put the phone in her pocket, it beeped again. Echo, this time, with a short text: "About to call you." Cinnamon answered with a thumbs-up emoji and waited the five seconds it took for Echo to start FaceTime.

"Were you baking?"

Despite being the older sister, Echo—after an all-nighter that included alcohol, drugs, and a slightly younger man who would refer to himself as a "player"—looked as fresh and well-rested as though she'd just left a spa. She was walking quickly down an indoor hallway Cinnamon recognized from CT headquarters.

"Are you going to tell me that's sisterly intuition? We're connected?"

"You've got chocolate on your forehead."

"What?" Cinnamon pulled the phone closer to look at the little square of herself. She clicked her tongue against her teeth and rubbed at the large smudge of chocolate. When it didn't budge, she licked her hand and tried again. "That's been there this whole time. Why didn't..." She sighed. "Croissants, earlier."

"Did you make extra for your favorite sister?"

"I have plans today, Echo. Entertaining you isn't one of them." At the thought of her sister visiting, she remembered that Starlight had used the espresso machine, and she went to clean it.

"Yeesh. Just wrap them up and leave them in a box on your porch. I'll send someone to pick them up. Chocolate?"

"And ham and cheese."

"Yeah, make me a care package, please. I'm about to earn it."

"So confident, and yet, such lies."

"I was wrong."

Cinnamon paused, the portafilter with its used coffee grounds in her grip. Her attention bounced back to Echo.

"Sorry, I thought I heard you say you were wrong."

"I did. Don't act so shocked. A good business leader can admit when they're wrong, and I'm the best."

"There she is. You had me worried for a minute."

"Be quiet so I can make amends."

Placing the portafilter in the sink, Cinnamon nodded for her sister to continue.

"I followed up on that Redgrave girl," Echo said, "and I don't think she's a threat. To the business, I mean. Socially, she's a disaster. Used to work for her family's company, but never in a position of power, and she quit a few years ago. Now she's an accountant at a small business management firm that doesn't seem to have any connection to Redgrave Group. The only thing I can't figure out is why someone as wealthy as she is would work as an accountant at a firm she doesn't even own."

"She's good at it?" Cinnamon knocked the coffee grounds into the compost bin. She was used to being paranoid, but Starlight's desire to work in a job she was good at and enjoyed made sense to her. "If she doesn't need the money, she must be doing it for the pleasure."

"As an accountant," Echo said flatly.

"People like different things, Echo."

"I don't know. The social train wreck, good with numbers, are you sure she's not autistic?"

Cinnamon closed her eyes and took a breath. "What if she is? You want me to rethink dating her? Because her brain works differently? I don't know which is worse, that you're willing to find any excuse to get me to stay away from her, or you're genuinely an ableist dickwad."

"Cinnamon."

"Uh-uh. First you said to avoid her because she might be a threat to the business. But then you do some digging and she's not. So now you're coming up with other reasons why I shouldn't see her. Honestly, Echo, just tell me what it is so we can move on. I like her. We've made plans for a date. So what is it?"

Echo had stopped walking, and she glanced around the empty hallway before answering. "You're right. I *am* looking for any excuse to keep you away from her, and it's not because she might be autistic, that was just me being an idiot. I'm sorry. I know it's been a while since you had feelings for someone, and whether she's autistic is not only totally fine either way, but none of my business."

"It doesn't matter to me if she is, but I definitely don't want you to be ableist about it." Cinnamon turned on the faucet and rinsed the portafilter. "And I'm not sure these are feelings yet. I only met her yesterday."

"Whatever it is," Echo continued with a wave of her hand, "I just don't want to see you hurt again. Every year that's gone by that you don't find someone else, I think, 'It's taken her a year to get over her. It's taken two years...three, four, *seven* years to get over her.' And I don't know if it's because you love hard, or if she was the one that got away, but I hate seeing you lonely now, when I remember how happy you were with a partner."

Cinnamon glanced away from the screen, her jaw clenched. "Echo, I—"

"I love you, Cin. But if someone is going to hurt you, I'm going to prevent it."

Ever the big sis. "I only met her yesterday," Cinnamon repeated. "And there's never a guarantee that it'll work out. Even if we're totally compatible. Even if there are no secrets, no shadowy motives. Sometimes it just doesn't work. But it sounds like you're trying to prevent me from getting my heart broken by making sure I don't date...anyone."

Echo bit her lip. "Well. Yeah. When you put it like that. But that wasn't my intent."

"No, I know. So just let me do my thing, okay? If dating Daphne isn't going to plunge the business into bankruptcy, I don't need your opinion about her at all."

"Harsh. But fair. If you get to a point where you aren't totally embarrassed of your older sister, I'd like to meet her in person."

"I'll need to exact a few promises from you before that happens."

"Understood. I just want you to be happy, meimei." Echo gave her a small smile and ended the call.

"Me too, jiejie," Cinnamon said to the empty kitchen. "Me too."

***

As Daphne sat down in one of the conference room chairs, she noticed the scent of chlorine still clinging to her. It had taken a half an hour to get home, and she needed another twenty minutes to get to the office, which left her ten minutes to gather her stuff, grab an external battery charger for her phone, change into not a cropped graphic tee and gym shorts, and throw on deodorant. Brushing and straightening her hair was more important than taking a shower, but now that she had to smell the consequences, she wasn't sure she'd made the right choice.

Nearly every seat at the table was taken. Violet had been at the front desk and told Daphne that the full team was being assembled for this one. It wasn't unusual, but it meant that the client was important. Daphne could only remember two other cases that required all hands on deck, and neither of them had been easy.

For one of them, she was instructed to dye her hair a dark chestnut brown, but one of the IT people introduced her to an amazing hair and makeup artist, and she was able to get away with a wig, some contouring, and chocolate-colored contact lenses. Such extreme subterfuge wasn't a requirement in most of their cases, but it was fun when it was.

Since Daphne had only gone super-platinum and bob-ish the week before, she might not have to do much more than contacts and makeup tricks for this one.

Once her phone had enough battery, she was able to get in touch with Mattie and Rin and make sure they were alive and well. They were at Mattie's apartment, basking in the glow of a satisfying night, nursing their hangovers with Chinese takeout and *Sense8*. Daphne wanted a full report of their evenings, but between the new case at work and trying to get an actual date with Cinnamon, story time would have to wait.

The rest of the team trickled in as it neared one o'clock. Daphne texted Cinnamon to let her know she made it and still wanted to do dinner, if work didn't get in the way.

"Daphne," Brad greeted her as he slid into the chair beside her. His clothes were clean and unwrinkled, but his hair stuck up at odd angles, and his blocky glasses couldn't hide the tiredness in his eyes. She raised an eyebrow at him.

"How long did you end up staying?" She asked.

He set down his iPad and took a sip from his travel mug. "I'm embarrassed to say."

Daphne made a thoughtful noise and reached for his mug, bringing it to her nose to discern the contents. "Coffee. No hair of the dog, that's a good sign. Unless it wasn't a choice."

"It was a choice," Brad said with a lilt. "Time will tell whether it was a good choice. You seem fine. How are Mattie and Rin?"

"Alive and content, eating greasy food and watching Netflix."

"Love it when everybody has a good time." He smiled slyly. "And you? Did you have a good time? Did you track her down?"

"I never said I was looking for anyone," she answered, mirroring his grin.

"And yet." Brad leaned in, peering at her face, and sniffed. "You needed to get to a specific party, when it was already late. You took a Lyft to Sea Cliff. You've been in a pool and didn't have time to shower, and since this is an afternoon meeting, you stayed up very late to have to rush here like this."

"My building has a pool, I could have been busy doing anything else to have to rush here, and how the fuck do you know I took a Lyft to Sea Cliff?"

He leaned back and tried to shrug casually. "It's my job to know these things."

Daphne rolled her eyes and opened her own iPad. "It's not your job to keep tabs on me."

"I have to practice somehow."

Before she could retort, Clarissa walked into the conference room and closed the glass door behind them. Their assistant used his tablet to dim the room's windows until they were opaque and set the overhead lights to a more comfortable level. Daphne glanced around the room, noting that she knew everyone by sight and at least first name. Some people sat at chairs against the walls, while others preferred to stand. Violet held the second door open for the last few stragglers before sinking into the last available chair.

"New case. Big client." Clarissa launched into the meeting without preamble or a roll call. Their boxy almost-suit caught Daphne's eye, from the sharp cut of the pants with a slit to the knee, showing off their black platform boots, to the seemingly random display of pixel-like colors and vertical lines across the wide-shouldered top. If Daphne had to guess, it was to confuse facial recognition software. She thought she had a pretty good fashion sense, but Clarissa put her to shame. After all, Clarissa wasn't the one who wore a crop top tee with "Maybe Baby" plastered across it to bed the night before. They would never.

"Real name is Need-To-Know, so we're calling it the Goldenrod Case. Let me remind you that if your role requires you to know the client's real name, it will appear on your assignment sheet. That doesn't mean you should use it outside of your role. When it leaves your lips it should sound like 'Goldenrod,' got it?"

The room answered with mumbled agreements and the sound of throat-clearing. Pseudonyms were a necessary precaution. "Diophantus Consulting" was the business name people would see if they tried to look up Daphne or any of the other employees who worked there. But the name their clients used—clients who could only hire them by referral—was "Lamarr Alkindi." Clarissa liked to be clever. Likewise, the clients' names were a secret to most of the Dio employees, and each case and client got a nickname of Clarissa's choosing.

Their assistant clicked a remote control, and an image of an office building with a blue, stylized "BDMT" appeared on the screen at the front of the room. A chorus of groans rose from the assembled spies.

"Yes, we're all sick of having to deal with these clowns," Clarissa said. "Luckily, Goldenrod is in the process of acquiring Bad Mountain Tech, so they won't be a problem for us much longer. And thanks to BDMT's sloppiness and my incredible foresight, we already have lots of dirt on them and a molothrus who has been planted there for almost a year." They looked up and smirked at their audience. "Goldenrod will be charged appropriately, so they feel like we did all this just for them."

Laughter tittered through the room, and Daphne glanced up from her iPad to grin at her boss.

"Most of you will be reviewing your previous discoveries at BDMT and pooling them for the team. With our long-term plant out for maternity leave, we're sending in four new molothri: Daphne in accounting, Rayna as a personal assistant, Ivan as a software developer, and of course, as a fellow creepy, white, cishet dudebro in management, Atticus."

"My husband would object to several of those adjectives," Atticus said, smiling like a devil. If Brad reminded Daphne of Thor, Atticus was more like Loki.

"I know Felix, and he'd rather have the money," Clarissa countered, to another round of laughter. They nodded to their assistant, who swiped at his tablet again. Across the room, everyone's phones and iPads beeped with new messages. "That's your roles. Review your assignments and get back to me within the hour if you have questions, concerns, or need a bigger team. Otherwise, happy digging."

Daphne was vaguely aware of people leaving the room, her focus already entirely on her assignment. In all her time working at Diophantus, she had only been a molothrus—what Clarissa called the infiltrators they'd plant in a company for espionage, like a cowbird hiding its egg in another bird's nest—for a handful of cases. Her acting skills weren't flawless, but Daphne was so good at accounting, they'd put her in regardless. Atticus was always one of the plants, able to blend in with the young guys in management, gain their trust, and uncover their secrets with the charm of a vampire, so Daphne would follow his advice when it came to deception.

For the Goldenrod case, it looked like her primary task was to find original records that the previous molothrus suspected were there and would prove that BDMT's amended records were cooked. Once Daphne retrieved them, she could review them here at the Diophantus office, or she could leave it for Andrej to work on while she was at BDMT looking for more evidence. No way to know how messy it was until she got there.

"See you in three hours," Brad whispered, standing up. "Security briefing. Check your schedule before diving into the data. I know you're bad at time. I'll send you a text five minutes before."

Daphne glanced up at him and nodded. "Thanks, bro. See you then."

She'd already accepted the assignment, so she would get an automated alert before each meeting, but she appreciated him looking out for her.

She gathered her things and moved to her office, where she could read over the material in peace. Dinner with Cinnamon was looking more and more unlikely, but there was still a chance she could take a break at a reasonable dinner hour. She set an alert to text her later, when she would know for sure, then turned back to her computer. This was going to be fun.

***

Cinnamon felt the lateness of the afternoon in her back—stiff from sitting at her desk for hours—and her stomach, grumbly and tight from the wine and nothing else since croissants. Starlight hadn't texted her since she arrived at work, and Cinnamon had no idea if they would be getting dinner together soon. A snack, then, satisfying but not too filling.

She stood and stretched, a loud crack in the middle of her spine making her groan. Five hours in one crunched position was too many hours. She shook out her hands and grabbed the empty wine glass on her way downstairs. There were definitely taquitos in the freezer. Leftovers from several restaurants in the fridge. She should try to eat some vegetables, or an apple or pear, but the taquitos were going to win out.

Starlight had thought Cinnamon might make them dinner. She laughed, thinking about it. Her breakfast pastries had impressed the moon-fae, and so she expected homecooked meals of the same caliber. Cinnamon could do that classic sneaky thing, ordering food in from a fancy place then plating it so it looked like she cooked it herself. Why were lies always so much more work than the truth? They'd go out, if Starlight was available, and Cinnamon would just explain that, with the exception of truly glorious pastries, her cooking skills most resembled those of Lorelei Gilmore. Takeout and frozen pizza for the win.

The microwave beeped at the same time as her phone, and she tried to take out the plate and read the text at the same time.

Starlight:

I won't be able to come out tonight :(

Numbers emergency.

Stupid numbers. Stupid for keeping me from you, though I do enjoy the puzzle.

Dinner tomorrow night?

I can make reservations.

Any allergies (I should have asked this before)

Cinnamon didn't understand exactly what Starlight did for work, but she couldn't even imagine what a "numbers emergency" would look like. Except that accounting was money, and people were rightly particular about their money, and the next day was Monday, so maybe there was a "by Monday" deadline.

Cinnamon:

I understand. No allergies, but I don't like seafood. I know, I know.

Starlight:

You live on the ocean.

Cinnamon:

I live by the ocean.

Starlight:

It's called Sea Cliff.

Cinnamon:

Still dislike seafood.

Starlight:

I bet your mom had a lot to say about that.

Cinnamon:

Well…

Starlight:

hooooooboy you never told her?

Cinnamon:

It was that or telling her I'm gay. Might be the only time someone came out to their mom because they're a coward.

Starlight:

Cinnamon. I will never tell your secret. Whenever we have dinner with them, I'll tell them I hate seafood, and you don't want me to feel bad, so you will also not eat seafood when I'm there. I will do this for you

Cinnamon:

Starlight. Make the reservations. Tell me when to be where.

Starlight:

Yes, dear. :-*

It was for the best that they couldn't see each other again that night. Cinnamon didn't have a lot of experience with dating, but she was pretty sure that things weren't supposed to move this fast.

She sighed. Maybe it had just been too long for her and she was desperate and didn't know it, even if her body and emotions did, and yearned.

The taquitos were still cold in the middle, so she put them in for another round and grabbed an apple. Makeshift dinner would be fine. The wine was still out, and she poured another glass. She needed to fortify herself for her Secret Hobby.

Before heading back upstairs, she re-checked the locks on the front and back doors and windows and made sure the security system was set to Home. When she once again sank into her office chair and set her plate and wine glass where they wouldn't spill on her keyboard or paperwork, she looked through the stack of notebooks in the desk drawer and pulled out the one for Erica.

A year ago, Cinnamon noticed a pattern among her clients. They were all engineers, developers, tech specialists, analysts, and the like, feeling enough pressure and anxiety from their jobs to seek help from her.

From what she could tell, the industry was just like that. A bunch of already-rich white guys would decide to launch an app or a website or whatever will disrupt, get the funding from other rich white guys, hire their friends to fuck around, and hire professionals at criminally low wages to pick up the slack. Fully stocked snack room instead of lunch breaks. Air hockey table instead of health insurance. Empty promises of fortune instead of respect.

And the people who came to her got the brunt of it when shit hit the fan. The worst part was that these were the people who believed in the product, the app, the value of the experience they were trying to create. They were the ones putting in the work, and the ones who were fired if everything wasn't perfect.

It was undeniably a toxic environment. It should have been unacceptable for even one company to try to get away with it. Yet that was the environment that took root, and people came to expect it, normalize it.

But among her clients, something stood out. Of all the people she'd seen in the past year, five of them told her about experiencing an assault at work with details so specific, they had to be committed by the same man. Start-up culture was appalling, but it hadn't occurred to her that it could be cultivating serial rapists. After everything she'd heard, it shouldn't have been a shock. She did what she normally would, listening and encouraging and emphasizing that it wasn't their fault.

But for some reason, she couldn't let it go.

She had clues, she could track down more evidence, she could find this guy and make sure he faced consequences for what he'd done. And make sure he didn't do it to anyone else. Didn't she have a duty to do whatever she could?

Several points had made her hesitate: First, digging into her clients' lives outside official means was discouraged, though not explicitly unethical, and she wasn't completely comfortable with the moral grayness of it. Second, if she didn't succeed and her investigation was exposed, she could lose her business, her license to practice, her reputation, and her career. She could be sued by both the clients she was trying to help as well as the abusers she had on her radar. Third, there was a strong delegation of internet trolls dedicated to defending their tech-lords through internet and real-life harassment. Cinnamon had seen firsthand how her only client who tried to speak up against her attacker had been blacklisted from their industry, threatened, harassed, and stalked, and she had heard plenty of other horror stories about people who speak out against anyone in power: threats of physical harm, swarming, doxxing, swatting.

Two months ago, Cinnamon received a slew of intimidating messages containing details about her life and told her to back off. The next day, she found a dead cat on her doorstep. She was almost certain that the anonymous accounts she used to go undercover in extremist forums for her investigation couldn't be tied to her real name, but she had been outspoken about sexism and labor practices in the tech industry on her personal accounts, and assumed that was why these people targeted her. Not for her investigation into sexual misconduct, but for simply saying, "Maybe the current model for tech industries isn't great."

Either way, Cinnamon installed the security cameras, nuked the dedicated accounts she had been using to investigate and made new ones, scrubbed her personal accounts of criticisms that might get her targeted, and started her new safety routines online and in real life. Since then, she had no reason to believe anyone suspected the link between her and the fake accounts she created. But the threat was always there.

A lot of things could go wrong if Cinnamon didn't stay anonymous. And since she needed to know she was exposed as soon as it happened, she set up two different apps to send her the equivalent of a Google Alert if her name popped up on any of the social media sites she had investigative accounts on. She hated to think about it, and knew she needed a plan, but besides the forethought of anonymity and the alerts if that anonymity was breached, that plan started and ended with her running to Echo for help and letting her use all her business connections to mitigate the fallout.

And her investigation may have been slow, but it had produced a lot of information. She'd narrowed the perpetrator down to two men earlier that month, but didn't know where to go from there. In her spare time, she would review her notes, over and over again, but she was stuck, and afraid she'd reached the end without changing a damn thing.

Her grip on the notebook tightened, and she took a deep breath. Perhaps a distraction would work. Let her mind do its thing in the background for a while instead of the foreground. Macarons. No, semla. No. Baklava. She imagined Starlight eating baklava, eyes closed in pleasure, like in the picture she took with the chocolate croissant, honey and nuts sticking to her fingers, her pink lips, laughing.

Yes, that might be distraction enough.

Chapter Ten

The restaurant Starlight had chosen was a modern, high-end place that reminded Cinnamon of all the other characterless places her parents liked to take her to. Black and glass, clean lines, the glittering crystal of wine glasses refracting light like the diamonds adorning the guests. Depressingly small portions at extortionate prices. And somehow, the dining room didn't even smell like food. Where were they cooking it? In a hermetically sealed room?

Even though it wasn't quite eight o'clock, Cinnamon worried that Starlight would stand her up. That was anxiety, but just because she could name it didn't mean she could control it. She hadn't been on an actual, out-of-the-house date with someone since college, and wondered if the protocols had changed. Five minutes early was fine. She texted Starlight that she was at the table already, and the typing ellipses appeared. No reply came. The dots disappeared. Her anxiety perked up as though saying *I told you so*.

A tinkling of laughter at the door cut through the conversations and low music, and moments later, Starlight walked into the dining room. She wore a white dress that hugged her body and fell mid-thigh, the neckline a sharp slope that left one arm bare and the other with a snug sleeve that covered to her wrist. Gold accents decorated the hem and cuff, and she had paired it with gold, strappy heels and matching sapphire earrings and necklace.

Between the cut of the dress and the meticulously straightened hair, Cinnamon had the fleeting thought that she looked like a villain. Before she could disperse the idea, it was followed by the sharp and unexpected desire to submit to whatever villainy the woman had planned.

Cinnamon stood as she approached the table, feeling awkward and underdressed in her halter-style black maxi and black sandals. But Starlight's eyes wandered over her, full of approval and mischief.

"You look hot," she murmured, leaning in to kiss Cinnamon on the cheek before sitting down.

"You—" Cinnamon stammered, lowering herself into her chair. "You look—" She settled for nodding. "Yeah."

Starlight smiled, her dark eyes and necklace catching the light. "I know the atmosphere isn't anything special, but there's a specific dish we need to get, because it's fun. Don't bother with anything else, it'll be too little and not as good. Can I order for us both? No seafood, I promise."

A tendril of fascination curled in Cinnamon's gut, and she found herself making a quick calculation: three and a half hours in Starlight's presence, eight hours of sleeping curled up together, another half hour with her awake, and a day and a half without her again. So little time together, yet Starlight remembered her aversion to seafood.

"Sure," she answered.

"Yeah? Are you okay? Am I being too much?"

"No, no." Cinnamon just wasn't used to it. "It's been a long day, is all. I know you have good taste. You liked my croissants."

"Oh." Starlight sighed a little. She looked into the distance, her gaze becoming soft. "Mmm. Yeah, those were better than the ones in Paris." She caught Cinnamon's eyes again with a little bit of panic. "Don't tell Paris that, okay?"

Cinnamon laughed. "They'll never hear it from me."

When the sommelier came to the table, they discussed their selection and the women settled on a bottle of white. Their waiter approached, recognized Starlight, and correctly guessed her order.

"You can't make the most delicious pasta in San Francisco and expect me to not come here as often as possible," Starlight explained. "What's in it this month?"

"Pancetta and asparagus," he answered, blushing. Cinnamon understood. Between Starlight's attention, sincerity, charm, and beauty, it was hard *not* to blush.

"Damn. Yes. Okay. Fettuccini alla ruota. Instead of the tuna niçoise, can we sub strawberry salads? And the chocolate souffle for dessert."

"Sure thing."

As he walked away, Starlight turned back to Cinnamon and waggled her eyebrows.

"You're in for a treat."

"You must come here pretty often. Do you take all your first dates here?"

"Nah. I've never met anyone I wanted to impress this much." She winked. "But I'm sure you've been to places just as nice up in..." She paused dramatically. "Sea Cliff."

"Wow, you're trying to diss my neighborhood. But it's unclear if you're hating on the fact that it's as wealthy as yours, or if you're making fun of the fact that there are no restaurants there."

"Whoa, you don't have any restaurants?"

"There are plenty within walking distance. Just not technically in Sea Cliff."

"Cinnamon, that's just sad. I can't make fun of you for that. I'll make fun of you for living in the snobby area."

"This from the woman who lives in Nob Hill."

"I prefer to say I live near Chinatown," Starlight said, wrinkling her nose.

"That sounds like code for 'I live in Nob Hill and have a complex about it.'"

Starlight sat back and nodded, licking her lips and stretching her arms onto the table, like she was preparing for an argument. "Cinnamon coming in hot with the diagnoses."

Cinnamon chuckled, and Starlight giggled and bit her lip, then rubbed at her eyes.

"Ugh. I spent all day in a room with physical records, tons of paperwork, and it must have dried out my eyes. My poor hands too." She rubbed her hands together, like she was remembering the torturous hours she didn't have access to hand lotion. "I hate cramped little offices like that. I don't love the outdoors, but I'd take an archery course over a cubicle any day."

"That's right, you mentioned archery yesterday. Are you any good?"

She blushed and seemed to struggle with the question. "I'm—actually, I'm really good. I'll take you, sometime. Saturday morning? When it's light out?"

"I'd love that," Cinnamon said with a smile.

"I bet." Starlight smirked.

They sat in silence for a comfortable minute before the conversation came back to Cinnamon. "You said you had a hard day, too," Starlight said. "Want to talk about it? I want to hear about it."

"Maybe you can tell me more about you, instead."

The wine and salads arrived at the same time, and they toasted in silence.

"So," Starlight said, twisting her wine glass by the stem. The golden liquid caught the light and sparkled, matching the glittering of her jewelry and her eyes. "I assume you've looked me up online."

"A bold assumption."

"Oh, so you didn't?" she asked, an eyebrow raised in question.

Cinnamon shook her head in wonder. "Are you ever not awash in confidence?"

"Rarely. I looked you up. I didn't find much, though."

The thrill of Starlight digging for more information about her mixed with the anxiety of anyone digging for her personal information online and the relief that nothing could be found, and the resulting tumult of emotion gave her a stomach ache.

"I don't have a big digital footprint," Cinnamon said, putting down her fork until her belly quieted. She would have left her explanation at that, but she had the feeling that Starlight would dig even more without an explanation. "I've had problems in the past with harassment, and I haven't found any social media to be worth the risk."

"You've been harassed?" Starlight's eyes darkened. "You need someone to harass them back? Track them down?"

"I appreciate it, but it's fine. It was vile before. I didn't want it to get worse, ramp up into swarming or doxxing or whatever new, awful thing trolls are doing, so I only really use anonymous accounts now."

Starlight put down her glass, reached across the table, and grabbed Cinnamon's hand. "I can help. If you wanted to give me some specifics, I can straighten everything out. Did something like that happen today?"

"No, no. Nothing like that." Cinnamon squeezed Starlight's hand and let go of it to take another sip of wine.

"Well, something happened today and it's bothering you," Starlight said, cocking her head. "You of all people should know it helps to talk about it."

"And you should know that I can't talk about my clients."

She shrugged. "So don't. Tell me about you. If not what happened, then how it made you feel."

"You sure you're the accountant and not the therapist here?"

"I know how to listen."

Cinnamon considered this. Took another sip of wine. If there was even a possibility of building something stable and lasting with Starlight, it would require, in part, sharing things like this. She could start small. Work up to more. Obviously avoid ethical violations. *Might as well see how difficult it is*, she thought.

"For a long time, growing up, I was sure I would be part of the family business."

At Cinnamon's change in tone, Starlight leaned closer, all her attention on her.

"Not that I wanted to be. It just felt inevitable. But, turns out, I was just excited about helping my family. I didn't like the industry at all. It didn't feel like there was any substance to it. Things, yes. Tangible, material product. But what was it all for?

"Dressing in a suit every day to manipulate people into buying things or selling things. I don't know. It felt useless. *I* felt useless. I wanted to help people, not sell something. So I went to school, got my degrees, became a therapist. I love knowing there are people out there whose lives have been improved by my expertise."

Starlight rested her chin in her hand and peered at Cinnamon with eyes that saw too much. "But it's hard sometimes, right?" she guessed. "Being in a position to help people means you meet them when they're at their lowest. When they're as unhappy with themselves as you were when you couldn't find your path in life."

Cinnamon glanced up and caught her eyes. There was sympathy in their depths, and strength, and...pride? She made herself look away before she thought too much about it.

"Sometimes it's really difficult," she agreed. "People come to me in pain. I can't help but empathize."

"I bet that helps you, though. Makes you good at your job."

She turned the base of her wine glass and pushed it an inch to the right. "Yeah." She shrugged. "Yeah, I'm pretty good at it."

Sparkling laughter bubbled up from Starlight again. "And so modest! Come on. You know you're good. And when you're good at difficult things, that means you're *really* good."

"So you must be pretty good, yourself."

"Oh, please. I fuck around with numbers all day." She took a sip of wine and shook her head. "And not in a manipulate-the-stock-market, exciting kind of way. I solve mysteries that are of interest to only a handful of people. Eight people would listen to my podcast, and six of them are doing it accidentally."

Cinnamon's bark of laughter echoed through the room, and she slapped a hand over her mouth in embarrassment, but that only got Starlight laughing, too, the both of them still giggling when the waiter rolled a cart to their table with half of a giant cheese wheel on it. The chef followed him, smiled and greeted the women, and began to make their entrée.

"What on earth did you order for us?" Cinnamon asked, in awe, but wary.

"Fettuccini alla ruota!" Starlight gestured toward the cart with both hands. "They make the pasta at the table *in the cheese wheel*. Part spectacle, part delicacy—"

"But mostly cheese."

"Part spectacle, part delicacy, several parts cheese." She counted off on her fingers. "The portions aren't huge. Honestly, if all you can do is just one bite, it'll be worth it."

"Oh, no," Cinnamon said. "I can smell the pancetta. I'm eating it all."

"Yes!" Starlight clapped. "You're gonna love it."

As her excited date launched into a list of the different types of pasta-in-a-wheel she'd had, Cinnamon felt the last remnants of her anxiety fade away like fog lifting. She let herself feel at ease without questioning it and the rest of their dinner felt like reconnecting with an old friend and discovering a new crush. When they left the restaurant two hours later, Cinnamon was reluctant to go home alone.

"We've been out on a date," she said, as they walked slowly down the well-lit street. "You've been to my house, worn my clothes, and slept in my bed. We've kissed. Quite a bit. But I still feel like asking you to come to my place tonight is too bold."

Starlight looked up at her, face open and true. The night was cool and quiet, with dark clouds censoring the sky. Lampposts shone orange, and stark, and still managed to make her sparkle, catching a glint in her hair, her eyes. She hooked her arm through Cinnamon's and put her head on her shoulder. "Not too bold," she said, just as she yawned. "Though I'd pass out on the ride there, and again once I made it to a couch or bed. I'd be a terrible houseguest tonight, and an even worse lover. Ugh. Don't tell anyone I said that."

Cinnamon smiled playfully and laced her fingers with Starlight's. "Who would I tell?"

"I don't know. The newspapers."

"The newspapers."

"I don't know!"

"Extra! Extra! Read all about it!" Cinnamon shouted far too loudly. "Daphne 'Starlight' Redgrave a terrible house guest, and an even worse lover!"

"Oh god."

When they reached the next streetlight, Starlight pulled Cinnamon to a stop and stepped in front of her, ducking her head.

"Is that what you're gonna call me?"

"What?"

"Starlight."

"Unless you hate it," Cinnamon said, moving a strand of hair out of her date's eyes. The wind put it right back. "But that's what I thought when I first saw you."

"I don't hate it," Starlight said, glancing up shyly. In the amber glow of the streetlamp, Cinnamon couldn't tell if she was blushing, but she was definitely staring at Cinnamon's lips.

"I know you said you don't kiss on the first date," Starlight said. "And that's fine." She ran her hands up and back down Cinnamon's arms. "I won't ask you to violate that rule. But you need to know that I really, really want to kiss you right now."

Her face was so earnest. Cinnamon knew that she could say she had a great time, thank her for dinner, call herself a ride, and leave without kissing her, and she would accept it.

But why would she want to do that?

She lifted her hands to either side of Starlight's face, brushing her hair back behind her ears again, letting herself memorize the smoothness, the soft, tiny hairs along her hairline. Her lips gave a hint of a smile, like she knew just what Cinnamon was thinking, and wholly approved. Her eyes invited mischief. Her body tensed in anticipation. And Cinnamon leaned into her, quickly, pressing their soft lips together, fingers sliding through Starlight's hair to hold her in place.

The night in woman form sighed and melted against her, arms circling behind her back and pulling her closer, as though they could occupy the same space if they tried hard enough. She flicked her tongue out, and Cinnamon took the suggestion, took the lead again, tracing her tongue along Starlight's lips before slipping between her teeth and finding her again.

Cinnamon moved a hand down her back, securing her in her arms as she pressed their lips harder together, afraid she would return to the heavens. Starlight let out a soft moan, and Cinnamon pulled back to plant two closed-mouth but very not-platonic kisses against her lips. She rested her forehead against Starlight's and waited for her to open her eyes.

"Are you asleep already?" she teased.

"Only if this has all been a dream." Starlight kept her eyes closed. Cinnamon leaned in to rub her cheek against hers, a light caress, memory of that night in the pool resurfacing as she caught the barest scent of raspberry. It was elusive, hiding beneath the perfume she had worn, light and floral-sweet.

"I always mean to kiss you first," Starlight murmured, her eyes blinking slowly open. "But then you kiss me, and I forget everything, because we're doing what I want and everything else can wait."

Going home without Starlight felt wrong, but as much as she wanted to take her back to Sea Cliff and kiss her until she fell asleep, she also wanted her to be healthy and well-rested. She brushed her lips against Starlight's forehead and kissed her tenderly.

"Let me walk you home."

***

They'd said goodbye at the door to Starlight's building. Cinnamon knew that if she walked her up to her condo, all Starlight would have to do was give her a lingering stare and bite her lip, and Cinnamon would have followed her in and kept her up too late.

Instead, she said goodbye and kissed her, then walked back to the restaurant just a few blocks away, so her rideshare would pick her up there. If anybody got the data from it, all they'd know was that she took a car to the restaurant and back to Sea Cliff. She rarely got picked up or dropped off where she actually meant to be. Between the problems with data privacy anyway, and everything she'd heard from her clients regarding their tech company employers, it was better to take precautions.

The restaurant was still full of people, and the valets outside gave her friendly nods as she finalized her ride. As she got the alert that the car was on its way, a new text message popped up.

Starlight:

Tonight was really great. Sorry I'm so tired, of course work has to be stupidly busy this week. Want to do this again tomorrow?

Cinnamon:

Shouldn't you be asleep by now?

Starlight:

Yes. Date? Tomorrow?

Cinnamon:

Tuesday nights are family dinner. Wednesday?

Starlight:

Am I not invited to Family Dinner

Cinnamon:

You want our second date to be a double date with two old Chinese Americans and an older sister who will grill you and judge you until she finds your secret shame and extorts whatever she wants from you?

Starlight:

Sounds like fun. What time should I be there?

Cinnamon:

Wednesday.

Starlight:

Cinnamon.

Cinnamon:

I can do Wednesday night. I'll pick the place this time.

Starlight:

No Family Dinner, and you won't be cooking for me either? Good luck with a third date. :(

Cinnamon:

Pretty sure it'll be easy.

Starlight:

Can't hide anything from you, can I?

Cinnamon:

You can certainly try.

Starlight:

I like you too much to try

Cinnamon:

Ah shit, I forgot your baklava.

Starlight:

?!

Cinnamon:

I made baklava last night and was going to bring you some.

Starlight:

I do get homecooked food?

Cinnamon:

Pastry. Give me your work address and I'll have it delivered to you tomorrow.

Starlight:

Can you send it to my condo instead?

Cinnamon:

Sure. You can't receive it at work?

Starlight:

Secured building. Sensitive financial stuff. Also, if you sent it to my work, Brad would eat it before I knew it was there.

Cinnamon:

Should I be sending pastry to your friends and family and coworkers? Should I be seeking their approval?

Starlight:

No! The pastry is for me!

Cinnamon:

lol

Starlight:

Well, it couldn't hurt. But they'll all like you anyway, with or without flaky crust cheesy savory chocolate sweet and can you send them tonight instead?

Cinnamon:

Go to sleep, Starlight. Thank you for dinner. I like being with you.

Starlight:

Get used to it. Night, Cinnamon.

Cinnamon:

Night.

Chapter Eleven

When Daphne had told Cinnamon that she spent most of her workday on Monday in a room filled with physical paperwork, it hadn't been a lie. It had been a massive inconvenience. It was 2015. Everything should have been digital. If BDMT had been founded in, like, the 1980s? Sure. Some paperwork would be expected. But this many hard copies for a firm that started four years ago was downright irresponsible.

And somewhere in that mess was a bundle of possibly mythical incriminating files that the long-term BDMT molothrus swore existed, though she couldn't pinpoint where. At the debriefing last night, Daphne had told Clarissa that she definitely needed Andrej to go through the digital BDMT stuff that had accumulated from past jobs. She could really use another set of eyes on the hard copies, too, but they weren't leaving the room unless it was definitive evidence, and it would raise suspicions to bring in another new hire so soon for a sensitive "project" that didn't have a deadline.

And the men on the management team were already acting squirrely. Or maybe that was just how guys like them acted normally, Daphne had no idea. Men who got away with everything usually had a douchebaggy confidence that mirrored the rest of their douchebaggy personality. But the ones that acted a little paranoid? Either they weren't very good at criming, or someone had already gotten close and hadn't been stealthy about it.

Luckily, Atticus was a consummate actor. Read the room like a book, charming, inoffensive. Immediately became one of the boys, accepted and embraced and initiated into their frat-boy enclave with a swiftness that was both impressive and slightly terrifying. He was as smooth and convincing as every con man in every movie about an endearing grifter. Ryan O'Neal had nothing on Atticus Michaels.

He had gotten good intel that first day, too. Daphne snorted. Men. They'd never question a guy who mirrored their looks, personality, money, prejudices, and vices. Meanwhile, Daphne's hazel contact lenses were drying out, the tag of her cheap blouse was scratching the back of her neck, and the fluorescent overhead lights were giving her a headache so bad she was convinced it was a deliberate attempt to drive her to violence. An attempt that was working.

She sighed and closed the report that was beginning to blur. Coffee would be a great excuse to stretch her legs and see if three hours was enough time for Rayna to access and pull up any files that management might have hidden on their computers off-network.

Grabbing her security badge, she left for the break room. The badge reminded her of Brad, which now reminded her of baklava, which would always remind her of Cinnamon. She let herself savor a moment of joy before readjusting her mask of frustration, impatience, and bewilderment. Prudish nerd, doesn't appreciate the disarray of the financial records, a little overwhelmed by the workload. At least the only part that required her sub-par acting skills was the nerd part.

An entire floor of the building was a dedicated employee down-time area, but since Daphne's evidence-gathering was through financial records, not people, she opted for the smaller break room down the hall from what they called her "office."

Only a few people there, absorbed in their laptops as their half-finished drinks cooled and their snacks or lunch—or with the weird, long hours everyone kept, possibly dinners—lay abandoned. Nobody looked up at her as she entered the wide, white-and-glass space, and a little bit of Daphne's anxiety evaporated. She didn't dislike people, but on a mission like this, she had to be as bland and forgettable as possible. Just another overworked cog getting some coffee. Nothing to see here.

"Oh hey, Olive, right?"

Damn it.

Daphne couldn't help a little jump at the unexpected greeting, but hopefully the nervousness went with her character. She continued her reach for the coffee pot and a Styrofoam cup, wishing she had grabbed them faster.

Props in place, she glanced at the person who spoke, starting with his shoes like a socially nervous person would (*thanks for the tip, Mattie*). Black and white sneakers, dark wash blue jeans, long-sleeved navy sweater with the collar of a white button-down shirt peeking out from under it. Being as wealthy as he was, no visible clothing labels or brand names probably meant that his casual-looking outfit had cost more than a car. His effortless chestnut-brown bedhead and five o'clock shadow at 11 a.m. were also meticulously constructed, though hopefully for an amount less than a car.

He could have been handsome. He certainly seemed to have the money to be handsome. But something was off. A flatness in his ice-blue eyes, or something in his easy tone. Maybe the fact that he was standing next to Atticus, who Daphne knew was genuinely sincere and handsome, even if he was playing a predator. The real predator next to him couldn't quite pull off the act of appearing normal.

"Oh. Hmm. Mmmhmm."

She turned back to the counter, poured her coffee and nodded nervously. Decided on the fly to make her voice a little softer, a little more breathy and unsure than usual. Michelle Pfeiffer as Selina Kyle, not Catwoman.

"Yes. Olive. I'm new." She hunched a little more as she replaced the coffee pot, wishing she had thought to add glasses to her disguise. The other people in the break room didn't seem to be paying any attention to them.

"It's great to meet you. I'm Collin, Collin Roday, CEO of BDMT." He held out his hand, and Daphne made a show of getting flustered and setting down the coffee pot. She tried to make their handshake quick, but he held her a little too tightly, a little too long. A chill spread up her spine, and she fought the urge to shiver. She had the sudden thought that Roday was the kind of guy who would go home from a long day of work and tell women on the internet he didn't know that they should kill themselves.

"Pleasure to meet you," she mumbled. Clarissa had said they had high employee turnover. Hair and makeup and clothes had transformed her into an unmemorable background character. She was tucked away in a makeshift office far away from everyone else. Roday should never have noticed her.

Daphne took a moment to consider the possibility that she had no idea what men like Roday would notice. Certainly, playing meek and shy and awkward should make him less interested. "I should be getting back to my paperwork—"

"Ah, nah, there's no rush." He leaned forward, finally letting go of her hand as he invaded her personal space. "I'm the boss, and I say you don't have to run back to work."

Roday glanced from her cup of coffee back to her anxious stare, a sly smile creeping over his face. Daphne knew there was nobody between her and the door, but she still had the feeling of being trapped. Pinned. "You know," he drawled, "I have an espresso machine in my office. You're welcome to stop by anytime, if you're ever looking for something stronger than that. Richer. Bolder. I bet you'd like it." He winked at her, and a thousand red flags bloomed in her vision.

Oh. So he was the kind of guy who would harass strangers *during* work, too.

"Ah, fuck," Atticus said, looking at his phone. Roday gave Daphne a once-over before turning away from her, and she briefly wondered what would happen if she threw the coffee in his face and walked out.

"Jared wants us," Atticus explained, typing on his screen. "Oh wait. He just wants you. I have to go to R&D anyway, want me to walk you there?"

"I'm not a fucking dog." Roday snorted, smiling. "Olive, be sure to stop by sometime. If I'm not there, my girl can tell you where to find me." He turned on his heel and sauntered out of the break room.

Daphne watched him go, needing to know when she was out of his sight. Her mind and body were coiled, tight, and it was a terrible, opposite feeling to her usual hedonism. She hated it, and hated him for making her feel that way.

The rim of the cup in her fingers squished into a flat oval, and Atticus gently put a hand around hers to steady it before plucking it out of her grip and onto the counter where it wouldn't spill. He made himself a cup of coffee, giving her a minute to get her breath back and gather her wits.

"Collin's such a dick. I'm Derrick, by the way. We met on Monday. I'm new here too. Can I walk you back to your desk?"

Atticus was with her. She was safe. Never in danger. She took a deep breath and tried to get back into character, picking up her coffee again and giving him a furtive glance. "Um. Oh. That's not—that's not necessary."

"It's no problem. It's my first time on this floor. I'd like to meet as many of my coworkers as I can." He flashed her a smile and threw the little metal coffee spoon to the sink. He missed, and it landed on the counter, but he didn't move to clean it up. Just stood there smiling at her. Perfect balance of charm and twat. Jealousy of his skill bubbled up, and Daphne almost laughed, her nervous system settling down with the familiarity of the emotion.

"Sure, yeah. I haven't met many people either."

They walked down the hall together, Atticus asking inane questions about work, Daphne acting like a shy violet. By the time they reached her office, she felt normal again.

"This is me," she said, gesturing to the door to the storage room she was using.

"Wow, your own office already."

"Heh. Not quite."

Atticus glanced around to make sure nobody was close enough to overhear them.

"Do not be alone with him," he said under his breath. "Under any circumstances. Boss works miracles but I'm not sure they could get you off for murder."

Daphne gave a light snort. "Worth it. I need to know if there are any off-network files for me."

He nodded. "I'll stop by Rayna." Atticus glanced away and clenched his jaw. "That spoon is going to bother me."

How he could play a role so anathema to him was impressive, but Daphne sympathized.

"I'll go back and get it in a minute," she said. "That's more Olive's personality than Derrick's."

He glanced at her knowingly and nodded his head in thanks.

"It was nice meeting you, Derrick," Daphne said, louder, smiling as she unlocked the door with her badge.

"You too, Olive. Hope to see you around."

***

It had been a light day for Cinnamon, and she was more than happy to get home early and spend some time in the pool and lounge on the patio. Even if it wasn't supposed to get warmer than seventy degrees.

She had texted Starlight, of course, but hadn't gotten a response. Work was busy for her, she knew, and if there was strict security protocol, it was possible she wasn't even allowed to have her personal phone on her while she was working. It had been nearly 7 p.m. by the time Starlight texted her last night, and she wouldn't be surprised if she got a response at about that time tonight, too. Right in the middle of dinner with her family.

After a few hours outside, Cinnamon had showered and settled in to work on her project until she had to leave for dinner. She copied the death and rape messages her anonymous accounts received to her Violent Threats folder, reported and blocked the accounts who sent her anything inappropriate, and flagged the worst or most credible threats for review later. Her personal accounts didn't seem to be compromised, which was the goal of using the fake accounts: investigate the abuse, poke the bear, but do it from a safe distance. Or the safest distance possible.

It wasn't anything worse than what the victims of GamerGate had to put up with for the past year, but it took an emotional toll, every time. It was just something she had to put up with if she was going to be outspoken about sexist practices in the tech industry.

Mainly, she worried for her clients. If anyone found anything to tie her to them, they would be harassed too, and blacklisted from the industry. The men in charge protected their own and shut out anyone who threatened them.

Cinnamon didn't get very far into her quest before the doorbell rang. She opened her security app and watched Ying-Li's tall, slender form lean to look into the camera and hold up a six-pack of bottled beer.

"Let's pre-game family dinner." Her voice warbled through the static.

Cinnamon frowned and pushed back from her desk, putting the computer in sleep mode. She opened the front door to Ying-Li slouched against the door frame. Her blonde hair fell into her eyes in a short, boyish cut, and her white tank top and shiny black track pants boasted large designer logos.

"Hong and Min invited me to dinner. Figured we could go together. Figured we could prepare together, too."

"Do my parents know you call them Hong and Min?" She stepped to the side and let Ying-Li walk in, shutting and locking the door behind her.

The woman shrugged and put two bottles of beer next to the D&D book on the coffee table before taking the rest to the fridge. "They love how 'Americanized' I am. I love how adorably slightly progressive they are. It works out."

Cinnamon followed her slowly, moving the cold, sweating bottles onto coasters. She chose a chair, knowing Ying-Li would crowd her on the couch, and pulled the Player's Handbook onto her lap, opening it to the half-orc ranger she had started the night she met Starlight. Ying-Li came back with the bottle opener and cracked both beers before Cinnamon could say she didn't want one.

"I couldn't let you suffer alone tonight," Ying-Li said, settling back into the couch and shifting so her feet stretched out onto the coffee table. Irritation flickered through Cinnamon. She had just told Echo the other night that Ying-Li was at most a friend and nothing more, yet here she was, invited to family dinner. Was this her sister's passive-aggressive way of saying, once again, that she disapproved of Cinnamon's pursuit of a Redgrave?

Then again, jiejie would hate to be thought of as passive-any-thing. She was more...assertive. With occasional aggression. It was more likely she would tell Cinnamon to her face she didn't like Daphne, since that's exactly what she already did. Maybe inviting Ying-Li had nothing to do with Cinnamon or her questionable new crush.

She gave a little snort and shook her head. Ying-Li joining them for dinner was probably her parents' idea. But showing up unannounced at her house felt wrong. Like an ambush.

Slow your roll, Little Spice, she told herself, pinching the bridge of her nose. *This isn't a healthy paranoia.*

"Dinner with them isn't agony," Cinnamon replied. "Beyond the usual generational disconnect."

"You know they can't hear you," Ying-Li said.

"Whether they hear me or not doesn't make it less true."

"So you find spending time with your parents enjoyable?"

"Usually."

Ying-Li raised her eyebrows and took a sip of beer. "From my own experience with parents, they suck. If I didn't know yours personally, I would never believe you. But they like me, so they can't be all bad." She wiggled her sneakers on the coffee table and Cinnamon gripped the book in her lap to disperse her annoyance.

"I just cleaned that table," she said, glad she didn't sound as unhinged aloud as she did in her head. "Please don't put your shoes on it."

Ying-Li moved her feet to the floor and sat up on the couch. "Yeah, of course, sorry, Cin."

"And I love my parents, but we don't need to spend the afternoon talking about them."

"You're right." She held up a hand and inclined her head in agreement. "What's new in your life?"

Starlight took up all the extra space in her brain, but she didn't want to talk about her, either. Especially since Ying-Li had acted jealous at the party. If she could get Ying-Li gossiping—her favorite activity—she would be preoccupied and wouldn't even notice if Cinnamon's mind wandered. Not a paragon of hospitality, but she shouldn't have invited herself over unannounced.

"Nothing new, really. Emma hinted that some crazy stuff went down at the Twinning's party after I left, but nobody has given me the details."

Ying-Li sat up straight, a sparkle of mischief in her eyes, a sure sign that Cinnamon would be subjected to plenty of irrelevant rumors, scandals, and backstabbing. "Let me tell you everything."

Sure enough, Ying-Li's account of the party was long-winded, petty, and ignorant of Cinnamon's lack of attention, which had been monopolized by Starlight and the limitless possibilities of what they might get up to together. By the time Ying-Li repeated herself several times, Cinnamon was hopelessly lost in her thoughts.

Cinnamon looked up from the D&D book she wasn't paying attention to. "What was that? Sorry."

Ying-Li gave her a tight smile. "I said I can set it up for you."

"What can you set up?" Cinnamon asked smoothly, trying to use confidence as a cover.

"Security for your computer."

A thin thread of panic wound its way through her stomach. What on earth had Ying-Li been talking about that came around to the security of Cinnamon's computer? "It already has a password."

Ying-Li gave her a pitying look. "That's the bare minimum. Do you have a camera hooked up to it?"

Cinnamon nodded. "Is that bad?"

"No, no, that's good. I can set it up so it'll take a picture whenever someone tries to log in. Send it to your email or phone so you'll know immediately."

A few months ago, when Cinnamon had received those suspiciously accurate private messages, she wasn't sure what to do or who to ask about what to do. She'd had enough presence of mind to get the new security system, but since the threat originated from the internet, she wanted to know what else she could do from that angle.

So she had asked Ying-Li, who wanted to know all the details but only received the excuse of general trolls and doxxing and being afraid of people coming to Cinnamon's house. She'd already taken care of the in-person part with the security cameras. Now she just needed help with the anonymity.

To her credit, Ying-Li didn't make her feel stupid or paranoid for wanting the extra security. She gave advice that was simple enough to implement. Maybe Ying-Li had been asking for an update on that situation, and that was how she'd come to the conclusion that Cinnamon needed the extra camera security on her computer.

"That's not a bad idea." Cinnamon bit her lip, thinking. "Could you set it up before we leave?"

"It'll only take a minute." She jumped up, bringing her beer with her.

They entered the office and Ying-Li nodded toward the chair. "Power it up then let me sit. I'll show you how I do it step by step."

A few minutes later, it was up and tested. Cinnamon got an email with an attached picture of Ying-Li sitting at her desk.

"That's so cool," she murmured. Ying-Li beamed. "So here's a question, possibly a dumb question, but is a VPN a good safety measure?"

Ying-Li shrugged. "Even with the best cybersecurity, nobody's really anonymous. I mean, *I* could find anybody, but that's because I have a 'very particular set of skills.'" She laughed at her own Liam Neeson impression. "And that's only if someone caught my attention in the first place. Are you doing anything online that would catch the attention of someone like that? Do you have a dark secret, Cinnamon?"

Well. Yeah. She shook her head, hoping Ying-Li wouldn't see her blush in the dark room. "I'm a woman online. People don't need more of a reason. I just don't want someone to find me, dox me, come to my house. Or do something to me that would jeopardize my career or my clients."

Cinnamon expected a sharp comeback or a brush-off, but Ying-Li looked thoughtful. With a groan, she stretched and stood up from the chair. "You're right," she said, "those kinds of people don't need a reason. But if anyone is bothering you, tell me, and I'll do more of this. I'll take care of you, Little Spice."

She winced. Her family nickname sounded wrong coming from Ying-Li. Condescending.

"Is that what you're wearing? Were you going to change?"

Cinnamon looked down, her irritation growing. Her outfit was fine for lounging. But maybe too casual for family dinner.

"I should."

Ying-Li nodded. "I'll finish your beer and wait for you downstairs. My car is outside, so we can leave whenever you're ready." As she stepped past Cinnamon into the hallway, she turned back and lowered her head.

"You know, if it was just you and me, I wouldn't make you change." She gave her a once-over that made Cinnamon cringe. Without waiting for an answer, Ying-Li bounded down the stairs.

Alone in her office, Cinnamon puffed out a breath and walked out, shutting and locking the door behind her.

It was going to be a long night.

Chapter Twelve

If Cinnamon had been told as recently as a week ago that her parents would not only invite an outsider to dinner, but let said stranger call them by their given names, she would have bet everything she had against it. And any other day, she would be right.

Ying-Li could be a lucrative contact for Cheung Technologies, and if that was what the fuss was about, Cinnamon could understand the attention she was getting. Still, after her recent conversations with Echo, it felt personal.

Since Echo had taken a more prominent position in the company, their parents had allowed more and more distractions to seep into what was once sacred and inviolable "family time." Cinnamon remembered how, years ago, her father would make a show of deliberately leaving his pager in his coat pocket before sitting down to dinner, a ritual that marked the shift from business to personal, from dealing with the outside world to finding joy in their private lives.

Now, more times than not, Echo would be on the phone while spooning braised duck onto her plate, and her father would drop his phone into the soup as he attempted to beat his high score on whatever game currently held his attention.

So with her family preoccupied, Cinnamon didn't see anything wrong with withdrawing from the conversation to reply to Starlight's text.

Starlight:

This week might kill me.

Cinnamon:

Is it the week's fault, or work's?

Starlight:

You're right. I should leave the week out of this.

Cinnamon:

And do you love the work enough to put up with it?

Starlight:

You're trying to therapize me.

Cinnamon:

Just gauging whether you'd feel justified quitting. Is it not just numbers?

Starlight:

It's not usually this bad. There are long stretches of boredom, but when the pressure's on, it's mayhem. Already tried the baklava and you're a goddess, thank you, you've ruined my dinner. Tell me about Family Dinner. What are you eating

Cinnamon:

Is this the Starlight version of "what are you wearing"?

Starlight:

No. What are you wearing.

Cinnamon:

Would you rather know that or the other?

Starlight:

> wearing

> Cinnamon:
>
> Blouse and slacks.

> Starlight:
>
> :(That does nothing for my imagination. What are you eating?

Cinnamon looked up to see that Ying-Li had already served her, the plate in front of her piled with rice, eggplant with garlic, and scallion ginger lobster. She just barely succeeded in keeping her face smooth.

"Welcome back," Ying-Li said, smiling. "I was worried I would have to feed you myself, too."

"Yes, Ying-Li is our guest," her father said lightly, "and it would be rude to ignore her for your phone."

"Oh, it's no problem, Hong. Cinnamon has a lot on her mind."

A wave of numbness rolled through Cinnamon's stomach. Ying-Li wouldn't just *tell* Cinnamon's family about her problems and worries, would she? She couldn't imagine any friend doing that, but something about Ying-Li's tone struck a chord. She hadn't said anything outright, but it still felt like a threat.

Opting to see where things went before deciding how to respond, Cinnamon slid her phone back into her purse and turned her attention to the people at the table.

"Is work very challenging, Cinnamon?" Her mother's tone was curious.

"It has to be," answered Ying-Li. "The world of tech start-ups is vicious. That's what you said you specialized in, right?"

Cinnamon picked up her chopsticks and started moving the food around on her plate, searching for pieces of eggplant that had survived the deluge of lobster. She had already had to skip the soup (crab and fish maw), swirling her spoon around and paying attention to whether anyone was paying attention to her. She would usually put a spoonful of the fish dish in the far corner of her plate and create a barrier between it and what she actually wanted to eat. Tonight would call for more aggressive action.

"I specialize in therapy," she answered. She took a sip from her wine glass and set it down dangerously close to her dish. "It would make sense if the majority of people I saw worked in a field that's popular here. But I like to think I could help anybody."

"Of course," Ying-Li said, giving her a small smile. "But it also makes sense that that popular field is cut-throat, and your clients more challenging because of it."

"Whatever the reason," Echo cut in, "I'm sure Cinnamon can get through one dinner without checking on her. It." She raised an eyebrow to make sure Cinnamon knew she was talking about Daphne.

And if it had just been their regular family dinner, that would have been fine. But with Ying-Li there, and her family acting out of character, she felt duped. Generally, she wasn't one to initiate drama, but she was feeling a little petty.

"Mama, Baba, what do you know about the Redgrave Group?"

Everyone at the table stilled. Her parents blinked, like they were trying to figure out why she was asking before they answered. Echo gave her an exasperated look, and even Ying-Li paused, chopsticks halfway to her mouth.

"Does one of your clients work for them, Little Spice?" her mother asked, glancing at Ying-Li.

"A new friend of mine used to. The name sounded familiar. They're one of our competitors, right?"

"Something like that," her father said. "But not exactly. They've tried, over the years, but they can't quite operate on our level."

"So they're not our sworn enemies? No blood feuds?"

Across the table, Echo rolled her eyes and began eating again.

"We've never had reason to collaborate, but we've also never had reason to retaliate." Min Cheung had a knack for putting things succinctly.

"The girl from the party, isn't it?" Ying-Li said under her breath, glancing up to meet Cinnamon's stare, but keeping her head bowed. Before Cinnamon could answer, Ying-Li turned away from her. "The Redgraves are into some really shady stuff," she told the rest of the table. "I might not blame them if it were lucrative, but to deliberately make risky decisions only to remain mediocre? They must have only made it this far on luck. They're too stupid otherwise."

How Ying-Li had connected the dots between the girl she saw Cinnamon making out with at the solstice party and the Redgrave Group, Cinnamon had no idea. Echo had said that Daphne wasn't a threat. Was that because Ying-Li was right, the Redgraves were too stupid to launch that kind of attack? Or was she making them look bad out of jealousy? Echo didn't correct her. Hong and Min laughed. Cinnamon, as usual, blushed.

Hong said, "I'm sure with your family's connections, you're more knowledgeable than most about what happens behind closed conference room doors."

"That kind of experience must make you a good resource for Cinnamon's job. If she has any questions about how these app companies work, she can ask you." Min had misread the heat in Cinnamon's cheeks.

"Definitely," Ying-Li said around a bite of lobster. "People have no idea the kinds of pressure the management is under. They're trying to build their dream and disrupt the system all while being beholden to shareholders. And hiring people to work on it is a total mess. Nobody wants to work. Everybody wants more money. They get generous benefits and still aren't happy. When ventures fail, it's not for lack of vision. It's because the worker bees get greedy."

On their first and only date, Cinnamon had asked Ying-Li what she thought could be going on at all these startups that put their employees in such a bad mental state. Her answer was evasive and full of speculation, but she was more interested in hearing the details of whatever gossip had prompted Cinnamon to ask in the first place. It hadn't been the only reason she felt Ying-Li wasn't right for her, but it was one of the reasons. Cinnamon had forgotten about it until tonight. The CEOs doing the racism and assault and embezzlement were the victims? Absolutely not.

Whatever remained of her desire not to cause drama dwindled to nothing, and she took a deep breath before responding. "The culture of harassment and exploitation that has taken hold of this industry is toxic." She tried her best not to shout, the adrenaline rushing through her veins making it difficult to modulate her voice.

"The workers are exploited in every possible way." Cinnamon stared at Ying-Li, whose face hardened at her rebuttal. "And when a project fails, the founder gets his rich friends to float him again, while anyone who rightfully complained about their treatment gets blacklisted. My parents were able to build an honorable business that respected every employee. The men running the start-up circuit just run grift after disgraceful grift."

It wasn't like her to launch into a rant, and she knew it wasn't the appropriate time or place. The argument was a good one, but she still felt embarrassed.

"Sorry," Cinnamon said, rubbing her temple. "It just upsets me when people doing their best get taken advantage of. For them, it's their livelihoods, but for those in power, it's a game."

Ying-Li's face softened, and she gave Cinnamon a half smile. "Is this what your clients tell you? Have you ever met someone who tried to launch their own tech business here?"

"I think," Echo interrupted, "we can all agree that both sides have their problems, and since none of us have first-hand experience with it, none of us can know just what it's like."

The rest of the table, eager for a quick resolution, nodded. Except Cinnamon. She reached for her glass of wine and accidentally knocked it into her plate—and it was an accident, even if she had planned to do it at some point.

She stood up with a sigh, watching the wine pool beneath the rice, staining everything burgundy. At least she understood what was making her so sensitive and had plenty of practice managing it. Sidling away from the table, she grabbed her purse.

"Excuse me," she said to no one in particular. "You're right, I do have a lot on my mind. I'm going to go outside for a few minutes and re-center myself so I can come back and fully participate in our dinner. Will you get me a new glass of wine? And a plate—leave it empty, I'm not sure what I'll want when I get back."

They let her leave without comment. As she walked away, she heard their conversation start up again, and Echo saying, "She always gets so eloquent when she's overwhelmed."

Sunset warmed the benches just outside the restaurant, and Cinnamon slumped into one with a sigh. Her bad attitude was all Ying-Li. Showing up at her house unexpectedly, the easy familiarity with her parents, then her comments defending the men Cinnamon had good reason to investigate. Cinnamon had planned to sit down and tell her clearly and directly that she wasn't interested in a romantic relationship, but after today, she wasn't sure she wanted a friendship with her, either.

What she needed was a bright reprieve. She pulled her phone out of her bag and remembered that she never responded to Starlight.

Cinnamon:

Sorry, distracted. No food yet, just wine. But I have my eye on some crispy fried bean curd and satay short ribs.

Starlight:

"That sounds amazing" she said while eating clam chowder in a bread bowl

Cinnamon:

Would you rather have mine?

Starlight:

Why not both?

Cinnamon:

Easy for you. The clam is the dealbreaker for me.

Starlight:

My plan was churros and crepes, but I was told those don't count as dinner? So now I will have soup AND churros AND crepes, and ice cream and some fudge at some point.

Cinnamon:

Sounds like you're at the pier. Are you going on the carousel? Who told you churros and crepes don't count?

Starlight:

lol no. I just told you I'll be eating my weight in treats. No carousel. I can barely keep it together on a bumpy car ride, I can't go round and round. I'm here with my sister and our best friend. Somebody has to keep me fed when you're not around, Cinnamon.

Cinnamon:

Why not both? I can come out with all of you next time.

Starlight:

How about Pride on Sunday? We're going to the parade and the park. Come with. Of course, if gay marriage is struck down before then, it'll be a protest, but I invite you either way.

Cinnamon:

Definitely. Send the details, I'll be there.

Starlight:

Have you decided where we're going for dinner tomorrow?

Cinnamon:

I have.

Starlight:

??? You gonna share?

Cinnamon:

Sure. When we get there.

Starlight:

How am I supposed to prepare!

Cinnamon:

Wear literally whatever you want and show up hungry.

Starlight:

Two of the three things I'm best at.

Cinnamon:
What's the third?

Starlight:
Oh you'll see.

Cinnamon:
...

Starlight:
And it's the number one thing I'm good at.

Cinnamon:
Making a scene?

Starlight:
You know, that's not a bad guess. Anyway I've got some clammies and sourdough to devour. Enjoy your tofu and other not-fish. Text me about tomorrow.

Cinnamon:
I will. Enjoy your churros etc.

The screen went black as Cinnamon stared at it, waiting to see if Starlight would say anything else. She brought her eyes up from the dark rectangle and stared across the city, harsh lines of buildings and emerald tufts of trees, all stained orange and pink by the tired sun. Of course she would be able to handle the rest of the dinner. It was just her family. And, yes, someone she would rather not spend time with at the moment, but an hour or two more would be fine. She couldn't always do what she wanted.

Starlight would disagree. If she'd been there, she would have already dragged Cinnamon away from the restaurant without another word to anyone. She smiled as she put her phone away. Just avoid talking about any business whatsoever, let thoughts of the woman she was dating flood her mind whenever what she really wanted to do was yell, and she might be able to salvage the evening.

***

"It has to be a new girl. It's certainly not us."

"I'm sitting right here, you know." Daphne narrowed her eyes at Mattie and Rin as she stowed her phone in her purse. "It's rude to talk about someone like they're not here."

"You weren't here," Rin said, letting her French dip sandwich soak up its au jus. "You were wherever you go when you think about the person who keeps texting you."

Daphne pursed her lips and looked out at the people on the pier. There was still daylight to be enjoyed for the next half hour, but the outdoor attractions and family-friendly entertainment closed before night fell, especially on a Tuesday, and the crowd was thin. Mattie and Rin had been there since early afternoon, when they went on a wine tour followed by an accidentally drunk aquarium visit. Daphne had wondered how "accidental" it could have been, since the order of activities had been planned when sober.

"Jealous, Rin-Rin?" she turned back to her Kiwi friend with a raised brow.

"Of course I'm jealous. I flew out to see you. But that means I want to *see* you."

"I know," Daphne said with a sigh, peeling off a warm strip of sourdough—soft on one side, crispy on the other—to dunk in the chowder. "We got a big client at work this week and it requires the participation of the entire office. In overtime. This is my second fourteenish-hour day, and the next three will be just as long. You're lucky I'm even awake right now. Friday should be our last day with it, and then the three of us will be able to spend more time together this weekend. And next week."

"Are you gonna try to tell me that that's work texting you, then?"

Oof. Nothing got by Rin.

"I made a friend," Daphne hedged. "And before you ask, I don't know if it's even anything yet, so, no, you can't meet her."

Mattie nearly choked on her grilled cheese. "You don't...you don't know if it's anything yet?" She and Rin exchanged a look before turning back to Daphne. "She isn't the love of your life?"

Of course she was. They all were, in the beginning. Up until Cinnamon, Daphne's constant declaration that the newest woman in her life was going to be her wife was a predictable and ongoing lesbian version of "The Boy Who Cried Wolf." It wasn't that she didn't learn. She was just that optimistic.

But something was different with Cinnamon. She had kissed Daphne first—rare enough—and wasn't put off by her admittedly chaotic intensity—rarer still. Maybe it was how she had escorted Daphne home the night before, genuinely wanting her to get a good night's sleep because she knew how long her days were and would be. The sincerity. Putting her first.

Maybe it was the small voice in Daphne's mind whispering that she didn't want to move on from this one. As much as she threw herself into every new relationship (real or perceived), she always knew she could bounce back, find love again. But this new commentary, quiet in case Daphne tried to smother it, was less concerned about the tedium of finding someone new, and more concerned with the no-longer-having-Cinnamon-specifi-cally part.

"Either she's depressed or it's actually serious," Rin mused.

Daphne snorted. "Or I'm growing up."

"We're too young to grow up," Mattie said.

The three of them sat in silence for a moment, letting Mattie's statement find a little bit of truth as they finished dinner. Daphne was pretty sure Mats and Rin were still a little tipsy, or had taken something else since their wine tour. She wished she could do the same, sand down the edges of her stress just a little, but she had to stay sharp for work.

Maybe she was growing up.

"What time is the escape room?" she asked them, scooping the last bit of clam into her mouth.

"Half past eight," Mattie said. "Enough time for a cookie?"

"Absolutely," Rin answered.

"And then karaoke."

"No karaoke for me," Daphne cut in. "My alarm is for just after five a.m. In the morning. Is it technically morning if the sun is still asleep? Either way, it should be illegal."

Mattie patted her hand. "Cookie, escape room, then bed for Daph. Are we gonna see you at all before Pride?"

Daphne flipped through the rest of the week in her head. Wednesday night with Cinnamon, Saturday night reservations at the Manu Ono popup restaurant that she was going to invite Cinnamon to. Saturday day had to be a buffer in case work needed her. That left Thursday and Friday night free. She wanted to tell her sister yes, but she wanted to see Cinnamon more, and she would most likely fall asleep too early to do either.

"I might fall asleep," she admitted. Her friends nodded.

"It's okay," Rin said sympathetically. "I'd rather spend time with you but if you're knackered, I found a promising-looking boxing gym nearby. Gonna convince Mattie to come with me."

Mats pulled a face but said, "Sure."

"Besides, Daph, you need the rest. You do look sort of like shit," Rin teased.

"Whoa now." Daphne held up her hands in surrender.

Mattie grimaced and glanced between the two of them. "Rude, Corinne. You know she's been working long hours. Where's the opportunity for a spa day in all that?"

"Emotionally like shit," Rin amended.

Daphne nodded and crossed her arms. "Not better."

Rin only smiled. "Forgive my bluntness, darling, but sometimes that's the only way you take us seriously."

What could Daphne say to that? "You're right. So let's get this escape room solved so I can get to bed. Oh wait. Are escape rooms like a real-life fantasy role-playing game?"

"You've been before," Mattie said, gathering the table's trash.

"I know what it is, but I don't know how it compares to RPGs. Similar?"

"Less physical than LARPing, more physical than tabletop RPGs." Rin added her empty dishes to the pile. "The 'RP' is the similarity. That's role-playing."

"So if I like escape rooms, do you think I'd like something like D&D?"

"Ah." Rin glanced at Mattie again. "Her new girlfriend has some nerdy interests."

Mattie laughed. "Be prepared to only hear about orcs and druids and dice for the next two to four weeks."

"Might be fun to play a game together," Daphne said, ignoring the bait. "I'm sure I can find some seasoned players to guide us."

"I'm sure you can," Rin teased. "Seriously, though, I'm in."

"Me too," Mattie said. "Obviously. If that's how you want to share your girlfr—uh, your new interests, then that's how we'll support you."

Daphne grinned. They were so easy.

The three of them left the restaurant, got cookies for the road, and made their way to the escape room. Sleepy as she was, Daphne felt the magic of the night, spending time with two of the people she most loved, beneath the stars, and about to once again practice the teamwork skills they were so good at.

Now all she needed was to add some Cinnamon.

Chapter Thirteen

An hour after her last patient left, Cinnamon was still sitting at her desk, staring at the shadows growing longer in her fourth-floor office as the day spun from afternoon to evening. Part of her had noted the change, while the rest of her thoughts spent equal time knotting themselves up and trying to untangle themselves.

Her pen was poised, forgotten, above Aoi's notebook, which was only closed because that was part of the ritual she used to end all her sessions. Thank them for coming in and sharing with her, close the notebook, reiterate that she looks forward to seeing them again, walk them to the door, and see them out with an "Until next time."

Two of her clients today were among the ones who had been assaulted at work. The earlier patient had been making a lot of progress since the year before, when she told Cinnamon about her job's toxic culture. Aoi, her last patient of the day, was struggling. Months ago, they had been vocal about calling out that same culture. Cinnamon had learned that public criticism of the industry made one a target and adjusted the visibility of her accounts, but Aoi didn't hide behind a mask. As a result, they'd been fired and left the industry altogether, but they continued to be harassed and threatened by a league of online trolls dedicated to making their life miserable.

Cinnamon knew the group well. They were the same ones harassing and threatening her. Rather, the accounts for her fake personas. It was clear they would go after anyone who had the audacity to condemn their favorite tech idols, nasty little cultists who used any excuse to make anyone else feel as small and scared and angry as they were.

Aoi was having a hard time today because they had read an article about their abuser recently winning an award. It was all Cinnamon could do to not grill them about which article, what website, which award, what was his *name*? It took a significant amount of concentration for her to pack away her personal curiosity, like an overstuffed suitcase she was trying to close by sitting on it. Even though she was able to navigate the session with Aoi, she still felt that she had let them down. She had a duty to focus on what would be in their best interest, and she had let her personal project distract her. Not very professional.

When they had left, Cinnamon rushed to her computer to search for whatever tech news would lead her to that article. People were making up awards for things all the time—usually a company associated with whoever wanted one, to pad their CV and generate good-sounding news about them—but only one of the two men on her most-likely list had won something in the previous two weeks.

Collin Roday.

Warmth spread through her body, into her cheeks. Was this it, then? Had she finally figured it out?

She'd been pursuing his identity for so long, she hadn't totally thought through what to do when she found it, and the thrill of potentially solving this year-long mystery stalled when she pondered the next step. If none of his victims were willing to come forward and name him, did it even matter? He was the CEO of a big company, debatably successful, criminally wealthy, and more of a tech icon than someone who actually solved problems.

Inching ever closer to being a cult leader, with his hate-filled fan base he could direct at will...

He would never be held responsible for anything.

The futility of the last year hit Cinnamon hard. Despite all her work, the man who violated her clients in so many ways would keep living his life free of consequences, and all the other people in similar positions of power would do the same. All those other names on her suspect list were there for a reason. According to her investigation, each one of them behaved reprehensibly, if not illegally.

So she let herself indulge in a bit of a spiral.

And that was how she came to be staring at shadows in her office an hour after she should have left, at exactly the time Starlight was supposed to meet her at home.

"Shit," she muttered, waking up her computer just to shut it down and sliding the notebooks into her leather messenger bag. She called a Lyft to her usual pickup spot and sent Starlight a text.

Cinnamon:

Running late at work, but I should be home in about 15.

Starlight:

Just got here. Can I go around back?

Cinnamon:

I have such a nice couch on the front porch.

Starlight:

You do. Should I lounge there as I await your return?

Cinnamon:

> Please. I also need a few minutes to shower. Sorry, I know you've had long days at work this week, I wanted to try for an early dinner.

Starlight:

> Aw Cinnamon. Looking out for me. You must like me. uwu

Cinnamon:

> You're okay.

Starlight:

> I am magnificent!

Cinnamon:

> We'll see. I'll be there in a few.

Starlight:

> I'll strive not to perish in the meantime.

Cinnamon rolled her eyes at her phone as she read Starlight's response. She never thought she would fall for such a drama queen, but if it was distraction enough from the day's setbacks, she'd take it.

***

Daphne had an itch to try to hack her way into Cinnamon's house past her security system, but she counted three cameras on the front porch and remembered from the last time she was there that the system looked pretty beefy. It seemed excessive for a therapist, though Daphne supposed if she dealt with potentially violent people, it might make sense.

Or it could be because of her family's business. If Daphne had still worked for her father, she might feel the need for extra precautions. And now that she knew how cutthroat corporate espionage was, if she ever worked for him again (unlikely), she would hire Brad to design and maintain the beefiest of systems.

Daphne stretched out on the pink and white striped cushions of the little couch and closed her eyes. Even if Cinnamon's car was electric, its crunch of tires on the driveway, and the garage door opening, would alert her to Cinnamon's arrival. No need to keep her dry, overworked eyes open if she didn't have to.

"Am I supposed to kiss you?"

Daphne jerked awake, her quick inhale thankfully more of a sniff than a snore, and blinked her eyes at a smiling and very close Cinnamon.

"Well," she said, clearing her throat. "Yeah."

Cinnamon leaned forward, and Daphne tilted her head to meet her halfway, rewarding each other with a slow and heartfelt kiss.

"Where did you come from?" Daphne murmured as their lips parted

"Work."

"I didn't hear your car."

"My ride dropped me off two blocks away."

"Why?"

Cinnamon pulled away to stand up, and Daphne swung her legs over the edge of the couch to join her.

"It's a long story," Cinnamon said. Her face was drawn, her shoulders sagging a little. Daphne had gotten up before the sun for three days in a row, but Cinnamon was the one who looked run ragged. She sighed as she pulled her keys out of her purse and went to open the front door. "Security measure, mostly. I don't know who's looking at my data. Don't want them to know where I live."

"Smart," Daphne said, hanging back while Cinnamon stepped inside and punched in the code for the alarm. "But why not take your car?"

"Don't have one. Rideshares and public transport suit me fine. When they don't, Echo sends me a driver."

Was she just paranoid, or did she have a good reason to be so cautious? She certainly looked like something was worrying her. Haunting her, even. At dinner the other night, Cinnamon had said that her job was stressing her out. Maybe it had gotten worse.

"How was work?" Daphne asked.

She stepped over the threshold at Cinnamon's beckoning, and her lover gave a quick glance outside before shutting and locking the door.

"Challenging," Cinnamon said, after a moment. "Do you want to stay down here? I'm going to put this in my office then take a shower. I'll be fast."

"Hmm. What are my options?"

"Anywhere down here."

Daphne pouted. "I could help. In the shower."

Cinnamon's cheeks glowed with a rosiness that Daphne found adorable. She might not be expecting anything so intimate so soon, but that didn't mean she couldn't tease her about it.

"You just seem really stressed out." Daphne stepped closer so she could grasp Cinnamon's shoulder affectionately. She wanted to be as considerate with her physical and mental needs as Cinnamon was with her. "If it's because of our date, it's no problem to reschedule. It sounds like we both had long days."

"No." Cinnamon shook her head. She reached up to grasp Daphne's hand. "No, I need our date. Work was just particularly awful today."

Daphne nodded. "You can talk to me about it, if you want."

Cinnamon shook her head. "I really can't." She blinked tears out of her eyes, and Daphne wanted to kidnap her away to where nothing bad could happen to her. Then return on her own and punish everyone responsible for her pain. Knowing that was unrealistic and embarrassingly cringe-worthy, she settled for squeezing Cinnamon's shoulder and giving her a reassuring smile.

"Go. Get clean." Daphne nodded toward the stairs. "I'll raid the fridge for snacks while I wait."

"Fifteen minutes, tops," Cinnamon said, taking the first few steps backward.

"Take your time. When I'm done in the fridge, I'm snooping through your record collection."

When Cinnamon had disappeared from view, Daphne moved far enough into the house that Cinnamon wouldn't be able to see her from the top of the stairs. A glance around the room confirmed what she thought she remembered: there weren't any cameras *inside* the house. That she could see. She heard a door being unlocked, opened, then closed again quickly. Cinnamon walking to the back of the house, then to the middle, and another door closing. When she heard the shower running, Daphne tiptoed up the stairs and knelt in front of Cinnamon's office door.

Of course she couldn't tell Daphne anything about work. Daphne wondered if she was able to talk about it in detail in her own therapy sessions, or if part of the ethics of being a mental health professional was that Cinnamon had to keep confidentiality all the way to her grave. She might love her job, but when anything caused as much suffering as she was obviously going through, it was time to take stock and decide what was the most important. What she really wanted from life.

Daphne might not be able to do a damn thing to help her, but she could certainly try to understand her. And, if she were to find the answers on her own, that would mean Cinnamon didn't have to violate any ethics. She wouldn't even have to know about it. And how ethical could it be, anyway, keeping hurtful things where she would keep experiencing them, but not being allowed to share the burden with anyone?

It only took a minute to pick the lock before she was inside, door shut behind her. It was a small room with no closet—definitely meant to be a nursery or office or even an enormous closet on its own. The one window on the far side illuminated the dusky purple walls and dove gray and black accents. The black wooden desk faced the window, away from the door, and a white built-in shelf behind it showcased books and knickknacks, a snowglobe that said "Vancouver" and a small wooden globe that looked hand carved. In the black leather chair, Cinnamon had set her briefcase, and Daphne moved it to the floor so she could sit down.

She moved the mouse, but the computer didn't wake up, so she pressed the power button and waited. Password protected. Daphne sighed. Cinnamon wasn't stupid. An admirable quality most of the time, but not so much when Daphne was trying to get information. She looked around, searching for a sticky note or something that might indicate where to look for one.

"Ah, there you are," she murmured as she flipped over the keyboard. A small piece of paper was taped to its underside. "KillerQueen0908#. Are you a Queen fan, darling? We'll have to do karaoke when we're not both sleep deprived."

She turned the keyboard right side up and typed in the password, finding a weird satisfaction in the clicky-ness of the keys.

The desktop opened showing a screen half filled with folders and files and programs that covered a background image of what looked like a group of five armed, fantasy-clothed characters fighting a huge, fire-breathing red dragon.

Somehow, out of everything, the picture was the thing that brought Daphne back to her senses.

"Jesus Christ," Daphne said, glancing at the icons. "What the fuck am I doing? I can't do this." There was so much she didn't know about Cinnamon, what she loved and hated, what she enjoyed, her secrets and the secret corners that, with time, she would feel comfortable sharing with Daphne. To force herself into those places was crossing a line, one that would be understandable justification for dumping Daphne immediately, if not pressing charges.

"Bad, bad, Daphne," she said, shutting down the computer without opening any files and putting the keyboard and briefcase back where she found them. "Literally everyone you love would be so disappointed in you. I'm disappointed in you."

She listened at the door, then opened it a crack. Hearing the water still running, she slipped out, locking the door and closing it behind her, and tiptoed back downstairs to wait. As much as she wanted Cinnamon to share herself, she knew that it had to be Cinnamon's choice. But when Daphne had seen how upset she was, her protection mode kicked in, and her brain narrowed its focus to a pinpoint. She was relieved, and surprised, that she had stopped herself before she ruined everything again.

Leftovers and records forgotten, Daphne plopped onto a chair in the living room and let herself have a little pity party. She was nearly thirty, how was she still such a fuck-up? Why had she learned to feel shame after the fact, but not to think things through more critically before taking action in the first place?

Well, she thought, *because I've been rewarded for my boldness more often than scolded.* It was how she found every next lover, crashing into lives and grabbing them, seeing how far they'd go together before she jetted off with a laugh into the next one. But if Cinnamon was the last one, that strategy wouldn't work anymore. If Cinnamon was the last one, that strategy might hurt Daphne.

But it would definitely hurt Cinnamon.

That was unacceptable. Was it too late to take a different approach? To change a lifetime of learned behavior? Maybe it couldn't be done. Shouldn't she try? She wanted to try.

"I'm not going to sit here and argue with myself," she mumbled aloud, looking for a distraction until she had the time and space to think about these things more clearly. The D&D book on the coffee table caught her eye.

Typical. Daphne running off, picking locks and hacking computers, doing everything the hard and illegal way to get to know her newest lover, when she could have just picked up a book. This was why Mattie usually planned their capers.

With a sigh, she grabbed it and started flipping through the pages. Too much information, too many details to get anything out of it in the few minutes she had, but she read the introduction and didn't hate it. Sliding the book back onto the table, Daphne decided that a D&D game would be a much more effective way to get to know Cinnamon than breaking in and snooping.

She slouched into the chair, crossed her arms, and closed her eyes. Assured herself she had shut off the computer, re-locked the office door. It would bother her to get caught, but for once, it bothered her more that she had acted so thoughtlessly toward someone she wanted to trust her.

When Cinnamon came downstairs fifteen minutes later, she must have assumed that Daphne had, once again, fallen asleep, and shook her gently. Daphne gave her a brilliant smile and a pithy quip, and the two left for their dinner date with only one of them worrying over Daphne's betrayal.

Chapter Fourteen

The twenty-minute walk to Cinnamon's favorite Indian restaurant nearly restored her mood. Starlight had said it wasn't a problem to walk that far in her high wedges, but Cinnamon suspected it was just better than potentially getting motion sick in a car. She'd told her to wear literally whatever she wanted, and the woman had shown up as stylish as casual could get, in red heels, distressed jeans, and a white peasant blouse with blue embroidery that matched her eyes. Cinnamon had chosen something more low-key: black midi skirt, aubergine-colored wrap-style sweater, and black flats that were comfortable enough for walking.

"Here we are," Cinnamon said, stopping in front of a locked gate. Starlight glanced around, to the door recessed in shadows behind the gate, the high terra-cotta walls, the lack of signage.

"Is this...someone's house? Where did you take me?"

Cinnamon smiled and leaned past Starlight to press a buzzer. "I might not know everything about you, but you definitely strike me as the type of person who has been to an exclusive venue before."

"Did you take me to a speakeasy?" Her voice squeaked with excitement. "I am not dressed for a speakeasy!"

That would have been much more Starlight, Cinnamon thought, with a twinge of regret. But she didn't know where to find one, and now she had to disappoint her date before they even got started. "No. Or, not how you're thinking. It's well-hidden, but not exactly secret. It just doesn't need advertising."

"Oh my god, Cinnamon, did you take me to a VIP sex party? Like at the Intermittent?"

The gate buzzed and Cinnamon opened it, wondering how she had gone from "dinner" to "sex party" based on one locked door.

"Uh, no. Are there sex parties at the Intermittent? No, don't answer that, I don't want to know." She let Starlight in first, making sure the gate locked behind them before she reached to open the wooden door for her. "Now I'm afraid I've set your expectations way too high, so let me bring them back down to achievable levels before we go in. We're at a restaurant to have dinner. The food is delicious, the atmosphere is chill, and the buzzer gives it an accidental air of mystery. That's all. No illegal substances, no sexual content. Are you okay with that?"

"Yes. But we should make plans to go to a speakeasy. And a sex party. Are you okay with that?"

Cinnamon paused, her hand on the doorknob, wondering how to answer.

"It's too dark to see it," Starlight continued, "but I'll assume you're blushing. We can hammer out the details later. I'm starving. Can we go in?"

Was it always going to be like this? Starlight saying aloud what Cinnamon wasn't sure she could even whisper to another person? The thought both terrified and thrilled her.

The wooden door creaked as it opened, revealing a short and winding enclosed hallway that hid the restaurant from them until they turned a corner and popped out into the courtyard. Plants dotted the stone-paved patio in brightly colored pots between wrought-iron tables, and some kind of climbing flower wove itself in the trellises and overhead slats, its white blossoms glowing in the strings of tiny lights zig-zagging across the living ceiling. Music filtered softly through the vines and tables and chatter, from a guitar duo on the far side of the enclosure.

"Whoa," Starlight whispered. "This is so cool."

Cinnamon breathed deep, letting the smells of coriander and lamb and simmered tomatoes and onions relax her even more. A server led them to a table, past a copper fountain and hemmed in by two tall, large-leafed plants in even larger pots, and left them menus.

"How did you even find this place?" Starlight let her gaze wander around the patio. She sniffed at the air and her eyes went wide. "I'm going to let you order for me."

Laughing, Cinnamon looked around too, remembering how magical it had felt the first time she'd been there. Hanging glass ornaments caught and reflected the gentle yellow light, and ribbons in deep and warm colors rippled in the breeze. "Echo," she finally answered. "Echo and I came here to celebrate my college graduation, because someone took her here, and that person discovered it when someone took them here, and so on. Just something beautiful to share. It always feels like the harshness of the world sloughs off me when I go through that gate."

She brought her eyes back to her date, who seemed to shimmer beneath the fairy lights, like the starlight Cinnamon liked to call her. For a moment, Cinnamon had to think back over what she had just said, Starlight's stare so intense, and she was worried she had said something inappropriate or too revealing. But maybe she was just enchanted.

"And of course I'll order for you. You can't go wrong with whatever you'd pick—I've tried most of it at this point—but I'm happy to guide you. After all, you introduced me to that pasta by your house."

"Mmm," Starlight hummed. "I trust you. You can't disappoint me." She leaned forward until her shoulders were almost touching the table. "I know we've only known each other a few days, but you seem so at ease here, you look like a different person."

"A more attractive person?" She tilted her head coyly.

"Someone I'd want to spend more time with, for sure." Starlight leaned back with a smile. "But I don't mean I want you without your problems. I'd rather like to help you with your problems." She frowned. "But I don't have, like, a fixing fetish or something. I'm saying this wrong. I like you, and it seems like you're under a lot of pressure lately. I have skills that would surprise you in both their content and depth, so I think you should let me be your teammate and we can tackle whatever's bothering you together."

A teammate, huh? A partner? Someone to confide in, to bounce theories off, to comfort her when her sympathy grew into despair. Someone who could go where the boundaries of her profession wouldn't allow her. The past year had made her cautious, and the past seven had made her cynical, so why did she want to agree to it immediately?

While she weighed how to respond, the server came and took their order, then left again.

"I'm sorry," Starlight said, before Cinnamon could say anything. "You already told me that you can't really talk about it. But it's obvious that something is bothering you, and if we're having such a good time even though you're upset, I can only imagine how incredible we would be together if you didn't have to lug around the weight of whatever burden you're carrying." She tilted her head back with an exasperated sigh. "God, I'm sorry, I sound so selfish. Even if we weren't together, I'd want to help you, and my help isn't dependent on a romantic relationship with you. I help people all the time who I don't even sleep with. You know what?

I'm going to be quiet now. I'm going to let you talk and eat—thank you—and I'm going to stuff this crispy cracker bread stuff in my mouth in the hope that it will prevent words from coming out."

Cinnamon watched her attack the bread with a look of amusement. With anyone else, she would have felt overwhelmed. If it had been Ying-Li, she would have cringed her way right out of dinner, made an excuse to go to the bathroom and disappear instead. With Starlight, it was endearing. The difference, she thought, was that she believed in her sincerity. She believed that her desire to make the world a better place, and her friends happier, came with no strings attached.

Rich. White. Privileged. Used to getting what she wanted. Cinnamon had wondered how that upbringing would shape a person. She expected it to create a monster who took what they wanted and disregarded everything and everyone else—she'd seen it herself again and again. But with Starlight, it appeared that it had, instead, given her the confidence to completely ignore the peer pressure to act like a jerk and just plow ahead doing what's right.

Loud? For sure. Inconsistent impulse control? Probably. Boundary issues? Obviously. Inconsiderate, demanding, condescending? Not so far. In Cinnamon's work and limited dating life, she had discovered that almost any problem could be addressed and managed, but the one thing that couldn't be learned was compassion. Compassion was the root of empathy, respect, and trust, and if she couldn't count on someone for that, she couldn't count on that person for anything.

She still had no idea what went wrong in her last relationship, but even up to the very end, she felt like she could trust her partner. So if she felt, now, that she could trust Starlight, did that even mean anything? When she had been so misled in the past, when it was still unclear whether it was her former partner's deception, or a lack within herself?

The patio-style iron tabletop was cool and rough beneath her fingers, and the guitar music flowed over and through her. Her life was fulfilling, but there was a constant, vague discomfort. Like a hard piece of fuzz in her sock—not full-out "pebble-in-shoe," but noticeable. And she had the feeling she'd never find comfort if she never let anyone in.

Starlight didn't seem anything like a safe bet.

"I love San Francisco," Cinnamon began, speaking before she could change her mind and crawl back into her safe solitude. "I grew up here. My family is here, my career, my friends. My D&D group. My house that I love, my favorite restaurants." She gestured across the patio, and Starlight grinned. "It has its issues. More than other cities? I doubt it. I've never lived anywhere else, so I couldn't say for sure. But nothing has ever been so bad that I thought about moving. Until this past year.

"I don't know if you remember when tech companies began moving here. When everyone deciding they wanted to 'disrupt' a system that already worked just fine chose here, collectively, somehow. I don't know the details, or the history, much," she lied, "but over the years, this industry of technological developments started cultivating a work environment that was, intentionally, infamously, hostile."

She paused to give Starlight an opportunity to say whether she needed more info or if she was familiar with these problematic reputations.

"Oh, yeah." She nodded slowly. "I know all too well."

That was encouraging. Or maybe not, considering what they were talking about. Cinnamon opened her mouth, but she wasn't sure what to say next. If Starlight had experienced something similar to what her clients had gone through, she didn't want to remind her of it during dinner. During a date.

Their food arrived then, and for a while, that's where their focus was. Starlight loved everything she tried, and Cinnamon found a visceral security in the familiar tastes and textures. She wanted to know what Starlight knew about tech company workplaces, but was afraid that turning the conversation back around to it would give too much away.

"Anyway," Cinnamon hedged, "like I said, I haven't worked in the industry, but I've heard stories, and it's infuriating that such a vile environment could be so commonplace and accepted in my city."

Starlight looked thoughtful, pushing a piece of naan around her curry. "I'm sorry to tell you the stories are true. My firm gets hired by companies like that pretty frequently, and if I have to go into their office to work, I see it every time. Sexual harassment. Unpaid overtime. Worker burnout. Especially if the people in charge were already rich.

"I can't do much on my own, since I'm hired as part of a team of business management people and the people acting like assholes are not my employer. But I do fuck with them when I can."

"How so?"

She shrugged. "Oh, you know, lock them out of their own files. Switch all their landline presets to dial OSHA and different union representatives. Set some computers' default language to Albanian. Set off stink bombs in their corner office. Classic tween boy pranks." Her smile fell, and she glanced at Cinnamon with a frown. "You're not going to tell anyone, right? We have doctor-patient confidentiality?"

"We don't, but I won't," Cinnamon said lightly. Might as well ask about the thing she really wanted to. "I don't want you to feel uncomfortable or like you have to answer either way, but have you ever had occasion to see what the work culture is like at BDMT?"

Starlight started, telegraphing worry, before she smiled and turned back to her dinner. "We say it stands for 'Big Douchey McTechbro.'"

Not really an answer. Cinnamon chuckled at the joke. "That's what I've heard, too. I had a friend who worked there when it started." A little fibbing was fine. "She said the worst offenders were these two guys. Jared Leyser and, what was it? Colin something. Rodrick. Colin Ramsey."

"Right, right. Uh. Roday. Collin Roday." Starlight finally popped the curry-soaked bread into her mouth.

Cinnamon nodded. "Yeah. I hate that they're giving my city a bad reputation. But even more, I hate that they're harassing my fellow San Franciscans."

"I've seen some stuff," Starlight said, reaching for her water. "Your friend is right, their behavior is unacceptable. They always seem to get away with it, though."

Don't say it. Don't do it. The line may be blurred, but this would be stepping right over it. Cinnamon ignored her better judgment and said, "If you wanted to talk about it, I'd like to hear about it. I'm apparently a pretty good listener."

"I've heard that," Starlight said with a nod. "And—I know I'm no expert on therapy, the medical profession, or morality, but—I'm pretty sure I'm not supposed to date my therapist? Like, I have to choose, right? And I'd rather date you. No offense. I'm sure you're amazing at your job."

Yeah, Cinnamon stepped right over that line. "Oh, no, no," she said, backtracking. "I meant as a friend. Or, rather, personal. Not in a professional sense. I wouldn't, or, I couldn't, if I did—"

Starlight clasped Cinnamon's hand to stop her stammering. "Hey, hey, I'm just kidding. Not about the choosing to have a personal relationship over a professional one. About the ethics stuff. Sorry. Though, who among us hasn't embarked on some ill-advised undertaking now and again?" She grimaced at Cinnamon and turned back to dinner. "I, myself, have been guilty of it."

Even when she knew she was about to say too much, Cinnamon couldn't help it. Starlight was being gracious about it, and Cinnamon wanted to get back to a place where she didn't feel like she was trying to manipulate information out of her—her what? Girlfriend? Lover?

"Let's...get away from such serious subjects," Cinnamon said. "You were with your sister and best friend last night. Tell me about them."

"You'll meet them Sunday and can judge for yourself. Tell me about your friend instead. The one you were with last night."

"What makes you think I was with a friend last night?"

She laughed. "I'm not stalking you, I swear. I was fucking around on Instagram while my sister was trying to solve our escape room by 'unraveling its narrative structure' instead of looking for clues. Someone tagged you in a picture, at your family dinner last night?" She pulled out her phone and brought it up. "Yep, here it is. Their username looks like random letters and numbers." She tilted the screen toward Cinnamon.

"Oh. That's Ying-Li. She's a family friend."

"I would have guessed girlfriend."

Cinnamon nearly choked on her lamb curry. "Why would you have guessed that?"

"The dirty look she gave me at the costume party when she caught us kissing. I don't mind being in a polycule, but I need to know about it first."

"Not a girlfriend." She took a drink of water to stall for time while she decided how much to tell her. "She has business ties that my family would like to explore. They found out she's a lesbian and went on to try to set us up."

"I'm not sure if that sounds nice of them."

"Their motives aren't pure," she muttered. "But I'm not interested, and I let them all know it." She paused, remembering how Ying-Li defended guys like Collin Roday. "Actually, I'm not even sure I like her much as a friend."

"Yikes. So at Family Dinner Featuring Ying-Li, there you were, trying to hide your phone beneath the table so you could text the woman you *are* interested in about clam chowder and what you're wearing. Sorry if I contributed to your discomfort."

"You didn't, and you didn't know."

"Good. And who's Little Spice?"

"What?"

"The text says 'dinner with the Cheungs and Little Spice.' Did you have another not-girlfriend there?"

"That," she said with a sigh, "would be my family's nickname for me."

"You're Little Spice?" Starlight's glee escaped as a squeal. "I love it. I'm going to use it."

Cinnamon groaned. "Only my family calls me that."

"Really? A second ago, Ying-Li was barely a friend, and she's using it."

"You're killing me, Starlight."

She grinned like a maniac. "You'll let me. You don't want me getting the wrong idea about that other girl."

"So you're jealous."

"Wildly." She reached out and grasped Cinnamon's hand. "But you invited me out tonight. And you came out with me on Monday. And after the party, you went home alone, and ended up with me anyway." She leaned across the table, Cinnamon mirroring her. "So I'm starting to think there's nothing to be jealous about, Little Spice." Their lips met. Cinnamon let the warmth sweep over her, every muscle relaxing, anticipating, like Starlight could make everything right and still promise more. From her mouth, her family nickname sounded perfect, like comfort.

Afraid she would get too emotional, Cinnamon pulled away first, glancing down and blinking fast to hide the moisture gathering in her eyes.

"Um." she reached between them and pulled one of Starlight's shirt tassels out of her soup.

"Dammit," Starlight muttered, grabbing a napkin and wrapping it around the tassel to squeeze out the excess liquid. "I'm gonna see if I can rinse it out so it doesn't leak tomato soup on my white shirt. Don't go anywhere."

Left alone for the moment, Cinnamon wondered again how someone like Starlight had ended up in her life. Well, she knew, really. She had crashed into it and wouldn't let go. And if she wanted to keep her, things would get messy. Whether it would be worth it was still unclear, but she was willing to try. Let in the chaos for a little while. See how it felt.

***

"Axe-throwing?!" Starlight screeched as they shut the doors of their Lyft.

"Have you been?"

"No, I keep forgetting it exists."

Cinnamon slid her hands into her pockets and came beside Starlight, basking in the pure joy radiating from her. *I did that,*

Cinnamon thought, self-satisfied. "You mentioned archery, and I can't compete with that. But I figured this was close enough that you might like it, but different enough that I wouldn't get my ass handed to me."

Starlight cocked her head. "I think you could give me a run for my money. Come on." She grabbed Cinnamon's hand and pulled her toward the building. "This is better than a speakeasy."

"But is it better than a sex party?" If this was going to work, Cinnamon had to get used to teasing Starlight on her level.

"No. But if it's done right, not much is."

Despite her regular hikes and smattering of other physical activities, Cinnamon's shoulders began hurting after a half hour of throwing different types of axes at different styles of targets. Their scores were close enough that she thought she might have a chance of beating Starlight, but she couldn't tell if her date was holding back to make it more interesting or make Cinnamon feel like she was doing better than she was.

"I've come to a decision," Starlight said with an oomph, letting the lightweight black axe fly toward the cartoon zombie on her target. The tip embedded in its gut with a *thwack*. "Body hit! One point!"

Cinnamon grunted and updated the score on the touchscreen. Conversations across the twelve lanes echoed over to them, blending with the irregular thuds of axes in wood. "And what have you decided?"

Starlight rocked the weapon out of the wood, walked back to the starting line with one hand on her hip, and gestured to Cinnamon with her axe. "I think you secretly want to be a hero."

Well. Cinnamon blushed, hoping Starlight would think it was from the exertion of the sport. *Yeah. Don't most people?* Except it was a selfish thing to want, and that selfishness would undercut the hero-ness, especially if admitted aloud. Unsure how to respond, Cinnamon adjusted her feet on the starting line and lifted her arms. She timed the throw with a slow exhale, and the blade stuck between a zombie's knees. Miss.

"Boo." Starlight tapped a zero into the scoreboard as Cinnamon retrieved the axe. "Anyway. I mean, you dressed as Mulan. You rescued me from a panic attack. Hell, you became a therapist. That's a lot of work just to help people."

"Wanting to help doesn't make someone a hero. In fact, I'd argue that the two have nothing to do with each other at all." She knew plenty of peers who wanted to improve people's lives, but she couldn't think of anyone she would call a hero.

"Hmm. Okay." Shuffling back to her lane, Starlight stretched her arms and took up the starting position again. "So what's...Uh—" Zombie leg. Another point. "What's your current RPG character?"

"That won't tell you anything. Unless the group decides as a team to be evil, everyone's a hero." Starlight was six points up now.

"Cool, yeah, that makes sense." She paused. "So what's your character?"

Cinnamon eyed the larger axe. She tallied the additional point and switched to a heavier weapon, hefting it in her hands to get a feel for its weight. "We're between campaigns."

"So what were you last time?"

"An elf."

She rolled her eyes. "You're making this unnecessarily difficult, darling. Your elf's occupation. Or whatever it's called. Your main skills."

Unless there was a class called Villain or Billionaire or Puppy Stomper, anything she said was going to prove Starlight's point.

"Healer."

"Oh? Healer? You don't say. Sounds very hero to me."

Channeling her frustration into the larger axe, Cinnamon threw it with a grunt.

"Head shot!" Starlight yelled, bouncing on her toes. "Two points! I knew you'd be good at this. Heroes usually are."

"Coincidence."

"Modest." She nodded. "Also very hero."

Cinnamon laughed and ran her hand through her hair, forgetting it was sticky with the talc dust meant to improve her grip. "You can't turn me into a savior just by repeating it enough times."

Starlight stored her axe and walked right up to Cinnamon. Those intense blue eyes saw everything, and they were looking into her depths, illuminating for Cinnamon the things she kept in the dark.

"I think you'll find that I can." Her eyes flicked to Cinnamon's lips, and she bit her own playfully. "You were working on a character the other night. What's that one?"

"Half-orc ranger," she answered, voice a little gravelly. She was sort of liking Starlight bossing her around.

"Ah," she said, holding up one finger. "Another hero!"

"You don't know," Cinnamon teased. "A ranger could be a villain."

"A ranger? Like Aragorn? Unlikely." She sauntered backward, letting her eyes roam over her date's body.

"Face it, Little Spice." Blush crept back into Cinnamon's cheeks at the nickname. Starlight shrugged. "You're a protector."

Was repetition all it took for her to believe it? Because she was sounding more and more convincing. All this and she didn't even know about her real-life campaign against Collin Roday, which would have only cemented the idea in her mind.

And as much as Cinnamon hated to admit it, being a protector sounded appealing. It wouldn't matter if she wasn't like anyone else. If she wasn't normal. Her worth would be in her work, in the long-reaching effects of improving lives.

Actually, it sounded incredibly appealing. She glanced at Starlight, who was lining up her next throw. If nothing else, *she* believed in Cinnamon's desire to do good.

She let her eyes wander over her body, really looking at her. Hot, of course, and pretty, too. Wild. Smart and savvy. And she thought Cinnamon was a hero.

Of course she was falling for her.

Chapter Fifteen

The city was only just flirting with the sunrise, the periwinkle heavens retracting toward the west like an eyelid opening on the day, in tandem with tens of thousands of people across the Bay Area. Daphne had been setting the auto-timer on her espresso maker for even earlier, so it would be ready to go when she eventually shuffled into the kitchen. Would she have rather stopped at the café on the corner? Of course. But making it at home meant she could sleep an extra ten minutes. And sometimes ten more minutes of sleep meant the difference between success and disaster.

It also helped that Violet brought her and the other molothri their favorite caffeinated beverages as they were getting their hair and makeup done for the day. In Daphne's case, one latte wouldn't cut it.

It hadn't been lost on her that she asked what was bothering Cinnamon and the answer mentioned two BDMT founders by name. After a moment of panicking that Cinnamon had somehow found out about her job—either the fictional one or the real one—she was able to collect herself and the things Cinnamon was leaving unspoken and deduced that someone she knew had suffered at one or both of those men's hands, and more than what might be expected at a demanding job.

Not Cinnamon herself, since she became a therapist right out of school. Not her sister, since she worked in the family business.

And Cinnamon said she only started hating these guys within the last year. So: a client.

Though why she was asking Daphne, of all people, about it, she had no idea.

"Okay my little cowbirds." Clarissa entered the disguise room with an energy and alertness that Daphne would have envied at any time of the day. "What's happening in our target's nest? Daphne. Look alive."

"What if I'm dead?" Daphne asked with a yawn, giving away her mental exhaustion even as her foot jiggled impatiently.

"Weekend-at-Bernie's it," Clarissa said, swiping across their tablet. "And go first, so I know you're awake enough to pay attention to the others."

Daphne took a long draw of her Mexican mocha and shifted in her seat to get comfortable. She'd walloped Cinnamon at axe throwing the night before, at the expense of soreness this morning. "The physical records are mostly duplicates of what's on the hard drive we got, but thanks to Atticus and his uncanny ability to blend among douchebags, he figured out where I can find the Super Secret Files in the bad mountain of paperwork I'm smothered by every day. That's my focus today."

"Unless they're hand-written, they had to be printed from somewhere," Clarissa said.

"There are files off-network on Roday's laptop," Rayna chimed in. "I'm working on that today, but he rarely leaves it unattended."

"Which means you'll have to be physically close to Roday?" Clarissa asked.

"That's a problem," Atticus said from the other side of the room. "If she's alone with him. If Daphne were there too, one of you could distract him while the other copies everything onto a thumb drive."

Daphne and Rayna both made a face.

"Nobody's getting groped today." Clarissa's voice was flat. "Spill something on him, slip eye drops into his coffee, find a similar enough computer in our storage to make a swap for a few minutes. If you can't do any of that, forget it. Hard copies will be enough for Goldenrod. I'll tell them where to find the original files and then it's their problem."

"Speaking of getting groped," Daphne cut in, frowning as she heard herself. "A friend told me Jared and Roday have reputations for being inappropriate. I mean, we've all seen it, but the subtext was that one or both of them are responsible for assaults. She didn't come out and say that, but in the context, she wouldn't have been able to."

"Does she know you're working there?" Worry lines bloomed between Clarissa's eyebrows.

"I'm not made, no. I worried for a minute, but she was very in her own head. And if she found out I was lying to her about anything, she would never speak to me again, so let's continue to keep it under wraps, folks."

Discomfort pooled in her psyche. Cinnamon wouldn't speak to her again if she was lying to her about anything. Or if she did something that would break her trust. Like break into her locked office and hack into her computer. That would definitely be the kind of thing that would make Daphne seem untrustworthy.

No, not seem. *Be* untrustworthy.

Fuck. Stupid, stupid Daphne. Cinnamon deserved better than that, and if Daphne found out that someone else had disregarded Cinnamon's boundaries and plowed ahead with whatever they wanted to do, she'd hunt them down and make them sorry for it.

Daphne knew she had boundary issues, but she thought they were cute. They were always cute in movies. They were never the reason anyone broke up, but often the reason people got back together.

Was it not like that in real life?

Her emotional whirlwind got to fear, and Daphne felt it in her belly, like a cold stone. If Cinnamon deserved better than that—and she did—then she deserved better than Daphne. And this time, it wouldn't be fate that ruined her new relationship. It wouldn't be timing or work or distance. This time, the thing that ruined Daphne's relationship would be, without a doubt, Daphne.

She looked around the room, wondering how everyone was acting so normal, when her skin was burning up and her mind was teetering on the edge of another panic attack.

"I've had minimal contact," Ivan said, his voice warbly and low, "but there's just something in the air."

"These guys have no problem saying the quiet part out loud," Atticus said, shifting in his chair as he finished inserting his blue contact lenses. "You've seen my reports. I have no idea how they've gotten this far without getting sued into oblivion. I would bet good money if I 'confess' to any of them about a crime, they'll tell me about the time they did the same thing. Do you want me to do that?"

Daphne watched Clarissa shake their head, but didn't hear what they said. She didn't want to lose Cinnamon, and she didn't want to hurt Cinnamon, so the only choice she had was to...become a person who didn't hurt her? It seemed easy enough, in theory. Just listen and respect what Cinnamon needed. But in practice? It would take practice. Which would include coming clean about getting into her computer. And having a plan for what to do after that to show that Daphne was serious.

Atticus was talking again. *He* was in a stable relationship. So much so that he had trusted his husband with the truth about what he did for a living.

A sliver of hope worked its way into Daphne's spiral and slowed the spin. Tell Cinnamon about getting into her computer and why she did it, promise to do better however she needed her to, and offer her own secret in return.

She put her coffee down on the makeup table and picked up her phone. Sent a quick text to Cinnamon that she wanted to share something important with her.

"Redgrave."

"I'm listening," Daphne said, typing faster.

Behind her, Clarissa grunted, and Violet swooped in out of nowhere and took Daphne's phone out of her hand.

"Sorry," Violet mouthed, before twirling away toward the lockers where they stored their real-life things.

"I repeat," Clarissa said, leveling a glare at Daphne that brought her back to the present. "We would need hard evidence. And while I would love to pursue this as a personal endeavor, it'll have to remain dormant until we complete what we're being paid to do. Don't highlight this side quest while the main quest is unfinished. What have you got for us, Ivan?"

Daphne sighed and took another sip of her coffee. The text to Cinnamon had sent, so that was her evening sorted. If she had the opportunity during work to look into what Cinnamon told her about Roday and Jared, she would take it. She should have been paying attention to her boss, but nobody said her name, so she didn't find her way back to their conversation until Clarissa clapped their hands.

"So it looks like we might get everything we need today. If that's the case, Daphne and Rayna, tomorrow will be your last day, just fuck around at your desks if that's what it takes to get you through it. Ivan will leave sometime next week. Atticus, next Friday. We'll get a firm date once Goldenrod has what they need. As for now, fly, my little birdies."

***

The Cheung Technologies building looked squat, despite its five stories, due in part to its sprawling design and large parking lots, and in part to the flat neighboring buildings and flatter topography. They'd had it built in the early 1990s, nestled against I-280 where the freeway nearly aligned on a north-south axis before gently turning west and flirting with Route 1. Over the years, the other companies renting office space moved on, and CT expanded until, as planned, the entire complex was theirs.

Cinnamon was there often as a child, when she didn't have tap lessons or oboe. She and Echo would make their nanny bring them, and the girls would play in the lobby or do homework beneath the stairs, measuring the hours until their parents might be finished with work by the changing light in the tall, west-facing windows. In the years since then, the lobby had changed, but the café thankfully stayed the same.

The hiss of the steam wand reminded Cinnamon of Starlight and their too-short Sunday morning together. That she'd had the tools to make herself something more delicious than burnt drip coffee, but never wanted to deviate from what she knew, was beginning to feel more like a character flaw than stability.

"Actually," Cinnamon said, as the barista moved to get her usual black coffee, "I was thinking a regular latte? With soy milk?"

The barista gasped, teasingly. "Why, Miss Cheung!"

"I know. I had one the other day. It was good."

"Wow. I can't wait for the morning four years from now when I convince you to get one pump of vanilla in your latte. World-changing."

The truth in it made her cringe, but she laughed anyway. "Let's not commit to anything too wild."

A few minutes later, she was on her way to her father's office, latte in hand. Cinnamon entered the elevator but let her mind wander back to Starlight. She'd sent a strange text that morning, saying she wanted to share something important with Cinnamon that night, but hadn't responded when asked if something was wrong. The woman was a mystery, and Cinnamon couldn't help turning the puzzle of her around and around. The biggest question on her mind was why, after so much time, this was the woman who caught her attention.

Not only caught but demanded it, and Cinnamon was eager to provide. She'd spent the last seven years trying to figure out why she couldn't connect with anyone, so not being able to understand why she *did* connect with someone now wasn't anything new. The question would be running in the background of her conscious-ness no matter what. Might as well give it a little more juice when she could.

As she stepped out of the elevator onto the fifth floor, she nearly ran into Echo.

"Whoa. You okay?" her sister asked, grabbing an arm to steady her. "Where'd you go?"

Cinnamon felt the side of the tumbler to make sure nothing had spilled. "Just...splashing in the shallow end of my thoughts. Sorry."

"And nearly splashing me with your coffee," Echo said, frowning down at her immaculate black suit, as though waiting for a stain to appear.

"The lid is closed, but again, I apologize. You off to a meeting?"

Echo stepped back to lean against the wall, an oddly casual pose in her business attire. The executive wrinkled her nose as she took in Cinnamon's outfit.

"I know therapists are supposed to embody comfort and approachability, but I was expecting something a little more professional than leggings and a sleeveless mock turtleneck."

"If it helps, I'll be adding a shawl when I get to my office," Cinnamon replied through a fake smile.

Echo snapped her fingers. "That's it. That's what was missing. The classic therapist shawl."

The two stood, staring at each other, nodding.

"Anyway," Cinnamon drawled. "You look like you were on your way somewhere in a hurry, so. Don't let me keep you."

"Oh, no." Echo pushed herself off the wall and walked backwards away from the elevators, nodding at Cinnamon to follow. "I was coming to make sure you were okay."

"Me?"

Echo shrugged. "It usually only takes you a few minutes to get from the front doors to coffee to Dad's office. You took longer today."

"Aw, jiejie, you love me."

"Pfft," Echo said. "Like you don't know."

A slow smile spread over Cinnamon's face, unstoppable in the radiant light of familial affection.

"I got a bar drink today. Mixing it up a bit."

"'Mixing it up a bit'?" Echo stopped in her tracks. "Because suddenly changing routine and being super casual about it is *so* you. Damn, Little Spice, what's gotten—" Understanding flickered across her face, and she tilted her head with a sigh. "Redgrave."

"It's Daphne," Cinnamon corrected her as she walked past, taking a sip of her out-of-character latte. "And last I heard, you gave me the all-clear to see her—which, by the way, I don't need. Your permission, I mean."

"Hey, I only said she probably wasn't a threat to the Cheung business," she answered, following. "I never said she wasn't a threat to the Cheung Cinnamon. As your older sister, I'm allowed—no, *expected*—to be judgmental about your girlfriends, and you haven't given me anything to work with in years."

"Oh, I am *so sorry* my love life has been such a bore for you. I'm rather surprised you even noticed, given how active yours is."

"'Rather surprised'? Tell me, are you naturally condescending, or do you practice?"

"Neither?"

They stopped outside their father's office, Echo pulling a pensive frown as she mused, Cinnamon wondering if she should apologize first.

"Can I give you some advice?" Echo asked.

"Absolutely not."

"Get what you can out of her while you can," she offered anyway. "Nothing is guaranteed. Maybe it'll work out, maybe it won't, but you have to make sure that—either way—you don't regret your time together."

"Why does this feel more like you covering your ass than you genuinely wanting to help me?"

"I'm helping," she said with a shrug, turning to go back to her office. "I also won't say 'I told you so' if it ends badly. Look at all the gifts I'm sharing with you, meimei." She glanced over her shoulder at Cinnamon. "You bringing her to the gala Saturday?"

The thing about not working in the family business was that Cinnamon often forgot about the many business events throughout the year that she had open invitations to.

"You forgot," Echo said matter-of-factly, but without malice.

"Do I get a plus-one?"

"You've always gotten a plus-one. Tell Lindsay ahead of time so she can include you in the count." She continued on her way. "Looking forward to meeting your Redgrave in person."

Cinnamon watched her sister turn a corner and called out, "I love you too, Echo."

"I know." Echo's voice carried to her clearly, and Cinnamon smiled and shook her head before entering her father's office.

Family Dinner on Tuesdays was a chance for the four of them to catch up, but Thursday Morning Coffee was just Cinnamon and her father. She'd sometimes see Echo or her mom in the halls when she stopped by, like that morning, but they didn't join them.

It would have been easy for the Cheungs to be distant from their daughters. Their business was successful and demanding, and they could have committed to it entirely. They could have expected their children to have the same drive for the same industry, tiny duplicates of themselves, burnout and all. It was a story Cinnamon heard often from her friends: the ambitious, challenging immigrant parents. Emotionally withdrawn but heavily invested in educational success and rapid career progress.

For whatever reason, Min and Hong Cheung never fit that stereotype. There were plenty of things they were sticklers about—there was a reason Cinnamon would rather tell her mother she was gay than tell her she didn't like seafood. And they would brag to anyone who would listen about their elder daughter taking over the family business while the younger daughter became a doctor. Cinnamon always corrected them, but they would wave her off with a "close enough" meant to reassure that they'd be proud of her no matter what.

So it wasn't a mystery to her why she got along so well with them. Especially when she saw how many of her peers suffered.

Lindsay, her dad's assistant, waved her into the office with a smile, used to their Thursday routine. She didn't say anything about Cinnamon's lack of RSVP to the upcoming event, but she had to be used to it by now. Cinnamon wanted to apologize, tell her whether she'd be there, but without talking to Starlight first, it was better not to say anything at all.

The heavy wooden doors to her father's inner office opened without a sound, a preview of the quiet sanctum within. A large antique desk sat in the corner, overlooking the rest of the room with a stately elegance. Cinnamon remembered the enormous computer that took up most of its desktop when she was a child, and how its replacement got smaller every year. It was mostly monitor, now, to accommodate her father's need for larger text and icons.

A stone fountain just inside the doors spanned from floor to ceiling, the gently trickling water reminding Cinnamon that she meant to look into getting a much, much smaller one for her own office. An easy addition to the soothing ambiance.

Hong looked up from the plate of pastries he was arranging on the coffee table and smiled at his daughter. Besides the silver in his hair and the wrinkles that seemed to increase every few years, he looked much like he always did. Tall and lean, with large hands and keen eyes.

"Daughter," he said, shuffling around the table and low chairs to give her a hug.

"Hello, baba," Cinnamon murmured, returning the embrace. "I just ran into Echo. She looks bored. Are you not giving her enough work?"

He laughed and sat on the couch, and Cinnamon joined him. "You girls were always so smart. If she has developed a way to reach her goals without doing so much work, I'm glad. But knowing her, she'll make it hard for herself again before long. It's our cyclical nature. When she's overwhelmed by industry, she finds a way to make it easier. When the easiness leads to boredom, she finds a way to give herself more work." He shrugged. "Sometimes, balance is struck over years, not hours. But here." He gestured to the plate. "I got us some continental."

Pastries, he meant, and Cinnamon grabbed a raspberry Danish off the top of the pile. When he was younger and traveling for work, he noticed that hotel continental breakfasts included pastries. He saw them as a symbol of Western business, and since founding Cheung Technologies, he offered them at every morning meeting for good luck and goodwill. Ham and cheese croissants were his favorite, so they were the first pastry Cinnamon taught herself how to make.

"They're not as good as Cinnamon Cheung continental, but you deserve a break, too." He picked up a croissant and moved his cup of black coffee away from the edge of the coffee table. "I'm sorry things aren't working out with you and Ying-Li."

Cinnamon nearly dropped her Danish. Well, that was unexpected. She took a bite of her continental and chewed slowly to stall.

"How do you think things should be working out between us?"

"It was never a 'should.' It was only a hope."

"And what did you hope?"

Her father smiled, a pastry flake stuck to his lip. "I can recognize your doctor training." He pushed the flake into his mouth with a finger. "We hoped for a companion for you. It would be...fortuitous...if that personal connection led to a business connection, true. As I said, it was just a hope."

"Are you sorry about the personal or the business part not working out?"

"Both," he said. "Of course. But I wouldn't ask or expect you to sacrifice something so important for the sake of the company. We're doing just fine. As you noticed, even Echo is not stressed."

He was mostly telling the truth. There were times he *would* ask, and setting her up with Ying-Li in the first place had definitely been a push.

"What makes you think that we're not happy together?"

"Oh, Little Spice. I do like my farming games, but I was paying attention at dinner. Ying-Li said something that upset you, and kept saying things that upset you. If you're invested in a person, you can work through that. But if you're not interested..." He trailed off. "You're not interested."

She hadn't realized he saw all that, but she should have guessed. When she was growing up, it seemed like he knew everything, saw everything. He was quietly observant and had great deduction skills and intuition, but she rarely saw him employ any of that in terms of his work, and he didn't press any issues when they had private conversations.

"I'm not interested," she agreed. "Ying-Li doesn't seem to value what I value. If you were going into a business partnership to get higher quality, but your partner was teaming up with you to get cheaper products, you would have to really think about whether the alliance was going to work, right? This is that, except with life stuff."

Hong nodded in agreement, but Cinnamon couldn't help but feel like she was still letting him down.

"I'm sorry I couldn't be your conduit to her network," she said.

Her father frowned and glanced out the window. Uncomfortable silences weren't a usual part of their Thursday morning talks, but then again, they didn't usually discuss Cinnamon's romantic relationships.

"I'm not sure I ever told you about the woman I was engaged to before your mother."

Cinnamon lifted her eyes to him slowly, not wanting to startle him into silence. Family gossip was usually confined to which auntie was mad at which other auntie, which cousin was embarrassing themself this week, whose spouse was in the doghouse. She had sometimes wished that there were juicy secrets to uncover—an older sibling given up for adoption, for the business to have been built on a foundation of mob-related favors, either of her parents being spies. Anything that would spice up her world with actual family drama. Then she grew up and was thankful for the stability of a boring upbringing.

But this little secret brought her right back to her childhood, and the idea of learning something they hadn't wanted her to know was too thrilling to pass up. And being able to tell Echo later would give her the upper hand for a while.

"No," she said carefully, tamping down her eagerness. "I'm not sure you ever told me about that."

Hong settled in, memory softening his gaze. "Long ago, before I met your mother, I was engaged to a girl. Pretty. Smart. She was working on her PhD. Took care of her parents and siblings. Put people at ease effortlessly. She was kind, quick-witted, well-connected, and I didn't feel anything for her at all. It was set up by my father, and I would have gone through with it, because he asked, and because it was no loss for me. I wasn't pining for someone else. I had never pined for anyone."

As his words sunk in, Cinnamon fought to keep her face still. The Cheung family had never forbidden sharing emotions, but they dealt with their own issues in their own ways. It felt too personal, hearing about her father having feelings, like seeing a teacher outside of school, or overhearing someone getting dumped on the phone. It felt too personal, too, that he was describing how Cinnamon had felt most of her life. The thing that made her think she was broken, because she was alone in it.

"I kept delaying the wedding," Hong continued. "My studies, her studies. The death of a relative. Inauspicious seasons. World events." He paused to take another bite of croissant, frowning as he chewed. Cinnamon wouldn't fill the silence before he spoke again. "At the time, I thought I was being prudent. Looking back, I was being ridiculous. I'm surprised, now, that no one ever pulled me aside. To tell me to stop. To ask me if I was all right. If I even wanted to marry.

"Finally, I had postponed the ceremony for the last time. Three years after the original wedding date, my studies were concluded, her studies were concluded, no more relatives had died, the numbers held good fortune, and the world had paused its horrors as much as it's able to, though it felt more like taking a deep breath before the wave hits you. And then: Min."

Hong's lips twitched a smile, and Cinnamon couldn't help joining him. She'd heard the next part of the story of how they met and married—without mention of this first engagement—and it was cute. Even when she was a teenager and had to act grossed out by it, she still thought it was cute.

"I didn't realize the wave I braced for was a woman. But it was. Min was a tsunami. A monsoon. She was the phases of the moon. She could destroy and create at will. She influenced everything she touched, and once our eyes met, it was then that I knew love.

"Your mother appeared out of nowhere and said I was hers, and she was right. We married within the month. You and your sister came along later, and you know the rest," he said quietly, picking up his mug. She mirrored him, wanting to draw out the moment to collect herself and contemplate the idea that she might not be defective after all. Her parents had the most stable relationship out of everyone she knew. And all it took was her father accepting it when it happened, no matter how unexpected or inconvenient.

"Don't settle for Ying-Li," Hong said, catching and holding his daughter's glance to underscore the importance of what he said. "In case you somehow missed the point of my story. You seem to be introspective right now, so it's possible you missed it, even though you're so smart."

Cinnamon gave him a small smile. "I didn't miss it, baba. I was just thinking that I've felt that way. The same as when you were engaged, and the same as when you met mama."

His eyes softened, and the hint of a frown appeared. Cinnamon wrestled with telling him more about Starlight, but she didn't want to get his hopes up. After all this time, she still liked keeping a little kernel of doubt about the good things that happened to her, in case, later, things went wrong and she had to comfort herself with the inadequate solace of being right.

"That girl, from years ago, she wasn't your Min," he told her.

Yet another unexpected statement by her father. She knew he was a detective at heart, but she had rarely been gifted with his insights so straightforwardly.

He was giving her an opportunity to talk about Starlight. Echo had bullied it out of her, their mother wouldn't bring it up even if she suspected anything, but her father had noticed and shared his story in a way that would make her comfortable with sharing her own.

So her reluctance felt like she was disappointing him all over again. Instead, she chose something adjacent, hoping he could do what her family always did and read between the lines.

"I have an unrelated question that isn't important," she said, breaking eye contact with him. "I'm just curious."

Hong smiled again. "Curiosity sparks the most important questions."

"What is your honest impression of the Redgraves? What have you heard, and what have you seen for yourself?"

He sat back against the couch and looked at Cinnamon with the same face he had when solving a puzzle.

"From a business perspective?" he asked. "Are you going to work for them, Little Spice?"

"No, no." She held up a hand in a gesture that was half dismissal and half promise. "Absolutely not. I have a friend who used to work for them, and she seems cool and not evil. But Echo thinks that anyone I meet is potentially using me in some vague, nefarious way to hurt the business, and I thought you could tell me if she's being paranoid or careful or right."

Hong took a breath and gazed across his office. "What we told you the other night was true. They're not quite our competition, but we move in the same circles, attend the same events. It would be sensible to learn what we can about them. I wouldn't want to be their direct competition. But I would like being their partner even less." He hesitated. "There is some truth in Echo's concern. We are investigating a few options that would lead to a restructuring in CT, and corporate espionage is possible. But I don't see how it would benefit anyone to target you."

His mouth formed a thin line and he nodded firmly, coming to a decision. "Your sister is being cautious. Make all the new friends you want, but maybe, don't bring them here?"

"Because I'm known for making friends and for bringing them to my parents' place of work," Cinnamon said, not quite filtering out the sarcasm.

"Life is predictable until it isn't." Hong shrugged. "The right person can change you forever. Will you bring her to the gala this weekend?"

"Mmm," Cinnamon answered, narrowing her eyes. "You think you're pretty clever, huh?"

"I am pretty clever," he said. "I'd also like to meet your Redgrave-adjacent friend you like so much you that you're seeking confirmation from your father that she isn't evil. Your personal life is closed to me, but you feel strongly enough to ask me about this. Bring her," he said with finality. "We will know she's evil if she doesn't like Claude."

Cinnamon did roll her eyes at that. "Baba, even terrible people love Claude. But I'll ask her. She might be busy."

"She'll make herself not-busy for you," he said with a confidence that Cinnamon shared but wouldn't admit. "Do I get to know her name?"

"On Saturday," she said. "If we can make it, I'll introduce you then."

Hong nodded and changed the subject, filling their conversation with the usual family gossip, to give Cinnamon space to recover from their unusual vulnerability.

Chapter Sixteen

No more texts from Starlight yet.

It was just after one in the afternoon, and Cinnamon sat by the window in the café where she usually had lunch. She left her phone face-down on the table, preferring to read a physical book during her break so she could feel like she did something enriching and worthwhile for thirty minutes a day. The internet didn't count, even if she read articles instead of doomscrolling.

She couldn't shake the feeling that she was forgetting something. Spending every free moment thinking about unmasking her clients' mystery rapist had taken up so much of her waking thoughts that now it was a noticeable absence.

Since the complex investigation had been replaced with a single name, there was no reason to keep any session notebooks at the house, and Cinnamon had brought them all back to the office that morning. She thought that that simple bit of housekeeping, of cleaning up when a project was finished, would reset her brain.

It didn't.

The phone dinged, and she frowned at the unfamiliar noise as she picked it up and read the alerts that her anonymous social media accounts had been compromised. Ice slid through her belly, reaching out through her limbs until they were numb. She read it over again until the words lost meaning.

She'd finally been doxxed.

Well, it happened, a more reasonable and unhelpful part of her brain declared as the rest of her started to panic. *Do you remember the plan we made to deal with this?*

She glanced around the café, wondering if anyone there had seen it, had cared, was a threat. Her thoughts kept trying to form, but fit together wrong, like in a dream where she had to get to the airport and tried to pack but again and again she was missing something she couldn't leave behind. She couldn't remember the plan for what—in retrospect—she should have assumed was an inevitability. Another alert came in, and she saw she had new Instagram and Facebook notifications.

She stood up quickly, knocking her chair over, leaving her half-eaten lunch on the table as she packed up her book and ran out the door. Instinct drove her back to the office, the closest safe place, but she had no idea if her work address was also compromised. She called her assistant, who picked up on the second ring.

"Cancel the rest of my sessions today," Cinnamon said, breathless from the fear and her haste. "And everything tomorrow. Tell them I had a family emergency."

"Oh my god, are you okay?"

"After you do that, take the rest of the day off." Cinnamon didn't have the capacity to answer whether she was okay, but she knew how to get other people safe in a crisis. "Tomorrow too. With pay. I'll call you this weekend to let you know about Monday." Beyond the call, her phone pinged with more notifications, and she scrolled through them to see exactly what had been leaked.

"Okay. I'm sorry, whatever's happening."

"I got doxxed. I don't want to take a chance that they have my office address too."

"Oh shit."

"No need to panic." Cinnamon was panicking enough for both of them. "Call the clients and go home. Lock up when you leave."

"I will. I'm so sorry, Ms Cheung."

One block away from the office, she froze. Why was she going back? Her briefcase and notebooks were locked up and safest there. Why would she take them home, to the address that was already being reposted across the internet? And she had to go home, that wasn't even a question. She needed to pack up anything valuable or sensitive in case she needed to leave quickly.

Turning on her heel, she walked back toward the café and three blocks past it before calling a rideshare to take her to Sea Cliff. Relying on an app that used sensitive data on the same internet that just leaked all her contact information wasn't ideal, but this time of day, public transportation would get her home in fifty minutes. A car would have her there in less than twenty. And she needed to get there fast.

The ride was a blur. Her mind was too busy bouncing between reviewing the next steps, worrying about how fast her harassers would move and what they would try to do, and fighting the panic that bubbled up every few minutes. The car dropped her off farther away than usual, and she walked past her house twice before going in—to see if anyone was parked nearby, or loitering, or waiting on her front stoop.

The house alarm hadn't been triggered, but she couldn't lean against the locked-again front door in relief until she checked the whole house. She started upstairs, closing blinds, curtains, and doors as she crossed off each room, finally ending up in a living room chair with her back to the wall, holding the metal baseball bat that she kept by her bed.

She was alone.

So she let herself cry like she was alone.

This was what she'd been afraid of. Really afraid of, more than not wanting to cross some ethical boundary with her clients, more than the idea of the bad guy getting away with it. She was exposed, and they were coming for her. They loved their tech lords and yearned to demonstrate their devotion—the more violently, the better.

She knew this was bullshit. Nobody deserved this for speaking out against injustice. She also knew that her clients had gone through much worse, and only because they worked at a job where someone in a position of power decided to take advantage of them. But knowing that didn't lessened her fear.

The phone she'd placed in front of her on the coffee table was lighting up with calls, texts, notifications. She'd suspended her voice mail. She wouldn't look at all the comments and DMs, but she couldn't help seeing a few as she switched accounts to private, or locked them, or suspended them. There were dozens now, threatening her, repeating her full name and home address and phone number and usernames. Letting her know they could find her. Letting her know she wouldn't be safe.

But they hadn't discovered where she worked. Not yet.

They also hadn't connected her to Starlight.

She brought up her text messages and found a dozen new threads, courtesy of her doxxing, but nothing yet from Starlight. Was it safe to text her? Could they somehow get her phone records?

Exhausted from fear and adrenaline, Cinnamon took a deep breath and walked back upstairs. She dumped her hiking gear out of her biggest backpack and filled it and a duffel bag with as much as she could. Clothes, sensitive documents, heirlooms, all the cash in the house. Phone left on her dresser, but she brought the baseball bat.

As she shut the patio door behind her, the sound of glass breaking echoed out to her, and she paused long enough to note the shattered front window before locking the door and sprinting through the grass, squeezing out of her backyard between the same bushes that Starlight had once used to find her way in.

***

Walking out of the Diophantus offices at 5 p.m., Daphne paused to breathe deep of her early release. Sure, the rest of the city might be ending their workday at their normal time, but even two extra hours of sunlight was enough to launch her into a good mood.

The "hidden" records were right where Atticus thought they would be, in a binder marked "2012 Duplicate Q3 Reformatted Standard P&L Reports." It was like trying to misdirect people from a box of porn by labeling it…well, "2012 Duplicate Q3 Reformatted Standard P&L Reports."

And hoo boy, was there a lot of information there. Daphne had no idea what Goldenrod would do with it, but with this much damning evidence, there were so many options—blackmail them, force them to sell the company for tens of millions less than asking price, get them prosecuted, leak it to the shareholders, leak it to a journalist. Imagining that they might feel even a fraction of the consequences they deserved made Daphne grin uncontrollably.

The team would make copies of the file tonight, and she would bring it back in Friday morning. She wouldn't know until the morning briefing whether Rayna was able to get anything off Roday's laptop, but Clarissa said that as far as Daphne was concerned, her primary directive was complete.

No texts from Cinnamon yet, as usual, since Daphne had told her it was unlikely she would be out before seven, and she'd also fibbed a bit about the security situation. Her phone really had been locked away where she couldn't get to it during business hours, but at the Dio offices across town. She sent a text anyway, hoping it wouldn't disturb her in the middle of someone's session.

Rin and Mats had gone to the Filoni Estate for the day, since they stayed open late on Thursdays in the summer. They'd stop for dinner in Redwood City or Belmont before coming home too late for Daphne to see them. Tomorrow would be another early day for her, but hopefully the last one for a while, and afterward, she could stay up as late as she needed to see her family.

Home, then. Text Cinnamon again. Ask her if she wanted to go out again tonight. Three dates and one overnight stay the first week of meeting someone wasn't too fast for Daphne, though it was something she rarely got. Cinnamon seemed fine with it. Daphne was still surprised that she kept saying yes to Daphne's ideas, never seemed annoyed by them, and somehow kept a level head the whole time. Was this love, or just acceptance?

On the ride home, she let her mind wander, but it didn't go very far. Just circled Cinnamon and worried that since she didn't know why dating her felt so much easier than dating anyone else, she couldn't know how to keep her when she inevitably messed up. Cinnamon was real. She didn't court drama. She was an actual adult who did what she liked and not what she thought she should.

Even when Daphne was deep in lust for someone, she could recognize a neediness in them and knew it wouldn't work. It was so similar to what she saw and disliked in herself. But Cinnamon had a steadiness, a confidence that didn't seek peer approval. And for all that, she was kind and compassionate and fun. No. There wasn't anything to worry about. If Cinnamon wasn't interested, she would just say so. Which meant she was. Which meant Daphne could daydream a little, planning their next date.

Which would be much sooner than she expected.

Daphne almost missed the woman sitting on the chair in her building's lobby, but the metal baseball bat caught her attention, then the huge backpack and duffel bag, then Cinnamon's face in the middle of all that.

"Cinnamon? What—" Daphne knelt beside her, noting her red eyes and sniffles. Something had happened. Something bad.

"I'm sorry, I think I overreacted," Cinnamon said, laughing. "I should have gone to my sister's, or checked into a hotel, I just didn't know if they could track me, so I came here."

Oh yeah. She was in trouble. Maybe even danger. Daphne grabbed the duffel and Cinnamon's hand and led her to the elevators.

"No, you're right to come here, for whatever reason. I'll take care of you—No! No! Not today, man! You just wait there!"

Some guy had tried to get on the elevator with them, and Daphne threw herself into the doorway with her arms and legs spread like an X to stop him.

"We are not stable enough to share an enclosed space with you right now, and if you want to argue about it, you'll experience my best impression of a feral cat, and I can't vouch for how accurate she is with a baseball bat."

As the doors started closing, the guy took a step back and held up his hands in surrender. Daphne stayed where she was, fixated on him until the gap closed, then she leaned to the side and swiped her hand up a row of buttons, illuminating eight floors, including her own.

She turned to face Cinnamon with a sigh. "How *are* you with a baseball bat?"

"Not as impressive as your impression of a feral cat."

Daphne gave her a sharp smile. "Then you came to the right place."

Nobody bothered them again, Daphne taking point and making sure the hallways were empty before waving Cinnamon to follow. Before long, they were in the condo, where she pointed to the kitchen and told Cinnamon to stay put while she made sure they were alone.

After checking every room, Daphne returned to the front hall holding a small, black device with blinking blue lights. "Okay, come on in." She waved Cinnamon in to the living room and set the device atop a stand on the coffee table. Cinnamon shuffled in, looking beaten, and Daphne gestured for her to make herself comfortable on the couch. "Do you have your phone on you?"

"No." Cinnamon shook her head, and Daphne pushed a button on the electronic device, making the lights a solid red. Cinnamon set her bags and bat down on the floor before sinking into the couch beside Daphne. "I didn't know if I could be tracked with it." She was about to say more, but her face crumpled, and she put her head in her hands.

"Hey, hey," Daphne murmured, scooching closer and pulling Cinnamon against her. "I don't know what's happening, but you're safe here. Like, really safe. See that little black flying saucer looking thing on the table? My friend gave it to me, he calls it a pimp. Because he's terrible about accidentally mispronouncing things to make them sound like sex things. He calls himself a sexpert, but what he means is sec-expert, like security-expert, and—you know, maybe it's not so accidental. He has a weird sense of humor. But this thing? It's a PEMP. Personal EMP. If there are any devices recording or transmitting around us, poof!"

She paused when Cinnamon didn't reply, still crying, so she decided to shut up for a while and just hold her. Daphne smoothed her hair and rubbed her shoulder, trying to piece together the clues. No phone because she thought someone would use it to track her. Needed to get out of her house because it wasn't safe. Brought a goddamn baseball bat as a weapon and honestly, good for her. If shit was that serious, Daphne would have done the same. Well, bow and arrows, but close enough.

Most likely, it had to do with whatever was making her so upset the past few days. Which she said had been making her upset for months.

"Okay," Cinnamon said, sitting up and wiping at her eyes. "Okay. I'm going to tell you the whole story."

"You know," Daphne cut in before she could continue. She leaned back to look Cinnamon in the face. "You don't have to. My help doesn't depend on knowing why you need it. Of course, the more you tell me, the more specifically I *can* help, but it's not necessary."

Cinnamon gave her a quick smile. "I know that. And I appreciate it." She paused, and Daphne got up to get her a glass of water. "Thanks. I forget we met less than a week ago."

"Yeah but in lesbian time that's like, pfft, four months."

She gave her head a small shake and took a sip of water. "It's never worked like that for me. So it's hard for me to believe it's working like that for me now." Cinnamon twisted the glass around on the coaster. "I'm choosing to trust you. But I'm not sure I had a choice."

"I won't let you down." Daphne nearly choked on the words, wanting more than anything for them to be true, knowing there wasn't a person alive that she hadn't disappointed at some point.

So Cinnamon told her everything. Except her clients' names, which didn't matter to the story, and which Daphne wouldn't have wanted to know. She detailed the increasingly disturbing harassment: the threats, threats with details, trolls finding her on other social media and liking all her posts there, a direct message saying they'll get her license revoked, and so much else.

Daphne did everything she could not to yell. She wanted to hunt them down, these men. She wanted them to be afraid to walk alone at night. And when Cinnamon got to the doxxing, to the broken window, to her flight, Daphne launched herself from the couch.

"I'm listening," she said, pacing, arms crossed. "I'm listening, I'm just so angry for you. I'm so sorry and I'm incandescent with rage and if I don't dispel some of it with movement, I'm going to implode."

Cinnamon gave her a weak smile. "Don't implode. That's the last thing I need." She sniffled. "I'm starting to think that the risks weren't worth it. I should have just prayed or found a coven and cast a hex on him or something."

Daphne rubbed hard at her eyes and plopped back down on the couch. "I knew Roday was a creep. This isn't surprising, but it is infuriating. Okay. First things first. You're safe here. So that's good. Next: who do you trust to go to your house, assess the damage, get your phone and anything else you might need, and bring it here?"

"My sister."

"Echo? The one taking over the business? That's good. She can help us in a couple of ways." Daphne reached over to turn off the pimp, went to the bedroom, and returned with her phone. "Call her. You don't have to tell her everything. Just that you've been doxxed, and what happened at your house. Ask her to go there to assess the damage and grab your phone, and—this is important—she has to turn it to airplane mode then turn it off completely before she leaves your house. Then she can meet me or, if you feel up to it, you, a few blocks away from here."

For a moment, Cinnamon just stared at the phone in her hands, then she stood up and wrapped her arms around Daphne. Daphne hugged her back, as tight as she could, and didn't let go.

Chapter Seventeen

An hour and a half later, an enormous black SUV with tinted windows pulled into the circular driveway of the Ritz-Carlton and stopped beside Daphne. She waited with her arms crossed over her chest, the lenses of her sunglasses as inscrutable as the car's darkened windows. The silky, dark-blue blouse, black stiletto booties, and black leather pants were terrible decisions as far as walking was concerned, but apparently Echo had doubts that Daphne could protect Cinnamon as well as their family could, and Daphne had taken that personally. So she had to look badass and serious, and she thought she was pulling it off.

Until the obviously ex-military guy in the passenger seat got out and opened the back door, and Echo descended to the earth.

Polished black dress shoes, as high as Daphne's and just as sharp, clicked on the sidewalk, and Daphne's eyes, drawn to the sound, followed Echo's bare legs up to the skirt of a black wiggle dress, long sleeves, wide black belt, and turtleneck. She wore a long gold necklace with a ring of jade hanging low, a pair of black sunglasses, and her onyx-black hair slicked into a tight bun.

"She should be with her family," Echo said, not waiting for any small talk or pleasantries. She crossed her arms over her chest, mirroring Daphne's stance. The resemblance between the sisters was stark, in the jawline and the shape of her mouth, but Echo was taller than Cinnamon, maybe as tall as Rin. With both of them wearing heels, she still had several good inches over Daphne. But people had told Daphne her whole life she just didn't know when to quit, and she wasn't about to start now.

"The truth is," Daphne said, smiling sweetly, "when they came for her, she went to the first place she thought she'd be safe, and that's with me." She had wanted to respond with a cutting retort, but she had to play nice, for Cinnamon's sake.

"And," she continued, "I'm the one who told her to call you, because even if I can help her all by myself, she deserves the benefit of all the tools at her disposal. And you're too big a tool to waste." Okay, she just couldn't help herself.

Echo didn't even seem to hear the devastating insult, and Daphne hmphed to herself. "So what's the plan here, Redgrave? Keep my sister at your undisclosed location indefinitely, magically make her phone less of a liability, and then what is she supposed to do? Move out of her house? Out of the city? Abandon her practice? That's not acceptable."

"I totally agree," Daphne said. If Cinnamon trusted them both, they must both want what's best for Cinnamon, but she hated that they had to play whatever game this was. "I have people who can help without putting Cinnamon in danger."

"I can put the full force of my family's connections to work. Get posts taken down, sue whoever posted it, whoever reposts it. Round-the-clock security team. I can make her as safe as Beyoncé."

"Great. Then we're on the same page. If Cinnamon wants any of that, I'm sure she'll be in touch."

Echo stared. Well, Daphne assumed she was staring, behind the sunglasses. She was utterly still, otherwise. Despite wanting to bounce on her toes or tap her feet, Daphne imitated her stillness.

From what Cinnamon had told her, the sisters' relationship was similar to what she had with Mattie. Protective and meddlesome, sometimes incomprehensible, sometimes infuriating, but always in each other's corner. It was possible that if the situation were reversed, Mattie would have eviscerated Cinnamon with cutting remarks, demanded to see Daphne, and finagled her way in. So the fact that Echo hadn't physically or verbally overpowered Daphne had to mean that things were going well.

Finally, the Cheung heir lowered her arms. She turned to the bodyguard guy, who reached into the backseat, pulled out a Louis Vuitton backpack, and handed it to her. As she started to pass it to Daphne, she suddenly pulled it back.

"You're not going to break her heart, are you?" Daphne recognized a note of pleading in her voice, like Echo was resigned to letting Cinnamon's heart get broken if that's what she wanted, like she had had to watch it happen again and again throughout the years.

And, god, if it had been anyone but Cinnamon, Daphne would have laughed and told the truth, which had always been: most likely. But Cinnamon had shaken everything up, and Daphne had no road map for it anymore. That little voice saying *please don't lose her* chimed in, and she swallowed down the fear that she would, that she would fuck it up and finally ruin her life for good.

Then there was the fact that Daphne had already done something to break her heart, but Cinnamon didn't know it yet. So really, they were both correct when they suspected that Cinnamon couldn't trust anyone. Awesome.

"No," Daphne said. Even if it meant more work. Even if it meant thinking before acting. Her answer was more hope than truth, but she hoped it would become truth. She had a plan, but it would have to wait until they got through this bigger crisis. "I'm not going to break her heart."

Echo stared at her for another moment before holding out the bag. Daphne grabbed it by the top handle. "Keep my number," Echo said, as close to a grumble as someone could manage and still seem totally put-together. "And call me if anything happens you think I should know about. I have someone coming first thing tomorrow to replace the broken window. Cops know about the harassment, so she shouldn't get swatted. A security team is keeping an eye on it, too, so Cinnamon will have to contact me before going back so I can let them know. Otherwise, it'll be ready for her to return whenever she feels comfortable."

Daphne nodded, appreciating what a good sister she was. "Once her phone is up and ready, I'll have her call you." She shifted on her heels. Time to balance the toughness demonstrating she could take care of Echo's little sister's physical safety with the sincerity needed to take care of her heart. "Thanks for doing this. I know, you're sisters, and close, so you would. It's just. Nice that people she cares about care about her. That there are people who know how great she is and don't take it for granted."

Echo cocked her head, slid her arms back into position crossed over her chest. "Didn't you meet each other for the first time on Saturday?"

Obviously Echo wasn't familiar with Daphne's infamously swift romances. No reason to tell her about it. "Do people not usually recognize her magnificence this quickly?"

"She doesn't usually let people this quickly."

Hmmm.

"I'd better hear from one of you again tonight," Echo said as she turned back to the car. "And when this is all settled, the three of us are going to dinner." She shook her head and mumbled as she slid into the back seat. "Why'd it have to be a Redgrave?"

A moment later, the SUV pulled out into traffic, and Daphne slung the backpack over her shoulders. That meeting wasn't as bad as she expected. Then again, she had expected to get knocked on her ass. Metaphorically, if not physically. Dinner wouldn't be so bad. But first they'd have to make it through the night.

***

By the time Brad showed up at Daphne's apartment with his backpack full of equipment and an armload of takeout, the women were already feeling better, if hungry. Daphne set Brad up at the big table while she and Cinnamon took seats at the kitchen island.

"Ooo, what did you bring us? It smells amazing." Daphne reached into the unmarked plastic bag and started pulling out foil-wrapped bundles.

"You only said 'no seafood,' so I got a bunch of vegetarian burritos. One of them's mine, please. Chips and queso too, if you don't mind."

"So what are you going to do, exactly?" Cinnamon unwrapped a burrito while Daphne made Brad a plate of chips.

"Uh." Brad didn't look up from connecting wires to devices. "Well, how much do you know about computers? And the internet?"

"I can't name most of the stuff you have spread out on the table."

Brad snorted. "Nothing wrong with that, that's why you've got people like me to help. The best way for me to explain it is to say I'm going to search the internet for your name and the other personal info that was shared, get it taken down, and flag the accounts that did it. It's more complicated than that, but that's the gist of it."

"Okay," Cinnamon drawled, pushing the overstuffed burrito in- gredients back into the tortilla. "But the information has been available to everyone online for a while, so some people already have my address and email and everything. Can that be fixed, or is it just something I'm going to have to deal with forever?"

Brad looked up and smiled at her. "I'm going to make sure they know it's in their best interest to forget it. Again, it's complicated. It'll take me an hour to do and a month to explain."

"If this happened to me, I'd trust Brad and only Brad to get everything back to normal," Daphne said as she set his dinner on the table. He continued plugging things in and setting up.

"And you work together?"

"Not directly," Daphne said, coming back to her own plate. "He does IT stuff at the firm, but he's capable of a lot more." From across the room, Brad snorted again.

"Okay, where's the phone?" he asked. "Oh, is this it?" He con- nected Cinnamon's powered-down phone to a cord leading to his laptop and slid the device into a little black pouch that he sealed like a plastic baggie, cord sticking out.

"Faraday bag," Daphne murmured. "The only info passing in or out of it is solely through the cord."

Cinnamon paused, the burrito halfway to her mouth, and glanced between Daphne and Brad. "Are you two spies?"

"Just rich." Daphne winked. Afraid that might not cut it, she threw in a little lie. "I have an affinity for useful gadgets, but my very brief time working for my father taught me to be a little paranoid. So, the pimp, the secure condo, some other things you can't and won't see, and my fascination with whatever Brad comes up with next."

Whether her performance was adequate or not, she couldn't tell, but Cinnamon didn't ask any more questions. With everything that had happened, Daphne wouldn't be surprised if her mental capacity just wouldn't accept any more new information.

When they finished eating, Cinnamon went to shower, while Daphne bothered Brad. The phone was clean, but he didn't want to give it back until he was sure that Cinnamon wouldn't be bothered with any more nonsense. Two more laptops were open beside the first one, and the table was strewn with a number of devices that Daphne didn't recognize. She wanted to pick up each one and ask what it was and could she have it. But Cinnamon had to come first.

"You're going to fuck up all of her harassers, right?" Daphne said under her breath. She could hear the water in the shower running but didn't want to take the chance that Cinnamon might overhear.

"Like they were my own," Brad said at the same volume.

"How? I want to revel in their pain."

He rolled his eyes but his fingers kept typing. "Oh, have you somehow become a computer expert in the last few hours?"

"Hey, I can use the programs at work pretty well."

"Because that's how I designed them, Daph. A monkey could use them. Your monkey could use them."

Confused for a second, Daphne had to wait for the slowly surfacing memory of Coco and the great monkey heist of—Christ, had it only been a week ago? It felt like a different life. She cringed, thinking of how over-the-top she had been, and for a woman who'd never met her. Oh, she'd still steal a monkey. For Cinnamon, she would even *stop herself* from stealing a monkey.

"Look," he said, nodding to the screens. "Can you understand what I'm doing right now just by looking at it?"

Daphne huffed. "No."

"So just trust me." His fingers paused over the keyboard. "Huh. That's weird."

"What's wrong?"

"Not wrong, just weird. I would think..." It only took him a second to get back to typing, but if Daphne didn't say something, he would tune her out as he worked on the mystery.

"You'd think what?" she prodded.

Brad glanced up at her with a frown. "Someone else is doing the exact same thing as me."

Daphne leaned toward one of the laptops, as if getting closer to it would help her understand anything she was seeing. "Could it be just a lag in the data?"

"That's a good guess, considering your level of understanding. I mean that as a compliment, I swear. No, it looks like someone is also focused on these terms, doing the same thing I am, in tandem. Tracking, flagging, scrubbing, doxxing. Deleting and corrupting accounts. Like we're working together. Or like an echo."

An echo, huh? Echo had said that she intended to use all her family's connections to make Cinnamon safe. Daphne smiled. She'd known they were on the same page.

"Treat them as friendly. I think it's someone Cinnamon's family hired to do the same thing as you're doing."

"Someone's getting paid for this?"

"Oof, Brad."

"Joking. You get the Daphne discount."

She leaned back from the monitor and crossed her arms. "I've already got something great for you through my costume designer. You know she worked on *Thor*, right?"

That got his attention. He stopped typing and stared at her with big, hopeful eyes.

"It'll take a few days to get here, so just keep doing your thing and act surprised when it shows up. I take care of my friends. So yeah just like, give that other good guy a handshake or whatever."

He turned back to the keyboard with a huff. "That's not what a handshake is, but I can't be mad. It won't take much longer. I'm tweaking a program that will do this automatically so someone doesn't have to spend every hour of the day on the lookout for more of the same bullshit."

His fingers flew over the keys and he shot her another look. "Me. To be clear. I'm the someone who doesn't want to spend every hour of the day troll hunting. Not that you're not worth it," he added hastily.

Daphne heard the water shut off in the bathroom and knew she didn't have much time. "One more thing. Can you do that and still pay attention to my unrelated thing?"

"Go on, but be direct."

"Collin Roday has sexually assaulted a number of people."

Brad clenched his jaw but didn't look up. "I heard rumors. But you sound sure. Clarissa would want hard evidence."

"They won't come forward. What you're seeing today, with Cinnamon? This is a fraction of what would happen to them."

"Roday's laptop. Phone. Ask Atticus?"

"I already suggested all that before I knew for sure Roday was guilty. I just wanted to know if you'd gotten anything incriminating."

"Sure. Embezzlement. Shorting stocks. Wage theft. About a dozen other things."

"Right, but no mention of sexual harassment?"

"It sounds like you're looking for a text or email that says, 'Hey friend, let me tell you in detail about this assault I just did in a way that can be corroborated and verified,' and as far as I know, we don't have that. Could it exist? Yes. Roday and his ilk are stupid like that. Does it exist on any of the systems I've seen? No. Seems like Roday and his ilk aren't stupid like that."

Daphne sighed. "Isn't there a way to make sure they're investigated? Prosecuted?"

Brad punched in a few more definitive keystrokes and leaned back in his chair. "No. Everything we found belongs to the client. Goldenrod. They get to do whatever they want with it. If we take the data they paid us to collect and go public with it when they were planning to blackmail them privately, or vice versa...that's just not good business. You know that, Daph."

She bit the inside of her cheek and let her eyes wander. "I know that look," Brad admonished, "so let me just remind you, as a friend: whatever you're planning to do, make sure it doesn't come back to Diophantus. Steal monkeys on your own time, under your own name. Do it with Diophantus resources, and you'll tank all of us. Not just yourself."

He was right, obviously. But she wasn't totally without her own resources.

Chapter Eighteen

When Cinnamon came back into the living room, clean and comfortable in her usual loungewear of leggings and tank top and wrapped in Starlight's floral scent, Brad was packing up his equipment.

"Done already?" she asked. Had she been afraid of something for six months that could have been undone in an hour? But she remembered her house, her flight, the shattering of glass that sounded like rain and the obliteration of her remaining sense of security.

"I make it look easy," he said, holding out her phone. "They did get your office address, since it was public information, but I didn't find anything mentioning your clients. Keep your phone locked with a code, not your fingerprint. There's a new app on the first page, dark purple with a squiggly teal thing that could be a J or a squid. If you get any threats—email, Insta, Facebook, texts, whatever—wherever you get them, you now have the option to move them to AK—that's the new app, Aetos Kaukasios. Move them there, they'll be deleted from wherever they originated from, but it'll send a backup of it to a remote server where they'll be saved in case you mount a legal defense. And of course, your personal information has been scrubbed from the internet as much as it can be. You're welcome."

Brad demonstrated the new app by sending her a text from one of his burner phones. It was easy enough.

As he was leaving, Cinnamon asked, "Why is the app named after the eagle that tortured Prometheus?"

Starlight and Brad exchanged a look, and she shrugged.

Turning back to Cinnamon, Brad shrugged, too. "The app gathers the data and feeds it into other programs that track down the real-life information of whoever sent it to you. From there, it can block the account or the IP address, suspend the account, connect it to an email address, website, physical address, phone number, other usernames from the same email address. And then dox the sender across a number of platforms as a bot. If it can get the sender's contact list—which it usually can—it'll send a copy of what he sent you to everyone on it. Mother, girlfriend, wife, boss. If they have a business website, it'll launch a DDoS attack. The app is basically constantly picking at the electronic guts of whoever's harassing you."

"Holy shit," Cinnamon said, looking down at the purple and teal icon.

"It's not my design, but I trust the person who made it. She got caught up in the GamerGate bullshit last year. It's not exactly legal, so, don't go bragging about it and it should be fine."

She barely heard him, lost in the wonders and horrors of technology. Starlight thanked him for the both of them and walked him out. When she returned, Cinnamon was still staring at her phone.

"I'm not sure I should have this much power," she murmured, setting it down on the table. Laughing, Starlight took her hands in her own.

"I think you're exactly who should have this much power." She kissed Cinnamon's fingers, one by one. "How are you feeling?"

Clean. Scared. Angry. No, livid. Worried. That burrito wasn't doing much for her, either.

"Glad to have such a capable friend who's willing to help me," she said instead. Starlight was more than a friend, but the shower had given Cinnamon time to worry about everything in her life, including things that were going well.

Starlight let go of her and bit her lip. "You must be talking about Brad, because I am much more than a friend to you." Cinnamon flinched, thinking she'd read her mind, but she didn't seem to notice. "Especially when I'm taking you to the Manu Ono sushi popup restaurant Saturday night."

"Oh you are, are you?"

"Yeah, and I wouldn't take just any friend there. I mean, okay, I made the reservation six months ago the minute it became available, and if I couldn't get a date, I would take my best friend or my sister, but the point is—"

"The point is, you want to take me. Even though I don't eat seafood."

"Pah!" She waved her hand. "The man is a genius, even the not-fish sushi is amazing."

"I'll be the judge of that. Or I would be, but I was going to ask you to be my date to my family's business gala that same night." Starlight's face fell, and Cinnamon laughed. "I can skip it. I usually do. Or we can put in a brief appearance before dinner. Maybe...introduce you to my parents? And Claude?"

Starlight narrowed her eyes. "Meeting parents sounds like a step in the right direction—I do know how to behave when I want to—but this Claude person. Sounds important."

"Oh, he is. You should be striving for his approval above all."

"Damn," she said. "Give me some tips."

"Adore him. Fawn over him. Tell him he's a handsome boy."

Starlight pursed her lips and lowered her head. "Claude isn't human, is he." It wasn't a question.

"You're just going to have to see for yourself." Cinnamon gave her a sly smile. "But I would abandon all of it for something as rare as a date with Starlight Redgrave to have—what was it? The exceptional cuisine stylings of Manu Ono?"

"We're going to circle back around to Claude in a minute, but yes. I went to Manu Ono's restaurant in New Zealand years ago and fell in love. As much as one can with sushi, which, I don't know if you know this, but that's a lot of love. I missed his last popup here because of work. But now work won't interfere, I have the reservations, and I have a date, and nothing can go wrong."

"You know something will go wrong now," Cinnamon said with a grin.

"Nope!" Starlight yelled. "I forbid it! And you need something to go right this week, besides meeting me."

"Was that this week?" she teased. "This same week?"

"Less than."

Cinnamon sighed and sank into a dining room chair.

"The good news," Starlight started, "is that your address is off the internet. So, yay. Your sister has a security detail at your house. Also, you should call her tonight, or she'll track me down and murder me. But you're welcome to stay here as long as you need. Ah." She glanced at the floor then slid herself into the chair beside Cinnamon. "It's possible that I might be able to get access to BDMT's financial records. I know it's not the kind of evidence you're looking for. It won't help get him caught for sexual assault, but he would feel the consequences of *something* he thought he was too rich and important to get heat for."

Cinnamon had a vague feeling that she should be more surprised by this information, but she was starting to think that the unexpected was integral to Starlight's personality. Of course she could get Roday's sketchy financial info. And of course she would offer it to help Cinnamon. Not exactly the justice she was looking for, but...something?

Like mob bosses, responsible for dozens of murders, who get put away for tax evasion. Did the people they hurt feel vindicated? If his victims knew he'd never see justice for what he did to them, *could* they be satisfied that he'd see justice for his other crimes? Was Cinnamon even in a position to decide, when she wasn't among those that Roday hurt?

"I would love to say that's enough," she told Starlight. "It doesn't surprise me that he's dabbled in a variety of crimes. It would be nice to know he can bleed, but if he isn't bleeding specifically for his assaults, I'm not sure it would feel like a win."

Cinnamon moved her phone a little so its sides lined up with the table's. "I also don't want you to put yourself in danger to get evidence that isn't what I need. I don't know how you would get it, and—no, don't tell me, I probably shouldn't know." Starlight closed her mouth, probably about to tell her just that. Or something close to it.

"What if there was an email saying, 'look at my sex crimes'?" Starlight asked anyway.

It was doubtful that anything less than video evidence would even put a dent in Roday's life. And even then, it might not be enough.

"Without any victims willing to come forward and bring charges, it would be like admitting to a murder without a body, a murder weapon, witnesses, and a motive." Cinnamon shook her head, feeling all of her hard work of the last six months slipping away. "I think it's over, for me. Playing detective. It might have been worth it, the fear, everything that happened today, if I could take him down, too. But it's all been for nothing. I can't keep putting myself through this."

A dozen emotions flickered across Starlight's face as she slid off the chair and knelt in front of Cinnamon, lips pressed into a flat line, eyes wide.

"Sunk cost fallacy," Starlight said, nodding. Cinnamon frowned, then laughed.

"The accountant would go to 'sunk cost fallacy.'"

"Hey, it's widely applicable. It takes a lot of soul-searching to assess a situation you've poured a lot of effort or time or money into and walk away before it buries you. And you're allowed to mourn what you lost in it."

Cinnamon sniffled. "Okay, Doctor Starlight."

She wrinkled her nose. "Keep insinuating I'm competent and I'll have to act extra helpless until you change your mind. Now..." She stood up and pulled Cinnamon to her feet.

"My couch is comfortable. That weird chair is a nap trap, and I also have a guest bedroom. But earlier this week, you invited me to stay in your bed when I needed one, and I'm extending to you the same invitation. Full disclosure: My alarm goes off at five thirty and I can be violent about it."

Starlight's hands were soft, and a little cold, but held Cinnamon's firmly. It had been such a long day. There had been so many things she couldn't control. And this midnight woman didn't push her or judge her, she just took over and made decisions that Cinnamon would have if she'd thought of it. If she had the contacts that were able to do what Brad did.

Her house would be repaired the next morning and she had a security team at her disposal. She owed Echo and would have to have a long conversation with her soon, but not tonight. She owed Starlight, too.

"Hold on." Cinnamon reached for her phone and texted her sister that it was working again. Her reply came quickly, and

Cinnamon assured her that it was really her and would call her the next morning before going home. She tried to think of anything else she had to take care of.

"I cancelled all my sessions tomorrow," she told her rescuer, setting her phone back down on the table. "In case that information was shared, too. I didn't want to put my clients at risk."

"Smart." Starlight tilted her head and looked Cinnamon over. "So, what—"

Without thinking, Cinnamon darted in to cover Starlight's mouth with her own, her hands coming up to encircle her, fingers tangling in her platinum hair. She was tired of putting off what she wanted just because she thought she shouldn't want it. And if she didn't stop her from talking, the woman would never stop.

Starlight's arms snaked around her back, pulling them closer, caressing Cinnamon's tongue with her own. Raspberry and mint from her lip balm brought Cinnamon back to the night in her pool, all slippery and chlorine and starlight and desire. She kissed her top lip, then bottom lip, then kissed a constellation across her pale, upturned face. Starlight was blushing already, breath heavy, and when she started to speak again, Cinnamon stopped her with her lips one more time.

Cinnamon had also muted the running commentary in the back of her mind: the doubts about herself and whatever their relationship was, whether Starlight really wanted her, whether this could be the start of something really big, the performance anxiety of not doing this with anyone else for...how long? And why was she trying to do math right now?

"I know you have to get up early," she murmured, letting her fingers wander from Starlight's hair, around her neck, following the deep V of her sapphire blouse between her breasts. "I won't keep you up too late."

"Yeah, I," she said breathlessly. "I don't think what you have planned will take long at all."

Cinnamon laughed against her smooth skin and licked from her jaw to behind her ear. Starlight jumped and Cinnamon held her tighter.

"Give me some credit," she muttered.

"Meant it...as a compliment..."

She playfully nipped at Starlight's neck and slipped her hand beneath the blouse and bra to knead at her, thumb rolling her nipple.

"Fuck, yup, bedroom, now," Starlight said, clutching at Cinnamon's back and kissing her hair. As Cinnamon straightened, Starlight grasped both sides of her face and pulled her in for a rough kiss, rubbing against her with a desperation Cinnamon knew well. She pulled Starlight's shirt out from her leather pants and pulled it up and off, while her lover walked backward, leading the way toward the bedroom.

Tongues entwined and hands everywhere, Starlight copied Cinnamon and pulled her tank top over her head, and they began the game of who could unhook whose bra first. Cinnamon won—she'd started first—and Starlight made a grunt of protest when she had to take her hands off Cinnamon long enough to take off the bra completely. Immediately, Cinnamon leaned Starlight back, licking from her neck to her breast as her hand trailed down her back and grabbed her ass possessively. Starlight tried to concentrate on undoing the remaining bra with one hand, but with Cinnamon's mouth on her breast and her tongue circling her tit, she wasn't capable of doing much more than moaning.

"Fuck," she exhaled. "Let me—"

"In a minute," Cinnamon whispered. She ran her hands across her body as she kissed her way to her other breast, her skin soft, back muscles dancing beneath her fingertips. She breathed her in and let the scent of flowers and skin and darkness fill her, like she could keep Starlight somehow within her if she could consume her. Starlight grasped Cinnamon's hair and lowered them to the floor.

"Okay," Starlight said. "This'll have to be where I make my stand. Bedroom is too far for this."

She leaned back and pulled Cinnamon with her, on top of her, and Cinnamon laughed against her mouth as she struggled with the bra.

"Fine, fine." Starlight pulled the straps down, and it was Cinnamon's turn to reluctantly let go to thread her arms through the straps. Instead of pulling it around to undo the hooks, she tugged it down just enough to expose Cinnamon's chest, just enough that she could pull her mouth up to one nipple and her hand up to the other. Cinnamon groaned and leaned into her, grasped her hair and rubbed her face in it, breathing deep. She reached a hand between them and played with the waist of Starlight's pants, but what would normally be a playful teasing felt too small, so she stretched her hand over the front of her pants and rubbed between her legs.

Starlight bucked against her, encouraging her, and shifted so she could reach the small of Cinnamon's back, where she grasped her leggings and pulled them and her underwear down to expose her ass. Her fingertips traced the outline of her cheeks, dividing her attention between Cinnamon's firm bottom and the breasts she nuzzled her face against. She stretched a little farther and her fingers brushed the hot folds of her vulva.

Cinnamon twitched, and shifted, and took her own hand away from Starlight long enough to unbutton and unzip Starlight's pants and slide her hand back in place, but this time, beneath the pants and underwear.

Starlight gasped and writhed against her, bit at her breast playfully, then used her free hand to pull Cinnamon to her in a desperate and sloppy kiss.

"I want you," Cinnamon whispered between sliding kisses, Starlight biting at her lip. "I wanted you in the pool, shimmering starlight in my darkness; I wanted you at the party, beneath the fairy lights, you trying to flirt. I was already yours. I should have taken you then."

"Take me now," she said, a sharpness in her plea. Cinnamon held Starlight's mouth against her, hard, taking her time with one more long, slow, crushing kiss, before sitting up and grasping the top of her lover's pants.

But Starlight was quicker, somehow, and already had Cinnamon's leggings pulled down to her knees before she could make a move. Cinnamon laughed.

"These too," Starlight said, like it was something she might forget. Cinnamon pulled them off the rest of the way, mumbling, "Who's in charge here?"

"Both of us," she answered with a grin.

"Is that so?" Cinnamon leaned over and ran her tongue across her stomach, just above the top of her pants.

"Mmm. You? Is you the right answer?"

Cinnamon grasped Starlight's pants again and looked up at her with a sly smile. "You tell me." She drew down the leather pants slowly, Starlight wiggling with impatience. Cinnamon held the material bunched at her ankles while she got more and more worked up.

"Cinnamon—"

"Well?"

"You are. You're in charge."

"Stay," she said, slipping the pants over her toes and tossing them to the side. Starlight did as she was told—Cinnamon knew, even now, that that was a rare event. Her eyes wandered over her, greedy and eager, this picture of desire she'd had in her mind since the day they met: this feral moonlight woman, naked and wanton, waiting for her, no lust lost just because she was sprawled against a thick white rug instead of Cinnamon's red sheets.

And she stayed there, waiting, in a torment of expectation, as Cinnamon kissed the inside of one knee, splaying a hand against Starlight's stomach. She placed a hand over Cinnamon's and closed her eyes, waiting for the next kiss that landed farther up her thigh. And the next, higher. The next against the last inch of flesh that would be called her leg, and Cinnamon dragged her tongue from there to plant a wet kiss against her center.

Starlight jumped and grabbed Cinnamon's hair while she kissed her again, and again, tongue lapping her slowly.

"My sweet Starlight, I'll take care of you," she murmured, running her hand down her pale, soft stomach to play at her folds before sliding a finger inside her.

"Yes, Yes, Cinnamon." Starlight whimpered and pressed against her hand, her mouth and tongue, clutching her hair and the rug beneath them. Cinnamon felt her twitches, breath faster and faster, and she wouldn't let up, wanting to bring Starlight to climax, wanting to watch her face contort, eyes pressed closed, biting her lip—Starlight's frown line creased her brow as she panted and jerked and squeaked and came with a moan that sounded surprised, whole body shuddering in wave after receding wave.

When Starlight could move again, she fluttered her eyes open, looked down at Cinnamon, and laughed in pure joy. "You're in charge. But I'm gonna take care of you now."

Cinnamon bit her lip and crawled up Starlight like a big cat, kissing and sucking and licking across large swathes of skin. "I want to be kissing you when I come," she said, sucking her lover's lower lip into her mouth.

"Fuck, yes."

"Touch me," Cinnamon said, guiding Starlight's hand between her legs. "Play with me, like this, while I kiss you."

"Yes," she breathed, her fingers sliding over Cinnamon's sensitive parts. She gasped as her fingers entered her, rocking against her to find a rhythm before kissing her again, clutching her hard, riding the high as well as Starlight's deft hand. She moaned against her mouth and lost herself in the feeling, the pleasure that had been building all day, all week, for hours, for years. Starlight grasped her hair again and tugged, never slowing her hand, her slippery lips and tongue dancing against Cinnamon's.

"Again," Cinnamon begged. "Harder. And don't stop. God—"

Starlight pulled at her hair again and grasped it harder. Cinnamon let out a sound halfway between a scream and a moan, her body tensing and shaking and releasing, all at once, everything, her mouth open in a silent scream, and her lips found their way back to Starlight's before she finished coming, body jerking in absolute pleasure.

Cinnamon rested her forehead against Starlight's as she fought to catch her breath. The hand that had been grasping her hair moved to caress her back in slow circles as she came back down.

"That was okay?" Starlight asked.

Seven years without romance, and a lifetime without the kind of physical and emotional connection that Starlight had just gifted her with. The emotions caught in her throat wouldn't let her speak, so she just nodded against her, rubbed her cheek with her own, and held her tighter.

"Mmm. Come here," she said, rolling Cinnamon onto her back. She pushed stray strands of silky black hair out of Cinnamon's face and trailed her fingers over her nose, cheekbones, jaw, and ear whorls, as if trying to memorize them by touch.

"This floor isn't the most comfortable of places," she continued, kissing her nose, her eyebrow, her hairline. "So if you want to move to the bed, I'm all for it. But I'm going to take some time to kiss you everywhere, and then I'm going to fall asleep making out with you." She shifted so she could kiss Cinnamon's shoulder. "And then I'll wake up violently at five thirty and you'll see a totally different side of me. But before then? All kisses. All the time. My fierce protector."

"My sweet Starlight."

Chapter Nineteen

It wasn't until Daphne was sitting in the windowless room at Bad Mountain Tech, surrounded by her own bad mountains of paperwork, that she realized how lucky she was that her only job for the day was putting the records she stole yesterday back in their pile. Her alarm had gone off before sunrise, and while she was glad to be conscious again so she could see and feel and smell and taste for herself that Cinnamon was, in fact, in bed beside her, she was also—as predicted—angry about having to *get up* out of her lover's arms, leave the room, the condo, the building, and that part of town, and go to work.

For hours.

After Daphne had slapped the alarm clock, she snuggled up against her barely awake lover and took a deep breath. Cinnamon's spicy scent flirted beneath Daphne's lotion and shampoo, and their combined smell was as powerful as any aphrodisiac, the scent of her now part of Cinnamon. She wondered if Cinnamon had felt the same way seeing Daphne in her borrowed pajamas that first night.

She was lucky, too, that other people were responsible for getting her hair, makeup, outfit, and props ready, because replaying the night before in her head had taken up ninety percent of her brain capacity.

The little voice saying *Don't lose Cinnamon* had been joined by a much louder and more conscious voice saying the same thing.

Not only because of the sex. Or maybe the sex was just a part of what happened that cracked Daphne open like a Kinder Egg. Even she didn't know what emotions she would find within it, but it was the opening, the sharing, the being vulnerable with Cinnamon that created a bond that Daphne might have never felt before.

When Cinnamon eventually got up, she would find a note from Daphne that said, simply, "To work. Text you later. p.s. We're girlfriends now." Never mind that she had called them girlfriends since they kissed in the pool and Cinnamon didn't kick her out. But now? Oh, she was in it.

And she was going to get that fucking evidence for her.

At the briefing, Clarissa told them that the client was happy with what they'd found, so the only job the molothri had left was to keep their cover until they no longer had to go in to BDMT. None of her fellow spies had found anything regarding Roday's assaults, and neither Roday nor his computer had appeared yet today for them to try again. So she went back to her poorly lit makeshift storage room and thought about Cinnamon until lunchtime.

Just before her break, someone knocked at the door.

"Hey, Olive. Still here, huh?"

Daphne sat up straighter and rearranged the documents in front of her to look like she was working before she realized it was just Atticus.

"Oh, uh, sure, um. I want to say...K—Kevin?"

"Derrick," Atticus corrected.

"Sorry, yeah. It's been a long first week." She gave him a smirk.

"I hear you," he said, holding the door open with a foot so he could lean his back against the frame. "So hey, we don't do this a lot, but Roday isn't going to be here today so he won't care. We're letting everyone go home early, to celebrate marriage equality.

The Supreme Court decision was announced a little while ago. I'm sure there are plenty of queers in this office who would love to get out there and celebrate."

"What?" Daphne screamed. "Atti—Derrick!" She glanced out the door to see if anyone was watching, and lowered her voice. "And Pride is this weekend!" she whispered loudly.

"Get out of here," he said, gesturing with a nod.

"Oh, I..." She'd finished her one job-related job, but she still had Cinnamon's evidence to find. "I was hoping to see Collin today. I had something to ask him about, uh, electronics?" She didn't know what kind of code to use, so she wiggled her eyebrows inappropriately.

Atticus shook his head. "He won't be here. But I'll be sure to look into it myself on Monday. You have my guarantee."

This had been her last chance to get the evidence Cinnamon needed. And she had wanted to get it for her personally. Historically, not many things had stood in her way when she wanted something. It was a new feeling and she hated it. But until she could come up with a better solution, trusting Atticus—and Ivan, too—to try their best would have to be enough.

"Thanks, Derrick. I owe you one."

"I accept payment in Bitcoin and sex," he said loudly. Daphne frowned at him, but a second later, Jared walked by and gave Atticus a passing high-five.

"Ha, nice," Jared said.

Atticus watched him leave, then shrugged at Daphne. "Sorry. Gotta keep up appearances."

She rolled her eyes and gathered her bags to leave. "Thanks again. See you later, co-worker."

***

From what Starlight had said, Cinnamon expected to be woken up in darkness by thrashing and screaming, things breaking, lights angrily switched on. Instead, she heard a quiet beeping, felt her lover shift to turn it off, and fell back asleep. So either Starlight had exaggerated, or she remembered Cinnamon was there and was extra careful to not scare her.

Not long after the alarm went off, she roused again, feeling fingertips moving hair out of her face, Starlight's body pushed against her long enough to press a gentle kiss in front of her ear.

"I'll see you after work," Starlight whispered.

Hours later, Cinnamon woke up for good when the light level in the bedroom was an inescapable mid-morning brightness. In the chaos of the afternoon and evening before, she hadn't really had a chance to look through Starlight's apartment. She had expected a place as quirky and messy as the woman herself, but it was tidy enough. Fashionable but comfortable and filled with easily ten times as much clothing as Cinnamon owned. A third room that could have been another bedroom or an office had been fitted as a second walk-in closet, and she loved everything in it. Not for herself, of course. The entire apartment was all very Starlight.

Right down to the fact that she didn't own a regular drip coffeemaker. Cinnamon sighed and stared at the well-loved but clean espresso machine, as if looking at it hard enough for long enough would make her spontaneously know how to use it.

She had found Starlight's note next to a set of keys and the alarm code. In case she wanted to go out before Starlight got home. Making it easy for Cinnamon to leave, if she chose, should have been a basic expectation from a partner, but after feeling the violation of getting doxxed and hunted, Cinnamon was just relieved that Starlight respected her autonomy.

Nob Hill wasn't an area Cinnamon knew very well, but she'd been to several cafés in Chinatown and could find her way there again if she couldn't find coffee any nearer. As she gathered her things into a purse, ready to go on a pilgrimage for coffee, her phone rang, with Echo's name appearing on the screen.

"Hello jiejie," she answered. "I survived the night. I know I owe you a longer explanation and apparently dinner with the three of us—"

"Where are you?" Echo demanded.

"I'm safe," Cinnamon said, frowning. Her sister knew that, she had texted her the night before to tell her so. "I cancelled all my sessions today, just in case. Did you want to do something?"

"Pack your bags and give me the address. You need to leave her place immediately."

Cinnamon's stomach flipped. Had they found her? "What happened, Echo?"

"I'm coming to pick you up."

"That's not an answer," she said, keeping her voice level. Why did Echo have to treat her like a child right when she needed to feel like a capable adult? "I'm not leaving until you tell me what happened. I know how secure this place is and I feel safe here. Tell me how it's not safe."

There was a pause on Echo's end, then mumbling like she had put her hand over the microphone before coming back to answer. "It's Daphne. I told you not to trust a Redgrave, and you didn't listen."

"We've had this conversation." Cinnamon rubbed her face. Her sister's yo-yoing was giving her emotional whiplash. "You jumped to conclusions the minute you found out I liked her and made me feel like an idiot for it. Then you changed your mind and said she was fine. Yesterday, you even teamed up to help me. And now she's somehow done you wrong again. You must love to see me miserable."

Her voice cracked and tears filled her eyes faster than she thought possible. She hadn't meant to get emotional, but, well. Things caught up to her.

"I know what I said," Echo said gently. "I have something I need you to see. It's important. I don't think you're an idiot. Leave your stuff there if you want. But let me come pick you up so we can talk. Humor your big sister. I'll come to the Ritz again, you can hop in, we can drive around for a while, and I'll bring you back if that's what you want, I promise."

"You're scaring me, Echo."

Her sister took a breath and let it out slowly. "You know I treat every problem as seriously as life or death. Daphne's at work, right? So let's go get an early lunch. Or a coffee. Bubble tea. It'll be fun."

Yeah, Cinnamon doubted that. But Echo was worried, and she did need caffeine. She had the keys and alarm code to get back in.

"Fine," she said. "I'll meet you at the hotel in twenty minutes. Bring me tea. A big one."

***

Echo picked her up in one of their black Escalades that was set up like a limo, so Echo's back was to the driver, and Cinnamon had to climb up into the vehicle to slide into a seat facing her sister. A large bubble tea was already in the cup holder, and Cinnamon grunted a reluctant thanks as she took a sip.

"I'm so glad to see you in person," Echo said, looking over her sister like she was searching for signs of violence, bruises, torn clothes, a favored wrist. "Tell me what happened last night."

"Some asshole posted my address and phone number, and someone came to my house and smashed my front window."

Echo shook her head. "No, I want to know what happened after I brought you your stuff."

Cinnamon blushed, one long and intimate memory standing out. "Nothing happened afterward."

"Your phone was fixed, did Redgrave do it herself?"

"Echo." She sighed. "It would be easier if you just told me what you're looking for specifically."

"Okay, okay. I'm going to send you a link to an app. I want you to download it."

"What is it?" she said warily. "This is weird, Echo."

Her phone chirped and she looked at the file.

"I have this already."

"What? No you don't."

"Yes, I do. Br—" Cinnamon caught herself. "I got it last night. The eagle app."

"The what?"

"Aetos Kaukasios. The eagle who—"

"Yeah, yeah, Prometheus. That can't be right." Echo frowned at her own phone. "Are you sure it's the same thing?"

"I forward threats to it and it isolates them and saves them but I don't have to see them, and then they fuck up the sender's life."

"Huh," Echo said. "Where did you get it?"

"Daphne."

"That can't be right," she repeated.

Cinnamon took a deep breath to steady herself and shoved the plastic cup into the cup holder with more force than she intended.

"Well, this has been a great ride, but I'm ready to go back to Daphne's now."

Echo glanced up, the look on her face a little sad, but resigned. "We're almost there. We're picking up one more person."

Instead of answering, Cinnamon watched the buildings as they passed by. A few minutes later, they pulled into a driveway, the car's back door opened, and Ying-Li slid in beside Cinnamon.

"Hey," she said, nodding to each of the Cheung sisters. "Did you tell her?"

Echo shook her head. "You're the one who found it, you can explain it better."

Cinnamon expected them to drive around again, but the car idled in Ying-Li's driveway.

"Echo called me yesterday and told me what happened. I'm sorry, Cinnamon. I've had friends who were doxxed and it sucks. Anyway, I went with her to your house to pack your things and take a look around. We were just talking about computer security the other day, and I worried that someone might have come through the broken window and tried to get on your computer."

Cinnamon stilled. She hadn't even thought about that. In her panic to get out of the house, she had checked that the desk drawers were locked, but that was it.

"Someone did try to get in. Actually, someone succeeded."

"Shit," Cinnamon said, lowering her head into her hands.

"I wouldn't even have known. I couldn't get in without your password, you know, like last time. But something was bugging me, so I checked my own email. When I set up your computer to take a photo, I had it send it to your email, but I must have put my own somewhere in the script, because I found an email from it to my own spam folder. I didn't even see it until last night, after I got home." Ying-Li took a breath and looked up to Cinnamon hesitantly. "I'm sorry I fucked it up, or you would have known about it Wednesday night when it happened.

"Here. Look." She tilted her phone to Cinnamon, who lifted her head to see. It was an email like the one she'd gotten when Ying-Li had set up the security measure. The photo attached was, clearly, Starlight.

Cinnamon didn't know what she was looking at. Starlight in a computer screen glow. A familiar bookshelf behind her.

"No. That's impossible. I was with her all afternoon. She was at work before that."

"This is from Wednesday night," Echo said. "Did you know she was at your house Wednesday night?"

"We went to dinner. But this is wrong, she never..." Cinnamon had been running late, lost in thought after her last client, and Starlight had arrived at her house first. But the house alarm hadn't been triggered by the time Cinnamon got home. She hadn't even left her alone.

Until she went to take a shower. Which wasn't enough time...

"That can't be right," she whispered, echoing her sister's earlier phrase.

Ying-Li and Echo exchanged a look.

"There's something else," Ying-Li said, licking her lips and ducking her head. "I don't want to show you because, well, I fucked up. When I set up that thing on your computer. It was a simple thing, I could do it in my sleep, but I think I was just nervous and excited about going out with you." She shifted uncomfortably. "I don't want you to feel like I've invaded your privacy, especially after everything that happened yesterday. But after Echo called me and I found this email, I looked further. It rerouted your entire security system to me. I've fixed it," she said quickly, holding up a hand. "It's reverted back to you, and I'm so sorry. I feel like shit, especially when it might have prevented all of this."

Cinnamon's head was reeling. The security she'd set up was going to Ying-Li. Starlight had tried to get into her computer.

"Is that all?" she asked from somewhere that wasn't her body, trapped in a car with her sister and Ying-Li while the trust and friendship and maybe even love she had been cultivating with Starlight the past week curdled in her gut.

"There's another video," Echo said softly, looking at her like she could see her life falling apart. Cinnamon nodded, and Ying-Li brought up camera footage from her porch. "This is from a few minutes before your computer took the picture."

Starlight got out of a Lyft at the curb, came to the front door, and rang the bell. When no one answered, she knocked on the door, then wandered to the porch railing, looking at her phone. Her fingers flew over the screen, and she let out a sigh.

"Poor Cinnamon," she said aloud, glancing at the couch. She went back to the door, peering at the doorbell camera, then the camera in the ceiling above. She backed up and looked up and down the street, like she was afraid of being seen, then went to the second camera in the far corner, the one that overlooked the couch, staring at it so long it felt less like curiosity and more like calculation. A sour taste crept under Cinnamon's tongue. Starlight turned to the couch and flopped down, getting comfortable lying across it. Slept for ten minutes, woke when Cinnamon appeared and crouched beside her.

Ying-Li paused the video. "You were there for the rest. And a few minutes later, she logged into your computer. She didn't just attempt to break in. She used the correct password."

Cinnamon nodded again. She wasn't sure her voice would work anymore.

"And then you were doxxed," Echo said quietly. As though Cinnamon hadn't gotten that far in their theory.

Starlight didn't seem inscrutable. If anything, she overshared. Unless it was all an act. If she wanted to get into her phone or computer, what could possibly be valuable enough to go through all this? What were the benefits of conning her?

"I keep my password taped to the bottom of my keyboard," Cinnamon said finally. "She's impulsive. I could believe she saw an opportunity to try to know more about me, and did it without thinking. But doxxing me?" Cinnamon shook her head. "I just don't see it."

Echo made a snort of disbelief. "She—did you ask her to log into your computer?"

"Echo—"

"No, meimei," she said, shifting in her seat to lean forward and point a disapproving finger at her younger sister. "This is important. Even if your password was easily found, that doesn't mean she wasn't looking for it in the first place. The chances that she wasn't involved in leaking your personal information across the internet are very, very small. And unless you're living a double life, unless you're involved in something so unsavory that people want to target you for that, it's because of Cheung Technologies. That makes it my responsibility."

Cinnamon couldn't argue. She couldn't tell her about Roday. Starlight only knew because Cinnamon needed help. Thinking her name churned her stomach, little balls of tapioca threatening to come up. Echo waited for her to acknowledge that her logic was sound.

"That must be it," Cinnamon said lightly.

"We'll get your bags, then bring you home," Echo said. She reached behind her to tap the partition. Ying-Li stowed her phone in a pocket and buckled in.

"I'd rather do it myself," Cinnamon told them. They exchanged another look.

"You don't have to do this alone, Cin. You don't have to be embarrassed about it, either. I liked her too." Echo gave her a sad smile.

"I'd like to confront her myself," Ying-Li said, her voice a rumble. "Let her know she made a mistake, targeting you."

"No." The word came out firmer than Cinnamon thought she was capable of at the moment, and she shook her head to emphasize it. "I'd rather you didn't come at all. Echo, if you want to drive me back, I would appreciate it. But I'll find my own way home from there."

"Cinnamon, if she's there—"

"She isn't. She's at work."

"Is she?" There was an edge to Echo's question, letting her anger show.

"She won't be home for hours. Please. I—" Cinnamon closed her eyes and exhaled slowly. "I need to do this on my own. I'll be safe. Drop me off. I'll bring out my bags, you can take them to my house. I'll stay, confront her, then take a Lyft back home. Is the window fixed?"

Echo nodded, fished a set of new keys out of her bag, and handed them to Cinnamon. "I've already been by to see it, and I locked up after they left. I'll tell the security detail that you'll be there."

"Thanks for your help, Ying-Li," Cinnamon said hollowly. "I'll text you when I'm in a better mood for company."

Ying-Li opened her mouth to speak but nodded instead, glanced at Echo, unbuckled, and left the car. With another knock to the driver, they began making their way back to Nob Hill, Cinnamon's mind looking at the tangles of the entire ordeal like a haruspex trying to read their own entrails, and her heart a leaking wound.

Chapter Twenty

Daphne couldn't help dancing down the sidewalk. Mattie and Rin had already texted her about the Supreme Court decision, and everyone's joy was palpable. Her Lyft was covered in rainbows, and she pointed at the driver as she got in and asked, "Lesbian?" The woman gestured to the décor and grinned. "Me too!" Daphne yelled. "Happy Marriage Equality Day!" That was a sign, if she believed in signs.

Cinnamon wasn't responding to her texts. She hoped she was still sleeping, recuperating from her ordeal the day before. She imagined waking her up with the good news, making out, more sex. They'd go out to dinner to celebrate. No one was in her lobby, so she didn't have anyone to high-five on the way to the elevator.

Although she wasn't able to get the personal evidence that Cinnamon needed to complete her year-long quest to out Collin Roday as an abuser, she knew Atticus and Ivan would do everything they could to get it. If they couldn't, then it couldn't be gotten. Goldenrod wouldn't have hired Dio if they didn't intend to fuck with BDMT, so Roday would at least be miserable for some reason soon. Cinnamon's front window would have been repaired by now, Brad had deleted her info off the net and electronically slapped the people who shared it, and there was a Cheung Technologies-funded and scary-Echo-coordinated security detail making sure Cinnamon would be safe back at her house.

She got to leave work early, gay marriage was nationally recognized, and her girlfriend was waiting for her at home. If Daphne were superstitious, she would have been worried that everything was about to go terribly wrong.

"Cinnamonnnnn!" she sang as she unlocked the door and entered her apartment. "Have you seen the news? We have to celebrate, and I have five things in mind—oh hey. What's wrong?"

Cinnamon leaned against the dining room table, facing the door, arms crossed. She didn't smile or move or even acknowledge that Daphne had come in.

"Hey," Daphne said, dropping her things and making a beeline to her. It looked like she was trying not to cry. "Hey, I texted you, what happened? Are you okay?"

She reached out to touch her, and Cinnamon sidestepped her and walked away.

Okay. Not good.

"Cinnamon? Are you okay? You know you don't have to tell me anything, I don't need details, but I do need to know if you're hurt."

Cinnamon laughed and wiped at her eyes, turning back to Daphne, who had stopped trying to approach her. "Of course you're okay with me not telling you everything. Because that gives you permission to not tell me everything."

Panic rose through her, but she concentrated on keeping her breath even. Had Cinnamon found something in the apartment? Something that would incriminate her? Daphne tried to think of anything she might have kept lying around, and what exactly it would have indicated that Cinnamon didn't like, but there was nothing. Had someone said something to her?

"Okay," she said levelly, holding her hands out at waist height as though Cinnamon were a wild animal she was trying to calm. "No,

I haven't told you everything. That's pretty normal for two people who've known each other for less than a week. But you could ask me about whatever is bothering you, and I'll answer you truthfully. Do you not trust me enough for that?"

There were so many things she could have been upset about. Daphne's real job, for one. That was the big one. Her entire life of acting selfish. Her family. Hacking Cinnamon's computer. Some people were upset simply by the number of women she'd dated. Maybe it was something she hadn't even done? The odds were against her on that one, but it was possible.

"I'd love to defend myself," she said, stepping back and to the side so she wasn't between Cinnamon and the door. So she didn't feel trapped. "But to do that, I'll need to know what you think I've done."

"Huh." Cinnamon frowned and nodded at the floor. She started pacing. "I wonder if you've done so many awful things, if you have so many secrets, you're not sure which one I could be talking about."

Bullseye. "In general? Yeah, I'm pretty carefree, and there have been times when I tip too far into carelessness," Daphne said, hating how exposed she felt. After lockpicking her way into Cinnamon's computer, she'd been re-evaluating her behavior. Or, well, evaluating her behavior, since it was possible she'd never done it before. And as much as she hated feeling exposed, she hated feeling like an insensitive asshole even more. "But with you? That list is very short."

"But not empty."

This wasn't how Daphne wanted to tell her. Not when Cinnamon was already upset with her, ready to run, reminding Daphne of all the times she did the same thing, when a relationship didn't work out and she wasn't interested in why or how or how to fix it.

She'd hesitated too long.

"Tell me," Cinnamon said, pulling out her phone and typing. "Is this one of those things on your 'short list'?"

Daphne's phone chirped and she looked at the picture Cinnamon had sent. Photo from a computer, Daphne's bright face, bookshelves behind her with a little wooden globe and—

"I can explain." It looked worse than it was. But even as she told herself there was a great explanation for it, Cinnamon's anger, the despair and hurt in her eyes, told her there wasn't. Nothing was worth making Cinnamon feel that way.

"I'd love to hear about why you broke into my office and then broke into my computer, but I also don't want to hear you lying to me, so."

"You were at work late. You came home upset. I wanted to help. You couldn't tell me, because patient confidentiality, so I decided to do a shitty thing and snoop. Then *you* wouldn't be the one violating ethics. I would be. And I wanted to do that for you, so I could understand—"

"That wasn't your choice to make!" Cinnamon shouted, shaking her phone at her. "I trusted you to listen to me instead of deciding you knew better than I did about my life. I trusted you not to literally pick the lock on my office door, and I trusted you not to break into my password-protected computer to find sensitive information about my work that I couldn't tell you even if I wanted to!"

"You did tell me. Yesterday, you came here, and you told me everything. So it wasn't something you couldn't do, it was something you chose." Daphne knew it was the wrong thing to say as soon as she heard herself say it aloud.

"This is about you betraying me."

Daphne sucked a breath through her teeth. Shit. That *was* it. That was why it had bothered Daphne so much this time. It wasn't a misunderstanding or incompatibility. She knew Cinnamon had issues around trust, and she just steamrolled right over them.

Daphne held her hands out, palms up, a pleading gesture. "I was going to tell you yesterday. It's been eating away at me because I don't want to be someone who does that to you, but I didn't know how to fix it—"

"There's video, too. You on my porch, scoping out my security cameras. Are you going to tell me you were just curious what model they are?"

"Honestly, that's exactly what I was doing."

"Just a coincidence, huh?" Cinnamon folded her arms again, stopping in her pacing to look at Daphne, who was slowly walking toward her. "You show up when my family's business is vulnerable and just when I start making progress with unmasking Roday. You make me think you like me, which I should have known from the start was suspicious."

"I do like you—"

"You check out my security system, finally get into my computer, and the next day, I'm doxxed."

Daphne stopped short, pinpricks of fear starting in her fingers, her toes. Cinnamon thought *Daphne* was the one who doxxed her? It didn't even make sense...but Cinnamon had laid it all out for her, connected the dots. Daphne's world shrunk. What could she even say?

"No."

"Yes." Cinnamon's conviction sounded as immovable as her defensive stance.

"No, I absolutely did not have anything to do with that. That doesn't make any sense. I helped you get *un*doxxed. And you—you came to *me* when it happened."

"Because in a few short days, you'd managed to get me to trust you. You seduced me." Cinnamon laughed. "How many months of recon did it take to make yourself into exactly the person I would fall in love with?"

Anger and desperation flooded Daphne's muscles, threatening to vibrate or lash out or shut down. "I would never do that to you. I fucked up, okay? I made a mistake. You're right to be angry with me. I did betray your trust. By breaking into your office and logging into your computer, which I didn't see as a betrayal at the time because all I could think about was what I could do to understand what was bothering you so I could help you. But your desktop popped up and I saw your wallpaper and realized there was so much I didn't know about you, and it was fucked up for me to try to force it instead of letting you tell me things at your own pace. I didn't even open any files. I shut it down and left and felt like shit the rest of the night. Did your security system tell you that?"

"Why should I believe you?"

"Why would I confess to half a crime?"

"Because you would think, for some reason, that even though I could never forgive you for giving my address to the men who have been threatening to kill me for six months, maybe I could forgive your unacceptable boundary issues."

Daphne had been prepared to have a conversation about trust. She'd done wrong, she knew it, she wanted to make it right. But if Cinnamon believed that she'd doxxed her, Daphne would never get the chance to fix her mistake. She started to panic. "Yes, I have boundary issues, I know. Freely admitted. You have the proof. But you don't have anything that tells you I doxxed you, because I didn't. Why would I?"

"Echo thinks you did. Ying-Li too. They think it's about Cheung Technologies, and that's a possibility. But the people threatening to dox me were Roday's, so at this point I think either could be true."

"And Echo and Ying-Li are the experts."

"Expert enough. And I trust them."

Unlike you, she didn't have to say.

"Cinnamon." Daphne's voice was small. She didn't try to wipe away the tears she could no longer successfully hold back. How were things going so wrong so quickly? "I wouldn't do that to you. It doesn't make any sense."

"There's no way for me to know that," Cinnamon said. "I have no evidence that you're trustworthy." She pinned Daphne with a sad look. "You know," she said softly, "before I met you, I thought I was broken. But now, I'm sure of it."

"You're wrong. Cinnamon, you're wrong." How was this happening? "I don't want to lose you. I swear I didn't dox you, I didn't seduce you for any reason other than I liked you."

"I can't believe you."

Daphne caught the sob before it left her throat. Cinnamon gave her a once-over and headed for the door.

"Please," Daphne begged, following her but stopping a few steps away. "Please don't leave. If I can prove I didn't dox you, will you give me another chance? If I can prove that I'm not malicious? That I'm just stupid and selfish but want to make it right?"

Cinnamon paused, and for one hopeful moment, Daphne thought she might stay, but even the tilt of her head told her how utterly furious she was. "You crossed a boundary I shouldn't have had to communicate. Goodbye, Daphne."

Cinnamon gave her one last glance, full of hurt and anger, then walked out the door.

***

Daphne wanted to rely on logic, even though she often failed at it, because the choice now was logic or emotions and her emotions were a goddamn mess. What did the evidence say? What was the likelihood of any given outcome? What did the numbers look like, and was there a pattern?

There was always a pattern. For instance, in romantic relationships. Daphne would see—or in some cases, simply hear—someone who caught her interest, crash into her life in a completely inappropriate, over-the-top scene, obsess over her for a few weeks or months, stall at the first and tiniest inkling of incompatibility, and be gone and onto the next girl before she had to think too deeply about why she couldn't make a relationship last longer than sixty days.

But then: Cinnamon.

While Daphne was sobbing on the couch, post-panic-attack and lost, she felt a brief, incongruous happiness at recognizing the parallel between the fight's logical breakdown and its aftermath of an emotional breakdown.

Because what could she *do*? What could prove she wasn't the one to dox Cinnamon, when she'd been convicted on...on coincidences and vibes?

Cinnamon thought it had to do with Roday, and the idea that Daphne would do his bidding for anything made her sick to her stomach. She remembered his eyes roving over her body, his unyielding grip as he tugged her closer to whisper innuendos in her ear. Until Atticus interrupted.

Oh.

That was something, wasn't it? Get all those personal files on his laptop. Brad had made fun of her for looking for an email that explicitly detailed Roday's wrongdoings, but what if there was something that proved he was behind Cinnamon's doxxing? Okay, it was just as delusional, but wouldn't it be worth it to try? And if nothing like that existed, maybe Daphne could get the rest of the personal information to someone who would make Roday pay.

So, best case scenario: proof of all of Roday's crimes, including how Daphne wasn't involved in the doxxing. Next best case scenario: enough to bring that man down, but nothing about the doxxing. Worst case scenario: getting caught, getting assaulted, getting arrested, getting no proof of any wrongdoing whatsoever.

Daphne wished it were easier. She would be putting a lot on the line.

But...Cinnamon.

Her heart clenched, like a fist, wringing out more sorrow than she thought was left in her.

She'd do it. But she needed help. And a milkshake.

***

When Daphne walked into Shake & Quake a few hours later, Rin and Mattie were already on the scene, seated in their booth. They rose when they saw her, noting her reddened eyes and splotchy cheeks. She hadn't told them much on the phone, just that she'd fucked up but had a plan and had promised to involve them the next time she had a plan, and she needed comfort food immediately. After much hugging, Rin sat beside Mattie so they could both face Daphne, and they ordered their usual.

"This is about a girl again, isn't it?" Mattie asked, twirling her straw in her snickerdoodle shake. "I'm not judging. I'm glad you're including us before you try to do anything. We always work better when we work together."

"I've been wondering when I was going to get a Daphne adventure," Rin said. "I've barely seen you this week. It felt like something was brewing."

Daphne had thought about what she was going to tell them. Obviously not everything. Not what she really did for a living, and not Cinnamon's secrets. She had wanted to keep Cinnamon herself secret, but that wasn't happening. Her partners in crime didn't need to know everything, but they needed to know some things.

The problem was, she wasn't sure how to convince them that it was for real this time. She glanced out the window, afternoon sun bouncing between the buildings as the shadows lengthened.

"I know you don't take me seriously," she said. "You make fun of my slutty heart and starry-eyed optimism and enthusiastic pursuits. And I agree, it's ridiculous. That's part of the fun. But it's also part of the problem."

"Daph," Mattie said, teary-eyed already as usual, "we love how you are. Whenever I start to worry I'll never find anyone, I just think about how much you believe in love."

"If we've done anything to make you think otherwise, tell us so we can stop immediately." Rin reached across to grasp one of her hands, and Daphne squeezed her back.

"It's not your fault. When I think that anyone who makes eye contact is my soul mate, and tell you so, I can't really blame you when you stop believing me after the four hundredth wrong soul mate. I mean. I kidnapped a monkey for a girl who'd never even spoken to me. Maybe that was cute when I was younger, but as an adult, that's...creepy."

Daphne hadn't known she was going to say that, but she realized it was true. Some part of her knew it, and her fear of not being true to her wild self had hidden it from her, had hidden the fact that she had learned, grown, even evolved. If that was true, who was she now?

A woman desperate to make amends? She shook her head. Her actions would tell her, but not until all the decisions were made and followed through. Existential examination could wait. Cinnamon couldn't.

"I met someone at the costume party," Daphne said, pushing ahead. "I like her. We've seen each other almost every day since then. But I did something stupid that violated her trust. Usually, I would just shrug it off and start looking for my next girlfriend. But I don't want to. I think this time, if I can't fix it, I'll be broken. And I don't know who broken-me is. Beyond that, though, I want to make amends. Then, I guess, see where it goes from there."

"What if it isn't enough?" Rin asked. Ever practical, though it still stung. "What if it doesn't get her back?"

Yeah, Daphne had thought of that too. It would suck.

"Well. That's not the point. I'd love to get her back. But I want to do something significant for her, to offset my behavior. Make her life better even if it doesn't benefit me. I think..." Daphne swallowed. "I think that a bit of selflessness, on my part, is what was missing from every other relationship, and I'd like to fix it with this one. Of course, to do that, I have to be more Daphne than ever. And hope I make it to the other side still myself, but grown."

Mattie reached over and took her hand. "I'm in. Tell me your plan. I'll make it better." Her friends grinned at her.

"An Honest Mischief Alliance dalliance, featuring one last Daph?" Rin asked.

Daphne barked with laughter. "Sure. One last Daph. Here's what I'm thinking..."

Chapter Twenty-One

FWIT-THUD.

Daphne's last arrow missed the target but at least hit the paper and not the tree or hill behind it. Luckily, there were few enough people around that nobody witnessed the embarrassing shot. Everyone she'd ever met at the range had been kind, helpful, and encouraging, but her ego wasn't in the right place for her to be perceived as a Katniss cosplayer and not a practiced archer.

She took a picture of her work, even though she wasn't proud of it, and retrieved her arrows. Her initial plan to do mischief immediately last night was overruled by Mattie, Rin, and herself, once she realized she didn't have enough information to run a successful heist. Plenty of drive, anger, and irrelevant ideas to make a mess, though.

All she had to do was think of the Makamerah incident to know her friends were right. One day of recon, then they'd move tonight. It was Saturday night, so it was unlikely that Roday would be glued to his laptop and not, like, clubbing or whatever super rich assholes did. Strip club? Yachting? Whatever form of exotic animal fighting was popular?

Daphne didn't know. She'd rather be shopping, shooting, or showing her girlfriend a good time. Or playing her part in a Mattie plan. She was ready to admit that it was fine that she sucked at strategy, that she needed a team.

Sliding the arrows into her quiver, she made her way to a nearby picnic table to take a short break before moving to the next course. Her silenced phone showed texts from Atticus, Mats, and Brad, but no Cinnamon. Fear gurgled in her gut. God, she'd fucked up. Some of it wasn't her fault, but the parts that were had directly led to the assumption of the parts that weren't, so actually, it was all her fault.

Daphne took a sip of water from her bottle and shook her head. She'd spent every hour since their fight poking at the memory, turning it around, demanding it give her the answer to how to undo it. But after all that, the best chance was still to steal that goddamn laptop. And that required help.

"Call when youre free i'm still to drunk to read tests," Atticus had texted.

"Why do you hate me?" he growled when she called, his voice sinking to the same register as the recently exhumed.

"You didn't have to answer," she said softly, accommodating his likely headache. "But I'm glad you did."

"You texted me thirteen times, what was I supposed to do? Hold on."

He said something unintelligible and far away from the microphone. His husband, Felix, knew about Atticus's actual work at Diophantus, and Daphne felt a familiar jealousy. If she could have told Cinnamon the truth about her job, and the details of this one contract, it would have prevented most of this fucking mess.

"Do you still need something, or was it an emergency situation that you miraculously found someone else to help you with?"

"I need to know where I can find your fake boss and his laptop tonight, especially if they'll be in separate places. I'm assuming his phone will be with him no matter what."

Atticus didn't respond for so long that if she hadn't heard Felix talking in the background, she would have thought Atticus had hung up on her.

"Um. Hello?"

"I heard you. I'm trying to figure out how stupid this will be."

"You could just ask."

"How stupid is it?"

"Stupid enough that you don't want details. Not so stupid that it could be traced back to Dio. Did he invite you out tonight?"

"This is a bad idea," Atticus confirmed.

"Yes. The worst. And you can get in the already long line of people who are going to tell me so when it's over. You'll retain full gloating rights for all of eternity."

"I can look into it Monday."

"I need it tonight."

Another pause.

With the patience and resignation of a parent giving up on their kid's bath time, Atticus sighed. "I'm not going to be able to talk you out of this, am I?"

"Many have tried. All have failed. You can't talk down a tornado."

"Maybe the tornado just needs to outline a little bit of her reasoning if she wants to get on her way."

It wasn't an unreasonable request. And it was Atticus.

"One: I suspect my girlfriend got doxxed because of Roday and I want to keep her safe. Two: I want to punish Roday for what he's done—the assaults and the doxxing. Three: no matter how else I fucked up with said girlfriend, I don't want to be framed for something I didn't do. Four: I'm mad. Five: I was planning to do it anyway. Six—"

Atticus laughed, coughed, and groaned. "Daphne, I think you skipped a couple important pieces of information."

"I'm on a deadline here. See back to points One, Two, Three, Four—"

"Okay, okay. I got stuck doing actual work yesterday. He came in around six. Left his laptop in his office. Forced me to go out with him. Strip club." Atticus paused to suck in a breath through his nose and groan it out in what was obviously a stretch. "He never got drunk enough for me to get away. Got home at five. Unless he's going back in today, the laptop is there without him. No idea if he's got anything planned for later."

Daphne brightened. "I can work with that. Thanks, Atticus. Text me if you know where he'll be tonight. I owe you."

"I'll add it to the tally."

She texted the criminal masterminds next.

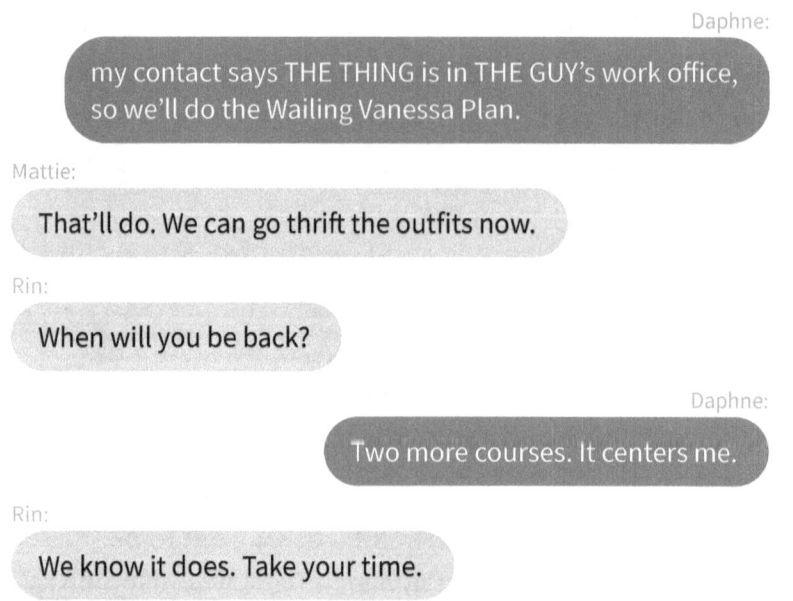

Daphne:

my contact says THE THING is in THE GUY's work office, so we'll do the Wailing Vanessa Plan.

Mattie:

That'll do. We can go thrift the outfits now.

Rin:

When will you be back?

Daphne:

Two more courses. It centers me.

Rin:

We know it does. Take your time.

And then there was Brad.

Brad:

Trying to plan my day, so let me know exactly what you need when.

Daphne:

Does my badge still work for YOU KNOW WHERE

Brad:

Yes, and it will through the week.

Daphne:

Can you give me a different name?

Brad:

Easily. Is that all you need?

Daphne:

That and have your burner phone close tonight in case I get in trouble

Brad:

Nobody chases trouble more than you.

Daphne:

And sometimes I even catch it!

Brad:

Make tonight not that night.

Daphne:

Does it not thrill you?

Brad:

Rushed, half-formed, high chance of failure? No.

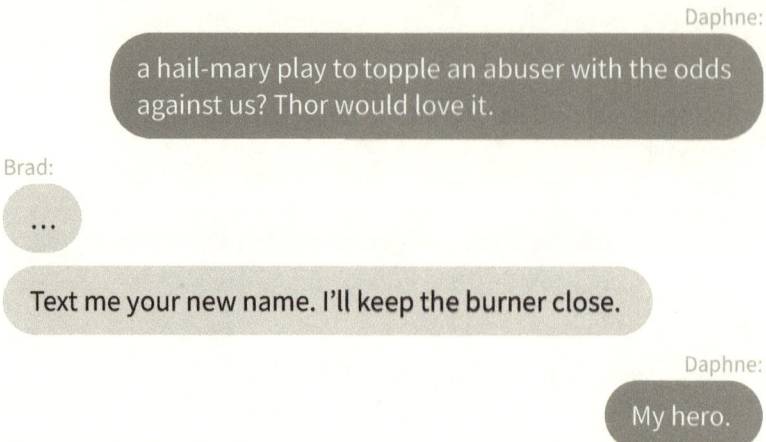

Now that they had more information and everyone was working on their part of the intrigue, Daphne was able to relax a fraction more. She might even be able to pull this off without Mattie or Rin finding out what she actually did for a living. They knew she loved being a part of whatever they cooked up, and that she was social and made lots of different kinds of friends, so hopefully it wasn't too suspicious that she knew people who could get sketchy stuff for them on short notice.

With the text app still open, she scrolled down to Cinnamon. The last few texts were from when she left BDMT early and wanted to celebrate the decision on marriage equality with Cinnamon. She'd never responded because, as Daphne had soon discovered, people who didn't know what they were talking about had told her that Daphne was responsible for ruining her life.

Cinnamon's last text was from Wednesday night, when Daphne had let her know she made it back to her place.

Cinnamon:

Cleaning my kitchen.

Daphne:

Gross. Do I need to come over there to stop you?

Cinnamon:

Then I wouldn't have a clean kitchen. Unless you were planning to clean it?

Daphne:

My mistake, please continue.

Cinnamon:

Don't you have to be up at 5:30 again tomorrow?

Daphne:

And Friday. But hopefully that will be the last time for a while.

Cinnamon:

I don't want to be responsible for you losing sleep.

Daphne:

Then I've got some bad news for you.

Cinnamon:

lol if I'm living rent free in your head, that's not my fault.

Daphne:

I believe you. But that doesn't change anything. In fact, I might lose LESS sleep if you were here…

Cinnamon:

Wow do you believe all of your own lies or?

Daphne:

Not a lie. Just a hypothesis. Wanna test it?

Cinnamon:

Always flirting.

Daphne:

By being sincere. Is that a no then :(

Cinnamon:

Get a few nights of 10+ hours of sleep, first. You need to be in your right mind when you make big decisions like that.

Daphne:

In that case I've got some more bad news for you.

Cinnamon:

I'll never tell you to eat your vegetables. I'll never force you to go hiking with me. I'll never shame you for your milkshake habit. But don't fuck with sleep. Seriously. It's the most important.

Daphne:

Yes mistress.

Cinnamon:

Hmm. Okay.

Daphne:

? Did I hit a nerve there?

Cinnamon:

We can talk about it later.

Daphne:

Ooooo I did! Cinnamon! We are going to have SO MUCH FUN. well, now I'm awake

Cinnamon:

I'll text you tomorrow. Night, Starlight.

Daphne blinked back tears and tapped the cursor to write a new text to her, but her thumbs hovered over the screen. What could she even say? Texting her wouldn't change anything. It would only make herself feel better for a moment, before she felt worse for trying to reach out when Cinnamon clearly didn't want to talk to her.

And besides that, if she did somehow clear her name on the doxxing thing, regaining Cinnamon's trust was going to be a process that would start with her giving Daphne another chance. That couldn't happen until Cinnamon knew for sure who really doxxed her.

Making the mature decision, Daphne put her phone away. She took a deep breath, recapped her water bottle, checked her equipment, and started walking to the next target. *A good mantra for this whole situation*, she thought. *One target at a time.*

***

The forest was anything but quiet. Birds and insects and people went about their normal day, singing or chirping or talking or hiking. The woods was its usual, seemingly unchanged, everyday self, but teeming with life and growth in ways that couldn't be seen during even the most leisurely of walks beneath its canopy.

Life went on. Even when Cinnamon's was in shambles.

She leaned against the wooden railing and peered into the undergrowth, moss and green ferns, reddish-brown earth and trunks. Midmorning sunlight struck small patches of clearing like illuminated museum dioramas missing the mannequins and narration. So her mind filled in her and Starlight for the dolls, and their argument for the voice-over.

Every emotion roiled just beneath her skin, fighting for supremacy, each achieving it for a moment before another took its place. Mostly, she let herself feel it all, even though it made her nauseous. But embarrassment kept elbowing its way up, and that was the one she would try to push back using the tools she offered to her clients. It wasn't her fault that she trusted the wrong person, and it wasn't her fault that that person had hurt her. Those were both Starlight's fault.

But why did Cinnamon trust her in the first place? What made her different from anyone else she'd met in the last decade? She'd known beautiful women. Confident. Good at their jobs. But being with Starlight felt like...everything would work out, but never how she expected it to. It was thrilling. There was a messiness, a shamelessness, a boldness. Like she could be counted upon to answer when Gondor called for aid. She might show up hungover, in sequins, and on a pig, but she'd be there. And she'd kick ass.

Maybe that was it, that Cinnamon had been attracted to her because she made real life feel like the best parts of a fantasy game. An adventure, but one where her heart was safe.

That was why the whole ordeal was tearing her apart. If she had suspected anything, if she had thought for a second that Starlight wasn't what she seemed, she would be able to point to it and tell herself, "Look. You knew." Instead, she was torn between "I never thought she would" and "but she did." She couldn't think of anyone else whose betrayal would surprise her as much as Starlight's.

There was no reason she should have felt so attached to her after only a week. But the most honest part of her that she didn't want to listen to said it hadn't taken that long at all.

If Cinnamon had to guess at Starlight's worst qualities, carelessness would have been number one, followed closely by entitlement. She had Daisy Buchanan written all over her. But her cruelty had been less obvious. That was what made it hurt so much.

"You're right," Echo said beside her, jarring her out of her introspection. They hadn't been in the middle of a conversation, and Cinnamon wondered if she had spoken her thoughts aloud. "I really should try to make it out here more. It's beautiful. I prefer more open spaces, but I can't deny the forest has a certain peacefulness."

Cinnamon looked back toward the trees, imagining worms writhing in the soil, the slugs, the butterflies she couldn't see but knew were there. The deer and foxes and turkeys, all trying to survive.

"It only looks peaceful because you don't see the struggles of the things that live here." Not overdramatic at all.

"Yikes," Echo said under her breath.

"Yeah. Sorry."

"Hey, if you can't wallow a little in front of your sister, when can you? I won't try to convince you that you'll heal with time, or that there's someone else out there for you. I will say that it's better you found out early. You weren't living together yet, no pets, no kids. This is the least messy it could have been."

If staring into the woods wasn't improving her mood, maybe changing scenery would. Cinnamon pushed away from the railing and nodded for Echo to follow her down the path. They walked in silence, as comfortable as possible when one of them was mourning the loss of a promising relationship and the other was the one who illuminated the problem.

"How sure are you that it was her?" Cinnamon had asked her a dozen times already. She just didn't find any comfort in the answer. It was easy for her to believe that Starlight had made a beeline to her computer for the reason she said: trying to find a way around Cinnamon's ethics so she could understand how to help her. It was less easy for her to believe the woman had leaked her personal information to the big, bad internet. Something about it didn't add up. Then again, Cinnamon didn't want it to.

"I mean," she continued, "I saw the video too. The picture from my computer. I'm not saying she's not guilty of *something*. But how do you know she's the one who leaked my information? And why...why do you think that would have anything to do with CT?"

Echo paused before answering, weighing her words. "I know you're not stupid. But I could explain everything that's going on with Cheung Technologies and it still wouldn't make sense unless you were steeped in years of experience. Not just in the company, but the industry, too." She glanced around, but the few other people on the walkway were too far away to hear. She lowered her voice anyway. "We've been anticipating something like this. Not with you specifically, but in general. This whole situation checks all the boxes. And despite the word 'technology' in our name, I'm not an expert in that aspect, though I've built a team I trust that is.

"I can get you a meeting with them if you want details. They can explain better than I can. Which means I don't know how well you would understand it, either." She paused, probably expecting the usual volley from her sister, but Cinnamon was too lost in thought.

Echo cleared her throat. "So. Are you coming to the dinner tonight? Do you want to, uh, hang out?"

Cinnamon blinked her way back to the conversation. "Do you?" she asked, surprised.

"Yeah, meimei. Of course."

She narrowed her eyes at her sister, measuring the likelihood that she meant it.

"I have—" She'd had a date with Starlight. Sushi. A reservation she'd made months ago, as though waiting for Cinnamon to appear in her life. "I'll be there tonight," she finished, sweeping the growing longing back into her subconscious.

"Oh good. I'm glad."

"I bet you are. It's Saturday night. Wouldn't you rather be on a date?"

"I will be. After the gala. I just have to meet him first."

"I don't know how you do it," Cinnamon admitted. "I don't know how anyone does it. Trust people serially, in quick succession. Enough to take them home, or leave with them, to share themselves so intimately, so quickly. I'm not slut-shaming," she emphasized. "I'm marveling at the confidence and self-knowledge someone must have to get to the place where they can assess a situation and within moments take a leap of faith in another person. You do it regularly with great success. I do it once and..."

"Mmm," Echo mused. "But am I happy?"

"Are you not happy?"

"I am. I just thought it would make you feel better if you thought I wasn't."

Cinnamon made a sound almost like a laugh. "That wouldn't make me feel better."

They were silent again, considering.

"I do what works for me for now," Echo said lightly. "If that changes in a month, or six, or a year, or whenever, then I'll do what works for me then. You have your own way of doing relationships. None of these ways are wrong. You found out that the woman you really liked was untrustworthy, but you aren't responsible for her. You're only responsible for yourself."

Is that true? She wondered. She knew she wasn't responsible for Starlight or anyone else in a parent or minder sort of way, and she didn't want to be. But there was a reason she got into health care, and it was to help people. That kind of responsibility, to care for others, was an important part of her life. Had it expanded into taking on other obligations, ones that she should have never shouldered?

Starlight's words from axe throwing echoed back to her, that with all that helping, Cinnamon must want to be a hero. Regardless of hero status, if Cinnamon was effectively helping people, that meant she had value.

And if she had value, that meant she wasn't broken, because broken things are useless.

She sucked in a breath. Her campaign to expose Roday may have sprouted from the desire to assist her clients, but had ended up consuming her entire life when it became the only way for her to feel validated, useful, whole.

And when it came to how she would achieve that, didn't she do something infuriatingly similar to what Starlight said *she* did? Saw someone struggling and used unethical means to bypass their reticence to "help" them without their permission or knowledge? If Starlight was telling the truth, she'd done it once. Cinnamon had been doing it continually for months. To several people. Who trusted her with their problems so much, they paid her. If someone had done *that* to Cinnamon...

The depth of the violation was staggering, and she reached out to steady herself against the fence post.

And all this time she thought Starlight was the hot mess.

"*Tt, whew*!" The call brought Cinnamon back to the present, the smell of the forest, the sharpness of pine needles. The birdsong bounced between the trees and she and Echo both looked up to find its source. It was a *tsk* of admonishment followed by a whistle of incredulity, repeated until the bird caught their eye and switched to a vulgar gargle of laughter directed at them.

"That's good luck," Echo said, pointing.

Cinnamon wiped her eyes and sniffled, angling her face so her sister couldn't see it. "Oh yeah? Then why does it sound like it's heckling me?"

"It's telling you to get out there and live your life. Survival requires boldness. Of course it's yelling at you."

They stopped and watched the jay as it hopped against a deep brown branch, stomping its feet like a toddler throwing a tantrum, mean strangling noise projected from its open throat. If it could, Cinnamon was sure, it would be pointing at her as it jeered. Still, it didn't feel hostile. More like a personal trainer whose brand was loud encouragement.

She couldn't change what'd happened between her and Starlight, but she could try to right a few of her own wrongs. All she had to do was channel the messiness and daring of the woman who'd broken her heart.

***

As a precaution, Cinnamon had deleted the AK app that Brad put on her phone, and she downloaded it again from the link that Echo had sent. There wasn't much to share to it anyway: the number of unsolicited messages and threats had dropped to nothing.

For one long day and one sleepless night, Cinnamon tortured herself trying to find answers to what Starlight actually got out of doxxing her. After all these hours, she arrived at the same conclusion again and again: *if* Starlight was the one who doxxed her, it was either because she had been working for Roday or his minions and wanted to tank Cinnamon's mental state to cast her credibility in doubt, or it was for the sex.

Alone in her home office, Cinnamon felt the bloom of heat in her cheeks. Thinking that the sex had been anything other than an honest, private delight compounded everything she was already feeling about being doxxed. Nobody could have known her deep and embarrassing insecurities about intimacy and romantic relationships. And nobody would have targeted them unless they were aiming to hurt. That was the main reason she suspected it was billionaire-sex-criminal related and not family-business-espionage related.

And the thing was—the really, really shitty thing was—the entire ordeal had absolutely no effect on her ability to bring Roday down. She was already at an impasse, unable to speak out unless she wanted to be sued for slander, unable to point to his victims unless she wanted to lose her license, and unable to produce any shred of meaningful evidence otherwise. If she hadn't been doxxed, her little investigation would still be finished. At this point, spreading her contact information around the internet was just adding insult to injury.

Her research into unmasking the man who'd preyed on her clients was a bust. She didn't know what, if anything, to do about Starlight, but she would give herself more time to think about it. That left her with the only other action that would make her feel better.

Cinnamon wrote up a loose script with bullet points of the most important things she had to say to her clients. A heartfelt apology. A pledge to do better. Asking what she could do to make things right. An explanation of why she had to cancel sessions for two days. Understanding if they didn't want to see her anymore. If they did, her office would be open again during the upcoming week. And finally, she'd ask if they wanted to be put in touch with the other clients who had experienced the same trauma.

If Starlight did something similar for her, would Cinnamon give her another chance?

She wanted to. But the hurt went too deep. Maybe, if she were telling the truth about what she had and hadn't done, Cinnamon could handle trying again. But indulging in the fantasy wouldn't achieve anything now.

She bent to her work, ready to make amends, intent on treating her clients and their needs with respect. It was what she should have been doing all along, instead of playing detective and avenger for a cause that wasn't her own.

It was a start.

Chapter Twenty-Two

The security checkpoint blinked green with a quick beep that sounded like a supermarket scanner, and Daphne walked through the metal arch with an inward sigh of relief. Her job at Diophantus didn't have her playing undercover very often, but it always thrilled her. The planning, the preparation, the improvisation when things didn't go right, the risk of getting caught. And, until this past week, the high of succeeding. Mattie and Rin had to agree, or they wouldn't all chase good trouble so often.

The guard on duty barely looked up at her, used to employees coming and going at hours that would be odd in a traditional office but was normal for a deadline-fueled tech company. Daphne schooled her expression anyway, not wanting to give away the buzz she got from getting away with something.

Her black boots echoed through the atrium as she made her way to the elevators, and her mind wandered back a week to her misnamed sneakers squeaking against the clean tiles of the basement laboratory at Makamerah. Of all the feelings the memory could have brought to the surface, Daphne was surprised that the clearest one was hope: hope that her current undertaking would win Cinnamon back so she wouldn't have to keep making disproportionate romantic gestures every week. She loved her capers, but she was getting tired of wasting them on continually abysmal ROI. Or ROR: Return on Romancement. Cinnamon had been the first and only crush that was worthy.

Daphne swallowed hard in an attempt to physically push down the rising feelings of regret and panic and Cinnamon.

Cinnamon.

In the reflective brass of the elevator doors, she picked at the soft bangs of her auburn wig and adjusted the white-framed glasses. She had half listened to Mattie's advice from last time. Last time, she had combined impressing a girl with pissing off her father, and wearing an entire outfit of reflective white to successfully liberate a lab animal from a secret basement was intended as an enormous "fuck you" to her dad. This time: black shoes, pants, long-sleeved shirt, dark wig, all for the stealthy part of her plan. Then, to disguise herself further and pass as an employee: fake glasses, peach headscarf and matching sweater, empty messenger bag.

The elevator arrived and she kept her head down as two men exited and passed her. She swiped her badge and pressed the button for the BDMT general employee break floor. Brad had changed the name on her badge but not the access, so it would have taken her anywhere except the executive floor. But it was better to start on a floor any employee would have a reason to visit. And she was going to have to take the stairs to Roday's offices anyway.

The phone in her pocket buzzed angrily, a foreign staccato from the cheap and oddly shaped flip phone. She remembered the camera placement in the elevator and waited to look at the text until she stepped out into the break room. All the lights were on, but nobody was there. It was Saturday night. Anyone still working would be doing only that until they could go home, not wasting time on the Teenage Mutant Ninja Turtles game and bowls of Froot Loops.

Vanessa:

> Vanessa and Fran in position. Awaiting signal.

Betty:

> hold for signal

Since there was a not-zero chance that any of them could be jailed for what they were doing, code names were a necessity. Fran—Rin—was dressed in the light blue polo and navy pants of building security, posing as one of them as she leaned next to an exit door by the main atrium, looking bored. Or she would be, if she were in position. Mattie, code name Vanessa, would be pacing the sidewalk in front of the building, sniffling and upset, in blue jeans and sneakers, an orange blouse, brown sweater, and oversized bag, waiting to launch into her act.

They were cutting it close, but Daphne needed it to be done yesterday, and she wasn't about to wait another two days for someone else to do it. And her dumb, too-evolved heart couldn't deal with the separation another minute. Breaking in, getting the info, getting it into the right hands, texting Cinnamon that she saved the day, convincing her to meet for their date, and making it to the restaurant in time for her reservation was ambitious but necessary.

Daphne weaved between the air hockey and foosball tables to a far nook with the least-used stairwell. It hadn't been updated with the rest of the offices when BDMT moved in, and the dingy walls, dim lights, and stale air gave a kind of murder-vibe she assumed people just naturally avoided. If she'd learned anything from scrutinizing their books the past week, it was that BDMT was cheap as fuck when it came to everyone else and extravagant when it came to their CEO's comfort.

That was fine. It suited tonight's purpose.

Halfway up her eight-floor climb, Daphne leaned against the wall to catch her breath. She should have taken Cinnamon up on that hiking thing. It still sounded awful. But it could have prepared her for this physical part of her plan. *Not after just one afternoon,* she told herself. *So that wouldn't have mattered.*

It would have been another afternoon with her, though. She should have known their time together would be cut short. It had felt too good to be true from the beginning. Different. Stable? For someone who thought every new date was The One, Daphne hadn't been sure she'd be able to sense the difference when—if—she found The Actual One. But looking back on the week, the difference was undeniable.

The thought of helping Cinnamon one last time (and in doing so possibly making it a continuation and not an end) fueled Daphne up the last few flights to the locked and alarmed door of the executive floor.

"Huh," she whispered. As cheap as BDMT was, Daphne had expected only a regular lock. None of her (sparse, last-minute) intel said anything about being connected to the alarm system. She pulled her phone back out and texted Mattie's burner: "Sad Vanessa a go in thirty seconds."

From another pocket, she brought out her lockpicking tools and started on the manual lock. If Brad had been an active part of her scheme, he would have been able to bypass the system for her. Instead, she had Mattie, and she smiled thinking of her sister and best friend downstairs, playing roles much different than Daphne's but equally important. Just like they'd always done.

Last tumbler in place, Daphne turned the knob and swung the door open, slipping inside as the alarm panel blinked red. It would send the alert to the security desk, but there was otherwise no indication she'd tripped the system, no flashing lights or siren. The girls would do what they could downstairs, but Daphne still had to hurry.

Thanks to a hastily drawn map of the floor that Atticus had sent her, Daphne found Roday's office quickly. He'd left the blinds open, and in the dim glow of the LEDS on the bar cart, she saw his laptop on the desk.

"I got you now, motherfucker," she said under her breath. The biometric lock was dark, deactivated months earlier when it stopped reading Roday's prints correctly, and had never been repaired. Maybe he'd done her a favor and left the whole thing unlocked. She tried the doorknob, but it wouldn't budge. No luck.

She had just gotten the second tumbler in place when the elevator at the end of the hall dinged its arrival and opened. Roday stepped out, loud on his phone, backlit by the slowly closing elevator doors.

"Son of a dick," Daphne murmured, scrambling away. His assistant's desk was just around the corner, minimalist and made of glass, and Daphne had to dive behind a white fuzzy chair to hide.

It wasn't difficult to hear his side of the conversation. He was the kind of guy who wouldn't think twice about having personal and inappropriate phone conversations at full volume in places like waiting rooms and school plays. Daphne peeked out from behind the chair. Roday tried his door and, finding it locked, grunted, and pulled the keys out of a sleek gray messenger bag that looked like it was made of seal skin. There was no reason to think it wasn't seal skin, and Daphne wrinkled her nose.

"I don't care, Vick, bus them in from a sorority. Have Jordan screen them. This shouldn't be my problem tonight, I told everyone what to do." Roday got the door open and turned on the overhead lights as he walked in. "Heh. I warned her. Can't take direction."

He passed by the desk and stopped in front of the bar cart, reaching into a drawer and pulling out a small yellow envelope.

"Tell me the boat is gassed up. Bars stocked." Roday paused as he slid the envelope into his jacket pocket. "I did my fucking part, and I did more than that, because I'm back in the fucking shithole of an office right now getting my own stash in case Brody fails in his job like the rest of you, so you get on the phone with Jessie or whoever the fuck is in charge now and if there's not a sorority's worth of girls when I get there, I'm taking my pills and I'm taking my pilot and I'm taking your fucking girlfriend and I'll have my own party, *bro*."

Daphne could hear the murmur of a quick apology, its speaker in enough of a panic over Roday's threat that his tone carried from the office to where she was hiding. Roday tapped the cart drawer closed, nodding and muttering as his friend continued talking. He walked back past his desk, not even sparing a glance at the laptop, flipped the lights off, shut the door, and left.

Either Mattie and Rin were an effective distraction, or Roday's arrival at the same time as Daphne's break-in gave the building's security an excuse to not investigate, because nobody else had come up to the floor since she tripped the alarm. She did a few calculations in her head and decided to stay hidden for another ten minutes before finishing her job and getting the data. Giving everyone who might interrupt her enough time to go away and stay out of her way.

"Fuck." The word bounced down the hall, and Daphne froze behind the chair, worried that he'd seen her. She could hear his footsteps coming closer.

"Forgot something. Look, I'll be there in a half hour...yeah, fuck you too." Keys rattled, and the office door opened again. Daphne stuck her head out to see what was happening as Roday entered the dark office, grabbed his laptop, and left again.

No, she thought, *no no no. What the fuck.*

She could tackle him. Hit him with something from behind and steal the computer. Cause a scene. Throw something at the wall so he'd come back and investigate, then grab it and run. Act hurt, lost, horny, to get him close...

None of that would work, but neither would wallowing in her indecision until he was back in the elevator, leaving.

"Shit," Daphne said, bursting from her hiding place as the elevator doors closed behind him. She ran down the hall and slid to a stop in front of the wall, frantically pressing the down button, willing another car to her floor as she watched the descending numbers above Roday's. She texted Rin as she waited, asking her to get Roday caught up in the scene, slow him down. When the muffled whoosh and electronic ding announced her car, she noted that he was on the fourth floor already, composed herself the best she could, and stepped into the elevator.

If only she had brought a decoy laptop, she could bump into him, they'd both drop their stuff, and she would take his. Or if the people she worked with had tried harder to get into his personal phone and email, she wouldn't have had to come up with increasingly absurd and drastic measures. The funny thing was, if Diophantus hadn't taken the job, it would have been easier for Daphne to recruit her coworkers to help her. But since it *might* be a conflict of interest with their client, her options were limited.

Limited to two amateur spies, basic-level security assistance from Brad, a map from Atticus, herself, and an appalling number of terrible ideas. And as she was well aware, the bigger the thing she had to improvise, the greater the chance of failure.

With her mind pinging in a dozen different directions, she hadn't formulated a plan by the time she got to the ground floor. Mattie's wailing was still going strong, echoing in the atrium and down the hall, and Daphne smiled. They hadn't been arrested yet.

As she turned the corner to pass by the security checkpoint again, she saw Roday leaving through the front doors. Mattie was sprawled on the floor, sobbing about a plant she left on her desk when she was fired earlier, three guards and undercover Rin standing over her. As much as she would have loved to watch their performance, her focus was on catching up to Roday. Dread spilled through her as she realized what she would have to do, and she took out her phone to text her friends it was time to go.

Betty:

I'm out. About to do something stupid. sorry

She texted Atticus next, as she watched Roday get into the back of a car and ride away. As soon as Atticus responded, she stuffed the phone, hair scarf, glasses, and sweater into the messenger bag and stashed the whole thing in the bushes. A panic crept up as Roday's car turned out of sight, and she had to reassure herself that she needed him to be a few minutes ahead of her. The third taxi she hailed finally stopped, and she thought back to the reflective jacket she wore at her last break-in. The cars would see her better to stop, but so would the people she was trying to hide from.

"St Francis Yacht Club," she told the driver, shutting the car door behind her. "And this is a weird question but, you guys still take cash, right?"

Chapter Twenty-Three

If the party at the Intermittent the previous Saturday was a celebration of chaos and possibility, the Cheung Family Gala one week later was an expensive reminder of order and responsibility. Cinnamon heard the ripple of voices and clinking silverware over the string quartet before she entered the room and remembered its theme that hadn't changed in twenty years just before she turned the corner and saw it again for herself. It had been so long since she attended, she had called Echo earlier in the evening and asked what she should wear. "Red," she answered quickly and hung up. So Cinnamon had shrugged and put on her sleeveless, poppy-colored silk midi dress with the lace shoulders and a pair of tan and gold heels.

Cinnamon didn't think Echo had deliberately led her astray. But once she stood awash in red lighting, she gave serious thought to going home to change. This was the event that always reminded her of the end of *Carrie:* the red lighting, red tablecloths, massive red planters with arrangements of red flowers. Wide Tuscan columns lined the hall, reaching to a ceiling several stories above them, and marking the sunken exhibit behind them where Claude lived. There was a good chance that she could walk through the room invisibly, her dress another tablecloth, her body a trick of the carmine light.

Should have worn black.

She nodded and smiled politely at the people she saw as she crossed the room, faces that were slightly more aged than the ones her memory plucked out of dusty bins and held up to her with a question mark. She remembered them from five, ten, twenty years before, looking old even then, to her child eyes.

Hong and Min Cheung were the easiest to find, at the center of the room, in the middle of a group of laughing, well-dressed guests. Cinnamon paused at the outskirts, wondering if they'd notice her, since she was the same color as the walls. Her parents were impeccably attired in a perfectly tailored black suit (dad) and long-sleeved dress with wide, gold slashes (mom). They had clearly remembered what the event hall would look like.

"Oh," her mother said, gesturing. "Of course, you all remember our younger daughter, Cinnamon."

She walked into the circle to a chorus of murmurs: they remembered her from years ago, of course, she looked unchanged, what was her secret? She smiled at them, unsure what to say, out of practice in dealing with groups of people she had to impress.

"Thank you all for coming," she said. "You're too kind. And it's so nice to see your lovely faces again. None of you have aged a day."

That got the round of laughter she was hoping for, and as the group protested and began talking among themselves, Cinnamon's mother leaned over and whispered in Mandarin, "Did Echo tell you to wear red?"

Luckily, the hue of the overhead lights hid her embarrassed blush, and she nodded as she glanced around the room, looking for said sister.

"You should have called me instead," Min said in English. "I would have looked out for you."

"I want to think it wasn't mean-spirited," Cinnamon said. "She's had a lot on her mind recently."

"So have you, Little Spice."

One of the tuxedo-clad men stepped up to Min then, taking her hands in greeting, and Cinnamon turned to her dad. "Your friend couldn't make it," he said. A statement, a little sad.

He had made it easier for her to open up to him, thanks to their heart-to-heart a few days before, but she still wasn't sure what to tell him. What would feel right, what was the truth, what wouldn't trigger an ugly-cry breakdown the moment her mouth tried to form the words. But her father knew this wasn't the place for that kind of conversation. He just wanted to let her know that he saw.

"No," she said, finally. "She couldn't make it."

It was after eight. Their reservation at the sushi place wasn't for an hour, and Cinnamon wondered what it might take for her and Starlight to reconcile and get there in time. Starlight would have to use her uncanny tracking skills to find the gala, take a car out here, find the chameleon that was Cinnamon, prove that she wasn't the one who doxxed her and convince Cinnamon to give her another chance, kiss and make up, then take a car over to the restaurant.

It sounded impossible to pull off and unlikely to happen anyway, but if anyone could do it, it would be Starlight.

Her father rested a hand on her shoulder, and Cinnamon realized they had been standing in silence for too long.

"Go on and get something from the buffet," he said, nodding toward the long table before leaning in closer. "There are plenty of options that aren't seafood," he whispered, giving her a wink and a gentle pat on the shoulder.

Yes, that man saw entirely too much.

She wanted to give Starlight time to get to her, even though it was a stupid desire that was causing a sensation like indigestion.

She'd make the rounds, have a drink, find Echo, and hit the buffet at nine if she was still there.

The Swamp hall of the California Academy of Sciences wasn't so big that she couldn't find her sister, hidden behind a pillar near Claude's enclosure and wearing a floor-length, one-sleeve dress made out of a crinkled and shiny black material Cinnamon couldn't name. With her hair pulled back, she looked like a movie star, descended from her heights to grace the commonfolk with her presence. Cinnamon had the passing thought that if her sister had worn her hair down, she would have looked like a Chinese Morticia Addams.

"Damn, meimei, if you didn't want to come, you could have stayed home," Echo said with a wince. "You don't have to camouflage yourself to hide from the guests."

"That's pretty funny, since you were the one who told me to wear red."

Echo gave her a patronizing smile. "I would never—wait. Was that why you called me earlier?"

Cinnamon raised her eyebrows in assent.

"Shit, I'm sorry, Little Spice." Echo puffed out a breath. "To be fair, I was trying to last-minute coordinate all of this, but yeah. It's my fault. Sorry I ninja'd you."

"They're going to think I'm another table. Or part of the entertainment."

"Nobody's going to mistake you for the entertainment when our favorite chonky boi is right here." Echo walked to the railing and looked down at Claude. Claude did his best impression of an albino alligator who didn't care what Echo Cheung thought of him.

"Hello, sweet boy," Cinnamon whispered. Their parents had been major donors to CAS for years, and of the many memorable behind-the-scenes tours they'd taken, anything having to do with Claude was Cinnamon's favorite. Introducing Starlight to him was supposed to have been the highlight of the night.

She glanced at her watch. Nearly eight thirty. Starlight was cutting it close if she wanted to make a grand gesture and celebrate with sushi. It had been one day, six hours, and thirty-two minutes since she last saw her.

"Ying-Li is here somewhere," Echo said.

Cinnamon snorted lightly and shook her head. "How is it that every time I'm thinking of Daphne, you mention Ying-Li?"

"You get a look in your eye that's wistful and sad, and I want to bring you back to a reality you can grab on to. I'm not pushing romance, but she seems steady and grounded."

"What is she doing here, anyway?" Cinnamon allowed herself a little bit of petulance.

"Oh, has it been so long that you mistook this for a party? It's an *event*, Cinnamon, for recognizing and renewing our strongest business ties, and cultivating the less strong ones. If you don't want to see her for personal reasons—if you're somehow mad at her for being the one to expose Daphne—you can pack that in for the evening and do your family a favor by treating her like you would any of the other two hundred or so guests here."

It did feel wrong that Ying-Li had been the one to expose Starlight, and Cinnamon knew that wasn't a rational feeling. But everything else about Ying-Li that irritated her all added up to a discomfort that she couldn't shake. She could deal with it for an evening if that's what it took. If she wasn't expected to be anything beyond polite and friendly.

"For you, Echo, I'll do my best. But I'm not going to be spending time with her after tonight, and it'll be up to you to keep the connection. And you owe me."

"I'll bring you to Paris in September," she vowed, hand over her heart. "I'll even pay you for your time tonight, if you want."

Cinnamon grunted and pushed away from the railing with a wave to Claude and a promise to herself that she would return to him before she left. "Just stop meddling in my love life."

"Get a love life and I'll stop meddling," Echo countered.

Another slow walk around the hall, and Cinnamon found Ying-Li back by the Reception Desk, talking with a young white guy in a suit. She looked stunning—more polished than Cinnamon had thought possible—in high-waisted dress pants that might have been a dark blue or plum, and a gold lamé blouse that was daringly open until it met the top of the pants in a plunging neckline.

Ying-Li didn't notice Cinnamon right away, laughing with the suited guy as Cinnamon approached in her accidentally stealthy outfit. It was only when the guy looked up and stuck out a hand to her in greeting that Ying-Li acknowledged her.

"Gerou, this is Cinnamon Cheung. Of Cheung Technologies. Gerou is the CEO of LabLabs."

"All the other lab-adjacent names were taken," he said with a mock sheepishness, shaking her hand. "But a 'lab' is also a type of bean, so we have the bean angle for marketing, and the repetition makes us memorable. What's your role at Cheung Technologies?"

"Daughter," Cinnamon said without hesitation. It had been her go-to answer years ago, and it was all coming back to her. Gerou laughed. Ying-Li looked around the hall with an air of boredom but finally nodded toward Cinnamon's empty hands.

"No drink?" she asked over her own cocktail glass. "Beer? Champagne? I'll get it."

"Champagne would be great."

She raised her glass in acknowledgment and went to fetch the drink.

"So. Gerou." One-on-one Cinnamon could do. After all, it was literally what she got paid for. "How do you know Ying-Li?"

"Oh, we've worked together on a lot of projects. LabLabs is just my most recent investment, but if—when—we need a fixer, I'm calling her first. These kind of ventures, they always end up needing someone like her." He shrugged and sipped his beer. "I'm sure you know how it is."

"Yeah, she helped me with some computer security issues the other day."

"Exactly. Like, it's like the way a private detective can get away with doing things that cops can't. Well, clean cops, anyway. The breaking in, the bugs and cameras and stuff, but then the malware and spyware too. I'd call her an artist, but she'd hate that."

Cinnamon's discomfort from earlier began creeping back in, more insistent, and with questions this time.

"It sounds like you've worked with her a lot more than I have." She kept her tone light and glanced around to make sure Ying-Li wouldn't take her by surprise. "If I wanted to hire her for something—something that I can't talk about, you know—would you say she's worth it? Like, has she ever messed up so bad that it compromised your entire business? I won't tell her you told me, I'd just like an honest review." She added the last part hurriedly, giving him a wink so he knew she was cool.

"Swear to god, nobody's better." He laughed and crossed his heart. "And if she's ever made any mistakes, you wouldn't know it, because everything works out in the end. One hundred percent success rate."

"Good to know." She joined in his laughter. "I wouldn't want to hire someone who would, like, accidentally put their own email address in when they meant to put the client's, you know? Rookie mistake like that."

"Nah, she's the real deal. If Cheung Technologies doesn't have their own guy to do it, she's good at hiding code. But hey—don't send her after LabLabs, all right? That's the deal. I share the weapon, and you don't use it on me."

"Truly, I wouldn't dream of it."

Ying-Li returned from the bar looking more put out than before, while Cinnamon and Gerou carried on like old friends. She took the flute of wine with a smile and turned back to Gerou.

"I'm surprised you're out," Ying-Li said. "With the death threats and all. She was doxxed on Thursday," she explained to Gerou.

"Oh," he said, looking between the two women. "That's—that sucks. I'm sorry to hear that. You know, Ying-Li is good about preventing things like that—"

"It happened *after* she set up the security on my computer," Cinnamon said, keeping the smile plastered on her face. "Never had that problem before, then, two days after Ying-Li works on my desktop, bam! Dudes who want to rape and kill me know every single way to find me."

"Where are you staying now?" Ying-Li pushed on. "I saw the security in front of your house, but that wouldn't stop someone motivated."

Gerou glanced between them again and shuffled past. "Cinnamon, it was a pleasure meeting you. Ying-Li." He nodded and left.

Cinnamon turned sharply to face Ying-Li head on. "Did you come to my parents' event tonight to share their daughter's personal problems with a stranger?"

"Lighten up, Little Spice," Ying-Li drawled, and Cinnamon's face warmed. "I'm here on business, and Gerou was getting too friendly with you. Now he knows we're on high alert for shady behavior."

Even if Cinnamon thought that were true, someone who knew the importance of safety and security shouldn't give anyone more information about her than they needed.

"Actually, we're back to low alert. I've been un-doxxed."

Ying-Li turned back to her curiously, meeting her eyes for the first time that night. "What the fuck does that mean?"

"Thought you'd be happy about it. My info is off the web. Harassment has trickled down to the same levels as—as before." Cinnamon had to stop herself from saying exactly what the turning point had been in the uptick of trolls. "And I guess, if someone posts it again, it gets deleted quickly enough that it doesn't get any traction."

"I don't know who told you that, but they lied. It's impossible."

"Echo got a team who did it for me." She didn't want to mention Starlight or Brad.

"No. No way." Ying-Li shook her head, placed her glass on a tall table, and brought out her phone. "If someone sees their post is gone, they'll just repost it. And plenty of people already have what they need, even if it's been removed. What did they do, exactly? Did they put something on your phone? Home computer?"

Cinnamon shrugged. "You know I don't know anything about that kind of stuff. But if they worked on my home computer, you would already know, right? Since you set it up for the camera to take a picture of everyone who logs in, and send it to you, instead of me."

Ying-Li frowned at her phone as her fingers flew across the screen. "Seriously, what's your problem? I already apologized for that."

"The problem is, it's weird that when you set it up and we tested it, I got the email immediately. But I didn't get them when I logged in afterward, and I didn't even think of it because I wasn't used to it."

"It's not weird," she said, still staring at the screen. "It was a mistake in the set-up. It only seems weird because you wouldn't understand it even if I explained it to you. But thanks for bringing it up again and making me feel like shit."

Cinnamon had been drawing out the conversation to give her brain time to unravel some things and put together others, and as she took a breath to give Ying-Li another verbal poke, she paused, mouth open, eyes going unfocused as her beautiful subconscious presented her with the fruits of its labor.

There were two reasons why someone would have set up her computer to send a login picture to a different email address. First, to pinpoint exactly when Cinnamon was in her office. And second, to prevent Cinnamon from seeing who else might try to log on to her personal computer. If, like Starlight, someone she trusted and invited into her home waited until she was occupied in another part of the house and tried to log in, she would never know.

Had she come up with the idea for it, or had Ying-Li? She'd been upset, thrown off by her unexpected visit, making herself at home uninvited. If Ying-Li needed to know what security measures were in place, she had to ask, and in asking, risked Cinnamon getting someone else to set it up. Better to do it herself and ensure the person receiving any evidence against her was, well, her.

Ying-Li knew there were no trade secrets on her computer. Nothing about Cheung Technologies proprietary IP, officers, partners, accounting, plans. She did, however, have a hoard of evidence in a trail that led from a number of abuse victims to Collin Roday.

Despite the orderly fashion in which her brain trotted out her initial revelation, chaos quickly took over, and everything it revealed fought for her attention all at once: Ying-Li had doxxed her. She'd used Cinnamon's flight to go into her house under the cover of friendship and concern. She probably found and copied everything she had on Roday and his crimes. Then, she had the good fortune to catch Starlight's unfortunate hacking and saw the opportunity to point the finger away from her for good. Gerou said she was a fixer, like a PI, willing to fight dirty. Had Roday hired her himself? Or was it just his idolaters? Starlight hadn't doxxed her.

Starlight hadn't doxxed her.

The thought pierced her panic and dread with relief, then grief, then hope, then grief again. She had to talk to Starlight. And she had to tell Echo about Ying-Li.

"It doesn't make any sense." Her voice sounded far away, like she was watching someone else speak.

"It wouldn't," Ying-Li said, thinking Cinnamon was speaking to her. "One misplaced character can mean the difference between a smooth-running program and critical failure."

"No, I mean, Daphne. Why would Daphne wait until after she got into my computer to dox me? She already had all my information."

"I don't know. Maybe she didn't need you anymore and it was just a parting shot."

"But that kind of aggression, that's personal," Cinnamon continued. "I can't imagine I did anything so bad that she would advertise my personal information—"

"Cinnamon, shut up." It was a bark, sharp enough to cut through the music and conversation, and the people closest to them turned to look. Ying-Li had finally turned away from her phone, and her gaze burned into Cinnamon. "You've been kicking hornets' nests across the internet and dragging good men through the mud, and you think you haven't done enough for someone to want to track you down, share where to find you so others can track you down, and shut you up themselves?"

The shift in Ying-Li's expression was subtle enough that someone paying less attention would have missed it, but Cinnamon was looking for it: the realization that she had said too much, given too much away. And Cinnamon must have reacted to it, too, because Ying-Li started, looked at her like she'd never seen her before, and shoved her phone into a pocket. She turned to walk away, but Cinnamon grabbed her by the arm and pulled her back.

Whatever Ying-Li saw in her eyes surprised her. It would. Cinnamon had been playing nice for weeks. Making friends at her family's insistence even though they didn't click. Hiding her feelings and opinions in case Ying-Li disagreed enough to sever her business relationship with CT. The entire time, she was the mark. But Ying-Li had tipped her hand.

Which meant Cinnamon Cheung didn't have to play nice anymore.

"What did you do?" Cinnamon growled, her fingers digging into Ying-Li's bicep. She tried to twist out of her grip, but she had no idea how strong Little Spice was. She never had.

"You. Vile. Snake. What did you do to me?" Louder this time, people turning to look, and a growing panic in Ying-Li's eyes.

Instead of trying to answer, she stepped in closer, catching Cinnamon off guard, and Ying-Li used that advantage to send Cinnamon toppling to the floor. Despite grabbing her arm first, she hadn't expected a physical fight, and the shock of it left Cinnamon paralyzed. Gasps echoed close by, and several party-goers moved in to see if she needed help.

Ying-Li saw her opportunity. "You're drunk," she said, pausing to down the last of her cocktail and readjust her blouse. "You want to start a fight, and I'm not here for it." She turned on her heel and stormed away, faster than appropriate at this type of event, and Cinnamon gave herself a moment to gather her wits before scrambling back on her feet and chasing her across the hall as fast as the packed room would allow.

Echo had been so paranoid about someone sabotaging the company through Cinnamon, and there was Ying-Li. She told Echo several times that they weren't compatible. There was the way Ying-Li acted at dinner. And Echo brushed it off every time. Gerou was right. Cheung Technologies did need a new security person, if Echo let this slip past.

As if thinking of her conjured her, Echo stepped in front of Cinnamon and grabbed her arms. She wasn't watching where she was going, besides following Ying-Li, and hadn't realized she was so close to her sister.

"Little Spice?"

Echo hadn't moved from her spot by Claude—it had only been a few moments, even though it felt much longer, a lifetime ago when Cinnamon was young and stupid—but she had attracted a large group of guests.

"Jiejie," she said, her voice firm but more gravelly than it should be.

More people pressed in, trying to get in position to see the alligator or hear their conversation, Cinnamon didn't know, so she switched to Mandarin.

"Ying-Li doxxed me. She just said as much. It isn't about the business, and there's no time to explain what it *is* about, so you just have to believe me. She ran out. I think she's leaving. I don't know what I have for evidence, so I don't know if we could even prosecute her. I didn't think she would hurt me, but now I don't know—"

Echo already had her phone out and was rapidly firing orders to the security detail, still in Mandarin. The gathered group looked at her curiously, and she paused to smile at them.

"A friend left her purse," she told them in English. "We're trying to catch her before she leaves. Just one of the many benefits of doing business with the Cheungs."

The party laughed, Echo took Cinnamon's hand, and the girls made a beeline to the exit Ying-Li had taken. They stopped just inside the door.

"I have to find her," Cinnamon said, about to push her way outside.

"I know," Echo said, tugging her back. "I know you want revenge by your own hands and believe me, I understand. But let me do this for you. Let me send my enormous security boys to do this for you. I don't want you getting hurt, and depending on how much Ying-Li doesn't want to get caught, you could get very hurt."

Cinnamon looked outside, scanning the area for Ying-Li, and rubbed the spot on her hip that was going to bloom into a nasty bruise later. She nodded and glanced at her sister, and couldn't remember her looking this angry before. Not even when she'd thought Starlight was the one who'd doxxed her.

Oh god, Starlight.

"I have to call Daphne," Cinnamon murmured, bringing out her phone.

Echo hadn't let go of her hand yet, and she squeezed it. "You just uncovered the real villain like we're at the end of an episode of Scooby-Doo, and you want to call your ex-girlfriend?"

"I appreciate you believing me," she said instead of answering the question. "I'll explain in detail later, I promise. Everything got out of hand because I'm not a detective and I'm not qualified or trained and I didn't protect myself as well as I should."

"Meimei," Echo said firmly. "What's this called in therapy?"

"A breakthrough?"

"Victim blaming."

"Oh. No. Maybe. What I meant was, you were right to worry about me. And if I told you what I was getting into, you might have been able to protect me. I accused the woman I love of betraying me. And now she's out there thinking I hate her for something she didn't do, and I don't even hate her for what she *did* do, and I have to apologize and tell her I know she didn't dox me. What's wrong? Why is your face doing that?"

Echo's grin had an unmistakable alligator vibe. "You love her," she said.

Cinnamon rewound their conversation in her mind.

"You said 'the woman I love,'" Echo repeated. "You love Daphne."

"Well of course I do," Cinnamon said, like her own brain wasn't telling her *You do, wow, you love her, you love her, you should have known, find her, get her, tell her, tell her now.* "And of course you're going to make fun of me for it."

"Never." Her sister reached out to grasp her with both hands. Cinnamon had never seen her so serious. "And you should have told me."

"I...didn't know," she said lightly. "I didn't even tell her."

Her sister's expression softened and she squeezed her hand again.

"We still have the photo of her. In your office."

"I know," Cinnamon said. Compared to giving internet trolls her home address, lockpicking her office door and logging into her computer seemed almost forgivable. "She had an explanation, and it seemed believable."

Echo's walkie app crackled and a male voice came through, saying they had Ying-Li and were escorting her to the security office.

"Can we even detain her?" If recent events were any indication, Cinnamon had no idea what lawfulness looked like. "I don't know what kind of evidence there is."

Her sister smiled again, this time her expression full of promise and mischief and illegal intent. "Don't worry about that. There's the legal system, and then there's the justice of the business world." Yeah, Echo made a much better business leader than Cinnamon ever would. Her expression changed, from ruthless mogul to older sister. "I won't make you stay if you don't want to, but I don't think you should be alone. I don't think you should try to contact Daphne, either—don't interrupt me—you've had a shock, and I'm sure your mind is chaos right now. Humor your jiejie and wait a day. Let me see what I can get out of Ying-Li first, before you go running to someone who, at the very least, blew past your reasonable boundaries with reckless abandon."

It was sound advice. But when the brick had shattered her front window and she'd run out the back door of her house, getting to safety had been her primary thought, and it'd brought her to Starlight. Her heart was racing with the same panic, telling her, again, to get to Starlight. Cinnamon wasn't sure she could be reasonable now.

"I think I'll just go home." Her voice sounded strangled.

"I'll get you a car," Echo said, letting go of Cinnamon's hands to make the call.

Nearly nine o'clock. Cinnamon was exhausted. Hungry. Heart-sick. She should have gone home. Instead, when the car picked her up, she gave them directions to the Manu Ono pop-up. It wasn't technically trying to contact Starlight, since Echo had asked her not to. If Starlight happened to be there, well. It wasn't like Cinnamon had called or texted her.

It didn't matter. Starlight wasn't there. Cinnamon took the table anyway, nursing the small hope that she was just running late. It didn't occur to her that Starlight might show up with another date, or that she wouldn't show up at all. The dinner had been on her radar for months, and if Cinnamon knew Starlight at all, she knew that she wouldn't miss sushi.

She missed the sushi.

Cinnamon ordered, and ate, and ordered more to go. She told herself it was too good not to, that she would eat it for breakfast. All the while, she thought about what she actually wanted from Starlight. What could be enough for her to re-open the door to the trust that Starlight had—as Echo so perfectly put it—blown past with reckless abandon?

When she got home, she put the sushi in the fridge, cried until her eyes were too puffy to open, slept fitfully, and hoped the woman she loved was having a better night than she was.

Chapter Twenty-Four

Daphne crouched in a dark corner at the back of the ship, clutching the metal railing and trying not to vomit. Every time she thought she had figured out the rhythm of the swaying, an unexpected wave would jostle everything out of time, the boat would bounce, her insides would clench, her skin would grow clammy, and she would have to fight to hold down whatever liquids and solids were preparing to make a reappearance.

And the yacht was still at the dock.

Why did it have to be boats? She tried breathing through her mouth. The brine and bitterness of the ocean didn't bother her normally, but somehow, combined with the irregular pushes and pulls of gravity, the smell triggered her motion sickness as much as the motion did. The thought of going out even farther into the ocean scared her more than getting caught. So she held tight and prayed that yacht parties thrown by rich, entitled douchebags usually stayed in dock, and didn't go out into choppy international waters to do things that would otherwise be illegal closer to land.

Daphne had to admit that this improvisation sucked. Not only because it might not work, or because she was on a boat for thirty seconds and already seasick, or because she was in danger, but because she didn't think they would hold her reservation at the Manu Ono sushi pop-up restaurant.

That was the thought that motivated her to try to stand and get this thing over with. If she missed the sushi for a failed mission?

She would be pissed. If she missed the sushi but got evidence of Roday's multitude or wrongdoings? *Worth it*. Her stomach writhed again. *In theory*.

"Christ," she muttered, wobbling as she stood, grateful Rin had talked her into sturdy boots. She patted her pockets to make sure the few items she brought were secure. Cash, lockpick set, USB drive in a thick rubber casing. Nothing that could identify her. No phone that could be tracked. It was just her, her noble goal, her wild ideas, her stubbornness, and her sensitive tummy. No problem.

She had arrived at the docks moments after Roday and hung back in the shadows to watch him. Three guys had been waiting on the jetty, including Jared from BDMT, and they hailed their leader with beers when he approached. They were too far away to be heard, but Roday took a beer and a cigarette and led two of them back on the boat. The last guy stayed on the dock, playing on his phone, his back to the vessel and the approaching Daphne.

She took advantage of that confidence, the distraction, the dark harbor, and her stealthy outfit, and snuck on board. The name plastered on the back of the ship was *Alphallic Envy*, and when she sussed out what it meant, she gave a tired shake of her head. One day, she wouldn't have to put up with entitled man-children, but today was not that day.

The walkway led to a door below decks, and with the first minor lurch, she went into the wall, the sweat of sickness beginning to prickle over her skin. Music thumped from deeper in the boat. The floor dipped and her stomach turned inside out, threatening to turn *her* inside out. No one was in the hall to stop her, so she clung to the wall and took a set of narrow stairs up to an open deck and fresh air.

After achieving a quiet corner in the dark, an open railing for when she threw up, and five minutes of gulping the cool and balmy air, she was ready to get on with it the best she could. But as she began walking toward the door that led below, to the terrible men and many girls—if Roday got his way—and the isolated data that would help Cinnamon bring that criminal down, the boards beneath her rumbled. And as the yacht made its slow path out of the wharf and toward the open sea, its gentle turn wasn't gentle enough to stop Daphne from finally throwing up.

She made it to the side of the boat. Mostly.

"Son of a dick, Daphne," she moaned as she slumped onto her knees, wiping her mouth. "Your ideas are shit. I'm never listening to you again."

"Oh nooooo, you poor thing!"

Her head snapped up. Daphne hadn't heard the barefoot woman approach over her own vomiting. Young, college-age, and wearing a short pink dress with spaghetti straps. One hand grasped her phone lightly, and the other gripped a bottle of beer.

"The trick is to drink so much that you don't care when you throw up." The girl hiccupped and shrugged, tossing back her hair to get the bottle to her lips without interference. "You just...haven't had enough to drink."

Daphne stared at her miserably as the idea came to her, and she told her body to be cool for a minute. "You know," she said, forcing herself to giggle. Using her abdomen muscles like that wasn't a great idea, but she pushed on. "You're totally right. But there's no beer here. Do you know where the beer is?"

The girl perked up, happy to be of service, and she held out the bottle to Daphne while reaching with her phone-occupied hand to help her up. How was it possible a drunk twenty-year-old had better balance than her? Daphne rinsed her mouth with the beer and spit it over the side to follow what she was trying to lose the taste of. She swallowed the next sip for courage, letting some spill down her chin onto her clothes.

"You're so pretty," the girl murmured, reaching a hand out to pat Daphne's wig and missing because her eyes were closed.

Daphne took her hand and sighed. "Did you come here with someone? Some girl friends?"

"Mmm. Boyfriend."

Daphne scrunched her nose. The boat turned a little more sharply and she shuffled to keep her balance. It wasn't that bad, but she was so sensitive to even the smallest movement.

"You came up here to get some fresh air, right? It's starting to smell like boys down there."

"Like boys do they even shower? They shower with the (*hiccup*). And girls have to shower because they smell too. My shower has a duck on it." She nodded like she had made a very good point.

"My shower has a duck on it too," Daphne lied, steering the girl to a secure-looking bench with cushions.

The girl gasped. "Ohmygod iss the same shower." She sat when Daphne gently set her down, and she let Daphne put her legs up so she was lying on her side. "I want a boat ride."

It was easy enough to find a pillow for her, and more cushions and pillows to hide her under. No rolling overboard, no choking if she vomited, and hidden from anyone who might see an opportunity to harm her. Not bad, considering what she had to work with.

"You got a boat ride. It's so nice, the waves rocking you to sleep." She stuffed another pillow behind the girl to keep her on her side. "Sleepy time, okay? I'll bring you some water if I can." The girl mumbled something, but she was already well on her way, and Daphne walked around to make sure she wasn't immediately noticeable from any angle.

The beer had been for show, and she didn't expect it to help with the nausea, but she did feel better after that sip. Whether it was real or in her head, Daphne didn't care.

A strand of music reached up to her through the stairwell, loud and driving, its bass joining the tremors from the engine. She didn't need a guide after all, following the noise below and to a large room at the front of the ship where dozens of people danced and drank and shouted conversations on low couches. Women outnumbered men three to one, easily, but Roday and his laptop were nowhere to be seen.

Even if she had brought the girl back with her, Daphne wouldn't have been able to blend in. No one else wore all black, because no one else was a stowaway trying to steal shit. And none of the other women wore full-length sleeves and pants. Or boots. Before going in, she tucked the bottom of her shirt up into her bra and rolled the waist of her pants down as much as she could, to show some midriff. She definitely wasn't as fit as the other girls, but that was from enjoying food with her friends. Like Cinnamon's croissants.

At the thought, she smelled those ham and cheese croissants again and remembered Cinnamon smiling at her, and her heart lurched in sorrow, quickly followed by her stomach lurching in protest, and she shook the memory out of her head before she threw up again.

Heist first. Love after. Snacks somewhere in between.

Hesitancy was what would attract attention more than anything, so Daphne strode into the room with a confidence she didn't quite feel but could easily fake. She moved from group to group, miming sips from her bottle, joining one group dancing, interrupting another to ask about Roday. Eventually, she made her way to the sunken area with couches and comfortable footstools.

The DJ turned down the music enough to make some kind of announcement, and in the relative quiet, everyone's conversations became loud. She heard the name "Vick" from a group of three guys to her right, and when the music came up again, she approached them.

"Hey," she said to no one in particular, sloppily leaning against the back of their couch. "Which one of you is Vick?"

The three of them checked her out, sneering a little at her outfit, but one of them raised his hand.

"I'm Vick," he said. "You okay, sweetheart? You look a little rough."

"A girl told me that you would know where to find Collin Roday." She let her eyes flutter closed and leaned harder into her hand. "She said, 'Vick would know, he always knows evthing I ask him.'"

Vick sat up straighter and smoothed his polo. "Was it Caroline? Caroline said that?"

Daphne opened her eyes and mouth in shock. "That's it! She's right. You knew. Oh. But do you know where Roday is?"

"His room. But honey, I'm not sure you're his type...well, never mind. 'Drunk' is one of his types." The guys laughed, and Daphne laughed with them, braying and snorting as annoyingly as possible. "Two decks below and just under us. There's a plaque. You're not so drunk you forgot how to read, are you?"

Daphne snickered and patted him on the head as she turned to leave. She stumbled a little, on purpose, but her belly didn't know that, and she had to lean against a column. A little beer helped her get this far. A little more might get her to the end. She took another real sip, a small one, remembering her stomach was totally empty.

This time, as she wound through the hallways, she encountered a number of people, partygoers and crew and staff alike. Instead of going straight to Roday's room, she took herself on a little tour of the ship, for recon. Late and incomplete, but better to do it first than to get caught and not know where to run or hide. They were on their way out to the ocean, it wasn't like Roday and his computer would somehow escape, so she made possibly the first smart decision of the evening and wandered, memorizing the deck plans. No one stopped her and no one bothered her. The half-full beer bottle and the motion sickness that could be mistaken for drunkenness were an excellent cover.

It was quieter when she got down to where Roday's room should be, the music a soft heartbeat. The press of the ship around her and the ocean below buffeted her from the world like a snug tomb. A number of doors lined the hall, named instead of numbered. After passing "Studio 69▯" and "Glory Whole," she wasn't sure she would be able to figure out which one was Roday's, but when she got to it, it would have been obvious. Besides having a set of double doors to the rest of the hallway's single ones, the plaque next to it read "The Khal Drogo Bedchamber."

"Barf," Daphne muttered. Her stomach threatened to comply, and she rested her head against the sign until her nausea passed. Well. Her nausea due to seasickness. Too many unexpected obstacles so far. Too much making it up as she went along. How to get into his room? How would a drunk girl get into his room?

Confidently, she thought, pulling down the door handle like it was her room and pushing it open like she did it every day. The handle turned without resistance, unlocked, and the door swung into the room easily. She paused, letting the door shut behind her, tossing the hair of her brown wig over her shoulder with a flick of her head and slouching on one leg as she took in the seemingly empty cabin.

The small foyer led into a large sitting area with dark furniture, marble tabletops, personality-free décor, and windows covered by beige curtains. The EDM from two decks above was reduced to the subtlest of vibrations, and Daphne wondered if the cabin was insulated and soundproofed. Within the room, there was no sound of a TV or anyone talking or moving around, so Daphne peeked around the corner. Eight-seater dining table with an impressively oversized bouquet of flowers that would ensure half the table couldn't see the other half while eating. Kitchen nook, fully stocked. Chips and other bags of snacks on the counter.

She ventured farther in to another hallway, where she paused again and listened, but there was still no sound of anyone else in the suite. Door on her left, a bathroom with a tub so big it had stairs. *Don't mind if I do*, she thought, wondering why she didn't have her own yacht. Doorway on the right led to an office-looking area. It was dark, and she closed the door behind her as she entered so no one would see when she turned on the light. There, on the desk, like a present just waiting for her, sat Roday's laptop.

Fuck. Yes. Finally. With one more quick pause to listen, she crossed the room and opened the computer. Battery not full, but full enough. She set down the beer and fished the USB drive out of her pocket. Before even looking for evidence, she started downloading everything, pulling up windows and typing commands. Reading and typing worsened her nausea, but luckily, being low in the boat meant a little more stability.

Files began downloading to the drive, and Daphne double-checked that she had followed Brad's instructions. The important thing was to get everything. If it was too risky to take the time to look through it now, she could review it at Diophantus once she was back on land. But...it was downloading slow enough. She went back to the closed door and listened again, heard nothing again, and decided to sift through some data while she waited. As a little treat.

For someone who ran a tech company, Roday's email was anarchy. No folders. No labels. No obvious system of organization. Over 200,000 unread emails. Daphne got contact anxiety simply witnessing it. She clicked the search bar in the program, and a dropdown of previously searched words appeared. The idea was for her to quickly discern what would give any hits, not specific ones, but the fact that he'd already tried to find emails based on things like "girl," "slut," and "liar" already told her what she wanted to know. And it looked like a jackpot, in terms of what Daphne was hoping to find.

"Oh, okay," she murmured after clicking a few words Roday had already searched for. "You belong in the bottom right corner of that D&D alignment meme. The most bad. What's it called? Most Evil. True Evil. Evil Evil." She couldn't say that trying to learn about Cinnamon's interests never taught her anything.

Too many emails to dive into. She moved to his desktop, where she found a folder simply titled "lawyer." Mostly NDAs and settlement agreements. She clicked another named "T2WC2" and found what looked like a kind of log of women he'd had sex with. Gross, but since he was the kind of guy that thought anywhere he put his dick must be willing, also an invaluable piece of evidence. The heading spelled out the file name as "Two Thousand Wolf Cub Club."

"What on earth is that?" she said with a sigh. Moving back to his email, she found "T2WC2" near the top of the search and read the most recent message with that subject, sent to Jared the night before.

> 263 and 264. Right on track. Alphallic Envy tomorrow
> night, that'll be another two if you're lucky, and more
> if you're not. Pussy.

Switching back to the spreadsheet, Daphne scrolled down to
the bottom entries: 263 and 264, with yesterday's date, a woman's
name on each line, and descriptions of what they did. She hit the
keyboard harder than she needed to, getting angrier the longer
she looked. The T2WC2 and lawyer folders were included in the
download: she checked again before closing the windows and
bringing up an incognito browser.

She paused before typing it in, dread mixing with the ever-pre-
sent seasickness, worrying that it would lead her to something
even more unsavory, but "Two Thousand Wolf Cub Club" brought
her to the website of a guy she recognized as a notorious pick-up
artist. T2WC2 was a challenge for his followers to try to sire two
thousand offspring before they die.

"Oh my god." Unbelievable that people took this shit seriously,
but here she was, looking at evidence, and even if it was all just
Roday lying to himself in his sex spreadsheet, it looked like he
roped other people into it. She wanted to roll her eyes at the utter
ridiculousness, but it felt too serious to take lightly.

Then she read the guy's explanation of how to achieve two
thousand children: "Women are fertile one week a month, which
means women spend 25% of the month capable of conceiving a
child. If you have sex with ten women a week, you should be able
to complete your T2WC2 challenge within fifteen years."

Daphne did roll her eyes then, offended on behalf of both
women and math. "That's not how either works," she snapped
at the website. And Roday ran an entire goddamn company, for

fuck's sake. The ability of even the dumbest of white men to fail into the stratosphere of success was something she would never forgive this world for.

The site went on to assure its participants that they didn't have to fear taking care of all those children themselves. If they were truly the alpha males they claimed to be, they could easily pay off all the women bearing their sons. Or, if they thought their DNA wasn't enough to ensure genius, they could pay for their offspring's education. But they certainly wouldn't have to *raise* them. After all, that was women's work.

There wasn't any time to dig deeper, and Daphne didn't have the stomach for it, anyway. She x'd out the browser with a tut of disgust and checked the file upload progress bar. Just over halfway done. She closed the rest of the programs to see if that would speed up the process, but she paused when she got back to Roday's email.

Goldenrod would be getting all the evidence they needed of Roday's business misdeeds, and Cinnamon would have the proof she'd been searching for that he was a serial abuser. That should have been enough. But Daphne wanted something that showed, definitively, that she wasn't the one who doxxed Cinnamon.

Without proof, she would never even get the chance to earn her trust again. She would remain unforgivable. But the doxxing had to originate from Roday's camp. And if they weren't dumb enough to email about it, maybe they were cocky enough to.

She used the search bar again, but no hits came back for Cinnamon's first or last name, and her initials brought up every email. Daphne grimaced. She had an idea of what terms they would use instead.

"Fuck you for making me do this, you racist assholes," she hissed, stabbing the keys as she typed out a Chinese slur.

Sure enough, there was a short back-and-forth between Roday and Jared from a few months ago, Jared concerned that someone had been asking certain questions online, Roday brushing him off and telling him to just deal with it. Jared saying it required delicacy because they didn't know how much she knew, and if they moved too aggressively too quickly, she could get spooked and dump whatever info she had online. He had hired someone to get information about a rival company, and she was close to the person asking questions. Roday reiterated his disinterest and told Jared to do whatever he had to do.

Then, a few days ago, Jared said their contact retrieved the info and launched a campaign against her online. Threat neutralized, thanks to the highly skilled, highly recommended corporate spy:

Ying-Li Wu.

"Oh fuck." Fingers paused over the keys, Daphne reread the name, remembering the sour-faced astronaut at the Intermittent solstice party. The Instagram post of Cheung Family Dinner where the woman called Cinnamon "Little Spice." Family friend and business contact.

Cinnamon was in danger.

"Fuck," she said again, feeling her feet and hands begin to disappear, the gray worms eating at the corners of her vision, tightness in her chest. No phone to call her. She squeezed her eyes shut, willing the panic attack to hold on for just a few goddamn minutes, and wondered what the fallout would be if she just forwarded the email to Cinnamon.

She was so deep in her thoughts, Daphne almost missed the sound of the door handle turning. Her body was already in a panic response, and the immediate crisis focused her attention just enough to push her into emergency mode. She glanced around the room, looking for anywhere to hide, finding none. The files weren't finished transferring. *Grab the drive, rush whoever comes in, run past them and*...she was on a boat. Where was she going to go? And what data would she be leaving behind?

A new wave of nausea, and she had an idea. She turned the computer to better hide the drive and opened Yelp. Elbows on the desk, slouched so her face was a few inches away from the keyboard, ass in the air and the first thing anyone coming into the room would see.

"And the crab Rangoon, and oh, dumplings. How many. Four. Four dumplings." She spoke at a normal volume, though slightly slurred, and typed with one finger, letting it hover before plunking it down again and again.

"What the fuck?"

Daphne twisted her body and leaned her head back at an exaggerated angle to try to see Roday from beneath her dark bangs.

"Oh hey."

"How'd you get in here? What are you doing on my computer?" He strode forward but didn't touch her or the laptop.

She pushed the bangs aside and tried a clumsy, sexy pose.

"I'm ordering Chinese food for us. I'm starving. Did you say you want a pupu platter? They can be here in twenty minutes."

He stared at her in confusion, glanced at the bottle on the desk, and relaxed. His predatory smile made an encore appearance, and a warning of danger sparked down Daphne's spine.

"You having a good time, sweetheart? You have some beer?"

"It's a good time but I need dumplings."

"I think I know exactly what you need." Roday pulled her to standing and pushed her against the desk, hands on her bare hips and moving higher. He was going to kiss her. She was gripped with a terror she hadn't felt in a decade and had apparently suppressed until that exact moment, remembering the last time she'd been cornered by a man who didn't like to hear "no."

The memory made her dizzy, her muscles contracting from remembered fear compounded by current fear. The thought of this entitled man even putting his lips on hers, taking what he wanted, made her stomach roil.

As Roday leaned in, Daphne realized the dips and squeezes in her belly were more physical than metaphorical.

Oh god, she thought, opening her mouth to shout or protest, to use her voice, but instead, the gently rocking boat drew forth her remaining stomach contents, and she threw up all over Collin Roday.

They both froze, shocked. She had never thrown up on anyone so fortuitously. Roday finally took a step back, disgust on his face (right alongside the vomit), and repeated, "What. The *fuck?*"

Daphne's answer was to double over with another round of watery foam bile, thin strands of saliva dripping from her mouth onto his shoes.

Well. That was one way to deter a rapist.

The computer dinged that the files had finished downloading, and before either of them knew what she was doing, Daphne grabbed the entire laptop and ran out the door.

Things are going great, she lied to herself, keeping her shoulder against the wall for support as she staggered down the corridor, clutching the laptop to her chest. Her ears felt full, but she still heard the DJ's music thrumming through the boat, a vibration separate from the engines propelling them farther and farther out to sea, and she successfully tamped the panic threatening to overtake her.

She wiped her mouth with the sleeve of her shirt, which was thankfully starting to come untucked from her bra. It would have been nice to have a moment to roll up the waist of her pants, too, but as in the rest of life, pants were not a top priority.

"Hey!" Roday's shout reached her just as she turned the corner to take the stairs to a higher deck. Daphne felt like shit, and it slowed her, and she could only hope that getting thrown-up upon would make a person feel gross enough to be slowed, as well.

Even if he was, it wasn't like she had a plan. She ran down one hall and turned another corner, adding new paths to the map of the ship in her mind. For a little while, Roday was far enough away that he couldn't reach her, but not so far that he couldn't see where she turned next. And he was catching up fast.

She found the first staircase she took down from the open deck. Roday was close enough for Daphne to hear him panting, the sound a spur to her foolishness, and she took the stairs two at a time before bursting out into the night air. A few steps onto the deck, a woman screamed at her to duck, and Daphne tried to crouch, at speed, and tripped. The laptop flew out of her hands and skittered across the planks, sliding to rest against a lounge chair, safe and sound.

She curled into a ball, thigh and palms stinging from her fall, anticipating Roday's attack, but he flew past her and picked up his computer instead.

"Duck!" the woman said again. "Duck!"

Daphne glanced over to find the girl from earlier, sitting up on her bench, surrounded by too many pillows and cushions, pointing at Daphne, who closed her eyes and rested her head against the deck with a thud. She wasn't telling her to duck. She was remembering Daphne was the one who shared a shower duck with her.

He has to believe I'm drunk, she reminded herself, trying to plan her next move. *Drunk and lost. Confused. Hungry. Have to be another dumb girl to him. Not a threat.*

People who had witnessed their chase below deck had followed them, out of curiosity or concern. Roday inspected his computer for damage. Daphne pushed herself up onto her knees and let a little bit of her panic back in. The whimper that escaped surprised her, and she wondered how she would be able to rein it in when she needed to.

"I was ordering dumplings," she sobbed. "Where's Ahmed? Where's Keisha?" She glanced around, looking for her imaginary friends, wiping her nose with a sleeve.

"You stole my fucking computer," Roday yelled, storming up to her and tossing it on a nearby couch so his hands were free to grab her by the shirt and pull her off the deck. He'd gotten her vomit off his face, but the smell lingered, and Daphne breathed through her mouth so she wouldn't do it again. "Do you have any idea what you could have cost me?"

Daphne sobbed louder. "I was getting us dinner."

"We're on a boat, you dumb bitch, they don't deliver to the fucking ocean."

She gasped in shock and let out her breath in a rising wail, as though not getting Chinese food delivery to a boat on the open sea was the paragon of tragedy. He shook her, hard, and she loosened up too much and bit her tongue, which gave her another reason to cry.

"Oh shit," a voice behind them said. "Dude, I think she's on the wrong boat."

The girl from earlier came up to them and took Daphne's hand. At some point during Daphne's running, the boat had come to a stop, and the more violent open-sea rocking made her stumble as Roday released her.

"Duck-duck," the girl said. "S'okay. Shh. I'm here now."

"I want Anthony," Daphne said with a hiccup. "And Laverne. Where are they? Where'd the rainbows go? They abandoned me!"

"Yeah, I don't think there's anyone here with those names," someone else said.

Roday looked down at Daphne, being held by her duck friend, and she hiccuped again and snorted snot out of her nose. He sneered at her and stepped away.

"We're not going back. I'm not going let some drunk stowaway ruin my night." He scooped up his laptop and walked away.

"So...what do we do with her?"

"Like I give a fuck."

A blinding light swept over the deck, and Daphne flinched, feeling her friend do the same. The people behind her yelled and muttered.

"*Alphallic Envy*," boomed a voice across the water. "This is the United States Coast Guard..."

Daphne didn't listen to the rest. She didn't want to be stuck on Roday's yacht another moment. She didn't necessarily want to dive into the arms of the United States military, but between what she'd seen on the laptop and what she'd seen of the rest of the ship, the assumption of lawfulness was better than the misogynistic bacchanalia of Roday's inescapable boys club.

She shook off the duck girl and ran down the steps at the very back of the ship, hoping they would take her to a kind of swim platform.

"Hey!" she shouted, waving her arms in the spotlight. "This isn't my boat! This isn't my boat!" The low platform meant the ocean was just a few feet away, and jumping in wouldn't be too dangerous. She hesitated anyway, knowing how cold it would be, how deep beneath her kicking feet, but as the USCG pulled their boat around, and she was sure they could see her, she took a deep breath and leapt into the water.

On the Coast Guard's boat a few minutes later, she cried as they wrapped her in a blanket, and it wasn't totally an act.

"It wasn't my friend's boat," she said, voice wavering. "It was some mean man's. He wouldn't let me get dumplings even though I can get married now. Can you take me to my friend's boat? I can pay you."

Sniffling, she brought the last of her wet bills out of her pocket and cupped them in her hands, offering them up to the men and women around her like a shivering, soaked orphan begging for love.

Chapter Twenty-Five

"You'll never beat this," Rin said, spoon clinking against the ceramic mug as she stirred her hot chocolate. Next to her, Mattie pushed up her oversized sunglasses and adjusted the bisexual flag scarf around her head. In her other hand, she held a cup of coffee, and in front of her were the last, uneaten bites of a fruit bowl and oatmeal. Crumbs were all that remained of Rin's monster chocolate croissant.

"Sunglasses alone aren't enough of a disguise." Mattie glanced around, but they were still the only people in the café's outdoor seating, and no one passing by stopped long enough to overhear them. "I'm sure there are cameras outside the station. They'll see you."

"They'll see a hot brunette sharing a Sunday morning coffee and walking to a Pride celebration with her queer great aunt."

Mattie snorted. "Because I'm in disguise."

"I'm in disguise as an American. You said my accent was good. Also, I've seen you wear this exact outfit before. You disguised yourself as Mattie, forever a queer great aunt. Is Grey Gardens a goal of yours, or an accident?"

"You know it's a goal," she said, hiding her smile behind her coffee mug.

When they'd lost Daphne the night before, Mattie and Rin had stayed calm for about ten minutes. She hadn't been responding to texts, and the last one she'd sent said she was about to do something stupid, which, of course. Luckily, since she'd included her sister and friend in the planning process, they knew what to do. Mats texted the Brad burner from her burner, and a few minutes later, he confirmed that he was tracking Daphne and would keep them updated.

Two hours later, he told them to wait for her outside a certain café at 8 a.m. and to be discreet. When Mattie rather forcefully exerted her older sister concern, Brad confessed that Daphne was in the drunk tank at the police station near Chinatown.

"I didn't think drunk tanks were real," Rin mused, casually glancing up the street to the station. "I thought they were just something on TV."

"I'm sure Daphne will tell you all about it."

"I stand by my assertion that you'll never beat this holiday, Mats."

Mattie straightened in her chair and turned up her nose. "It's not a competition, Corinne. And she doesn't need the encouragement."

A dark-haired woman dressed in black stepped from the shadows of the station entrance and glanced around as though she were trying to orient herself.

"That's her," Rin said.

"Yup."

Rin pushed back her chair and stood over Mattie, took a deep breath, and yelled, "Dogs *can't* look up, Vanessa!"

Mattie tried her best not to smile or laugh as she scrambled to follow her down the sidewalk, away from the police. Daphne would hear their code phrase and catch up to them, or she would find her way home without them. It was barely a twenty-minute walk to her condo. Daphne could find her way back on her own. It didn't mean she *had* to.

***

A few minutes later, a voice behind Mattie and Rin said, "Excardon me, ma'am…"

Mats turned so Daphne could walk between them, but pulled away as the smell hit her.

"Holy shit Daph, you smell…really bad."

"Woo, yeah, what is that? Dumpster? Low tide?" Rin held her nose but put her arm around her anyway.

"Close enough," Daphne answered, pulling Mattie to her, too. Clothes and bodies were both washable, so they could deal with it. Her shirt and pants were dry, and the wig had miraculously stayed in place, even if it was tangled and as pungent as the rest of her.

"Who's got their burner phone?" Daphne asked. "I need it."

Mats pulled hers from her purse and handed it over. Daphne dialed Cinnamon's number and waited for her to pick up.

"I have so many questions," Rin said quietly. Mattie shrugged.

The call went to voicemail, a robotic voice confirming the number and giving instructions on how to leave a message as though there were someone left in the world who still didn't understand how it worked.

"It was Ying-Li." Daphne spoke quickly, not knowing how much of the message Cinnamon would listen to before deleting it. "If she's around, get away from her. Get to Echo. She'll know what to look for."

She hesitated before ending the call, wanting to say more, wanting to apologize or tell her she loved her. Instead, she hit the end button and handed the phone back to Mattie. It was all she could do at the moment.

Rin and Mattie exchanged a look. "Do you want to talk about it?" Mattie asked Daphne.

What Daphne wanted was for everything to be over and back to how it was before. She clenched and opened her fists, closed her eyes and took a breath, the smell of herself intruding on her attempt to find a spot of calm.

"Later," she muttered, shaking her head to try to knock her thoughts back into place.

"Yeah. We can debrief later," Mats said, leaning in to hug her sister. "The most important thing is that you're back in one piece. You worried us."

Past Daphne would have laughed it off with bravado, playing her part as the wildest of the three of them: unafraid and bold, to the point of foolishness. Present Daphne just wasn't up to it. Maybe it was the danger that had only been a theory until it met her face to face. Maybe it was the late-night dip in the cold and uncaring Pacific. Or maybe she was just achy and tired and itchy and stinky, her bit tongue still throbbing, body bruised from her fall on the boat, stomach wrung out and distrustful even though they were on land.

"Yeah," she admitted. She'd been worried, too. If she said more now, she would be spending all day with two people afraid to leave her alone. "I'm going to need some time to become human again. Shower, obviously. Sleep for a few hours. Get back into fighting Daphne shape."

Mattie and Rin caught each other's eye. Daphne didn't need to read minds to guess what they were thinking. She'd had decades to learn how they thought.

"Someone say something," Daphne said. "Your brooding isn't helping."

They'd all been friends long enough to understand each other without words. They could tell Daphne had failed in her mission, at great cost, and didn't want to push her before she was ready to talk.

"What can we do?" Rin asked. "What do you need?"

Daphne couldn't help it. She got a little teary. Her friends were the best, but there wasn't much they could do. "I left the messenger bag from last night in the bushes in front of BDMT. The phone's in there, and the clothes I left behind."

"We'll get it," Rin said with a nod.

"Did you bring anything with you to the unexpected part two of the evening?" Mattie noted her empty-looking pockets.

"Some cash," she replied. "I hung onto it, but it's still wet. I had to drop my lockpick set in the ocean. It would have been too suspicious. That was my favorite set, too."

To their credit, neither Mattie nor Rin pushed her for answers, though their curiosity was potent enough to ask on its own.

"We'll get the bag," Mattie said. "And we'll get you a new lock-picking set."

A chirping came from Mattie's purse and she brought out the flip phone again.

"Brad," she murmured, answering it. "Hello?"

She listened for a minute, nodded, and said, "Here she is."

Daphne took the phone gingerly, expecting a barrage of questions, having a number of her own.

"Brad?" She asked.

"I thought you got seasick," Brad said playfully.

"You have no idea," she said, laughing. It wasn't Mattie's or Rin's fault that the three of them were broody, but Brad's tone made her feel closer to herself. "You'll have to tell me how you did...some of the things you pulled off last night." She didn't want to blow his cover with Mats and Rin listening.

"Same, sister. Unfortunately, that will have to wait, because Clarissa wants to see you at the Dio offices. Like, right now."

"Oh, shit."

"Yeah."

"So they know about all of this."

"Well, someone had to approve the extraction."

"Yeah, tell me about that, by the way."

"What's to tell?" he asked innocently.

"How?"

"How what?"

"Brad," she whined.

After a moment of trying to be strong, he sighed. "I'll tell you, but you can't ask any questions about it, or let anyone know I told you, or ever bring it up again, okay?"

"Promise to all those things."

He paused, letting her stew in silence for a moment, before he said, "I tracked your microchip."

It took Daphne a minute to understand what he said, but when she did, she stopped in the middle of the sidewalk and blinked.

"You can't respond," he said quickly. "No questions."

Right. Microchip. Okay. The hacker who still wore makeup in a way to confuse facial recognition had somehow tagged Daphne with a microchip. She had no doubt there was language in her contract that allowed it, but it was still a breathtaking violation of privacy. But...it'd probably saved her life.

Mattie and Rin had kept walking, but stopped to look back at her and wait.

"Clarissa can't know that I told you," Brad said. "I need verbal confirmation that you understand."

"Understood," she said. "I...appreciate it? In this instance. Things were getting real up on that boat. I knew I should have brought my slingshot."

He laughed, clearly relieved by her acceptance. "I did what I could."

"No, really, thank you. I'll fill you in later."

"You going to Pride?"

"I'm going to bed. Well, after this meeting. But maybe. I'll text from my regular phone."

"Good luck, Daph. Glad to have you back."

She rejoined her friends and handed Mattie the phone. "I have to go take care of something. Why don't you two go back to Mattie's and wash up, since you smell like me now."

"Are you okay? Should we come with you?" Ever the concerned older sister. To be fair, the concern was usually warranted.

"Nah, I'm fine. Seriously. I just have to take care of this one last thing first."

Rin squinted at her for a moment and asked, "Is it Cinnamon?"

Most of Daphne's sleepless night was due to thinking and re-thinking her life choices that had led her to getting caught for the third time in a week. And for the second time in a week, it concluded with her locked in a room by the authorities, waiting for a release that was beyond her control.

All of it was her own fault. Atticus would have gone in on Monday and found a way to get the information. There was no rush, except that Daphne chafed at being blamed for something she didn't do, and the faster she got said information, the faster Roday and his lackeys would have bigger things to worry about than Cinnamon Cheung.

Daphne wanted to make her as safe and protected and cared for as she made Daphne feel, whether or not she ever wanted to see

Daphne again. Even if Cinnamon couldn't forgive her for breaking her trust, it was important she knew for a fact that Daphne did not dox her. Being mistaken for an idiot was fine. Being mislabeled a monster was not.

But step one of getting to that point was to solve Cinnamon's Roday problem. If Daphne were the one who exposed him, she couldn't be the one who doxxed Cinnamon, and that was the plan. That she stumbled onto emails confirming it was Ying-Li all along was like a sign from the universe that she was on the right track. Now she just had to cross her fingers and hope that Cinnamon listened to the message, took it seriously, talked to Echo...

Actually, it might take a while.

"I'll call her later," Daphne answered Rin, with a shake of her head. She needed Cinnamon to trust her again, and there were a dozen things that had to happen first to even have a chance at that. Trying to contact Cinnamon could wait until after shower, breakfast, and sleep. "This is different."

The three of them parted ways and Daphne took a circuitous route to the office, in case she was being followed. She cut through a pharmacy, stopping just long enough to buy a small tote bag and a clean T-shirt, which she quickly changed into in the alley. The wig took a little longer to remove, but she eventually stuffed it in the bag on top of her black shirt and made a mental note to get everything cleaned by professionals.

The Diophantus offices weren't busy, but they were never empty. Despite making a much-needed five-minute detour into the restrooms to wash her face and fix her real hair, she still got a couple weird looks. Clarissa's assistant sat outside their office, and his eyebrows shot up when Daphne stopped in front of him.

"I just got out of jail," she said brightly. "Please give me a break."

He shrugged and tapped his tablet. "Go ahead in." She nodded her thanks, but he caught her arm before she could enter and sprayed her down with an apple-scented bottle of something on his desk. Daphne coughed and grimaced at him.

"Sorry," he said. "You reek." He raised the bottle again, sniffed, and let her go. "Don't sit on anything."

Daphne sighed. "That's fair."

Clarissa sat at their computer, typing faster than most other humans could. Sometimes, Daphne thought they might be part android, though that seemed like an insult to their humanity. Knowing Clarissa, they might take it as a compliment.

Normally, she would take a seat and wait for them to finish. Daphne stood, trying not to fidget, in case it looked like she was being impatient. When Clarissa finally looked up, they nodded toward the chair. Daphne shook her head.

"I was told not to sit on anything."

If her boss noticed her criming-sweat, seasick-vomit, dried-ocean, or awake-in-jail-all-night odor, they didn't say anything about it. Instead, they nodded toward the seat again, with emphasis, and Daphne did as she was told. Clarissa looked her over and settled on her eyes. It was never not unnerving, but Daphne had gotten better at not worrying about it. Boss stared, weighing, assessing, in silence, and it could take a while. They would speak when they had finished sifting through the data of whoever was in front of them. It only took a few minutes this time, and tired as she was, Daphne was grateful.

"Is it true?" they asked. Vague, as usual. Testing her mental capacity?

"Most likely," Daphne admitted. If Clarissa had come to the conclusion that something was true, it was. "But a lot of things are true. If you want my firsthand account, you'll have to be more specific."

"Do you heart SF?"

Daphne blinked at her in confusion, then squinted into the distance, trying to figure it out, before she remembered the white tee from the pharmacy.

"Oh," she said, looking down and tugging the hem of the shirt. "Um."

When she glanced back up, Clarissa was trying not to laugh. Relief washed through Daphne, and she chuckled, too.

"Am I in trouble?" she asked.

Boss sighed and fixed her with another penetrating stare. "Have you done anything you think you should be in trouble for?" A trick question.

"...yes?" she asked slowly.

"Fuck yes," they answered, and Daphne winced. "You used Diophantus resources, personnel, and proprietary intelligence just enough to start trouble but not enough to finish it, and made a series of astoundingly selfish decisions that resulted in me having to personally contact the Coast Guard. You put yourself at risk, and I know that's sometimes how things have to be, but you put others at risk, too, as well as this entire operation." They leaned their elbows on the desk and clasped their hands under their chin. "Start from the beginning. Don't leave anything out."

Clarissa was one of the few people Daphne trusted implicitly, so she told them everything, and it didn't take long. After all, it had only been one week since she met Cinnamon, and that's where she started the story. She included Mattie and Rin, Echo, Brad, Atticus, and everyone she encountered at BDMT. Clarissa perked up when Daphne described what she found on Roday's computer, and shadows gathered in their face when she told them how he'd cornered then chased her.

"Oh shit," Daphne said, slapping her forehead. "Aetos Kaukasios."

Clarissa raised a questioning eyebrow.

Daphne groaned and stood up from her chair. "The AK app automatically redirects unknown numbers. My voicemail went right to spam. Is there a secure line I can use?"

Of course there was one in Clarissa's office, and Daphne started to punch in Cinnamon's number.

"This'll go straight to AK too," she said with a sigh. Echo, then. Good thing her strangely wired brain remembered numbers so well.

The elder Cheung sister picked up on the second ring. "Echo. Go."

"Ying-Li doxxed Cinnamon. I don't know if I can get you proof, but if your team is as good at tech stuff as you claim, you should be able to figure it out."

"Redgrave?"

"I just want Cinnamon to be safe. Keep her away from Ying-Li."

Daphne hung up abruptly, not wanting them to waste any time arguing when Cinnamon could be in danger at that very moment. She exhaled with a growl and collapsed back into her chair. Between Echo and Clarissa and their networks and talents, Daphne had to trust that the right people were doing everything they could. Brad might be able to find her too. Not in the same way he had tracked Daphne the night before, but...

She narrowed her eyes at Clarissa, thinking.

Following Daphne's train of thought, Clarissa said, "Brad told you about the microchip."

"How did you—okay." Daphne snorted a laugh that was half exasperation. "Please don't hold it against him. I can be very persuasive."

"It's not a secret," they said, sitting back in the chair. "We just don't talk about it."

That sounded pretty secretive to Daphne, but she wasn't about to argue.

"We have protocols for a reason," they continued, shifting their gaze to the monitor. "You're lucky Roday didn't recognize you. Look. Next time, use all the resources at your disposal. I'm one of your resources. If I set you free on the world today, are you going to get in trouble again? Or are you going to keep a low profile? No, wait, don't answer that. Just keep your phone on you. Go enjoy Pride."

It had always been Daphne's belief that Clarissa was cool, but she felt like she had just gotten away with murder. If nothing else, she had put the company in danger: of exposure by BDMT if she got caught and of violating their client, Goldenrod's, contract. And all she got was a "keep your phone on"?

"Am...am I not fired?"

"Should you be fired?"

Honesty had worked so well the first time, she tried again. "No," she answered definitively.

"Then I trust that you've learned your lesson. I'll contact you when we get something for you to do." They leaned toward the monitor and began typing again, and Daphne knew she was dismissed. She stood and turned to go, but hesitated, and turned back to Clarissa.

Daphne sighed. "Time to come clean." She reached down her shirt and into her bra, pulled out the USB drive—undamaged by the water thanks to its rugged rubber casing—and placed it on the desk.

Clarissa's hands paused over the keyboard, and they stared at the drive.

"I wouldn't know what to do with that data," Daphne admitted. "And neither would Cinnamon. She's just a therapist, and I...well, I've fucked up enough." She shifted her weight from one foot to the other, swaying slightly. She was taking a chance, and her gut told her it was the right thing to do, even if other parts of her were yelling that she'd got it for Cinnamon, she'd thrown up and gotten manhandled and oceaned and jailed all for her, and she was going to leave it with someone else? "I know you'll bring him down if you can. You know Goldenrod, so you know what's appropriate regarding our contract with them."

Before she turned to leave, she watched Clarissa reach out and close their hand over the thumb drive and Daphne suddenly felt like she was about to be given an entire chocolate factory.

"I think you'll find I can do a lot with this," they said with a wicked smile that made Daphne shiver.

**

The doorbell rang, and for the first time in six months, Cinnamon didn't check the cameras to see who it was. Partly because, after getting enough sleep for her brain to resume normal function, she believed that Brad's uncanny computer skills had effectively derailed the campaign against her, and partly because anyone who came to her door must have personal business, which meant that maybe it was Starlight. And while she still wasn't sure what to say or how to move forward or even if she really wanted to see her, she did have sushi in the fridge, and a day with plenty of free time to sit and talk.

Starlight hadn't tried to contact her, hadn't left her any messages, and while the implication was clear (she didn't want to talk), Cinnamon's feelings about it were mixed. She hadn't reached out, either. Maybe it would just take time.

The security detail was still stationed outside and hadn't texted Cinnamon about her visitor, so she should have known it was her sister. As she opened the door, she couldn't hide her disappointment.

"Well don't get too excited," Echo drawled, stepping into the house. "I only brought you bubble tea and a lemon cookie and a trusted professional who's going to undo whatever shit Ying-Li did to your phone and computer."

"Of course," Cinnamon said with a sigh, motioning them inside and shutting the door behind them. "I was wondering about that. What do you need from me?"

Echo handed her the tea and made a beeline for the espresso machine while Cinnamon took the CT tech to her office and set her up, leaving her with the computer and phone. Hopefully that was everything Ying-Li had corrupted. When she went back to the kitchen, Echo was leaning across the island, reaching for a still-warm cinnamon roll.

"Not for you," she said, swooping in just in time to move the plate out of her reach.

"Trade you for a lemon cookie." Echo waggled her eyebrows suggestively.

"You said the cookie was for me before you saw the cinnamon rolls."

"Yeah, but then I saw the cinnamon rolls."

Cinnamon pushed the plate back and let Echo take one in exchange for the cookie.

"Mmm," she mumbled. "I hate when you're stressed, but I love the results of your stress-baking."

The lemon cookie was from an expensive bakery near Echo's house. Cinnamon broke off a piece and ate it, pushing the soft dough against the roof of her mouth and letting the icing melt against her tongue. It tasted the same as usual, but for some reason, she didn't get as much joy from it.

"One might begin to think that you would orchestrate stress for me simply to take advantage of that." If Echo wanted pastries, she would just ask her to make them, but Cinnamon's calm had been upended and she hadn't been able to right it yet.

Echo just shrugged. "I'm not sorry that I worry about you enough to launch a full-scale attack against someone who's harming you. But I am sorry that I did that and was wrong. My gut was right but pointed in the wrong direction." Echo put down the pastry long enough to sip her latte. "I'm willing to be just as driven and vicious about getting her back for you, if that's what you want."

The tassel on her shawl suddenly got very interesting, and Cinnamon smoothed it between her fingers, remembering how Starlight couldn't help touching new textures. "I don't know what I want."

Her sister's gaze was heavy, and after a moment of consideration, Echo wiped her buttery icing fingers off on a cloth napkin, folded her arms, and crossed her legs.

"Alright, Little Spice. Time to come clean. What did you do, who's after you, and how can I help?"

"Was Ying-Li not as chatty as you'd hoped?"

Echo pinned her with a sharp stare, mouth twitched into a half-smile. "I have her story. I want yours."

She'd already told Starlight, thinking she could do anything about it, so Cinnamon no longer had the excuse that she didn't want to break her clients' trust. And while confessing her most embarrassing righteous ambitions and moral failures to her sister wasn't ideal, watching how Echo expertly handled the doxxing and Ying-Li, as a business professional and a sister, sparked a new kind of trust. So for the second time that week, she told a confidant the whole story.

Before she'd finished, Echo was laughing.

"It's not funny," Cinnamon said flatly. "I got death threats. Someone broke my front window!"

"I know," Echo said, fighting for breath. "That's not what's funny. Please, continue."

"People were hurt." She paused. "Are you laughing because you thought Daphne was a corporate spy sent to get to CT through me, when the entire time, you and mom and dad were the ones who set me up with the person who was sent to get to CT through me?"

"No, but that is what happened, and I appreciate the irony. Finish your story and I'll tell you what's funny."

She did, and Echo sat in silence, processing it all. The CT tech came back downstairs, gave Cinnamon her phone, and declared her house and electronics free from spies and spyware. Echo offered her a beer from the fridge and asked her to wait outside. Once the tech was settled on the patio, Echo tried to explain herself to her sister. She opened her mouth to speak, but closed it again, thinking.

"Is it so complicated?" Cinnamon asked.

"The complication is in the confidentiality. There are people and firms and strategies involved that can't be revealed. I'm trying to parse out what I can say without saying anything."

"Well, you're going to have to say *something*." She'd been working to expose an abuser for months, slinking through the dark of the internet, which of course followed her into reality. Then Ying-Li targeted her and upended her life, and Echo—who had nothing to do with any of it—was going to decide what Cinnamon needed to know?

"Roday and Ying-Li are my problem, not yours," Cinnamon said, too upset to hide it. Echo had all of her attention. "I don't know what's confidential about it, but since I'm the one who was doxxed, I need to know everything Ying-Li told you. Do you have any idea how scared I've been? Not just since Thursday, but for months." Despite ordering herself not to cry, she had to wipe tears from her lashes. "It all got out of control, and you've helped, but if I don't know what's going on, I can't know the best way for me to handle it. For *me* to handle it, Echo. Beyond what you and your computer wizards can do. I want to be less afraid, and part of that is making my own choices."

"Hey," Echo said lightly, reaching across the island and taking Cinnamon's hands in her own. "I will tell you everything Ying-Li said. You're right, she was hired by someone at BDMT to look into Cheung Technologies. Her family already had ties with us, so I guess it was a no-brainer. And the first thing we did was set her up with you. I know, I said I didn't have anything to do with it, but you know what? You've been unhappy, and maybe it wasn't about finding a romantic partner, but maybe it was, and what was the harm in pointing the two of your toward each other?"

Echo grabbed the cinnamon roll off the plate and tore a chunk of it away with her teeth. The look in her eye told Cinnamon not to interrupt while she paused her story to steal another bite.

"Ying-Li was pissed," Echo continued around a mouthful. "We'd shunted her off to the one person in the family who had nothing to do with the business. And you were—well, you. Not very forth-coming. She was about to call it quits when you mentioned BDMT by name, and that piqued her interest."

She'd mentioned BDMT? That didn't seem likely. Echo must have recognized her confusion, and clarified, "You asked her about tech industries or something, mentioned BDMT, said something about how the trolls online love going to battle for their little tech lords. Not untrue, by the way, but it caught Ying-Li's attention. She told the guy who hired her and asked to focus on you instead. He said sure.

"At some point, the only thing Ying-Li could do was try to get into your computer, so she brought up that security picture email thing in the hope that she'd get the chance to mess around in there. She was going to bug out afterward, but stupid Daphne gave her someone else to blame. That's when she doxxed you. Ying-Li doxxed you. Not Daphne. As far as I can tell. I'm paraphrasing here. You can watch the video of her confession later."

"Video?" Cinnamon asked, sniffling. "Confession?"

"Don't worry about it. The thing that's confidential doesn't have anything to do with you or your project or Ying-Li. The most I can say is that Cheung Technologies has been trying to buy out BDMT, and, using independent resources, we've gotten a ton of stuff on Roday and his illegal and morally bankrupt business practices. It's enough to make him uncomfortable, so he'll sell to us for a bargain."

"Well. That's, just, extortion?" Cinnamon ventured.

Echo shrugged, more of a *so what?* than an *I couldn't say*. "The thing that's funny, though, is that the firm we hired to get all that dirt on him gave us a cache of his personal data this morning. Now, after we buy his company at a literally criminally low price, we can expose what a jackass he is, too. He's going down, meimei. We'll make sure of it."

Cinnamon scrunched her face up, trying not to cry again. Despite her terrible, morally gray, insufficient detective work, the bad guy was going to experience consequences. Between this and Starlight in the clear, getting doxxed was almost worth it.

"And I might get in trouble for saying this," Echo added, "but his downfall wouldn't have been possible without Daphne."

With all the crying, there was too much snot to be able to snort, so Cinnamon rolled her eyes and grabbed a tissue to blow her nose. "Echo, I love you, but you have to either pick a side or admit that Daphne contains multitudes, because every time you mention her, you switch between having her on your shit list and your gratitude list."

"Would it help to know she's perpetually on both?"

"It would not. You'll have to explain yourself."

"She—" Echo stopped short and squinted at the ceiling. "It isn't my place to say. But. I will say that Daphne fucked up, but she also did something for you without caring if she got credit for it. I know she hurt you, and as Older Sister, I want to hurt her back. Thanks to Ying-Li's slip-up, you know the true extent of what she did, so you have a better idea of whether there's a way forward for you two. I reserve the right to contradict myself tomorrow, but for now, I'm on team Give Her A Chance To Fix Her Shit. If you want to."

The memory of their last fight coiled in Cinnamon's belly, like the fear and anger that sickened her from the moment she was doxxed through the moment she left Starlight's apartment. She would feel it again the next time they met, and it would be tangled with desire and reason and unreasonable-ness, making the whole ordeal very uncomfortable. What she wanted was for Starlight to never have picked that lock in the first place. The way back would be so much harder now.

But with the truth exposed, they could have an honest conversation. Take it slowly. See what happened.

"I don't have the mental capacity right now to know where to start or what to say."

Echo patted her arm and smiled. "I bet she's tired, but you could text her. She'll reply when she can. Maybe say something like, 'I know you didn't dox me. I'm open to having a conversation.' Then tell her when you're available."

Once Echo and the CT tech left—with plans for the sisters to meet Tuesday morning to review the whole Ying-Li debacle in detail—Cinnamon did text Starlight. She couldn't come up with anything better than what Echo suggested, so she left it at that.

When Starlight didn't text back right away, Cinnamon cleaned her house and reorganized her office. Two of her clients had already replied to her personalized confessions, and both of them wanted to talk about it at their sessions next week, and after reading their emails, Cinnamon had to lie down. Their grace and kindness made her feel even worse about how she'd used them, though she was grateful that neither had flat-out said they were going to sue her or get her license revoked. It softened her.

She could give Starlight the opening to apologize and discuss where to go from there. Maybe it wasn't rational. But it was what Cinnamon wanted, and it was past time to give her desire the attention it deserved.

Chapter Twenty-Six

Despite scrubbing herself with the hottest water and strongest soaps and flushing out her nasal passages with the teapot thing she used when she was sick, Daphne woke up from her nap four hours later with the smell of dead ocean things still stuck in her nose. *I deserve this*, she thought, throwing back the covers and sitting on the edge of her bed.

After her meeting with Clarissa, Daphne had shuffled home, depressed and exhausted, kicking at pebbles like a disappointed child in the olden times. Safe in her condo, she peeled off her clothes, showered (with bonus mini panic attack), quickly ate a leftover burrito, and slept for several hours. She had expected the day to go on without her, but it was only early afternoon. Restlessness pricked at her, even though she had performed all the rituals correctly and technically slept for four hours. The sun still shone as though her mood didn't affect it at all.

She hadn't even looked at her phone since returning home. Mattie and Rin would be waiting for her whenever she was ready. Clarissa and Brad already knew she was safe. If she approached it, if she got too close, she would want to text Cinnamon a hundred times. And every time she thought about contacting her, a little brick formed in her belly, and she chickened out. She'd warned Echo that Ying-Li was the threat—the best she could do, as long as the flash drive was with her boss—and without the drive in hand, Daphne didn't have the proof she needed to convince

Cinnamon she didn't dox her. She wouldn't go so far to say she was innocent. That ship sailed a long time ago. Her stomach-brick bounced, remembering the ship the night before, and she stood up to stretch and walk it out.

A stop in the kitchen first, to pick up chopsticks and a bag of Cheetos, then Daphne went on a little tour of her place. Beyond the leftover briny smell in her nostrils, freshly ground coffee dominated her rooms. Near the bathroom and clothes room, her dark and floral perfume subtly twined with the coffee scent in a not-unpleasant combination.

But there was a weight as she walked, toeing the soft rugs, running her hand along the wooden furniture and through the leaves of her meager plants. Like the fog when it got thick, when every sound was distorted and every breath a chore. The weight of a silence she didn't want anymore.

The loft was comfortable, but she didn't spend much time there alone. The steep angle of the afternoon sunlight shining through the living room windows was a rare sight for her, and added to the weirdness she felt wandering around the quiet and empty apartment. More often than not, she would be out. Work, dinner, parties, meeting people, dating people, spending time with Mats. It was the location, more than the space and the baubles, that she needed, but she would be willing to sacrifice it in exchange for a loving and stable partner.

Maybe even a partner as far out as Sea Cliff.

Daphne shook her head as if that could loosen the hold of her memories with Cinnamon. She gazed out the window, trying to find something to distract her. Outside, it looked like a normal summer afternoon, but she knew that the streets were teeming with joy, with life, with an abundance of pride and relief and costumes and acceptance that dwarfed the solstice party where they'd met. She wanted to go out in it, and she wanted Cinnamon with her.

And why couldn't she? She paused, Cheeto halfway to her open mouth. Cinnamon hadn't said she needed space. She didn't say she never wanted to see Daphne again. That was Daphne's assumption, based on how terribly she'd hurt her, and how this kind of thing had gone in the past, with other lovers. But wasn't that the whole problem? That she'd assumed things about Cinnamon and their relationship because if she asked, she might get an answer she didn't like, and would go on to do what she wanted anyway?

She hadn't called or texted Cinnamon since their fight because that's what she always did: argued with her partner, assumed things were done, and moved on. If they contacted her days or even hours later, it was possible she was already onto someone new. It was a habit. A bad one, though Daphne never saw it that way in the past. As problematic as it felt now, it wasn't any worse than when she'd done it before.

But another habit was just as responsible, and that was Daphne's desire to present loved ones with something amazing without any forewarning, so they would be dazzled and overwhelmed and more likely to agree to whatever Daphne wanted. She'd used this setup just a week ago, when she liberated Coco the monkey for a girl she'd never met. And again to impress Mattie and Rin with her solo capering skills and a new, fully-formed girlfriend before they even realized she had a plan or a crush. She was doing it now: why put in the effort of having a necessary and painful conversation, when she could just stow away on a millionaire's yacht to steal evidence of his multitude of wrongdoings instead?

It wouldn't work this time (did it ever?), but more importantly, Daphne didn't want it to. She didn't want to be off the hook. She wanted to be a good partner. Have the tough conversations.

Respect boundaries, especially when she didn't have the same ones. Until Cinnamon, Daphne thought that love was about how easy it was to be with someone. Not easy? Not a match. But now...

"I'll just text her real quick," she said into the empty room, setting her snack down on the table. One text shouldn't have felt like this big of a deal. "I'll apologize and then it's up to her, and I won't obsess about it or do anything stupid. No expectations."

The room wasn't convinced and neither was Daphne (lots—she had lots of expectations), but that didn't stop her from snatching her phone off its charger too quickly to look believably casual.

The screen was awash with notifications. Surely some were from her sister and Rin, some from Brad, but they knew she didn't have access to her regular phone until a few hours ago, and wouldn't keep trying to contact her that way. For a split second, she thought she, too, had been doxxed, karma catching up to her.

Order of importance meant voicemails first, and surprise surprise, it was everyone who knew she was on a heist and had left her phone back home. But then she opened her texts, and waiting for her at the top of the screen—sent a mere hour before—was a message from Cinnamon.

Daphne's sob cut through the silence, phone screen blurring from her sudden tears. The text wasn't sentimental. Cinnamon didn't declare her love or ask Daphne to come back to her. "I know you didn't dox me," it said. "I'm open to having a conversation." Succinct and emotionless and the most beautiful words Daphne could have read.

"I'm glad you're safe," Daphne typed, then deleted, then re-typed. She meant it. And if Cinnamon knew that Daphne hadn't betrayed her like that, she knew who did, and had put distance between them. Unless Ying-Li had gotten into her phone and was luring Daphne out for nefarious purposes. She shook her head. If that was the case, Ying-Li was going to be sorely disappointed. Daphne wasn't dumb enough to give up sensitive information, and she had a squad at the ready to come to her aid and zero reservations about walking around San Francisco with a bow and arrow.

Well. Maybe a slingshot.

"I'm free all day," she added, and sent it.

Would it have been too much to type out everything else she wanted to say? That she was sorry, that she wanted another chance, that she wanted to support Cinnamon however she needed and would do whatever it took? Daphne's heart was pounding, blood galloping through her veins at a pace that made her dizzy. Tears still blurred her vision, and the taste of Cheetos coating her mouth at such an important moment was slightly embarrassing.

It was unlikely Cinnamon would get back to her quickly. In the meantime, she could rehearse what she wanted to say. Get dressed and wash her face, to feel a little more human. Find that slingshot.

"I'm going to Pride," Cinnamon replied moments later. "Want to meet at the park?"

I'll meet you anywhere. I'll give you anything. I'll think before I speak and listen to what you need instead of doing what I wish you wanted.

"Give me the details. I'll be there."

The most measured response Daphne had ever had.

***

Not long after Cinnamon arrived at the park, wound her way through the costumed bodies of queer and friendly revelers, and found the best bench to camp on to watch for Starlight, the sun began its hottest few hours in the heavens, and Cinnamon's resolve began to lag. The happiest people on the planet surrounded her, and while some of their bliss was undoubtedly from the celebratory drugs, most of it was from pure emotion—the new ruling on marriage equality, the crowd's energy, the bright and beautiful outfits, living out loud, outside, on an unparalleled summer afternoon.

It caught her up in it, of course it did. That was the force that kept her upright and on guard, waiting for Starlight.

The smart thing to do would be to keep her expectations low. If nothing else, it was possible that Starlight wanted to make amends, but had no idea how to do that, or wouldn't want to put in the amount of effort needed. Because it would take a lot of work. And for someone whose MO was "cut and run," Starlight might not have the right tools to "stay and mend." As much as Cinnamon loved helping people, she shouldn't have to teach her girlfriend how to be a partner.

Getting ahead of herself. She fidgeted on the wooden bench and set the cooler of sushi on the ground by her feet. A sprawling tree shaded her from the afternoon sun, and she took a deep breath, trying to ground herself in the present. The whisper of leaves in the wind. Dance music from the speakers of a party picnicking on the grass. People running and laughing, many in brightly colored clothes, sometimes abundant and flowing, sometimes revealing and tight.

The world felt at peace, for once, and Cinnamon closed her eyes and breathed it in, along with the scent of dirt heated by the sun, a soft and dissipating waft of pot from a passerby, and her own perfume.

"Hey," came a familiar voice, small and tentative.

Cinnamon's heart jumped, and she opened her eyes slowly. Starlight was usually loud, assertive, undeniable. Hearing the uncertainty in that one word nearly broke her heart.

There had been a not-zero chance that Starlight would dress in her Mucha costume for this. Romance, Starlight had no problem with, so showing up in dark skinny jeans, flat strappy black sandals, and an ink-blue sweater so thin it could be called threadbare was a choice. There was a hope that Starlight was actually taking this seriously.

Her hair had been brushed but not straightened, and however she'd gotten there had mussed it up a bit. In the brightness of the afternoon, the midnight blue of her eyes was striking and Cinnamon couldn't help thinking of all those RPG and science fiction characters whose eyes were filled with one color, the pupils gone, the whites overtaken by a glowing magic or alien force.

In her hands, she held what looked like the kind of small white box that contained a variety of pastries or an oversized cupcake.

"Hey," Cinnamon responded, crossing her arms. She'd meant to say more, but by the end of the short syllable, emotion had crowded her throat, and she coughed to cover it.

"So," Starlight said, drawing out the word, swaying a little as she looked Cinnamon over. It reminded her of the night they met, when their kissing had been interrupted and they weren't sure what to say next. "What have you got there?" she nodded to the cooler.

"Just some sushi."

A glimmer flashed in Starlight's eyes, and she bit her lip. "Kind of a hot day to bring sushi out to the park. But I bet you have a good reason."

"Bait," Cinnamon answered, cocking her head and pinning Starlight with her own striking gaze. "What did you bring?"

Starlight froze, then shuddered like she was shaking off a spell. "Pavlova."

"That's..." Cinnamon trailed off, frowning. "Somehow that seems weirder than sushi."

"Well," Starlight started, "I really like this girl, and she bakes. And I want to impress her, but I don't bake. But my favorite dessert is pavlova, and I thought I could bring her some, and then I could share my favorite dessert with my favorite person." She tilted her chin down and glanced up at Cinnamon, shyly.

"To impress her?"

"Yes. Well. No." Starlight shifted her weight from one foot to the other, and Cinnamon almost pitied her, looking so lost. "To apologize. I hurt her. I'm a mess. And I know—god, this is hard to say, but—I know pavlova can't solve all my problems. And when I'm having a really good day, pavlova not being able to solve problems is my only problem. But I'm hoping that offering to share it will at least get me in the door, and then I can try to make things right again like a responsible human adult."

"A responsible human adult who needs dessert to get you in the door?"

"It was my best idea."

"Don't you usually use lockpicks for that?"

Her pale cheeks reddened, and her face twisted into an embarrassed grimace. "When I'm at my worst," she mumbled. "But they're at the bottom of the ocean now, so. Not an option either way."

Cinnamon blinked. "The bottom of the ocean."

Starlight nodded without the slightest suggestion of sarcasm. "Yeah."

"How...?"

"Well, if I wanted to convince the Coast Guard that I was harmless, I couldn't be caught with a set of lockpicks, so I had to take them out of my pocket and drop them into the sea. But don't worry, they didn't see me do it. I was already swimming out to them."

Over the course of the last week, there had been a few hints that Starlight's life included otherwise unbelievable adventures. She'd tracked down Cinnamon in the dead of night knowing nothing but her name. She knew people who could undox her and give her less-than-legal and morally questionable software to fight back. And if Echo was to be believed, she had something to do with getting enough dirt on Roday that he would lose his business and maybe even his freedom.

After six months of Amateur Investigator Hour, Cinnamon didn't want to play detective ever again. Unless it was a role-playing game.

Or maybe she just needed the right partner.

"I'm out of your life for one day," Cinnamon drawled, "and you get caught by the Coast Guard?"

Starlight shrugged. "I'd love to say it doesn't happen often. I can say that it will happen less often?"

"Can you say that with a straight face?"

"I can't say anything with a straight anything. Ba-dum tisk!" She gave a pained smile. "That felt inappropriate. I came to—Can I?" She gestured with the pavlova box toward the empty side of the bench, and Cinnamon waved a hand over it in invitation.

Starlight sat down in a huff, and stilled, her gaze fixed on nothing in the distance. She took a deep breath and brought her attention back to Cinnamon.

"I am so sorry," she said, blinking back tears. "I thought I knew better than you. About you. I thought you wanted me to be able to sympathize with what you were going through, and I was ready to break down the thing that was standing in the way of that. If I had listened to you, I would have known that what you wanted was for me to be trustworthy. For me to trust that you would tell me what you need. And not to take matters into my own hands, which I did, and I have to confess, I did it twice."

Despite the summer heat, Cinnamon shivered, a numbing anxiety creeping from the pit of her stomach. Starlight had said she stopped herself from opening any files. That once she saw the picture on her desktop, she shut it down without snooping at all. What else had she done?

"What did you do?" She didn't try to keep the edge out of her voice.

"I had a whole speech prepared—"

"Just tell me."

Starlight sighed. "I went after Roday. You told me not to. But I did anyway. After we argued. I was trying to get my hands on anything that would incriminate him."

Cinnamon's heart skipped a beat. Starlight had a way of throwing herself into problems. She knew how dangerous he was, but she'd still tried. That was what Cinnamon had been working toward, and failing toward, and Starlight wanted to give her what she wanted.

"In the ocean?"

"Well, before the ocean. But yeah. I had the resources I needed to attempt something, and I succeeded, and—wait. Let me tell it in order. And I have something more important to say first." Her hands clenched the sides of the pastry box and she took another breath.

"I know there's no one immediate thing I could say or do that would prove to you that I respect your boundaries and understand how important it is for you to be able to trust. That's something I have to prove again and again, over time, and that's what I plan to do, if you give me the chance, which is totally up to you." She fidgeted on the bench and stared down at the box in her lap. "But I wanted to offer you something now. Beyond promises and apologies. I want to give you the gift of a secret about me that no one else knows."

It had only been a week since they met, but to Cinnamon, it felt like a lifetime and the blink of an eye, and she could never have imagined Starlight being so serious about something.

"Is it that you baked that pavlova all by yourself?"

Starlight snorted, then glanced around furtively. "I wish. No. Actually, I-I'm a corporate spy."

Cinnamon let Starlight's confession settle in her brain. A corporate spy. That might be the least shocking thing she could ever have admitted to.

"Fuck." Cinnamon huffed a laugh. "So Echo was right about you."

"Only that that's my job. I've never investigated Cheung Technologies. I was spying on BDMT. So at the Indian place, when you asked if I knew of Roday, I panicked that somehow you'd found me out. Nobody knows what I do. Not even my sister or best friend. It's safer for all of us that way."

"But now you're telling me."

"I'm trusting you," Starlight emphasized. "If you tell anyone, I could get in trouble or lose my job, or the whole firm could go under. If you don't want to see me again, then you have a nice little piece of blackmail. But if you do want to see me again, this might be a good foundation to build on. Honesty. Trust. Respect."

For a moment, neither spoke. The park had filled with more vibrant people funneled in from nearby Pride events who danced with abandon to three different songs warring at full volume from various corners of the green space. The world was overflowing with the unfettered joy of being seen, acknowledged, embraced, and encouraged. Of finding family, a partner, a place. Cinnamon hadn't felt much of that...possibly ever. Now, she knew she could. It didn't have to be with Starlight.

She looked up at her, the moon-fae sparkling in midnight and silver, even in the middle of the day. Impulsive and beautiful and enamored of Cinnamon to the point of foolishness. It didn't have to be with Starlight. But she wanted it to be.

Rebuilding their relationship would be a long process. And there wasn't any guarantee that it would work out.

But they could try. And Starlight would be right there with her. Listening, this time, and without any major secrets between them. As partners.

Cinnamon reached down, pulled two forks from the cooler, and handed one to Starlight, whose worry transformed into a hopeful smile.

"Let's share that dessert," Cinnamon said. "And tell me absolutely everything."

Epilogue

For the fifth time in a half hour, Daphne walked out of the Sea Cliff former guest bedroom and current closet overflow room in an outfit that could only be described as impractical.

"Why do you keep putting on heels?" Cinnamon whined as she flopped back on their bed. "I said to find something casual like for hiking, do you hike in heels?"

"They're wedges," Daphne explained, turning her foot so she could see. "So they're more stable."

"I know you own sneakers. I saw them once."

"Do you want to come in here and dress me yourself?" She said it innocently enough, but the exaggerated, wide-eyed lash fluttering suggested a different meaning altogether. Also, she knew that Cinnamon would never willingly go through her hundreds of clothing items. Not happily.

"Sturdy pants. A top you like but won't mourn if it's damaged. Sneakers or boots—hiking or work boots, not stiletto booties, or fashion boots, or whatever," she quickly amended.

Daphne turned with a shrug and went to change again. "I don't want us to be late," she called from the closet room, her tone too deliberate to be truth.

"Please just trust me," Cinnamon answered, her words soft with, if Daphne had to guess, desperation. She appeared a few minutes later in white sneakers, white leggings, and a cornflower blue fitted sweatshirt. Cinnamon beamed. "I knew you had it in you."

"You," Starlight said, pointing. "I have you in me. This is a you outfit. Is this what you wanted?"

Comfortable as the bed was, they had to be somewhere, and Cinnamon pushed herself up to encourage her lover with a quick embrace and a peck on the cheek. "I would never wear white leggings. My legs are shaped too weird for that kind of attention."

"I beg your pardon." Daphne punctuated each word with exaggerated diction. "Your legs are perfect. Take off your pants and I'll show you." She reached toward Cinnamon's waist, but she jumped back, laughing.

"Starlight, no. We have to leave. I promise this is the only time I'll ask you to dress like me. I know it's a huge sacrifice for you, especially because you don't know what you're dressing for, but like I said, you just have to trust me."

She did trust her. This wasn't the first time Cinnamon had been so secretive. A few weeks ago, she was acting very similar to today, but the surprise was taking Starlight to meet Claude the albino alligator. Which of course made it the best day of her life (okay maybe like the fifth best day). So she couldn't be too upset that Cinnamon was being secretive again, because it might lead to another Claude-level surprise.

But that didn't stop her from being suspicious. And impressed. Cinnamon had been able to keep whatever it was a secret from her, and until that morning, Daphne had no idea there was even a secret to keep. Mattie and Rin had already bestowed upon Cinnamon a codename—Oracle—which meant they not only accepted her as Daphne's partner, but recognized her ability to caper. Secret notwithstanding, she was proud of her girlfriend.

But when the car dropped them off in front of the Makamerah building a half hour later, Daphne was also wary. A crowd had gathered, news crews and reporters set up around a podium where a tall woman chatted off-mic with two men in suits. Mattie waved to them from the front row of bystanders, and they joined her there.

"Just in time," Mattie said with a grin, holding up her phone so Rin could see them through the video call.

"I forgot to lie about the time so we would have a half-hour buffer," Cinnamon explained. Rin and Mattie groaned.

"That's clutch," Rin said from the phone, shaking her head.

"I'm learning." Cinnamon smiled with a shyness Daphne hadn't seen before, and she loved her more for it.

"You all are very mean," Daphne said loftily. "I can be perfectly on time when I want to be, and you can't blame me for dragging my heels for an event that all three of you managed to keep hidden from me, you sly vixens."

A loud pop as the mic was turned on, and the woman at the podium began speaking. The crowd quieted to listen as she spoke about policy and responsibility, compassion and justice. Daphne tried to keep up, but she was also trying to untangle whatever mystery it was, and she finally understood why her boss assigned her numbers instead of people. Her strategy was shit, but so were her interpersonal skills, if she had to play a role at the same time. She couldn't reconcile that many moving parts for more than a few moments.

"...Cinnamon Cheung, with the help of Daphne Redgrave. Come on up, ladies."

Cinnamon tugged Starlight forward, up the few steps to the wide landing, and squeezed her hand. She must have seen the look of panic in Daphne's eyes.

"Little Spice, what's happening?" she whispered through her fake smile, looking over the crowd as if they would give her any answers. Mattie was biting her lip, and Rin leaned toward her phone's camera with a hand over her mouth. Were they excited, or were they trying not to laugh?

"I wanted to do something for you, like you helped me with Roday," Cinnamon whispered in her ear. "Something big. Mattie and Rin helped me."

Well, that was concerning. Daphne narrowed her eyes at her sister. Oh yeah, they were definitely laughing.

"...they've all found their home in sanctuaries, but there is one very special girl that we wanted to reunite with her rescuer before she went to her refuge." The speaker gestured to the building behind them, where a woman in a blue uniform held the door open with one hand, her other hand in the small grip of a chimpanzee wearing a pink dress with a matching bow and diaper.

"Coco..." Daphne whispered.

"Coco!" the speaker announced, leading the applause amid the *ooh*'s and *aah*'s of the gathered animal lovers.

The chimp glanced around at the people, the sounds, then turned and pointed at Daphne. Daphne also pointed at herself, and Coco tottered over and reached her hands up, wanting to be picked up, and she obliged.

"You made it," she told the monkey. Coco burbled and played with Daphne's shaggy hair.

"Mattie and Rin told me about your caper here," Cinnamon said, over the murmurs of the besotted crowd. "I didn't realize you were such an animal activist. I wanted to say thank you, for all your help with my big problem, and since I have a good network of people who can get stuff done..." She nodded toward Mattie. "I decided to call in my own favors and do this for you. We shut down the lab. She's free now."

Tears crowded Daphne's eyes, as full as her heart. Cinnamon would see and think it was relief, knowing animals were safe, and she panicked for a moment that she would have to be vegan for the rest of her life to keep up the appearance. But it was Cinnamon. The woman had basically stolen a monkey for her, an outrageous Daphne-level gesture of affection, done in the most un-Daphne of ways: successfully.

She locked eyes with her girlfriend. She could see tears there, too, and she wondered how a chimp could make them so emotional.

"You're my person," Starlight told Cinnamon.

"You're my person." The finality in Cinnamon's voice was an anchor, promising to keep her and keep her close, a precious thing, loved, and deserving.

   * * *

Acknowledgments

I've never been good at moderation. My style is more feast-or-famine and vibe-based. But I'll try for a temperate acknowledgment section, because you deserve sincerity.

There's no universe where I would have been able to write and publish this book without the love, support, and computer knowledge of my husband. Thank you for all of that and for beta-reading *Starlight and Cinnamon* even though it isn't a D&D book. Love you.

Thanks to my mom, whose love of my fanfic spurred me to write for a living while also writing her sequels to my fanfic. To Donna, who's been supporting all my endeavors, both brilliant and foolhardy, for literally decades. You can't get rid of me. To Ámá, for being a beta reader even though this is not her genre at all. You're a good sport and a great sister. To May, whose innate sense of narrative and eagle eye for editing mishaps have saved me from some of my worst mistakes.

And a shoutout to those who have helped me get to this point: Sal, Joan, Mackenna, Amanda, Dad, Lauren, Morm and Morf, and all the cats who assisted me in various unhelpful ways. It takes a village to keep me alive and motivated and you've all got your work cut out for you.

Lastly, I want to thank everyone reading this. I wrote the story I wanted to read, and I knew I couldn't be alone. I hope you love it as much as I do.

About the Author

Somewhere in the Midwest, when the sun dips below the horizon, if it's not too humid, you can catch a wild Jem Spears in her natural habitat: napping beneath a number of cats. The rest of the time, she's at her computer, making characters kiss and distributing happy endings like they're candy. Her alter egos produce poetry, translations, and fanfic. *Starlight and Cinnamon* is her debut novel.

***

Find out more about the author online at www.jemspears.com.